DUEL TO THE DEATH!

The armored men slashed with electrical arcs which sprang from their empty gauntlets. Blue-white discharges crackled like ball lightning when they crossed one another, until one of the arcs failed or both combatants stepped back to break the contact.

A pine tree burst into flame as an arc brushed it; then a fighter's armor failed in omnidirectional coruscance. Bits of burning metal and superheated ceramic flew from the heart of a hissing electrical corona.

The man whose armor had exploded was toppling forward. His head was missing. . . .

≡ *Northworld* ≡

The electrifying new future war series by the bestselling master of military science fiction, David Drake, author of the classic *Hammer's Slammers*.

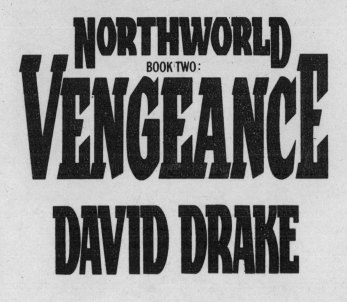

NORTHWORLD
BOOK TWO:
VENGEANCE

DAVID DRAKE

ACE BOOKS, NEW YORK

NORTHWORLD 2: VENGEANCE

An Ace Book / published by arrangement with
the author

PRINTING HISTORY
Ace edition / April 1991

To my son Jonathan,
who liked the first one.

≡1≡

As Nils Hansen lay on the grass of the grave mound, staring toward the black pines silhouetted against the sunset, he heard a shout in the near distance and the *sring!* of a sword coming out of its scabbard. Hansen jumped up from the warm earth, though he'd come here unarmed and there was no need for him to take a local quarrel as his own anyway.

No external need.

The approach of men on ponies—several men, judging from the voices raised as they yipped to their mounts— had been hidden by the snorts and clicks of the herd of giant peccaries being driven to the stockade at Peace Rock for the night. Vague skyglow glinted on the riders' harness and weapon-edges as they spread to encircle the herds-man.

Three men, one carrying a curved saber and the other pair pointing lances as they walked their ponies forward, Hansen thought as his legs took him into trouble because that was what they'd always done, ever since Nils Hansen was able to stand.

"You keep away from me!" bellowed the herdsman as he pivoted clumsily. He aimed his crossbow at first one of the intruders, then another. "You keep away or I'll shoot!"

Peccaries trailing the main herd grunted and clashed their tusks. The pigs stood belly-high to a pony. They were more than dangerous when they chose to be—but for now the beasts were less interested in a fight than they were in the swill awaiting them in the compound. They made way for the riders.

They made way for Hansen as well. With the dusk and the tension, none of the four actors noticed that a fifth man was joining them.

"And what d'ye suppose'll happen then *after* you shoot, boyo?" demanded the rider with a saber.

"Yeah, is that the way Peace Rock treats travelers asking guest rights, pig-smell?" added a lancer.

The riders halted like the spokes of a wheel, each about five meters from the herdsman at the hub.

"I don't have anything to do with guest rights!" cried the herdsman desperately. "You'll have to ask the Lord Waldron!"

The herdsman was trying to face all directions at once, but his real concern was for the lances whose points were already half the distance to his chest.

Hansen knew that was a mistake. The danger wasn't from weapons but rather from the men carrying them. The rider with the saber was the one deciding what would happen next. If Hansen were in the herdsman's place—

He'd shoot the leader at once and take his chances with the others. The lancers would run away or at least freeze for the moment it'd take to snatch the saber and the reins of the loose pony—

But Nils Hansen had the advantage of being a killer himself, with training and experience to hone a great natural talent.

"Listen to that!" said one of the lancers. "No respect for travelers nor his master neither! You know, we oughta—"

The peccaries were faint clicks in the distance. The sky had faded enough that whole constellations were visible in the east.

"You ought to learn civil speech," Hansen said, close enough to touch the nearest pony before it shied from his voice, "or the lord won't have any more respect for you than I do—*boyo*."

He'd had to speak up. The jingle of harness as the leader hunched over the neck of his mount meant that the fellow was about to lurch forward and cut the herdsman down from behind.

The leader straightened, trying instinctively to conceal the saber behind his right leg as the lancer nearest to Hansen sawed the reins with his left hand to control the startled pony. For an instant, the herdsman's crossbow pointed at the center of Hansen's chest; then the square-headed bolt twitched sideways to follow the lancer who steadied his mount a few meters away.

"Who the hell are you?" snarled the leader.

"I'm a traveler passing through these parts," said Hansen easily. He watched the teeth glinting in the leader's black beard and, in the corner of his eyes, the wink of the nearer lancehead. "Maybe I'll want to claim guest rights at Peace Rock myself."

Then, because he saw it was about to happen and he liked to tell himself that it wasn't what he wanted, it was never what *he* wanted, Hansen said, "Friends, we don't need a prob—"

The leader said, "Take 'im, Steith!" and the horseman to Hansen's left thrust forward with his lance.

Hansen was already moving, shifting his torso backward by its own depth so that the lancehead grazed Hansen's tunic of blue-dyed linen instead of grating in through one set of ribs and out through the other.

The herdsman shouted and jumped free of the circle. He still waved his crossbow, but the fellow's instincts told him it was a weapon for wolves, not men, and his fingers refused to squeeze the trigger bar.

Hansen gripped the spear shaft with both hands. The wood had been shaped with curve-bladed knives, not by lathe-turning. Hansen could feel the ridges through the calluses of his palms as he tugged.

The rider lurched forward. He dropped the lance to catch himself on the saddle pommel. His pony, slapped alongside the muzzle by the lanceshaft, shied again.

Steith shouted as he tried to control his mount. The leader was shouting also, but Steith was between him and Hansen, and the second lancer couldn't seem to decide whether to track Hansen or the yammering herdsman.

Hansen didn't say a word as he slammed the butt of the weapon into Steith.

The lance wasn't fitted with a metal buttspike. Hansen's shoulder muscles were powerful even when he was calm, and now his blood bubbled with adrenaline from fear and rage. He thrust the blunt wooden pole a hand's breadth deep in Steith's chest, catapulting the man over the cantle of his saddle.

The man with the saber kneed his mount forward as Steith's pony bolted out of the way. The lanceshaft cut an arc in the air as Hansen swapped it end for end. The leader couldn't be sure what had happened in the confused darkness, but he understood the wink of the lancehead centered on his chest. He drew up his mount with a curse.

Steith's pony, panicked by the smell of the pulmonary blood that sprayed its neck and mane, galloped into the forest with a terrified blat of sound. The other lancer shouted, "Abel! Abel! What should—"

"Get the fuck outa here!" the leader replied, yanking the head of his pony to the left and digging in with the same-side spur.

Both riders cantered off, the leader a pony's length ahead of the surviving lancer. The lancer was still bleating demands for an explanation as they disappeared.

"Eat *this*!" cried the herdsman as he aimed his crossbow.

Hansen lifted the crossbow's muzzle with the tip of his lance.

"What?" said the herdsman. "What?" He did not shoot.

The lance trembled like a willow in a windstorm. Hansen threw the weapon down and hugged his arms tight against his chest.

Blood and death stank in the air and in his mind.

The light was gone. The treetops stood out against the sky, but the trunks and the ground and the corpse lying there on its back were only blurs in blackness. Hansen squatted, trying to control his body as hormones burned themselves off in nervous shudders.

"My lord?" said the herdsman as he bent over Hansen. "Were you struck? My lord?"

"Just back off!" Hansen snarled. The herdsman hopped away in terror.

It was the adrenaline. Mostly the adrenaline.

Hansen stood up. "Look, I'm okay now," he said.

His voice had a rasp in it. He must have been shouting. There'd been a lot of noise and confusion; it was hard to keep the sequence of events straight, even though they had just happened.

"My lord," said the herdsman, "I'm Peter. May I guide you to Lord Waldron?"

"At Peace Rock?" Hansen said. He flexed his hands. He'd strained them in the brief moments of his grip on the lance. "Yeah, I'd appreciate that. I could use . . . "

Rest. Food. Some answers.

"Who were those—folk?" he asked aloud. "Has the Peace of Golsingh broken down?"

"Oh, them," said Peter, scornful now that he'd seen the backs of the men who would have killed him.

He'd dropped the crossbow when Hansen struck up the muzzle. Now he searched for the weapon, finding it beside the narrow track which the hooves of his peccaries had worn. "There's a lot of rovers from Solfygg to the east, recently. Warriors. They stay within the law, mostly, but they go from stead to stead and call out to a duel anybody who looks at them crossways."

Peter set off along the trail. Familiarity and the odor of pig droppings guided his steps where the faint light could not. Hansen followed along. He was glad to be moving again, but the big muscles of his thighs still fluttered with hormones and reaction.

"Those weren't warriors, surely?" he said. The hill ahead of them showed the ragged rim of a stockade, and the air held a tang of woodsmoke.

It didn't seem so very long ago that Hansen had last been in Peace Rock.

"Them warriors?" the herdsman said. "No, just retainers, the sort you'd find who'd follow a rover."

He spat. "A murderer, to give them their proper name. But the rovers now have battlesuits like the gods themselves wear, so they say. With armor like that, they kill whoever it is they call out."

"Do they just?" Hansen murmured too softly for Peter to hear.

He was beginning to tremble again. He should never have come back.

"Peace Rock was the king's seat in the time of the great Golsingh, King Prandia's grandfather, did you know?" the herdsman went on. "Before he moved to Frekka. And even then, his wife—"

"His wife Unn," Hansen said.

He thought only his mind had spoken, but the herdsman looked over at his companion in surprise and said, "Yes, Unn was her name. Do you know the story?"

"Tell me," Hansen said, flexing his broad hands in the darkness.

"Queen Unn asked to be buried here at Peace Rock," Peter said, "because it was here that she learned to love King Golsingh, so they say. That was her grave mound back there where the scuts waylaid us.

"Waylaid *me*," the herdsman corrected, but Hansen's mind was lost in another time.

A party of men, visible only as three bobbing torches, had just issued from the gate of the stockade a hundred meters away. "Peter! Peter, is that you?" one of them bellowed.

"I'm all right, Cayley!" the herdsman shouted back to the search that had been organized when the herd of peccaries returned without him.

"Well, where in North's name have you been?" one of the searchers demanded peevishly.

"She was supposed to be a beautiful woman," Peter said to his silent companion. "Blond hair and eyes the color of the summer sky."

"She was the most beautiful woman I've ever seen," Hansen said; but this time, the whisper was too soft to be overheard except by the pines.

≡ 2 ≡

WHEN THE SUN rose high enough to penetrate the valley, its light turned the ice-covered pines into dazzles of beauty outside the door of the brothers' lodge.

Sparrow paused with his armload of wood and stared up at the rainbow sparkles. Slats of ice popped and tinkled, dancing down through the lower branches as they melted from the first sun-warmed needles.

The forest would be dangerous today. When tufts of pine needles lost their covering of ice and flicked upward, the strain of their release would provide the final stress on some of the parent branches. Great limbs would crash down to crush anything beneath them—even a mammoth; even a man as powerful as Sparrow the Smith.

Sparrow chuckled. The forest was always dangerous.

"Shut the damned door, will you?" bellowed Gordon from within the lodge.

"Shut it yourself," Sparrow replied as he pivoted through the doorway carefully, because the logs he carried were each longer than the door was wide. "I'm the one who's doing something useful."

Gordon got up to close the door flapping on its leather hinges; Sparrow clumped past him to the lodge's central hearth. Sledd, the third of the brothers, lay stripped to a loincloth on a bench beside the hearth.

Sledd was in a trance. On the side opposite the fire from him was a carefully-arranged pile of scrap and ores. The materials shifted in response to unseen pressures and choosings. Sledd's mind worked within the Matrix, seeking through chaos.

The Matrix was the pattern of all patterns. Events moved in all temporal directions the way a tossed stone sends circular ripples across the two-dimensional surface of a pond. Sledd searched the infinite possibilities for a template that matched the form he wished to create in crystal and metal. When desire meshed with the reality of the Matrix, atoms of raw material realigned themselves into one of the patterns chance could cause them to take—

And an object of great sophistication formed within the pile of rocks and junk.

A man who could find templates within the Matrix was a smith.

A man who could ride the event waves of the Matrix to any reality—who could focus his mind in the raging chaos and form a palace or a world—a man with *that* power was a god.

But short of the gods, there was no smith on Northworld the equal of Sparrow and his brothers; and Sparrow was the greatest of the three.

"We're going to have to replace the hinges," Gordon complained. "I don't think Sledd tanned them through this last time. They're starting to crack already."

"It was a cold winter," Sparrow said without concern. He bent at the knees to lower the wood to the puncheon floor. If he simply opened his arms, the dozen ten-kilo billets would crash and bounce in all directions. "And sometimes the hide has flaws. Even mammoth hide."

The wonders the brothers had created stood or moved about the interior of the lodge.

In the center of the single long room, nine balls of light wove a sphere of intersecting circles around an invisible hub. The balls trailed luminous lines that faded gradually until the next slow circuit renewed them. Smoke from the hearth dimmed the illumination, but the soot that coated the ridge pole and the open gable ends through which the smoke escaped in lieu of a chimney did nothing to tarnish the insubstantial balls themselves.

A water clock hung from the wall opposite Sparrow's bed closet. A simulacrum of a wolf worked from tin lifted its leg to spurt droplets into a crystal cylinder scored to mark the minutes. On cold nights the water would have frozen, save that Gordon had fitted it with heating coils powered by energy differentials within the Matrix itself.

A battlesuit stood before each of the bed closets. Most of the objects the brothers had created were unique, but any smith could find the template for the suits of powered armor with which warriors clashed in dazzling radiance across the face of Northworld. Battlesuits like these, however, approached the ideal of the Matrix as closely as physical objects could do.

Sparrow stepped back from the pile of fresh logs and worked the thong and peg which fastened his cape out of the eyelet on the other side. He shook the garment to clear it of drops of melt water, then tossed it on one of the chests which served for clothing storage as well as benches when the brothers sat.

The cape, lifted whole from a cinnamon bear, was nearly the color of the smith's own hair and beard. Shortly after the brothers came to the valley three years before, Sparrow had strangled the beast with his bare hands when he surprised it raiding one of his snares. His forearms still bore scars from that battle.

Sledd began to murmur, coming out of his trance. Sparrow glanced to see what his brother had been creating, but a pile of reduced ores still covered the object like the crust of clay over a lost-wax casting.

Gordon put another log on the hearth. Sparrow walked over to the shelf built onto the front panel of his bed closet and took from it the mirror he kept there.

The polished bronze surface was a circle only about ten centimeters in diameter. For a moment it showed Sparrow his own face and whiskers, tinted even ruddier by the metal's hue.

The smith's fingers manipulated the controls on the back of the circle. Metallic luster cleared into a scene of figures moving against the brilliant green of summer foliage.

"Gods but it's cold!" Sledd mumbled. "Stoke up the fire, won't you?"

"Sledd," Sparrow said. "Gordon. Look at this."

His brothers' faces blanked as they joined him, one to either side. Sledd reached down to work a cramp out of his right thigh.

"Can you make them bigger?" Gordon asked.

"A little," said Sparrow. His index finger stroked the controls. The face of the nearest figure, a woman with perfect features and long black hair, filled the mirror's small field.

"No one we know," said Gordon as Sparrow panned the image back to capture the surroundings again.

"They're Searchers," said Sledd. "And that's the spring at the foot of this valley."

The other two women were blonds, both of them larger than their black-haired companion. As the Searchers ran down the flower-carpeted slope to the spring, Sparrow shifted the image in his mirror to examine the equipment the women had left on the knoll behind them.

Sledd trembled with the chill of the Matrix. He picked up his brother's cape because it was handy and slipped it over his own shoulders. "What are Searchers doing here?" he said.

"How did you find them?" asked Gordon simultaneously.

"Unless I ask the mirror for something in particular," said Sparrow, "it shows me what's nearby that it thinks will most interest me. The picture is near in time. A few months from now."

Three battlesuits stood on the wooded knoll. Each of the frontal plates which covered the wearer's face and thorax was swung open against the hinges on the left side of the join.

The brothers' eyes narrowed as they surveyed the armor. Even with the image shrunken to fit the mirror, they could see that the suits were of excellent quality.

That was to be expected of battlesuits which clothed the servants of North the War God.

Behind the armor were the mounts which had brought the Searchers to the brothers' valley: electronic dragonflies.

For the moment, at rest with their gear stowed, the fragile-seeming vehicles looked more like long-legged cave crickets.

When the gossamer antennas unfolded like wings to shroud the saddle in a bubble of separate spacetime, the Searchers could slip between the worlds of the Matrix.

When they were on North's business, the dragonflies hovered over battlefields, just out of temporal phase with the struggle going on below, while their receptor antennas drank and stored the minds of the dying. Flickering shutters of black radiance marked the Searchers passage to the humans of the Open Lands.

"Go back to the women," Sledd murmured thickly. "It's been a long time."

"Don't be a fool!" Gordon said. "They're Searchers."

Sparrow adjusted his image. "Why not Searchers?" he said. "They're women too."

The women were splashing one another in the cold water of the spring. They had left their tunics on the bank.

"These are the god's servants," Gordon said. "We can find other women."

"If we want to trek for a week we can find other women," Sledd replied tartly. "And who would we find then worthy to bring back here? Our father is a king!"

"If there's any justice," said Gordon, "our father is freezing in Hell."

"*And* his new wife," said Sledd. "*And* their bastard whelps."

One of the women sprang to the bank laughing and ran into the woods. Her companions followed a moment later. The black-haired Searcher was as lithe and compact as a lynx.

Sparrow stroked his ginger beard. "The Searchers have lives beyond the god's orders," he said. "These three aren't on North's business now."

His lips pursed. "They won't be on North's business next summer, I mean."

He shifted the image again. The women were picking fruit from a blackberry tangle at the edge of the woods. They reached carefully to avoid scratching their bare flesh.

"If we do," said Gordon cautiously, "we'll have to wear our battlesuits."

"No," said Sparrow.

The black-haired woman flicked a ripe berry at one of her companions. It burst in a purple blotch on flesh so clear that the veins showed blue beneath the surface. The blond laughed and flung back a handful of the fruit.

"Sparrow," Sledd protested, "you're forgetting they're Searchers. If we try to take them unarmed, they'll put their own armor on and cut us down."

Sparrow focused the image down again on the face of the black-haired woman. "No," he said slowly, "I'm not forgetting who they are. But if they're worthy of us, then we have to be worthy of them. We can't force this sort."

Gordon nodded agreement. "Not and live," he said. "We have to sleep sometime ourselves."

Sparrow reached out as though he were going to stroke the woman's smooth, tanned cheek; but his fingers paused just short of the mirror's surface.

"It may be," he said, "that we can convince them of our worth. . . . "

≡ 3 ≡

"LORD WALDRON," ANNOUNCED the herdsman in a cracked attempt at grandiloquence, "here is the worthy stranger who saved me from attack by bandits. Ah, and saved your pigs."

In good light—illuminated by the fat-soaked rushes within the Great Hall of Peace Rock, at any rate—Peter was a squat man of sixty or so, twice Hansen's apparent age. He wore a peaked pigskin cap, bristle side in, which he snatched off belatedly as he spoke with his master. Despite the age obvious in the lines of Peter's face, his hair was as black and stiff as the peccary bristles.

"The other pigs, you mean," said the warrior seated to the right, just below Lord Waldron's crosstable. "Phew, man, don't stand so close."

"Arnor," said the lord. "Not now."

Lord Waldron was as old as Peter, though his hair was white. Standing, he would be half a head taller than Hansen. Waldron looked fit rather than active, and there was an aura of intelligent calculation in his eyes as they touched his visitor.

"What do you mean—" Waldron said to his herdsman, before breaking off and shifting his steady gaze to Hansen.

"If you're a traveling warrior who claims guest rights, sir," Waldron said, "then you must tell us your name."

The Great Hall was the same thatch-roofed structure it had been when it was the king's seat in past ages; but because all the circumstances had changed, the physical surroundings seemed different as well.

Most of the bed closets in which the lord's warriors slept had been removed from the long walls. The benches and trestle tables to either side of the central hearth were still occupied at dinner, but only because freemen now sat on the lower benches and ate with the lord and his warriors.

Lord Waldron sat at the crosstable with his wife, a woman as old as he, who hennaed her hair. There were only three warriors on each of the parallel benches below them.

Hansen blinked away his memory of the long room filled with over a hundred drunken, shouting warriors. He liked this better, though the other was a more proper milieu for *his* sort.

"My name's Hansen," he said aloud. "And I would be grateful for a meal and a night's lodging, my lord."

"You do claim to be a warrior, don't you?" asked Arnor. He was a big man in his mid-thirties; running now to fat. Judging from where he sat below the lord, Arnor was probably Waldron's chief advisor and leading warrior . . . to the extent that Peace Rock in its present guise had military requirements.

Arnor spoke in a tone whose studious calm attempted to take the sting out of what could easily be construed as an insult; but it was a proper question to a stranger who appeared without battlesuit or retinue. Arnor, as the lord's champion, had the duty of asking—at the risk of a challenge if Hansen turned out to be a hot-blooded spark who felt his honor had been impugned.

Enough fights had come Hansen's way already without him needing to look for another. He opened his mouth to make a suitably mild reply—

But before he could speak, Peter the herdsman cackled, "A warrior? You bet he is! He killed six bandits with his bare hands. And *they* had swords and lances!"

Everyone stared at the guest.

Hansen chuckled. "There were only three of them," he said. "Two—"

And he paused because his voice broke. All the humor of Peter's overstatement had drained from Nils Hansen's soul when his mind remembered fury as red and real as steel glinting in the dusk.

Something unmeant must have showed in Hansen's face. The lord's wife gasped. Waldron's sudden flatness showed that he too had known battle in his day.

Hansen clamped his palms together. He knew the sweat and trembling would pass in a moment. Just a memory of blood and terror, one of too many memories to count. Soon his mind would scab it over with the rest.

"Two of them rode away," Hansen resumed, forcing the corners of his mouth up into a smile. "Anyway, I wasn't bare-handed after I took the lance from the first . . . but yes, my lord, I'm a warrior. Though I have no equipment."

Arnor laughed, breaking the ice around the table. "Even on your telling of it," he remarked, "I'd say your father chose right when he named you after the god Hansen."

He turned to the crosstable and added, "Milord, let's seat our friend with us now, and—"

"Yes, of course," said Waldron, nodding.

"And," Arnor continued, "since we've got some spare equipment that might fit him, I wouldn't mind trying him out on the practice field in the morning. For a regular place in your household."

"At least if he comes without armor of his own, we know he's not a rover," said a warrior on the other side of the hearth.

"Do be seated, Hansen," the lord said. His face clouded. "Armed riders like that, though. . . It means there probably *is* a rover about."

Lord Waldron hadn't assigned the guest a specific seat. There were gaps on the benches to separate warriors from the community's freemen. Hansen noted general relief as he chose to sit at the end of three warriors on his side of the hall.

Arnor shrugged. "They've missed us so far," he said. He lifted a drumstick. It had been stewed so long that the meat fell back on Arnor's plate before it reached his mouth.

A buxom serving woman handed Arnor a torn wedge of bread. He shoveled meat onto the wedge with the fingers of his other hand. "Maybe the reception they got from Lord

Hansen here'll make them . . ."

The remainder of the comment was lost in the wad of bread and chicken.

The two warriors seated down-bench from Arnor were middle-aged and even less imposing than their leader. They nodded cautiously to Hansen. The serving woman handed him a plate of meat and vegetables and a massive pewter tankard of beer.

The fire on the central hearth had been allowed to go out as soon as the meal was cooked, but woodsmoke lingered to spice the air which entered through the open gables and chinks in the low log walls. There were walkways for servants between the hearth and the lines of tables to either side of it.

The warriors opposite Hansen were much the same as those beside him, though the trio across the hearth appeared to be somewhat younger. Peace Rock wasn't the place a warrior went if he hoped for action.

Hansen drank. The beer was surprisingly good, but the tankard gave it a metallic undertaste.

"Lord Hansen," said Waldron's wife, "was it your parents who named you after the god, or is it a name you chose when you decided to travel?"

"Amelia," said her husband, "we don't quiz strangers."

But Lord Waldron wasn't frowning; and of course the folk here *did* quiz strangers. Anybody who lived in a community as isolated as present-day Peace Rock sought all the entertainment they could get when someone came in from the outer world.

"No, it's the name my parents gave me, lady," Hansen said, carefully limiting himself to a truth he could tell without causing a furor. He added, "I come from far away, and there's no one in this whole kingdom likely to know me."

Arnor leaned forward to look past his two fellows to glare at Hansen.

"Do you come from Solfygg, then?" Peace Rock's champion asked. His voice was harder than Hansen had thought him capable of using.

"I do not," Hansen said flatly. He met Arnor's eyes. "I come from much farther away than that."

To break the discussion, Hansen raised his tankard, drank, and found to his surprise that he had emptied the vessel. *Killing was a dry business, but he never remembered that at the times in between.*

Lady Amelia's sex and position made her arbiter of when to pry and when to ease off on the stranger. Now she said to her husband, "The king should do something about these rovers."

Waldron responded promptly, "If they stay within the law . . . ," and the conversation involved the members of the household while Hansen devoted himself to his meal.

The woman serving on this end of the table was older than Hansen had first thought, somewhere in her mid-thirties. She set a wedge of bread on Hansen's plate and gave him another of the bright-cheeked smiles that had caused him to underestimate her age.

"My name's Holly, sir," she said. "Will you have more ale?"

Hansen grinned and held out his tankard. "You wouldn't have another wooden masar in the cupboard for me to drink out of, would you?" he asked the big woman as she poured.

Holly paused in surprise. She wore a dress of dark material, cut very low in the bodice. For modesty a handkerchief was pinned to the shoulders of the dress, but the show she provided when she lifted the kerchief to mop her face, as now, was almost professionally intriguing.

"You want to drink from wood like a freeman, milord?" she asked in puzzlement.

"A whim," Hansen said. He grinned over the rim of his mug as he drank.

"Of course, sir!" said the servant as she turned.

Hansen sipped his ale, noting again the bitterness which alcohol leached from the metal. This wasn't the only society in which the wealthy and powerful proved their status by being more conspicuously uncomfortable than lesser folk.

For all that, Peace Rock seemed a happy place now that it had become a backwater. There'd been affection rather than fear in Peter's voice when he addressed his lord, and the muted chatter along the benches at dinner was generally cheerful.

Hansen mopped stewed chicken onto his bread and let the bland dullness of Peace Rock drift around him.

"A masar, milord," said the serving woman, giving Hansen another of her brilliant smiles. She set down a broad elm cup and filled it with a flourish of her pitcher.

They were willing to take him in, Waldron and Arnor and Holly, clearly Holly.

"Call me Hansen," he said, "or I'll start calling you Lady Holly."

Holly giggled and covered her mouth with the lower edge of her pinned kerchief.

Hansen knew he didn't belong here, of course.

But then, Nils Hansen didn't belong much of anywhere; and for the moment, at least, it was good to spend time with people who found their lives happy.

≡ 4 ≡

ONE, THEN THREE armored figures rode their dragonflies out of time. They trembled at the edge of visibility as if they were sliding in and out between the fracture planes of mica schist.

In the millisecond intervals when they were visible, happy laughter caroled from the external speaker of the black battlesuit.

Gordon crouched lower and muttered, "Just like your mirror showed. When and where . . . and especially who."

Sparrow laid a hand the size of an ice-bear's paw on Gordon's shoulder to remind him to be silent.

The dragonflies sharpened into perfect temporal focus. Brush crackled under the weight of the vehicles and their armored riders. There was a brief trail of steam; dew which the sun missed had touched hot metal.

The riders dismounted. The Searcher in black armor reached down to the latch below her right armpit and pulled the front of the battlesuit open. When the latch released, it shut off all the battlesuit's systems—including the servos which ordinarily powered the articulated joints of the armor.

The black-haired woman inside the suit swung the dead weight of the massive frontal armor as easily as if she were a man with triceps twice the size of those of her own trim arms.

Sledd wrinkled his nose; Sparrow's and Gordon's eyes prickled a moment later. The dragonflies ionized air when they appeared. A tendril of ozone drifted twenty meters to where the brothers hid.

The fire-orange battlesuit with bronze highlights opened as well. The blond Searcher inside coughed.

"For North's own sake, Krita!" she complained. "Why can't you let the stink blow off at least? We aren't on a deadline."

"Krita's always on a deadline, Race," said the other of the big blonds, waving her hand back and forth to dissipate the ozone. "She thinks if she runs fast enough, death won't catch her."

Krita laughed again. She pulled herself out of her battlesuit, both legs together—an awkward task that her muscular grace made look easy. She wore a singlet of doeskin; her feet and long legs were bare.

"Come along, Race, Julia," she called as she pushed through the screening brush to reach the flowered slope beyond. "Last one to the water never gets to touch a man again."

The two blonds climbed out of their armor as lithely as Krita. They were both taller than their companion, and they looked softer—the way oak cudgels seem softer than chipped flint.

"*That*," called Race as she and Julia loped along after Krita, "I wouldn't wish on my worst enemy!"

The blonds wore linen shifts. They were already lifting the garments over their heads as they disappeared downhill from the brothers.

Gordon exhaled heavily. "You're right," he said to Sparrow. "It *is* worth it."

"I didn't remember how long it had been," Sledd murmured.

Sparrow said nothing. He was watching the image in his mirror, the shrunken figures of women sprinting down the hundred meters of gentle slope.

The blonds' longer strides made up distance, but Krita held her lead to the sedges where water spilled from the rocks. The three women plunged together into the deep pool in the spring's center. Their clothing lay on the bank.

"Now," said Sparrow as he got up deliberately and walked to the equipment which the Searchers thought they had left concealed.

Sledd ignored the dragonflies on their spindly, wonderfully strong, monocrystalline legs. Instead he caressed one of the battlesuits whose quality he could fully appreciate. The suit's pattern of scarlet, silver, and mauve scales was not painted on, as Sledd had assumed, but rather integral with the outer sheathing.

"I still say we ought of worn our own armor," he said.

"There's nothing I want from those three that I can get with a battlesuit on," Gordon replied.

Some of the nearby foliage was shriveled. Ozone had bleached the green out of it.

Sparrow bent over Krita's dragonfly, then squatted. There was a set of manual controls on the underside of the saddle's edge. He did not touch them. Instead, the master smith adjusted the image in his mirror to show the same controls.

"What are you doing?" Gordon asked.

"Sledd, don't show yourself," Sparrow grunted absently. The third brother was peering through the brush in the direction the women had gone.

Sledd grimaced and squatted beside Sparrow. "Well, what *are* you doing?" he demanded.

"When the Searchers see us," Sparrow explained, "they'll either run away or they'll attack. We can't keep them from killing us, sooner or later, unless we're willing to kill *them*."

Sledd spat. "That'd be crazy," he said.

"Yes," said Sparrow. The image of the dragonfly controls blurred, then focused. There was a subtle difference between reality and the form in the mirror. "But it may be that we can keep them from running."

Sparrow poked a broad finger *through* the surface of his mirror and touched a control switch.

There was a dull pop. The dragonfly beside him vanished, but the image in the mirror remained.

The big man let out a long sigh of relief. "Like that," he said as he rose and moved to the next vehicle.

"Where did you send it?" Gordon asked with a frown. He

looked at the black battlesuit standing as a monument to the vanished dragonfly.

"It's still *here*," said Sparrow as he focused his mirror on the controls of Race's dragonfly. "But it isn't now, not quite. It's waiting—"

His finger jabbed. The second vehicle vanished from the brothers' present.

"*They're* waiting in a time state just out of phase with the space around them," Sparrow went on as his mirror blurred and sharpened. "It's in the regular controls; it's where they stay when they ride the battle plains."

"Where Searchers ride," Gordon said.

"Of course Searchers!" Sledd snarled. "We knew that before we started, didn't we?" He shivered in the summer shade.

A trill of laughter echoed from the spring. Sparrow looked at his brothers. "Calm down," he said in a firm voice. "There's risk. We don't have to make the risk worse."

Gordon grimaced. "Sorry," he said. "Sorry."

The last dragonfly puffed out of sight. Sparrow panned the image back momentarily, showing all three of the vehicles still on the knoll . . . with the empty battlesuits, and in the presence of the brothers.

Sledd muttered a curse. He felt in the air where the mirror said a vehicle should be. His hand met nothing, though a stray beam of sunlight danced across the ginger hairs on the backs of his fingers.

Sparrow switched the mirror's image back into a mere reflection in polished metal. He hung the artifact around his neck by a rope whose gold and silver strands were as fine as those of a battlesuit's circuits.

"What do we do now, Sparrow?" Gordon asked. Below, the Searchers giggled like young girls as they climbed from the water to look for berry bushes.

"Now . . . ," said the master smith. He combed absently at his beard as his eyes focused on a possible future. "Now we wait. And hope."

The women chattered as they walked up the slope. There were damp patches on their garments where their skin had not dried when they pulled the clothing on. Krita and Race held hands.

Julia had lifted the hem of her shift to cup a double handful of fresh blackberries. She yelped, then giggled, as a branch whipped back and caught her where the linen would normally have been some protection.

Krita saw the three big men standing beside the battlesuits. They were dressed in breeches and jerkins of tanned leather, crudely sewn but ornamented with metalwork of exquisite quality.

Krita took her hand from Race's and said, "There," in a quiet, charged voice.

Julia shook the berries from her garment. The groups were poised like packs of dogs meeting at the boundary of their ranges . . . or a pack of wolves, and a family of bears.

For a moment, Krita could imagine that it was the men's bulk which hid the dragonflies from her. She edged to the side, and her keen eyesight pricked the life out of that hope.

"We mean you no harm, ladies," Sparrow said. He stepped forward slowly, as though he were taking part in a ritual. He lifted the mirror from his breast. "We hold you in honor."

"We want nothing of you," Race called threateningly. "Do you realize who we are? Do you want the gods to blot away the very memory of you?"

"You are kings' daughters and Searchers, lady," said Gordon. Sparrow took another slow step. His brothers remained as motionless as the empty battlesuits beside which they stood. "But we are the sons of a king ourselves."

"We're smiths like no others that ever lived," said Sledd. "We'll make you wonderful things."

"Where are our vehicles?" Krita asked in a voice like frozen steel.

"You can't catch us, you know!" snapped Julia.

"And if you did," added Race in an unknowing echo of Gordon's words of months before, "then—you'll have to sleep sometime." Her teeth as she smiled were as bright and sharp as those of a predator.

"Your armor is here, ladies," Sparrow said. "You can kill

us now if you like. We are a king's sons, and we wish you only honor as our wives."

Sparrow had crossed half the distance separating him from the women. He held the mirror out to Krita and said, "Take it. It's for you."

The sleeveless jerkin showed deep pink scars from the bear's claws on the inside of Sparrow's forearm.

Krita stepped forward with brisk certainty instead of making a quick, rodentlike grab for the dangling object. Her eyes met Sparrow's. She took the mirror, then backed away.

"Give us our vehicles," she said flatly.

"Anything but your dragonflies, Lady Krita," Sparrow said.

The shaggy form of the master smith contrasted sharply with his cultured voice. His pale eyes were calm, but no one could look into them and hope that prayer or threats would make Sparrow draw back from the words he had just spoken.

"Wonders that not even the gods can match," Sledd boasted.

Julia glanced at him. She chuckled.

"Look into the mirror, Lady Krita," Sparrow coaxed. "Yes, like that. Ask it to show you something—anything, anyone."

Race played with a spot of berry juice on her garment. "You can make it change by speaking to it?" she asked, flicking her gaze from the object to its maker.

Krita murmured to the mirror. Its surface blurred.

Sparrow nodded. "Like a battlesuit's controls," he said. "Many smiths build battlesuits, lady. Only I could have created *that*."

"Well, is it true, Krita?" Julia demanded. "Does it work?"

"Oh, yes, it's true," Krita agreed in a distant voice. There was a decisive hardness in her expression that had been missing before. She hung the mirror's cord over a bare twig to free her hands.

"We wish only to honor you as our wives, lady," the master smith repeated.

Krita barked a short, harsh laugh. All five of the others watched her.

"Well, girls," Krita said in a bright voice. "We came here to relax for a while, didn't we?"

She reached down and began deliberately to pull her singlet over her head.

Race sighed, then smiled at Julia. The blond women lifted off their shifts. The brothers stepped forward in increasing haste.

Birds chirped and fluttered among the foliage. The mirror rotated lazily on its cord. Its surface showed the face of Nils Hansen.

≡ 5 ≡

THE DOOR AT the low end of the Great Hall banged open. Hansen jumped when instinct tried to throw him under the table to cover.

"Lord Waldron!" bleated Cayley, the watchman from the gate in the stockade. "They're coming, the rover! He's got his armor, and he's got mebbe a dozen riders with him besides mammoths for baggage!"

Lord Waldron rose to his feet with a grim expression. "Silence!" he boomed, quashing the sudden jabber of nervousness throughout the big room.

Lady Amelia raised her knuckles to her lips; most of those in the hall stared raptly at their lord.

A mammoth tethered in the Peace Rock compound screamed welcome to the newcomers it scented.

"Cayley," Lord Waldron said, "go back to the gate and admit them with all honor. Do whatever they tell you to do."

"Right," said Arnor. "Don't argue about anything."

Several of the warriors nodded nervous agreement.

Hansen's face went blank. He didn't understand what was going on, so he watched and listened . . . and waited until he knew enough to act, or until he had to act anyway.

Cayley ducked out of the hall. The door missed the notch of its wooden latch. It slapped the post and swung open again.

A freeman on the lowest bench hopped up to close the panel, then froze in terrified awareness that all the normal rules had changed. He scuttled back to his seat, leaving the door ajar.

"Now for the rest of you," Waldron continued, "there's none of us going to make trouble, do you understand? He wouldn't be coming here unless he had a battlesuit that can mince ours like forcemeat. No matter what he says, we're going to agree with him!"

"He'll leave in a day or two if he can't get a duel out of any of us," Arnor said with a glum shake of his head. "It wouldn't do a bit of good to get killed."

Lady Amelia stood up. Her thin face had flushed; now it was white. "There's seven of you, aren't there?"

Her eyes swept the room, skimming across her husband and the other warriors before resting a moment on Hansen's expressionless visage. "Eight now. This battlesuit isn't so good that eight of you can't cure him, is it?"

The squeals of the giant peccaries provided a jumbled warp through which baggage mammoths wove their louder, even shriller, calls.

"The Peace of Golsingh gives every man the right to travel through—" Lord Waldron said.

"He's coming here to *kill* you!" Amelia said.

Her control cracked. Hansen saw in her eyes love—and terror for her husband's life.

"He's coming here to fight a duel under the law!" Waldron said sharply. "*If* we give him the excuse. And we're not going to do that."

"Too right," muttered a young warrior. "I didn't hire on to here t'be outlawed for murder."

"Why *did* you promise to serve my husband?" Lady Amelia shouted. "To eat and drink and skulk when your lord is at risk?"

The old woman turned quickly to hide her tears.

Amelia and her husband sat on chairs, not benches. Her seat wobbled as she brushed past it, then rattled back onto its legs. She ran up the stairs to the chambers the lord's immediate family shared above the back of the Great Hall.

The warrior to whom Amelia had spoken hunched his shoulders and stared at the table in front of him.

"She's upset," said Lord Waldron to his retainers. His voice quavered.

He controlled it with an obvious effort and went on, "We're all upset. But remember: stay calm or it's your life. And it may be my life as well."

"We'll get out of this just fine if we all stay calm," Arnor added.

Hansen sucked at his lips. He drank the rest of the ale in his wooden masar, then toyed with the pewter mug again.

Cayley flung the door open. "All hail the noble Lord Borley!" the watchman shouted in a voice pitched even higher than that with which he had warned of the rover's approach. "Come from far Solfygg to claim guest rights with Lord Waldron!"

To Hansen's surprise, when Borley entered—pushing Cayley aside with deliberate brutality—he was already wearing his battlesuit. "That's right!" boomed the warrior's voice through the speaker in the faceplate of his powered armor. "My name's Borley, *Lord* Borley to you lot unless you're willing to challenge me. Any of you man enough for that?"

No one answered. Most of those in the hall grimaced with downcast eyes. Hansen took a tiny sip of ale, just enough to sluice around in an attempt to moisten the dryness of his mouth.

Borley's retainers spilled into the hall behind him. The leading man's face was familiar to Hansen: Abel, the black-bearded rider who had turned and run from Hansen's lance.

Abel carried his saber slung over his back where it wouldn't knock against objects when he was dismounted. Several of Borley's other retainers also brought edged weapons into the hall in defiance of custom and courtesy.

Hansen wondered if Abel would recognize him. Probably not. The fading sky had done a better job of lighting the horsemen than it did men on foot, a meter lower in the shadow of the pines.

Probably not.

Borley walked toward Lord Waldron at the crosstable at the far end of the room. The rover chose the aisle on the side opposite Hansen to make his deliberate progress. His battlesuit weighed over a hundred kilos. Every time his foot crashed down on the puncheons, sparks jumped from the sole to scar the wood.

The rover's battlesuit was of remarkably high quality, the sort of armor that a king might wear. Just as Lord Waldron had expected. . . . A wandering thug had no business owning equipment like that.

"What's the matter?" snarled Borley's amplified voice. "Dumb insolence, is it? Refusing to greet me with the honor I'm due?"

"Lord Borley," Waldron said promptly, "be welcome to my hall. Sit at my right hand, if you will—or in my own seat."

Arnor had been correct also. None of the warriors in a place like Peace Rock could afford armor that would last more than one swipe in a duel with a royal suit like Borley's.

Borley's retainers poured into the hall behind him. There were eight of them all told, not the dozen Cayley reported.

And not nine, either. Not since the ninth met Hansen.

The retainers split into two groups and pushed into the benches where the leading Peace Rock freemen sat. The locals scrambled to get out of the way, but Borley's men kicked and shoved them anyway.

"You don't mind accommodating my boys, do you, Waldron?" Borley demanded as he continued his slow progress toward the crosstable. "You don't think that maybe because they're the sons of thieves 'n whores that they aren't better than anybody in your lot?"

"Not at all, Lord Borley," Waldron said in a steady voice. "Your servants are welcome to sit wherever they choose in this hall."

Abel climbed into the seat at Hansen's left and jostled him. Hansen met his eyes.

The leader of Borley's retainers was young, smart, and fit, despite a certain puffiness of his features which suggested that drink would catch up with him soon—if a rope didn't. Abel's left thumb and forefinger were missing; the wound had been cauterized with hot iron that left a glistening pink scar.

He opened his mouth to snarl at Hansen but changed his mind. "Give me some room!" he grunted to the man on his own left.

Hansen sipped ale that tasted of metal and bile.

"You know," said the rover, "I'm kinda disappointed in you, Waldron. I'd heard you been telling folks that you're a tough bunch here at Peace Rock. Tougher than me, I'd heard. I figgered you guys'd like to try me in a duel so we could see who was really tough."

Servants were pouring ale into mugs for the newcomers. Holly put a tall jack of tarred leather in front of Abel.

"No, not here, Lord Borley," said Waldron. "There's nobody here as strong and brave as you."

Abel grabbed Holly's wrist as she set the jack down. He gripped the kerchief over her bodice and tore it loose.

Holly tried to stifle a scream.

"You don't mind my boys finding a little entertainment while they're here, do you?" the rover asked in a voice like that of a hog who had learned human speech.

Waldron swallowed. "If that's what pleases you, Lord Borley," he said.

Abel levered one of the woman's heavy breasts out of the dress with his three-fingered hand. Holly squeezed her eyes shut. She was murmuring a prayer.

Hansen's eyes watered. Microswitches in the powered armor must be arcing to leave a trail of ionized air.

"Some of 'em haven't had anything better than a mare t'stick their dick into fer weeks," Borley said. "Course, some of 'em *like* mares."

Hansen's wrist jerked, oversetting his pewter tankard. The half of its contents remaining sluiced across the trestles and down over Abel's lap.

The retainer jumped backward with a shout. The bench and the fellow to Abel's left trapped him in the path of the stream.

Holly pulled away to stand in the ashes of the cold hearth, out of reach from either row of benches. Her arms were crossed over her chest; her head was bowed.

Abel stood at a twisted angle between the bench and the table, staring at Hansen.

"Sorry," Hansen said. "I've always been the clumsy sort." He spoke softly, and his voice trembled.

"Fucking moron's the sort you are," Abel muttered; but

he sat down again and ostentatiously turned his back toward Hansen.

If Borley had noticed the incident, he made no comment.

"Well, what about you lot?" the rover demanded. He pointed to the warriors on his side of the hearth with the thumb and forefinger of his gauntlet spread—the gesture that would spread a blade of ravening electricity if Borley gave his battlesuit a verbal order to *Cut!* "Think you're as tough as me?"

"Oh, not me/not me/Nobody I know's as tough as you, Lord Borley," the three young warriors chorused. One of them stared at the table, one of them offered the rover a smile as false as a wax doll's, and the third warrior let his eyes dance across the sloping thatch roof of the hall as he spoke.

The tip of Hansen's right index finger traced the rim of his empty mug.

Borley strode across the back of the crosstable. "You've already told me you're a coward, haven't you, Waldron?" he said.

"That's right, Lord Borley," Waldron said. He faced the door at the far end of the room. His eyes looked like bits of glass. "You're welcome to sit here in my seat for the full three days of your guest rights."

"How about you, then?" Borley demanded as he paused in front of Arnor. "You're the champion of this shitpile, aren't you? Is that your name? Sir Shitpile?"

"That's right, Lord Borley, if you say it is," Arnor said in a choking voice.

"Hell take you all!" the man in armor grumbled in what might have been real disgust. "You really are a lot of dog-turds here, aren't you?"

Hansen hunched over his mug, staring at the pewter but not seeing even that.

"That's right," Arnor said as the two warriors seated below him bobbed agreement. "We're nothing but dog-turds compared to a hero like you, Lord Borley."

The stink of ozone was very close behind Hansen now.

"Well, what about you, *boy*?" the rover asked. "Do you think I'm tough?"

Hansen neither moved nor spoke. Abel stared at him with a look of avid anticipation.

"I *spoke* to you, boy!" Borley thundered. Hansen's body twitched with the shock as a powered gauntlet gripped his shoulder and spun him to face the rover.

Close up, Hansen could see that the limbs of the battlesuit had been joined to the thorax by a smith less able than the one who constructed the component parts. The lustrous power of those components shone through the painted skulls with which Borley had ornamented the armor.

"I'm a stranger here myself," said Nils Hansen, "so I don't know how tough you are. Where I come from, though, we'd think you were just a blowhard."

The blat of noise from the battlesuit's speaker was inarticulate in its rage. Borley raised his right hand to smash Hansen where he sat.

Hansen grabbed the catch under the rover's armpit and pulled the suit open. For a moment, Borley's broad, droopmoustached face stared out of the unpowered coffin his armor had become as soon as it came unlatched.

Hansen slammed his pewter mug against the rover's forehead.

Abel bawled in surprise. He tried to snatch his saber from its sheath. Hansen backhanded the retainer across the temple, knocking him sprawling into his fellows.

Everyone in the hall was shouting. Arnor lifted himself from the bench with a smooth grace that belied his appearance of softness and vanished into the bed closet directly behind him.

Hansen's face was white and staring. He pounded the mug into Borley. Stiff joints kept the depowered battlesuit upright, but the man within slumped forward so that Hansen's fourth blow thudded against the suede which lined the armor.

Gasping with reaction, Hansen stepped back. He tried to survey the rest of what was going on in the Great Hall.

Borley's retainers stood back to back, a tiny clot on either side of the hearth. Those who were armed had drawn their weapons, but there was nothing but fear in their eyes.

Arnor strode out of his bed closet, wearing a tan-and-gray

battlesuit. A blue-white arc snapped from his right gauntlet, fluctuating in length from a few centimeters to a meter and a half as Peace Rock's champion spread or closed the gap between his thumb and forefinger.

Extended, the arc quivered close enough to one of Borley's terrified men that his beard began to shrivel.

"All right, you slime!" Arnor shouted. The suit's external speaker gave his voice an eerie resemblance to that of Borley moments before. "Time for you to leave!"

The three retainers standing on Arnor's side of the hall rushed for the door; those across the room followed a half pace later. They paused on the threshold.

Torchlight wavered through the open doorway and winked on metal. The slaves of Peace Rock were gathered outside the hall. They carried hayforks, flails, and iron-shod staves.

Arnor's arc weapon sizzled into a thin ellipse almost four meters long. He crashed a massive step in the direction of Borley's men. They bolted through the door and began screaming as the farm implements landed their first blows.

Abel had knocked over one of the tables as he fell. His face was slack; there were dribbles of blood from his ear and nostrils. For a moment, the stertorous breathing of his master was the only sound to be heard within the Great Hall.

Hansen dropped his mug; it rang on the wooden floor. The metal was as distorted as though it had been hammered on an anvil.

He shouted to the staring faces, "He touched me as if I were a slave, not a warrior. He acted like a dog, and I treated him like a dog deserves."

"Oh, may the gods bless you!" Holly blurted in a high, clear voice.

Lord Waldron and his warriors crowded toward Hansen with their hands outstretched.

Hansen turned and gripped Borley beneath the arms. He dragged the rover out of the legs of his battlesuit, then let the man drop to the puncheons.

"Somebody get him outdoors," Hansen said in a throaty, terrible voice. "He'll void his bowels when he dies, and we don't need the smell in here."

"We didn't need the smell of him alive," said Lord Waldron as he embraced Nils Hansen.

Out in the courtyard, a mammoth screamed at the scent of fresh blood.

≡ 6 ≡

SPARROW RAN TO the left of the mammoth's tracks rather than between the double row of huge footprints. Otherwise he would have to break stride to avoid skidding on broad splotches of the beast's dung. The trail was now so fresh that the pine-scented droppings steamed on a thin bed of snow.

Sparrow and the mammoth were both pacers who matched their strides to the long haul. Krita ran like a deer. She loped and bounded over obstacles, wasting energy that the others conserved by never changing the length or rhythm of their steps. . . .

But the hunters were in sight of the mammoth now, and Krita was closing the gap while the smith was still a hundred meters behind her.

"Not—" Sparrow shouted as his right heel struck the ground.

"—yet," he boomed out at the completion of the next stride.

"Wait!"

Krita would do as her own whim directed. Sparrow shortened his pace by a centimeter, quickened his legs' scissoring by a few heartbeats, and began to draw minusculely nearer to his companion and their prey.

They had no business hunting a mammoth at all, just the two of them. Sparrow and Krita had been checking their trapline when they struck the trail of the beast. It was a lone bull who had passed by so recently that the edges of his footprints in the fresh snow still showed flakes whose individuality had not melted into a blur.

"Come on!" Krita had cried.

She unfastened her cloak and slung it onto the snow as she sprinted off in the unexpected direction. If the smith had not followed, she would have gone on alone.

Sparrow had stripped to the waist as he ran. He still sweated. The air was cold and dry. The tiny snowflakes of the evening before had ceased to fall before midnight, while the temperature continued to drop.

Sparrow would have taken off his fur leggings as well, but that would require him to break stride; and he would not break stride.

The mammoth's ivory tusks gleamed in intervals of sunlight through the pine boughs. As Krita drew nearer, she slanted her course slightly to the right. She was parallel to the beast's haunches and closer than the length of her spear.

Krita still wore her doeskin chemise. Though she was a small woman with a taut, trim body, her breasts were too heavy for her to run comfortably with them unrestrained. She had twisted her belt so that the sheath of her broad-bladed knife waggled like a tail.

Sparrow's quickened stride forced him to suck in deeper breaths. Needles of ice danced in his lungs.

The mammoth paced onward. Its legs moved deceptively slowly, but each step carried the beast another three meters across pine straw and snow. Either the animal was unaware that it was being pursued, or it was too certain of its own black-haired, mountainous strength to pay attention to mere humans.

Krita drew level with the mammoth's right shoulder. She poised the spear above her head.

"*Wait!*"

Krita stabbed, using the full strength of her upper body. Her left boot anchored the thrust. It slipped on pine needles iced into a mat and kicked the other leg out from under her as well.

Instead of plunging through the forward lobe of her quarry's lung and into the heart, Krita's spear ripped a long gouge across the mammoth's ribs.

The mammoth flared its small ears and pivoted like a dancer. Its trunk lifted. The beast shrieked outrage and fury as Krita tried to roll to her feet.

Sparrow hurled his own long-bladed spear from ten meters away. It sank to the shaft in the roll of fat and gristle on top of the mammoth's head.

"Ho! Mammoth!" Sparrow shouted as he waved his arms.

The beast's eyes glittered beneath its deep brow ridges. Ignoring Krita, as Sparrow intended it to do, the mammoth strode forward with the inexorable power of an avalanche.

Sparrow turned; and, turning, fell. He didn't feel the impact of the frozen ground because of the molten pain in his lungs.

The mammoth paced forward, right rear and left front legs together. Sunlight flared as Krita swung her heavy knife.

Left rear and right front—

The mammoth staggered and slid down on its left haunch. Sparrow stared up at the ribbed red dome of its palate.

The mammoth trumpeted in raging fury. It tried to turn. Krita, moving behind the huge animal with the grace of an ermine pouncing, cut the beast's other hamstring as well.

Sparrow rose. His spear wobbled high in the air. Its point was in the spongy bone of the mammoth's skull—useless to the hunter and harmless to his prey.

Krita backed away from the beast she had crippled. She set both palms against the trunk of a pine tree and leaned against her arms with her head bowed. Her black hair, loosened by the run, covered her face like a veil of mourning.

With the major tendons to its heels cut, the mammoth was unable to lift its hind legs. It was anchored where it stood as surely as if it had frozen in ice.

Sparrow walked around the beast, just beyond the circle its trunk could lash in desperate attempts to reach him. The mammoth lifted its right foreleg: once, twice . . . and settled again into the pose in which it now knew it would die.

Sparrow met the animal's black, glittering eyes. He blinked before the mammoth did. Sparrow walked the rest of the way to his goal. His vision was beginning to settle, and the air felt cold on his bare, trembling skin.

"I was wrong," Krita said. "I'm sorry."

She did not raise her head. Her chest heaved with the violence of her breaths. Her right shoulder and forearm were scraped where she had struck the frozen ground.

Sparrow found the woman's spear a few paces away in the snow. The tip was dappled with blood. He hefted the weapon, then stepped close to the mammoth from the rear. The gash above its heel was drawn back in a bloody smile by the white, severed ends of the hamstring tendon.

The beast slapped its ears twice, but it did not turn its head.

Sparrow set the point behind the mammoth's shoulder with a craftsman's precision, then drove it home. The steel passed between the ribs with only a faint grating sound, but the mammoth's hide and muscles were thick and its fat was a sucking blanket to clog the stroke.

Sparrow bellowed: with his effort, and in an access of pity. The steel slid in. A meter of the ash shaft followed it. There was a great sigh as the mammoth's settling weight drove the air out of its lungs.

Krita touched his shoulder from behind. "We'd better get back," she said. "Before we freeze."

"Yes," Sparrow agreed without turning.

Krita stepped in front of the smith and kissed him fiercely. "Back to the lodge," she said. "And to bed."

≡ 7 ≡

IN THE DARKNESS of his bed closet, Nils Hansen ran his fingertips over the surface of the battlesuit that had been Borley's. An amazing piece of workmanship—except for the joins between limbs and body, and even those were the work of a competent smith.

Enough. The cool solidity of the armor was the last physical sensation Hansen felt as he—a man who had become a god, and who was still very much a man—let his being merge with the Matrix that bound the eight planes of Northworld.

It was like diving into a slush of salt and snow, except that the chill was mental as well as physical. He rode the infinite possibilities spawned by every event, expanding into the future and past together—

Dawn breaks.

Dawn breaks in a solar flare that scours the land and seas of all life.

Dawn never comes and the world hangs in twilight.

—all possible, all real; unbounded—

Except that something blocked and channeled Hansen's course across the event waves.

For an instant without time Hansen struggled, spreading his consciousness across the eight worlds and the Matrix. He knew everything that could be and had been and was . . .and the other moved with him, as fast and as far, immersed in perfect interpenetrating cold without end—

without end

without

Hansen let himself be guided and slammed into individual being. He stood in North's hall of frozen light.

Hansen shook and trembled. It was a grim pleasure to him that the tall, one-eyed man on the High Seat also shuddered with the greater-than-cold.

North straightened from an attempt to hug himself into a fetal ball. He shook his head to clear it, then ran the fingers of both hands through his hair to settle it into smooth gray waves.

North smiled at Hansen, then glanced at the clear container on a stand beside his High Seat. "Well, Dowson," he said, "you should have joined us. We had a very interesting game, Commissioner Hansen and I. Didn't we, Kommissar?"

He smiled again. There was no more humor on North's craggy features than there had been the first time.

A brain floated in fluid within the container. Scales of light sublimed from the outside of the tank and expanded across the hall like the shockwaves of supernovae. As the colors swept through Hansen, his mind heard Dowson's voice say, "There are no games, North. Only the Matrix. Only reality."

"For you, perhaps, Dowson," said North. "But not for the rest of us."

"I'm not your plaything, North," Hansen said. His voice trembled, not so much from the freezing Matrix as with Hansen's need to control his own cold rage. "I was never *that.*"

"For all of you, North," whispered a wash of color. "Only reality."

"No . . . ," said North.

His eye bored at Hansen. Hansen stared back as though his heart were hard as an awl.

"Don't interfere with *my* affairs, Kommissar," North said. "In the West Kingdom."

Planes and solids of pure radiance swept around North to form vaults of unimaginable height. His nose, hooked like a raven's beak, flung a hard shadow over his chin as he glared at Hansen.

"The West Kingdom's my own affair, North," the younger

man said flatly. "It's been my affair since I was a warrior there with King Golsingh."

North spat. The floor was black and clear in intricate marquetry. His saliva splashed as speckles of blue light.

"Golsingh is dead," said North.

"The Peace of Golsingh isn't dead," Hansen retorted. Then he grinned, and his expression was as stark as the smiles of the one-eyed man. "But you'd like to change that, wouldn't you, North? What do you have against peace?"

North shrugged. "What do you have for it, Commissioner Hansen?" he asked in a reasonable tone. "If there's anyone in the West Kingdom who knew you before, by now they're old and on the point of death."

Color trembled from Dowson's container. "Men die in peace as surely as in war," the brain said. *"We* will die, North."

North's face went hard again. He wore the jumpsuit uniform of the Colonial Bureau of the Consensus of Worlds; his collar tabs bore a field-grade officer's shimmering holograms. "Yes," he said. "Queen Unn died in peace, but she died young for all that."

Hansen shrugged. *Letting them get to you is letting them win*.

"Then just say it's my whim," said Hansen. "I spent my life before I came—here, before I came to Northworld . . . I spent my life keeping the peace."

He could feel his cheek muscles tensing, changing the planes of his face. He must look like a grinning skull. "That's what we called it in the Department of Security, keeping the peace. So I'm going to keep one island of peace here on Northworld, too."

"And if I say you will not . . . Kommissar?" North asked.

Above the men and the tank containing what had been a man, coffers of light shifted down through the spectrum, orange and red and finally a red near to black. A sudden, soundless jolt of ruby lightning raked across the arches.

Hansen laughed. Jets of violet as saturated as the discharges from a Tesla coil ripped from every finial of the vaulted ceiling. Their crackling was scarcely distinguishable from Hansen's laughter.

North laughed as well. The hall brightened to its former purity.

"All right," said the one-eyed man in apparent good humor. "Will you play me a game, Commissioner Nils Hansen? To see whether the Peace of Golsingh will hold . . . or not hold."

"It'll hold," said Hansen.

"I won't interfere," said North. "But if you play, Hansen, you'll play as a man—not a god. If you intervene in the Open Lands as a god, I will crush the West Kingdom so completely that men will whisper when they speak of it. Do you understand?"

Hansen spat. A section of the floor dissolved into blue fire, then re-formed. "I hear you talking," Hansen said.

North nodded as if well pleased by the response. "One more thing, Kommissar," he said. "If you play in the Open Lands as a man . . . you can die as a man."

Dowson said, "All men die . . . ," in a veil of light.

Hansen shrugged. "All men die," he said. "I'll play your game."

He raised his arm. In another instant, he would have slipped back into the Matrix, but the one-eyed man called, "Speaking of Queen Unn . . . she died in childbirth, didn't she?"

Hansen looked at North. *He felt nothing at all*—

"Yes, I believe she did," he said.

—except the urge to kill.

Then he was gone from North's palace.

North chuckled mirthlessly. Dowson's voice washed over him, saying, "Hansen is not a hard man, North."

North stared at the tank with his one eye. "What do you mean?" he said. "He's a killer. You know that."

Colors—blue and mauve and orange—shimmered away from the tank. "Oh, yes," said Dowson. "But Hansen doesn't plot all the time to win his point."

The ripples of speech continued to expand and fade until they merged with the radiant walls.

North got up from his seat. He turned away from the man in a bottle; the god who had no life except in the Matrix, which was all lives.

"You know I'll need warriors at the end, Dowson," North said. "How am I to find them if there isn't war in the Open Lands? Constant war!"

"Hansen isn't a hard man, North," Dowson's words rang. "But you are a hard man."

North raised his arm. "Then he'll lose our game, won't he, Dowson?" he shouted as he dissolved into the Matrix.

"Perhaps some day he will lose . . . ," whispered the brain through the infinite paths that North followed.

≡ 8 ≡

HANSEN FLED THROUGH the paths of the Matrix. All times, all knowledge, all possibility; expanding before him as a wilderness of needles hiding one needle.

In a forest valley, three women lay on a flowered hillside and waited for their men to return from hunting. Above them, clouds scudded in a blue summer sky. . . .

One cloud was a bear, Krita thought; and one cloud was a horse.

And one cloud was an electronic dragonfly, sailing through the universe in perfect freedom.

"Forever," Race muttered, and Krita knew that her companions were thinking the same thing that she was.

"We should have gone with them," said Julia.

Krita closed her eyes and let the back of a finger rub the leaf of a violet. The contact was almost too subtle to notice. Her mirror lay flat on her chest, below her breasts, where its metal cord hung when she was upright.

Race snorted. "How many times can you walk a trapline?" she demanded.

"The men like it," said Julia in half protest.

"The men," said Krita, "have their craft. We have—"

She rose to a sitting position and plucked the violet up by its roots. "*This* is what we have," she concluded.

She tossed the flower contemptuously behind her, toward

the knoll on which the Searchers had left their vehicles for the last time.

"I miss being able to move," Julia said. "Of course, we could leave here on foot. . . . "

"Oh, aye, that's a *fine* idea," Race said. "Three women with no protector and nothing but what we could carry on our backs—what do you suppose we'd find for a fate then?"

She looked to Krita for support, but the black-haired woman was playing morosely with images in the mirror Sparrow had given her.

"*I* miss the fighting," Race continued. "Where North sent us, we were warriors as good as any man . . . but not on our own, not in any kingdom in the Open Lands."

"What I miss . . . ," Krita said, but she spoke so quietly that the others heard the words as only a sighing breath.

"They love us in their way," Julia said. "They're good to us."

The mirror showed Hansen, looking much as he had when Krita first saw him two years or two lifetimes before. He was seated with a lord and his warriors, as much at rest as a lounging cat—

And, unless Hansen had changed, as willing to leap with his claws out.

"Well, what of that?" Race protested. "Sledd gives me as much pleasure as any man I've met . . . but not *forever*! Not with him, not with anybody."

Hansen got up from the bench and walked toward the door of the hall. A chestnut-haired servant, fat and nearly forty, watched him leave with an expression that Krita had seen before.

Krita's lips tightened minutely. The image focused down on the face of the man she had known first as an outcast, then as a warrior. Now as a god.

"There's more to their lives than to ours," Julia said sadly. "There always will be unless they give us back our dragonflies . . . and they won't do that, because they're afraid we'd leave."

"They're right about *that*," Race snorted.

Hansen's face grew as though he were walking toward the

*back of the mirror. He smiled, a little crooked but warm, not
something that a carnivore would offer as it sprang. Krita had
seen both expressions on Hansen's face, and both expressions
were real.*

"Fagh!" Race continued. "If I have to endure this for *another* year—"

Krita bent forward to kiss the surface of the mirror. Her
lips met warm lips which returned the kiss.

She jumped up with a cry of blurring emotions. The mirror
jounced at the end of its looped cord. Had the mirror not been
attached, Krita's convulsive motion would have flung it as
far as the spring below.

Race and Julia, warriors both in all but sex, were on their
feet. Their senses scanned the placid hillside for the source
of Krita's surprise.

"The—it's all right," Krita said. She slipped the cord from
around her neck and held the mirror where all three Searchers could view it with ease. Its face quivered with glimpses
of clouds, trees, and the women staring at a polished metal
surface.

Race and Julia were still and watchful. Krita's visage was
transfigured.

"Show us . . . ," Krita said; paused, and continued, "Show
us the lodge."

The mirror obediently filled with the image of the rough-
hewn building that had been the Searchers' home for the past
year. It was roofed with fir shakes, not thatch, because grassy
glades were rare this deep in the forest.

"Closer," Krita said.

The image shifted and swelled, centering on a corner where
the eaves swept down to knee height above the ground.

"There . . . ," said Krita. The mirror trembled in her left
hand, but she controlled the spasm of hope and fear.

Krita reached through the mirror with her right thumb and
forefinger. She plucked a weathered, gray splinter from the
lowest shake and brought the bits of wood out into sunlight
and flowers.

"Show me my dragonfly," Krita said softly.

The mirror focused on a life-sized portion of a dragonfly's

manual controls. The image was as sharp as if it were real.

"Oh North . . . ," Julia whispered. "Oh gods."

"We're saved," murmured Race. Her eyes held the soft incandescence of a perfect sexual climax.

Krita reached into the image. Her dragonfly popped into present existence in the brush where she had left it.

"Not North," she said. "But yes, we're saved."

Her companions sprinted up the hillside. Their vehicles appeared on the knoll before the Searchers reached it. . . .

The three women paused for a moment with their dragonflies quivering in the interior of the lodge they had entered through the Matrix. Their battlesuits stood in front of the bed closets the Searchers had shared for a year with the three brothers.

Race and Julia moved quickly to don their armor. Krita hesitated for a moment. She took off the mirror; held it; and then set it on the wooded floor between the armored feet of Sparrow's battlesuit.

Before she put it down for the last time, Krita kissed the rim of the mirror which the greatest smith on Northworld had crafted with consummate skill.

≡ 9 ≡

THE CONCUBINE WAS oblivious to the skill with which Ritter designed electronic shielding so that it wrapped the tank in his holographic monitor with minimal surface area and no dangerous sidelobes. That wasn't her job.

Her gown was a pale diaphanous blue. It was cut off-the-shoulder and down to the waist, so that one breast was always bare and the dark nipple of the other shifted visibly beneath the folds of the garment when she moved. She took a moment to adjust the strap and give her master time to notice her.

Ritter didn't turn around. He reshaped the force envelope slightly to smooth a concavity that showed orange in the wall of blue-level protection.

"We were wondering, sir," the concubine finally said, "which of us you'd be wanting for tonight?"

Ritter muttered a curse.

"What's that?" he demanded, glancing over his shoulder. The butt of the holstered pistol, no less real for being a symbol of Ritter's status among the lesser nobility, clacked against the chair arm. "What—"

"It's only that the duke's second lady's giving a party tonight," the concubine said, tumbling the words out rapidly as though their torrent could quench the engineer's possible anger. She was a squat woman, heavy with muscle but perfectly formed on her big-boned design. "And it's getting late, sir, and we were just wondering if some of us could, you know, sir, could go, please?"

"Late?" said Ritter.

Inset over the exterior doorway of Ritter's huge workroom was a screen which showed the water-meadows outside Keep Greville in realtime. He glanced up at it. The sun had set hours before; the light of a full moon silvered the backs of the herd of short-legged rhinoceroses which had come from the swamps to feed.

"Yes, of course, all of you go along," Ritter said. "But don't bother me again!"

The workroom was positioned at the center of Keep Greville, the most protected place in the huge, self-contained installation. Even the duke's own apartments on the level above would be destroyed before an enemy reached the sanctum of the duke's chief engineer.

The high ceiling and circuit of the walls could be converted to vision apparatus, so that if Ritter wished, he could pretend to be working in the unspoiled wilderness that existed in past ages before the founding of Keep Greville.

For a time after his skill had won him his present rank, the engineer had done just that; but only for a time. He knew that, whatever his eyes told him, he was held forever within multiple impenetrable shells of forcefields and ferro-concrete.

Ritter's immediate work area glowed in the soft, shadowless illumination thrown by an array of micro-spots with optical fiber lenses. The remainder of the room was lighted only by diffusion, instrument tell-tales, and the dim rectangle of the screen above the door out of Ritter's suite.

Occasionally a piece of machinery clopped or gurgled, but for the most part the large chamber was still.

"The frontal slope should be proof to a flux density of three hundred kilojoules per square centimeter," Ritter muttered, talking himself back into the problem from which the concubine had recalled him. "But the volume of the field generator must be less than . . . "

The engineer's fingers tapped commands even as his voice trailed off. The tank's schematic changed shape, becoming more fishlike; the colored overlay of the forcefield modified also.

The concubine had been squat. Ritter himself appeared to be as wide as he was tall, though that was an illusion. He was forty-one years old, but he had looked much the same when he was a decade younger. His massive features would not age appreciably until he was sixty or older.

His hands moved as gracefully as those of a juggler as he controlled the information patterns of his design console.

Ritter paused, waiting for the thought that he needed to form in his mind and, almost as one, to extrude through his fingertips into the display growing in hologram. There was a whisper of sound behind him.

"Will you bitches all—" Ritter bellowed as he spun around in his chair.

Instead of one of his concubines, a man taller and much more slender than Ritter stood two meters behind the engineer's console.

"Who the *hell* are you?" Ritter demanded. Carefully, to avoid calling attention to what he was doing, he shifted his hips forward on the seat cushion.

"My name's Hansen," the stranger said. He wore a one-piece garment of unfamiliar cut. "I've come to make you an offer, Master Ritter."

"I'd like to know just how you *did* come here," Ritter said. He swiveled the chair beneath him carefully with his heel, so that the arm no longer interfered with his gun hand. "I didn't think it was possible for another man to get through the door to my harem."

"I didn't come through your harem," Hansen said easily. "And more important than how I came—"

Ritter snatched the pistol out of its holster. As the muzzle started to rise, Hansen's boot moved in a perfectly-calculated arc and kicked the weapon out of Ritter's hand. The pistol sailed beyond the lighted area and clanged into an ultrasonic density tester.

The engineer lunged up from his chair.

"I wouldn't," said Hansen. His hands were spread at about hip height, and his torso was cocked forward in a slight crouch.

Ritter was twice the stranger's bulk and strong for his size;

Hansen held no visible weapon. Ritter looked into Hansen's blank, cold eyes—and sat back in his chair.

Hansen relaxed. "More important than how I came here, Master Ritter," he resumed as if there had been no interruption, "is what I'm able to do for you. I need help, and I'm willing to help you in return."

"What can you offer *me*?" Ritter said. "What can *anybody* offer me that I don't have?"

He gestured with his left hand; lights went up across the whole room. Equipment, both electronic and mechanical, stood in separate cubicles. Racks held flasks of gases, fluids, and powders—as well as armor plate in slabs large enough for full-scale testing.

The workmanship throughout was of the highest quality, and nothing in the complex arrangements appeared to be out of place.

"And there," said Hansen, waving behind him toward the door of Ritter's living quarters, "is every luxury your world can offer . . . but that isn't what you mention when you talk about your status. That's why I want you and not somebody else to help me, Ritter."

"Do you know what power I've got?" the engineer demanded. He stood up and paced toward Hansen. "I could have anybody—outside the duke's immediate family—executed, Hansen."

Ritter pointed with an index finger as thick as a broomstick. "I could have the duke's first lady in *my* bed if I demanded it. I'm the best engineer in the world! There's nothing the duke wouldn't give me to keep me building armaments for him and his soldiers."

Hansen grinned. "Can you leave Keep Greville, Master Ritter?" he asked as softly as a stiletto penetrating silk.

Ritter's face set like flesh-toned concrete. He shrugged. "No," he said.

"Now you can leave," said Hansen. "If you want to come with me."

The engineer did not react.

"You'll need an airpack," Hansen added as though he were unaware of Ritter's hesitation.

Without speaking, Ritter walked to a freestanding cabinet. It opened when his hand approached its latch. He removed an airpack and helmet from the ranks of protective gear.

He looked over his shoulder at Hansen. "Do you want to borrow something?" he asked.

Hansen shook his head. "I won't need it," he said. "For that matter, you won't need the helmet for the time we'll be out. Just a face mask."

Ritter put the helmet back on its shelf and closed the cabinet.

Hansen walked into a nearby cubicle, ducked out of sight, and reappeared. "Here," he said, holding out butt-forward the pistol he had kicked from Ritter's hand. "You won't need this—but there's no reason you shouldn't have it."

Ritter reholstered the weapon impassively. "Where are we going?" he asked.

"To my home," Hansen said, "though I'll take you by the scenic route. I'm going to guide you with my arm. You don't have to do anything except step forward when I do."

Hansen's eyes hardened. "But *don't* panic and run," he went on. "Even if you don't see me for a moment or two. There's nothing along the way that's as bad as being left there with it. And you *will* be left if you run."

"I don't panic," said the engineer. His voice rumbled like a glacier calving icebergs.

"That's good," said Hansen without expression. He put his left arm around—partway around—the big man's shoulders. "Keep the airpack to your face and step for—"

Ritter's right leg swung forward in unison with Hansen's. The air shimmered opaque and *rotated* in a plane that was not one of the normal three dimensions.

Points of light in infinite number surrounded Ritter. For a moment they were chaos, but when he realized the alignment, he saw that all the beads were segments of lines focused on *him*.

They were as cold as the duke's charity.

Ritter was alone—without the stranger who'd promised to guide him; without even his own powerful body. He was a point in a pattern of intersecting lines, and when he moved (because he had been moving when he entered this limbo without soul or warmth) the lines shifted also and kept him at their focus until—

"You tricked me!" Ritter shouted as his heel shocked down on solid ground. He realized simultaneously that his voice and body worked again, and that his guide had not entrapped him forever in a waste as dead as the circuits of a computer's memory.

Hansen still held ʌim. "What was—" Ritter began before his eyes took in his new surroundings.

"Step," said Hansen.

The soil was frozen and crusted with snow. Ritter had never seen snow, even when he was young and not yet too valuable to be permitted to leave the armored fastness of Keep Greville. He and his guide stood behind one of a pair of lines of men who wore personal armor as they fought one another.

The armored men slashed with electrical arcs which sprang from their empty gauntlets. Blue-white discharges crackled like ball lightning when they crossed one another, until one of the arcs failed or both combatants stepped back to break the contact.

A pine tree burst into flame as an arc brushed it; then a fighter's armor failed in omnidirectional coruscance. Bits of burning metal and superheated ceramic flew from the heart of a hissing electrical corona.

"Step," Hansen repeated. The pressure of his arm was greater than a man so slender should have been able to exert.

The man whose armor had exploded was toppling forward. His head was missing, and the top of his chest plate still bubbled with the heat of its destruction. Ritter strode—

Into a world of crystal and cold so intense that the surface of Ritter's skin steamed. Around him stood pillars of glass—pillars of glassy ice—figures of ice! They were figures, because Ritter *knew* they moved though they were so glacially slow that he and his guide could wait here an age and see nothing.

"Step," said Hansen, but the engineer was already striding into—

A swamp. Ritter's weight plunged him over his boot tops in muck. The metal fittings of his airpack frosted momentarily as the hot, humid atmosphere thawed them. Drops of dew condensed on each of Ritter's exposed body hairs.

He took the mask away from his face.

"Step," Hansen urged from beside him.

"Wait," said Ritter. He drew in a deep breath redolent of vegetable decay.

This wasn't the swamp outside Keep Greville or any other swamp on Ritter's world. Large trees growing in the distance had branches like the limbs of hydras rather than anything vegetable. Leaves tufted from each of the joints of the meter-high reeds nearby. There was no true ground cover, only flat creeping greenery that looked at first glance like slime.

But after the frozen horror of one moment—one *step*—before, Ritter needed a rest in the familiarity of sucking mud and air as moist as the breath from a steam kettle.

"Those *things* were alive," he muttered to Hansen.

"At one time they were," Hansen agreed. "I suppose you could say they still are."

Watchful though not especially concerned, Hansen's eyes flickered over sheets of still water and the reed tussocks where the mud formed islands. Nothing of significant size moved, but something hidden in the mist bellowed a challenge.

Ritter straightened. "What kind of hell was that?" he demanded.

His guide looked at him with eyes momentarily as bleak as the waste the men were discussing. "The only kind of Hell there is, I think," he said. "Just Hell."

Hansen's mouth moved in what might have been either a grimace or a shiver. "Put your airpack on," he said. "We have to go."

With the mask clasped firmly on his face again, Ritter tried to take a step forward. The mud clung to his boot, and he didn't think his leg was moving until the invisible plane rotated him—

Onto a gravel strand under a huge sun hanging motionless on the horizon in a frozen dawn. The vacuum sucked greedily at the waste valve of his airpack. He felt his skin prickle against the pressure of his cells' internal fluids.

There was a wink of blue from a distant corniche. Something with its own light source had moved, because the sun and all it illuminated were dull red.

Hansen's lips moved. Though Ritter could not hear the word, he stepped into—

An upland forest of tall evergreens, and a beast so huge that for the first instant Ritter thought he had appeared next to a gray-green boulder.

The rock sighed with flatulence. Ritter looked up to see, browsing needles fifteen meters above him, a small head . . . on the end of a serpentine neck . . . attached to a ten-tonne body, now upright and hugging the treetrunk with its forelegs to stabilize itself during the meal.

There were dozens or even hundreds of the creatures around him, hidden in plain sight by their size and the cathedral gloom of the forest.

"Step," said his guide, and—

The men were on an island. Its shore was being combed by a breaker kilometers long. The air was fresh with the tang of salt. Sea oats bowed away from the off-shore breeze.

Ritter lowered his face mask. "Were they dangerous?" he asked. "The animals?"

Hansen shrugged. "One of them could have stepped on you, I suppose," he said. "But no real danger from them, no."

He looked over the breakers. A few kilometers out, a storm covered as much of the horizon as the two men could see from where they stood. Lightning quivered in and from the clouds, but the thunder was lost in the constant pulse of breaking waves.

There was more that Hansen wasn't saying. Ritter looked at his guide. "You were worried about carnivores, then?" he pressed. "What is it?"

Hansen shrugged again. "Not the carnivores," he said, "though they could be bad enough on the wrong day. The

Lomeri live there on Plane Two. But we weren't there long enough for them to find us."

"I don't know who the Lomeri are," said Ritter. He noticed that he was nearly shouting. Because the surf was omnipresent, it did not seem loud—until he tried to speak over the water's sound.

"Lizardmen," said Hansen, still looking at the flickering horizon. "It doesn't matter. Come, we're almost there."

Ritter thrust his boot forward and felt his heel strike hard—

On the floor of an open-fronted shower stall. Instead of water sluicing down, Ritter's ears sang with harmonics in the audible range as beams of ultrasound bathed him. The mud shook off his clothing as fine dust which hidden vents sucked away.

"Welcome to my home," Hansen said with an expression that appeared both mocking and wry to the point of being bitter. "At any rate, I call it that."

Somewhere in the background, a male voice sang that *Spanish is the loving tongue,* but no humans were visible. The engineer glanced at a couch. It shifted and became broad enough for his massive form.

Ritter stepped out of the shower stall. They were in a circular room whose walls were so clear that only slight vertical discontinuities between the panes of crystalline material proved that the ceiling was not suspended over open air. The furnishings were sparse, though the way the couch returned to its former configuration in the corner of Ritter's eye suggested that flexibility would make up for number.

"*I don't look much like a lover . . . ,*" sang the cracked tenor voice, "*yet I say her love words over. . . .*"

Ritter walked over to the clear wall. The dwelling was built into a sideslope. Their upper-story room was level with a flowered prairie on one side, while on the other it overlooked a valley floor. A breeze drew swathes of shadow through the grass heads below, but there was no sign of large animals for as far as Ritter could see.

He turned abruptly to Hansen. "Where are we?" he demanded.

"In my home," said his guide. "On Northworld."

"No," said Ritter. "Northworld is where we left. Where *I* live."

He frowned, then noticed that his right index finger was playing with the butt of the pistol Hansen had returned to him. He snatched his hand away. "That was the old name, at least," he said. "We call it Earth now. Most people."

Hansen nodded. "That *is* Northworld," he said, speaking calmly. "So is this, and so were the seven other stops we made. All equally real."

He smiled. "Or equally false, of course," he added. "Take your pick."

Ritter swallowed. He jerked his right hand down again. "I don't—" he said.

His tongue hesitated over 'understand,' then concluded, "—believe you!"

"I don't really care whether you believe me or not, Master Ritter," said Hansen. His look of amusement underscored the truth of what he said. "That's not why I brought you here."

Ritter's mouth opened, then closed. He had spent his life working to the whim of Duke Greville, who was a fool. This man, whatever he might be, was not a fool. . . .

"Go on," said Ritter.

"I brought you here to show you something," Hansen said with a smile of appreciation for his guest's attitude. "I'd like you to copy it for me."

He gestured at a slab of wall. The crystal frosted, then began to seethe with images.

"Why me, Hansen?" Ritter said bluntly.

"Because it has to be done without me manipulating the Matrix directly," explained the slim man with ice-gray eyes. "And there's no one anywhere, anytime, on Northworld who can do that as well as you can, Master Ritter."

The engineer looked from the speaker to the images forming in the wall, then back again. Figures moved inside a room built entirely of natural materials.

"What do you want copied?" Ritter asked.

"One of these," said Hansen as he pointed.

The image in the wall froze. "They're called dragonflies. I want a dragonfly like the ones these Searchers are riding."

≡ 10 ≡

SPARROW KNEW THE Searchers were gone before he took in the fact that their battlesuits were missing. The lodge felt empty; as empty as a tomb.

The mirror he had given to Krita winked from between the boots of his own armor.

"And except for that damned fox, we'd have another three martens," Gordon grumbled to Sledd as they entered behind their brother. "Hey, Julia!"

"They've left," said Sparrow in a quiet voice.

"Race!" called Sledd as he shifted the straps of his pack that doubled in apparent weight as he tried to get it off. "Damn. Help me with this, Sparrow."

"They've left us," Sparrow repeated. He didn't move from where he stood when the realization hit him.

"Hey, where's the battlesu . . . ," Gordon began. His voice trailed off. He and Sledd stared at their brother, finally taking in his words.

"They can't have gone!" Sledd insisted. He hunched his shoulders and flexed himself away from the straps of his pack. The bundle of fresh furs hit the floor with a thump.

"Are they walking, then?" said Gordon. "But they took their battlesuits."

"They've found their dragonflies," said Sparrow as certainly as if he had watched the women leave, "and they've ridden away on them."

Sledd ran his fingers over the carved wooden panel of his

bed closet. Race's battlesuit had stood there.

"I don't believe—" Sledd began; but he did believe, and his bunched fist slammed through the lindenwood panel with a sound like the first stroke of lightning.

"Why did they . . . ?" Gordon said. He knelt and removed his own pack, thumbs beneath the straps. His eyes were closed in concentration.

Gordon couldn't get out the rest of the question; and anyway, the brothers all knew the answer.

Sledd flexed and massaged his right hand as he wandered toward the farther end of the room. Objects that he and his brothers had made winked in perfect wonder. A silver cabinet opened for him as he came near. Its trays held every piece of the splendid jewelry he had fashioned for Race.

Sledd kicked at the cabinet morosely.

"It doesn't matter, does it?" he said. "We can go back to the way things were, that was plenty good enough. If we want women, we can always buy time from the nomads down south, the way we did before."

"Wait, there *is* a way!" said Gordon gleefully. "Sparrow, we'll use that mirror of yours to find them again, and then we'll—"

As Gordon spoke, he bent down and reached for the mirror. "—talk with them, conv—"

"No!" said Sparrow, bear huge and bear quick as his bulk slid between his brother and the object. "That's Krita's. Nobody touches it but—"

"You made it!" Sledd objected.

"Nobody but Krita!"

No one spoke for a moment. The beads of light continued their stately dance in the center of the lodge. Their illumination was dimmed by the blaze of sunlight through the east gable and the open door.

"We can still find them, you know," said Gordon, the words coming out faster as the wish clothed itself in the trappings of reality. "We can! They'll go—"

"They'll go back to the gods," said Sledd. He sucked the knuckles of his right hand. "We'll never see or hear of them again."

Sparrow turned slowly, lost in his own thoughts. His pack bumped the bed closet. He absentmindedly twisted one hand behind him to lift the massive weight, then removed the other arm from the unloaded strap.

"They'll want to see their homes, won't they?" Gordon protested. "They'll spend some time back where they were born, now that they're free."

Sparrow opened his bed closet. While the men were gone, Krita had pinned sprays of fresh flowers to the railing within. The stems had wilted and half the petals were scattered on the bedding.

"That was years ago," Sledd said, but he was commenting on the proposal rather than dismissing it out of hand. "Time isn't the same with the gods."

"It's not so long for Julia," Gordon said. He threw open a clothing chest, choosing quickly among the linens and woolen garments for which the brothers traded on their infrequent journeys to the fringe of the settled world. "Her father was King Tournalits. He may still be alive."

"Race had brothers," Sledd remarked. Though he spoke softly to hide the hope that might tempt fate to deny him, his normally harsh voice trembled with something close to tenderness. "But that was in the far south, Pallaia."

"Then we'll go to Pallaia!" Gordon said. "And to Tournalits' fortress in Armory. If they aren't there, they'll at least visit sometime—and we can c-c-convince them. To return."

Sledd opened a chest and began to set out a trading assortment—rings and bracelets and lights brighter than jewels; pots that heated by themselves, and boxes that sang in tones of inhuman purity. The brothers did not keep baggage animals, but their own massive shoulders could carry enough of the products of their craft to buy a duchy.

Gordon paused. "Sparrow?" he said. "Your Krita . . . ?"

Sparrow looked at his brothers. "Oh, she'll come back to me, you know," he said. There was no emotion in his voice. "You go on, yes, look for your, your . . . "

The smith's mind hesitated between 'women' and 'wives.' In the end he chose neither and continued, "You go look for Race and Julia, and maybe you'll find them. But I'll stay here, because I know my Krita will come back to me one day."

Sparrow's brothers stared at him. The master smith's eyes were opaque.

If Sparrow was looking at anything, it was deep within his heart.

But his heart was probably empty as well.

≡ 11 ≡

HANSEN SAT IN the empty bed closet to which he had returned, staring at memories. Someone tapped on the door.

He rose from the bed, but the door wasn't barred. He collided with the figure who slipped in as Hansen reached for the lifter.

Contact made his guest a woman whose low bodice was embroidered. The moon rising beyond the opening in the east gable woke a sheen from Holly's chestnut hair.

She closed the door quickly. "I—" she began stiffly, but then the rest of the words came out in a rush "—wondered if there might be something I could do for you, sir? I owe, we all owe—"

"Oh, nothing like that," Hansen said in surprise, though it *shouldn't* have been surprising.

He always forgot that people thought he was doing things for them. He wasn't. He did what was in front of him, what people forced him to do. It was never what Nils Hansen wanted, just that he was there when it had to be done.

"Oh," said Holly. "Oh, I'm s-s-sorry—"

Air stirred as the servant whipped the cloak back over her front and turned to leave.

"Wait," said Hansen.

He heard her fumbling in the dark for the latch lifter. When she couldn't find it, she slapped the thin doorpanel in frustration.

"Wait," Hansen repeated.

For a moment, Holly resisted the pressure of his hands. Hansen was stronger than the servant, stronger than any woman he had met, and he would not be denied.

"It's all right, really," Holly said in a voice which suggested she believed her own words. "You want someone younger and, and not so fat. I'll tell—"

"No, wait," Hansen murmured.

"Any of the younger ones would be honored, but I said that—"

Hansen's arms were around Holly's shoulders. "Stop," he said. He kissed her forehead and felt her relax.

"Just wait," he repeated, and as she turned her face upward, he kissed her on the lips.

"I rattle on when I, when I'm nervous," Holly said. She tugged her cloak open and pulled his right hand to her bosom. "I—what you did for us—"

Hansen bent. Holly was wearing a clean dress, not the one in which she'd been pawed by Abel, but the pattern was similar. He kissed the curve of her right breast, just above the nipple.

"Oh," Holly said. She put her arms around him. "Oh dear."

"But not here," Hansen said, straightening. "I—"

He paused. "There's too many memories."

"Oh . . . ," Holly said in a different tone. "Oh, of course, the killing tonight. . . Oh, I see."

For an instant, Hansen trembled with a vision of Unn shaking her blond hair out in a cascade across her breasts and the firm, pale flesh of her abdomen.

"Yeah," he said. "That's . . . "

He didn't have the heart to continue with the lie, but it was all right. The woman misunderstood as Hansen meant her to do.

"Right," he went on softly. "Ah, don't you have a place of your, your own?"

"The children are—" she muttered, thinking aloud. "But I could move—" She focused on Hansen. "It will take a little time, that's all, but—"

"Wait," Hansen murmured, kissing her lips again as the

only practical way of interrupting Holly's nervous flow. "We'll just go walking, shall we? It's a warm night."

Children might mean a husband.

Some questions are none of a third party's business, and no one benefits from the third party asking them.

"Yes, the meadow's lovely with the moon over it," Holly said. She led the way out of the bed closet and into the silent hall. "There's a wicket through the palisade, and there's no watchman there. Not that it . . . . "

The mud streets of the village were almost as quiet as the lord's hall had been. Penned animals grunted and gurgled with the noises of digestion, but the beasts showed no interest in the two humans on the board walkways.

The moon was brilliant: full, and halfway now to zenith.

Holly nimbly jumped a gap where streets crossed, then hugged Hansen fiercely as he followed her. "It seems like everything is getting different," she murmured.

"I didn't have anything terribly exotic in mind," he said dryly.

"Silly!" she said, kissing his cheek and striding on toward the gap in the palisade at a quicker pace. "Though that would be . . . I mean, *almost* anything, at least."

The circle of withies intended to loop the wicket closed had rotted away. Holly turned the wooden grating open, then leaned it back against its posts when Hansen had followed her.

"What I really meant was the rovers, of course," she continued. "And the king summoning levies to Frekka for his army."

The meadow was scythed, not cropped by the teeth of animals whose hooves would damage the roots. It had not been long since the last mowing.

"Umm, prickly," Holly said as she bent to brush the stubble. "We'll put my cloak down."

She giggled. "And besides, I don't care!"

The field sloped gradually. By now, irregularities in the ground would hide the couple from anyone looking down from the palisade. Holly paused.

"Lord Waldron has been summoned to Frekka?" Hansen

said as his fingers fumbled deliberately with the brooch clasping Holly's cloak.

"No, it's not a full summons," she said as her own hands, gently but firmly, took over the task from Hansen. "Two warriors only from here, that would be Arnor and Cholmsky, I suppose. . . . "

She turned and spread the garment in a graceful motion. She lifted her face to Hansen; the moonlight showed concern in her expression. "Unless you go, milord."

Holly gripped him fiercely before he could decide how to react. "Oh lord. Something has to be done to stop the rovers. Or—"

She shuddered with reaction. "Or everything will change," she closed simply, and began to unlace the sides of her dress.

If Hansen had ever thought the serving woman was stupid, he would have been disabused by that simple and accurate assessment of the kingdom's plight.

They knelt on the cloak, then lay on it and one another, changing positions several times. It wasn't love, but it was something both of them needed.

And perhaps in its way it was love.

≡ 12 ≡

ON THE THIRD day that Platt watched the isolated lodge, he got the chance he needed. The smith left, carrying a pack and a hunting crossbow.

Even so, Platt waited an hour before he risked leaving his hiding place in the gorse at the edge of the clearing. So long as he was sober, the spy—the exile—the *outlaw*—was cautious as a fox. Platt had been sober perforce for most of the past three years; and, cautious, he had made sure he was alone on the occasions he had stolen enough liquor to get drunk.

The tendons of Platt's legs complained when he got up. He carefully walked the stiffness out of them in the forest before he attempted the hundred meters of clear area surrounding the lodge. If challenged, he would claim to be a wanderer and lost; the first true, the second very nearly true, for he'd had no idea he would find a dwelling this deep in the forest.

There had been an incident a month before, and the house-holders had hunted him with dogs. Platt had moved fast, because it was his life at stake, and he had deliberately struck off into the wastes; habitation meant support for those chasing and no shelter for their quarry. By the time Platt had lost the pursuit, he had also lost all but the barest notion of his whereabouts.

In the empty nights, with his belt tied to a branch to prevent him falling from his squirrel-nook in a pine tree, Platt had time to reflect on the fact that his life had long ago lost all purpose.

The clearing was a carpet of pine straw near the trees, bare earth as Platt neared the lodge. He had decided to go to the door opposite the one from which the smith had left. The outlaw stepped lightly, careful not to stir the ground cover or leave footprints in the dirt—which fortunately was dry.

Platt's head moved only the slight amount that an honest traveler would look around as he approached haven in the wilderness. His eyes flicked constantly ahead and to the sides, and his ears strained to hear the squeal of a crossbow being cocked behind him.

The smith looked like a powerful man, but the real proof of his strength lay in the size of the crossbow he carried— and cocked with a lever, not a windlass.

But the big man had no reason to believe that his lodge was being watched. It was only chance that Platt had decided to follow the faint trail from the spring at the head of this valley. He'd thought it might be an animal track along which he could set snares to supplement the nuts and berries which had sustained him since he fled.

The lodge had been a surprise. Platt dropped from instinct. It was a hot, still day and the doors in the gable ends were open. The outlaw could see directly down the long room.

Platt could also see wonders of which he had never dreamed, not even when he strutted around the royal court secure in his position and his cunning. Platt was third cousin to King Hermann—

But the child's father had been kin to the king as well; and because Platt had been drunk, he hadn't murdered the witness after he raped her.

"Hello the house," Platt called, too softly to be heard any distance into the forest. The smith's pack had implied a long trek, but Platt never took needless risks.

When he was sober.

The latch string was rawhide, old and cracked. No one had used this door in years.

"Hello?" Platt repeated. He teased the latch open carefully to keep the string from parting.

What had been wonders to the outlaw watching from a distance were unbelievable when he stood within the lodge.

They lighted *themselves,* some of them, and the intricate motions of the rest were like a dream of a god's palace. Platt began to shiver with anticipation and—for the first time in three years—hope.

With this to offer King Hermann. . . .

Platt opened the door only wide enough for his thin body to slip through like a mouse squeezing into a cupboard. He looked around in amazement. Half of the devices were beyond his ability to guess their purpose.

In every sweep, Platt's eyes paused at the far door through which the smith might at any moment return.

The moving spirals that lighted the room hung in the air without any physical support. Platt's long knife probed beneath them, hoping to find a wire thinner than hair or a crystal column that passed light as the air itself did.

Nothing. Perhaps there was a support overhead, attached to the ceiling . . . but in the midst of so many marvels, it became easier to accept the truth of the inexplicable.

There were three bed closets. Platt froze as he considered the implications, but instinct assured the outlaw that the lodge was empty though he had seen only one man leave it.

A battlesuit stood open before the nearest closet. Aided by the artificial light overhead, Platt peered at the suit. It was not painted. After a moment's examination, the outlaw realized that paint on armor of this quality would be like paint on a knife-blade—defilement, not decoration.

His fingers ran over the glass-smooth joints of the finest battlesuit he had ever seen. Even the mechanical connections were perfect: though the suit was unoccupied and cold, the frontal plate swung as easily as if the hinges were balanced on jewels.

Platt breathed very softly. Many of the articles of the smith's craft were unique; and, because there was nothing with which to compare them, some of Hermann's courtiers would be unable to see their value.

But all warriors understood battlesuits. *Everyone* would see the supernally high quality of this suit.

He started to leave then, because he would gain only further amazement by staying—and Platt, even cunning, grasping Platt, had been bludgeoned to awe by the wonders he had already seen. When the shadow of his body moved, a mirror winked from between the battlesuit's legs.

The outlaw bent down, intrigued more by the placement than by the object itself. He raised the little mirror, though the caution that kept him alive against the odds was screaming that he *must* leave, that the lodge's owner might be anywhere—

The smith's face stared out of the mirror's surface.

Platt screamed like a rabbit as the snare tightens. He spun with his knife thrusting, knowing that its blade was keen enough to shave; knowing also that a man of the smith's size and strength would snap the intruder's neck like a twig even after being disemboweled.

Platt was alone in the lodge.

The outlaw picked up the mirror again from where terror had flung it. It had not been damaged by its skid along the puncheons—but now it was only a mirror which reflected Platt's terrified face.

But it *had* shown the smith—

As soon as Platt thought of him, the smith's image filled the metal surface again. He was trudging forward stolidly against a background of tree boles. His crossbow was in his arms because it would interfere with his pack if he slung it, but he had not bothered to cock the weapon.

The smith was several kilometers away from his lodge, but Platt was watching him.

The outlaw hugged the mirror to his breast for a moment, feeling in the object's hard outline the certainty of his own return to society. Then, cautious even in triumph, he set the mirror back where he had found it.

Platt latched the door behind him carefully as he left— for the time being—the lodge and the objects of wonderful craftsmanship within it.

≡ 13 ≡

RITTER SCOWLED GRUDGINGLY at the craftsmanship of the dragonfly which he viewed through the window of Hansen's house/palace/eyrie.

"This isn't going to be easy, you know," the engineer said. "I'll need the vehicle itself to examine."

"Yeah," said Hansen. "We'll go get it."

Ritter frowned. "How long can I keep it?" he asked.

"As long as you need," Hansen replied with a shrug. He looked out through the panes to the east, toward the horizon of gently waving grass. "Duration doesn't matter here."

The exterior of Hansen's dwelling was of cast plastic with windows of preternatural clarity. North had told him that the building had no soul, but it was the architecture to which Hansen had become accustomed when he was a security officer on a far world, in a distant time.

Besides, Hansen wasn't sure that he had a soul either. If he did, then he shouldn't have felt empty inside most of the time.

"But won't the owner miss it?" Ritter protested. He knelt beside the perfect image and took an electronic magnifier from his sleeve pocket.

The dragonfly's control module *was* a seamless monomer casting, at least down to the level the portable unit could magnify. He'd probably have to cut—and that meant analyzing the material so he could learn how to weld it before he started to dismantle the dragonfly.

"It'll go back to the niche in time where Krita finds it again, never fear," Hansen explained. There was movement on the horizon, not just the grass bending and rising in its slow dance with the wind.

"It's not going to be easy," Ritter repeated as he spot-checked radiation from various points on the vehicle while it was at rest. "And I'll have to take it back to my own laboratory. . . . "

The squat engineer looked up, half expecting to be told that he must perform the work *here,* away from his familiar equipment and support structure—

Which would give Ritter the excuse he needed to bow out of the project and go home to what he knew.

Hansen turned and nodded. "Yeah, I assumed you'd want to do that," he agreed without concern. "Though I could duplicate your equipment here, if you'd prefer."

"No, I . . . ," Ritter said. "I'll be all right, back in my lab. No one questions what *I'm* working on."

He was afraid of the unknown. Every human being feared the unknown.

But Chief Engineer Ritter wasn't so frightened of learning the unexpected that he would refuse a unique opportunity.

Ritter resumed his preliminary examination of the dragon-fly by measuring the dielectric potential across ten centimeters of the casing material. For the readings to be valid, the 'window' had to be as transparent across the whole spectrum as it was in the optical wavelengths. . . .

Hansen opened the door and looked out to the east. He could barely hear the clatter of the swans' pinions, but the car they drew was hidden behind the cloud of feathers rowing against the air.

"Just so long," he said to Ritter, "as you can do the job."

"Matter is matter," the engineer grunted. "I can analyze it; and if anybody can build it, then *I* can copy what he did."

He scowled at the reading he'd just taken. He checked it against similar lengths of the control panel and a leg strut, then swore in appreciation.

"All right," Ritter said, "I've seen enough to know that it's no good me fooling around with pocket instruments on a project like this. You deliver—"

His eyes focused past Hansen's shoulder. "What in *hell* is that?" he demanded.

Hansen laughed with some amusement but no humor. "My visitor, you mean?" he said, following the engineer's eyes. "She drops by when she has nothing better to do . . . and tries to do *me*."

The swan car swept in a circle that brought it to a halt broadside before the men. Between fifty and a hundred of the birds had been somehow harnessed to the gold lacework vehicle.

The swans held their positions well enough in flight, but as soon as they settled, they began to hiss at one another like a knot of vipers.

The driver was a haughty youth with broad shoulders, a wasp waist, and a pointed black moustache which perfectly matched the color of the minuscule briefs that were his only garment. He glanced at Hansen, then Ritter, sniffed, and began polishing the slim-spoked wheels with a chamois rag.

Ritter blinked in amazement at the queenly woman who descended from the car.

She was tall, and her hair and clinging dress were both the exact color of the golden car. When she moved, for instants that were almost subliminally brief, the dress seemed to vanish and leave her as perfectly naked—except for the jewel between her breasts—as she was perfectly formed.

Hansen slid open a crystal door. "Hello, Penny," he said with the wry smile of a man who'd been impressed despite himself. "You know, I've been meaning to ask you—how do you train those birds?"

Penny waved a languid hand. "It's taken care of for me," she said in a voice of studied culture.

Then she looked over her shoulder at the swan car and snapped in a very different tone, "Myron! Move it away, won't you? How is anyone supposed to think with all that racket?"

Ritter expected the driver to react sullenly, if at all. He knew the type, and they weren't all male.

Instead, Myron dropped his chammy and touched the controls—electronic, not mechanical reins, the engineer saw. The birds settled into the traces and began to beat their wings in unison.

Whatever else Penny might be, this surly young stud behaved as if she held his life in the palm of her hand.

Which meant that she probably did.

The car trundled off a few hundred meters, where the swans' noise was lost in the breeze.

"I have an idea you'll like, Hansen," the woman resumed in her false cultured tones again. "And I promise that you won't believe how *much* you like it until you've tried. . . . "

She touched Hansen's chin with long, perfect fingers and turned his face to a three-quarter profile.

Hansen disengaged Penny's hand. "I'm busy, Penny," he said.

"Do you want me dark-haired?" she asked.

Light struck from the jewel on her breast and abruptly she *was* dark, with hair like a rippling ebony carving and lips a fuller, darker red to match. "You know that time doesn't matter here, whatever you're doing. Busy doesn't exist for us."

"I'm always going to be too busy for you, Penny," Hansen said. "I wish you could understand that."

His face hardened into the expression Ritter had seen momentarily when Hansen kicked the pistol from his hand. "I'd appreciate the offer more," he went on, "if I didn't know you'd say the same thing to a Shetland pony you hadn't met before."

Penny sniffed. She didn't appear to be upset by the insult. "You don't know what you're missing," she said.

Her jewel flashed. She changed again, her body rather than merely her hair and features. Ritter's mouth was dry. Now Penny was a heavy, shorter woman whose chestnut hair had flecks of gray.

"I watch you with other women, you know," she said archly to Hansen.

He laughed. "I can't stop you," he said.

"I can *be* those other women," Penny said with a sudden fierce edge. "Look at me, Hansen! I can be—"

The jewel winked. Penny was blond, not quite so tall as before, not quite so statuesque, and Hansen shouted, "*No!*" as his fist rose mantis-quick for a blow that would crumble bone—

Penny was a teenage girl, not unattractive, who wore cover-alls of gray synthetic and an expression of blended fear and desire.

Hansen squeezed his right fist with the fingers of his left hand. "Penny," he whispered to the ground in a ragged voice, "don't show me Unn again. Don't."

He looked up at the girl. She simultaneously shifted to the woman's form in which she had arrived.

"It isn't just a body, Penny," Hansen went on, his voice filling to its normal timbre. "And it especially isn't just that body."

"You're wrong, you know," Penny said, without rancor but flatly certain; as certain as Hansen was in his own belief.

She turned and looked Ritter up and down appraisingly. "Your slave's from Plane Five, isn't he?" she said. "They're all such squatty fellows."

Ritter had seen men eye women that way—Duke Greville, for instance, whether the woman was a new concubine or the daughter of a peer; but it was a surprise to see the look on a woman's face.

"He's not a slave," said Hansen easily. "We're helping one another. Partners."

Ritter didn't stare devouringly at women. A unique piece of equipment—like the dragonflies waiting across a dimensional window—might elicit the same expression from him, he supposed.

"I haven't had one of your type for . . . ," Penny said, walking around the engineer as if he were a garment displayed on a mannequin. She giggled. "There *I* go, talking about duration."

Ritter rotated to face her. The jewel on her breast twinkled. At each flash, Penny was a different female form. Each time, along with changes in hair color and facial features, she was slightly shorter and a few kilos heavier—tending toward the somatotype with which the engineer was familiar.

"Turn around," Penny said sharply, making a brusque gesture with her hand. "I want to see your profile."

"Go to hell," said Ritter. He turned his back on her and knelt to study the dragonfly again.

The sonic imager he carried lacked power to penetrate the casing material. He'd need the full-scale X-ray equipment of his lab, and—

The woman giggled again and leaned over Ritter's shoulder. One bare, heavy breast lay on the back of his neck; the nipple of the other brushed his right biceps. "What's your name, then?" she asked coyly.

Ritter stood up slowly and turned.

"Penny," said Hansen in a dangerous voice, "he's under my protection."

"I'm not going to hurt him, you know," Penny replied with a touch of steel herself. "Just the opposite."

"My name's Ritter," Ritter said. "I'm an engineer."

The form Penny had settled on—for the moment—was that of a twenty-year-old woman, five centimeters shorter than the engineer. She had red hair—nearly orange on her head, duller and mixed with brown on her armpits and pubic triangle. Her body was thick, but powerful muscles dimpled the fat sheathing her hips and thighs.

Apart from the jewel, she was completely nude.

"Penny, we have business to take care of," Hansen said in a tone that thinned as he noticed the way Ritter met the woman's eyes.

Penny put a hand on the engineer's shoulder. She turned to Hansen and said haughtily, "What's the matter? Is he really your slave after all, and you control his breeding rights?"

Hansen took a deep breath. "Master Ritter?" he said, letting the context serve as the remainder of the question.

Ritter touched his lip with the point of his tongue. He didn't understand the powers of the people he was dealing with; but he didn't doubt that those powers went beyond the ability to appear and disappear, went beyond the capacity to change shape.

Went possibly to life, and certainly to death.

"Duration really doesn't matter?" he asked. "Time spent

here doesn't mean time taken away from the job?"

"No problem," Hansen said. He gave Ritter a genuine grin. "Go have fun, partner."

The engineer ran his hand over the plane which displayed the dragonfly, careful to avoid touching the curved surface.

"*This*," he said to his guide, "is the kind of fun I've never had before."

He looked at Penny. "All right, lady," he said. "I'll go for a ride with you, if that's what you want."

Hansen smiled. "I want to talk to Penny alone for a moment, Ritter," he said. "If you could—"

"I'll tell Myron to bring the car by," Ritter said with a grin of his own, pride and anticipation. "Let's see if he gives me a hard time."

He stalked off, a powerful man wearing bright, loose clothing that bulged with equipment. Very sure of himself, of his ability and of his manhood.

Hansen's smile faded as he transferred his attention to Penny. Before the expression was wholly gone, it had become a leopard's snarl.

"He's my responsibility, Penny," Hansen said. "If you get—"

"I won't hurt him!" the woman blazed.

"We can't bring the dead to life, Penny," Hansen continued as inexorably as a train on rails. "If you do something in a fit of pique that can't be undone, then I'll come after you. Do you understand?"

"You'd bring down the Matrix if you did," Penny said. "All of us. All of Northworld."

"Do you doubt me, Penny?" Hansen said in what was barely a whisper.

"No," the woman said. For a moment there was nothing in her eyes but calm intelligence. "I don't doubt you at all, Hansen. There won't be a problem."

Penny took the man's hard right hand between both of hers, raised it, and kissed the tip of Hansen's trigger finger.

She turned to meet the swan car. Her driver cringed like a whipped puppy in front of the big engineer as they approached Hansen's house.

≡ 14 ≡

A TEMPORARY STAGE had been erected before the House of Audience in the center of Frekka. The rest of the stone-flagged square was filled with warriors summoned from all across the kingdom and their attendants.

"You really wanted to be sent with the royal levy, didn't you, Hansen?" Arnor asked. His voice was tinged with wonder and a little bitterness.

Sunlight had not yet burned off the chill fog. The waiting men coughed and grumbled and spat.

"Sure," said Hansen, shrugging to bring the collar of his fur cloak tighter against his ears. "I'm a warrior, so I want to go where the fighting is. Right?"

He gave his companion a thin smile. "Didn't you want to come, Arnor?"

"Now stop milling around, gentlemen!" ordered the only person on the stage at the moment, a brightly-dressed usher. "King Prandia will be out to address you momentarily."

"Then you ponce off someplace else and get the king out here where he belongs!" snarled a lord with good lungs and too much rank to cool his heels willingly.

"It's my duty," Arnor muttered. "I'm the champion of Peace Rock, and the lord himself is too old to attend the levy."

"You could say it's my duty too," said Hansen as he eyed the crowd.

There seemed to be about a hundred warriors present.

Close up, a warrior's bearing distinguished him from his freeman attendants even when the warrior wasn't wearing his powered armor. In diffuse light and a mixed crowd, though, it was hard to be sure.

"Anyway," Hansen added, "I've got the best battlesuit in the hall. Thanks to my benefactor, the Solfygg rover."

The House of Audience was a tall building with spires at the corners; it antedated the year two generations ago that Frekka became the royal capital. Four trumpeters stepped out of the front door. Their trumpets were slender cones, each with a broad flange soldered onto the bell more for appearance than to affect sound quality.

Three of the instrumentalists managed a clear fanfare, but fog had gotten into the throat of the fourth man. His call sputtered. Even at best, the echoes from the old buildings surrounding the square were thin on this dismal morning.

"A bad omen," Arnor muttered.

"Balls," said Hansen in sudden anger. "Men make their own luck!"

Warriors in battlesuits shifted to block the streets entering the square. Instead of individual paint schemes on their armor, these men wore only patterns of stripes on their right arms. The color and width of the stripe indicated the warriors' unit and rank within it.

Professionals. The standing army—the Royal Household— of the West Kingdom.

"Hail to King Prandia the Just!" cried the usher. He hopped off the stage as a stocky, fortyish man mounted the steps behind him.

Prandia wore hose and a puffed black doublet that would crush flat without discomfort when a battlesuit closed over it. The spangles on his beret were as likely jewels as they were metal sparklers, but neither the cap nor the rest of his garb made any concessions to the cold.

Prandia's breath plumed from his nostrils as he eyed the assembly. Warriors in fur tried to control their shivering.

"Hail, King Prandia!" chorused the crowd.

A number of people cheered with genuine affection. The

interest of a few warriors was primarily on the armored professionals who now surrounded the square.

That only meant that Prandia the Just wasn't Prandia the Sucker.

The king's skin was pale and he had blue eyes. He looked nothing at all like his grandfather, Golsingh the Peacegiver . . . though his coloring was very similar to that of his grandmother.

Queen Unn.

"Lords and warriors of my kingdom," Prandia said. His tenor voice carried across the square with surprising power. "The Duke of Colimore, my friend and son-in-law—"

Breath fluffed again from Prandia's nostrils. He drew in a deep breath and continued, "The Duke of Colimore has been murdered with all his family by Ontell . . . who was his counselor, and claimed to be his friend."

"Happened at midsummer," Arnor muttered to Hansen. "Ontell's got a way about him, but he's mean as a snake inside."

"Ontell has usurped Colimore," Prandia continued as coldly as though he had not just mentioned his daughter's murder, "though the duchy is of my kingdom and in my gift. It would appear that Ontell is receiving support from the King of Solfygg . . . but that will be a matter for another time, after we do justice in Colimore."

"Princess Unn was the apple of her father's eye," Arnor said. "She was the prettiest little thing you ever saw."

"Was she indeed?" Hansen said. His lips were as pale as bone.

"I will not be leading you against Colimore in person," Prandia continued. "That duty will be performed by my marshal, the Duke of Thrasey, who will handle it ably and professionally—"

The tremors which shook the king's body could have been a reaction to the cold, but Hansen was shaking also within his furs.

"As I do not trust myself to do," the king added, getting control of his voice midway through the clause.

"Because the kingdom has been at peace during my reign

and that of my father," Prandia went on in his original cold, powerful tones, "it is necessary to organize you gentlemen of the levy for the first time. To that end, your battlesuits have been set within the House of Assembly."

The king gestured at the building behind him. The crowd murmured. Warriors were considering the matter of greatest concern to them: their status within the first army of the West Kingdom in generations.

"Please enter the building—only warriors!" Prandia said, raising his voice to a sufficient degree. "Enter the building and stand beside your own armor. Duke Maharg and several of his champions will speak with each of you individually before making their assignments."

"Duke *Maharg* of Thrasey?" Hansen said to Arnor as the push to the House of Assembly's doors began. "How old is he?"

"Hmm?" said Arnor. He eyed the rush doubtfully, then settled back to let the crowd thin before he moved toward the hall himself. "Maharg? Oh, he's the king's age. They were raised together when Prandia was fostered by the first duke, that was Malcolm, Maharg's father."

"What . . . ?" Hansen began. He sucked his lips between his teeth for a moment. "What happened to the old duke, then?"

"Well," said Arnor, "I think he's still alive, though he must be older than the hills. He abdicated in favor of his son, oh, must be ten years ago."

The square around them was full of chattering freemen, but all the nearby warriors had made their way to the queue snaking around both edges of the stage. Prandia looked down and caught Hansen's eye for a moment.

"I guess we better go," Hansen said to his companion. They moved ahead. Freemen jumped out of the way of their greater status.

"Why were you wondering about old Malcolm?" Arnor asked.

"Oh . . . ," said Hansen. He could feel the eyes of the king focused on his back, but he did not look up as he passed the stage. "I used to know him, a long time ago."

The champion snorted. "As young as you are?" he said.

They had reached the doors of the House of Assembly. Voices and hardware echoed within. Warriors looked for their battlesuits and objected to where the armor had been placed, as though a preliminary sorting had already occurred.

"If you did," Arnor added, "you must've been just a boy."

≡ 15 ≡

A PUPPY YOWLED pitiably as Bran and Brech, the king's twin boys, held its hind legs in the fire.

From the look of King Hermann and Stella, his hard-eyed queen, they would willingly be treating Platt as their six-year-olds were the dog.

"Like nothing you ever dreamed of seeing, Excellency," Platt whined.

The outlaw knelt in front of the royal chairs with his forehead to the floor. When he spoke, dust and ash puffed away from his nervous lips. "Lights that hang in the air and move. A mirror that shows far places."

"Pah!" said Salem, a young baron who'd joined Hermann's council since Platt was outlawed. "His breath fouls your hall, majesty. Let me stop it for good."

"Armor fit for the gods to wear!" Platt wailed against the flagstones.

"Wait," said King Hermann.

The outlaw exhaled bubblingly in relief.

Platt had taken the only chance he would ever have of being rehabilitated; but it had looked, and it might still be, that he had lost that final necessary toss of the dice. Unless the king believed Platt's story, the outlaw had nothing to trade for his life; and even before his exile, Platt's word had done little to compel belief.

"But I'll lead you there!" Platt whined to the scorn echoing in his own mind.

"For pity's sake, Hermann," said Stella in a voice like
chilled steel. "Tell him to get up out of that ridiculous
pose."

Her tongue clicked against the roof of her mouth. "Or kill
him. That might be better."

"All right," said the king. "Get up. For now."

Platt scrambled to his feet. He bobbed and touched his
forehead to each of the hard, sneering faces around him.

The thrones were on one end of the large, rectangular
audience chamber. Hermann's councilors stood to either side
with their uniquely-decorated battlesuits behind them as iden-
tification and insignia of rank.

The barons hated one another; but they hated Platt more.
If the king had suggested it, they would all have cooperated
to drown the outlaw in a cesspit.

There was a huge hooded fireplace in each of the sidewalls,
cold now except for the fire the twins had lighted for their
fun. During the morning levee, the chamber would be filled
by suppliants; but Platt had been brought to the king in late
afternoon, when Princess Miriam and her ladies-in-waiting
used the room's acoustics for their lute playing.

King Hermann was forty and fleshy rather than fat. His
queen was younger by ten years, but she had never been
beautiful or even striking, in the positive sense. Her eyes
were intelligent and cruel. Very cruel.

"Milord, he lives alone on the northern edge of your kingdom, deep in the forest, and he has treasures beyond belief, I
swear to you," Platt said quickly. The words tumbled out like
a cascade of smooth, stream-washed pebbles. "He's a smith,
and he makes wonders, not just battlesuits. But his battlesuit
is, milord, I can't describe its perfection—but I can show
you. For my life."

There was a sudden crash and screeching from among the
girls on the opposite end of the chamber. Princess Miriam
lashed at a servant with her lute.

"How *dare* you not serve me first?" Miriam shrieked.
Fragments of the sound chamber of her instrument flew.
She swung again. A string twanged.

The servant, a girl little younger than the fourteen-year-old princess, hunched on the floor. She was afraid to run or even raise her arms to shield against the blows. A platter of candied fruit lay scattered over the stones.

The six ladies-in-waiting sat rigidly on their stools as if they too were pieces of furniture.

"Miriam, my dear," called the queen in a peremptory voice. "Keep your voice down, please."

The princess looked at the broken neck of her lute and the bits of sound chamber dangling from the strings. She kicked the servant and hissed, "See what you did? Get out of here!"

The servant ran, scuttling the first few steps hunched over like a frog. The puppy had also escaped from the twins during the commotion. It moved with surprising speed on its two good legs and waited until it was beyond the doorway to begin yowling again.

Baron Tealer, an old man and kin by marriage to the girl who caused Platt's exile, cleared his throat. "If this place is in the forest, milord," he said, "then it's not in your kingdom. Our writ doesn't run through the uninhabited wastelands."

"If there's someone living there," said Hermann as he stroked his pointed beard, "then it's not uninhabited." The king smiled at his manicured hand. "And if there's such wealth there, Tealer," he continued, "then it must be royal wealth, mustn't it?"

Several of the barons shrugged a grudging acceptance of what they saw would be King Hermann's decision.

Stella looked at her husband. "Hermann," she said.

"My dear?" Even the king looked uncomfortable when he heard that tone of voice.

"If you're going to rob a man of such power, a smith . . . ," the queen said deliberately, "make sure you kill him as well. You'll remember that, won't you?"

"I'm his king and he owes me tribute," Hermann muttered without meeting his wife's eyes. "That isn't stealing."

≡ 16 ≡

"DID YOU THINK I'd stolen him, Hansen?" Penny called in a tone of harsh challenge as Ritter brought the aircar to a halt in front of Hansen's dwelling.

Hansen noted that the engineer flared the ducted fans fore and aft so that they wouldn't spray grit over Hansen's legs as the car settled. Ritter was a good man; an amazingly good man.

But then, Nils Hansen always needed the best when there was a job *he* couldn't do.

"Master Ritter isn't a chattel you could steal, Penny," Hansen said with a cool smile; but he was glad to see Ritter returning, glad not to have to check on the situation . . . gladder yet not to have checked and learned something that he didn't want to know, and then to act because he said he would act.

Hansen didn't want to die. Not really. Not most of the time.

Ritter shut off the engines and spread his blade pitch to maximum so that air would brake the drive fans to a halt in the least amount of time. Though the car rested solidly on the ground, it rocked when the engineer lifted his heavy body out of it.

He grinned at Hansen and said, "Tsk. Didn't think I'd stay away from a puzzle like this one just to screw, did you?"

Ritter raised his arms over his head, interlaced his fingers with the backs of his hands downward, and stretched up onto his tiptoes, still smiling. His clothing looked the same as that in which he had left with Penny, but Hansen's practiced eye noted that these garments were perfectly clean and of a softer fabric than the originals—though whatever synthetic Penny chose would certainly wear like iron despite its comfort.

Otherwise the engineer—otherwise *Ritter*—wouldn't have accepted the replacements.

Hansen smiled again, this time with more humor than before. "You're ready for work, then?" he asked.

"I'm always ready for work," Ritter replied, and he quite clearly meant it. They walked through the simple doorway into the observation level of the house.

Penny followed them. Her face was twisted into an expression too dismal to be described as a pout.

Penny's garb was normal enough for her: a macramé bra, briefs cut to expose rather than conceal, and net stockings. Her body, however, was unusual.

Penny now wore the form of a nineteen-year-old with vaguely blond hair, slightly overweight in a puppyish sort of way. She was neither stunningly beautiful nor strikingly grotesque. A mildly attractive young woman, but not the appearance most folk would pick from an infinite choice of features and bodies.

Unless it was the way they had looked before they received the power to choose; and if so, that was a fact Penny had been working to conceal for as long as Hansen knew her.

"Unusual vehicle there," Hansen said. He gestured with his thumb, but he did not look back toward the aircar.

Ritter blinked. "You're joking!" he said. "It's dead standard. Besides, nothing could be unusual after that whatever-you-call-it pulled by all those birds."

"Swans," said Penny quietly.

"You'd be surprised what people will come up with when any whim works as well as the next," Hansen said. "It *does* all work, you know. When all times are the same time; and when any idea has power if a—"

Hansen swallowed but managed not to lose his calm expression. "If a god chooses to think it."

Penny stared morosely out a window. For the moment the

view was only waving grass the aircar had overflown on its way here.

"Penny just . . . ," Ritter said, rubbing his chin and scowling at the memory. "She said, 'All right,' and there it was, a car like the ones we build for Duke Greville's scouts on campaign. I don't understand."

"It's a matter of arranging the correct point on the correct event wave to intersect with present reality," Hansen said.

Ritter turned in sudden fury—looked for a solid object within his reach—saw nothing. He slammed his right fist into his left palm with a tremendous smack.

"That's just words!" he shouted. "It means nothing!"

Penny flinched at the engineer's anger. She turned around.

"How would you," Hansen said coolly, "describe to a blind man the process of sorting red and yellow objects without touching them, Master Ritter?"

The engineer grimaced at his display of temper. Frustration carved his face into harsh angles like those of a tumbled wall. "Sorry," he muttered.

"Sorting event waves through the Matrix works in much of Northworld," Hansen continued, "for some people."

His voice had less of an edge than a moment before. "It didn't work where I came from, not that I knew about, anyway. And it doesn't work for *any* damnbody on the plane you come from. But that doesn't mean it isn't real."

"I remember when we put them on Plane Five," Penny said without emotion. "The first fleet the Consensus sent looking for us after we'd disappeared."

Ritter looked at the woman in fresh horror. "You *remember* the colonization?" he said. "That was—tens of thousands of years ago!"

Hansen put a hand on the engineer's shoulder and kept exerting pressure until the big man noticed and turned to face him.

"Time isn't the same here," Hansen said gently, though part of his mind noted that if Penny wanted to convince her latest stud that she was some kind of ageless monster, she couldn't have picked a better way. "And anyway, you're thinking of duration again. Besides—"

He grinned honestly, infectiously. "—you 'n me have got a job to do."

Ritter laughed, loose again. Whatever else Penny might be, Ritter knew she was a woman; and a woman was nothing to worry about when there was a uniquely challenging task to accomplish.

He looked around the observation room with a slight frown. "Ah," he asked. "Do you have a—"

"Toilet?" completed Hansen. "You bet. Down there—" he pointed to a drop shaft with a coaming of molded plastic "—and just to the right of the door."

"Back in a minute," the engineer muttered as he stepped into the shaft.

Now that they were alone, Hansen nodded a cautious greeting to Penny. "I guess things worked out for the two of you," he said.

It disturbed Hansen to see the woman acting . . . different. Hansen's fellow gods, who had the power to do virtually *any*thing, always seemed to do the same thing again and again.

It was easy for Penny to create an aircar in place of the swan-drawn vehicle she always used. It was amazing to see her do something because of a man's whim.

Penny hugged herself, squeezing her full breasts almost out of their slight restraint. "Well enough," she said.

She looked at Hansen with the disconcerting intelligence that sometimes glinted from her brown eyes. *Out of place in a trollop who thought only of sex and her appearance.* "How much danger is there going to be?" she asked.

"On this?" Hansen said in surprise. He waved at a section of window. The clear surface suddenly showed a thicket of magnolia bushes and tall, scale-trunked trees.

Krita's dragonfly and those of her two companions nestled into the vegetation. Their spindly legs compensated automatically for the slope, keeping the saddles level.

Hansen's eyes went flat as he calculated. "Not a lot of risk," he said. "None at all, if things go as they should."

"You're armed," said Penny, nodding toward the cutaway holster high on Hansen's right hip.

Not stupid at all.

"Well, you know what they say," Hansen replied with a chuckle. "You carry a pistol when you *don't* expect trouble. When you know the shit's going to hit the fan, then you lug something serious along."

Except that pistols were Nils Hansen's weapon of choice, because he pointed handguns as though they were his own fingers. Not that he really expected trouble.

"And those damned things—" Penny turned and spat in the direction of the dragonflies "—are there with the Lomeri."

The spittle vanished in a puff of light at the surface of what was still a window, not a physical opening onto another plane of the Matrix.

"I can make you as many as you—" Penny said.

She spread her pudgy right hand. Five dragonflies, indistinguishable from those sitting in the magnolia scrub, appeared in the gazebo.

Hansen brushed them back into nonexistence with a flick of his own hand. "North and I have an agreement, Penny," he said mildly. "We're going to do a quick in-and-out, Ritter and me. We'll be gone before the Lomeri know we were there. No sweat."

"Easy for you!" the woman blazed. "He isn't a, isn't a killer like you, Hansen."

"Ritter isn't exactly a babe in arms, you know," Hansen said with the care he would have displayed if his dog began yelping and snapping at the air. "Besides, nobody's going to be doing any fighting. We're just going to pick up a piece of hardware."

The engineer rose through the shaft, hitching up his equipment belt and checking the flap of the pistol holster dangling from it. He waved cheerfully toward Penny and Hansen.

Penny walked out of the observation room. She leaned against the aircar with her back to both men.

Hansen heard her mutter, "Bastard!"

Hansen supposed Penny meant the epithet for him; but he wasn't quite sure.

≡ 17 ≡

"WHAT'S THE STUPID bastard waiting for?" muttered King Hermann to Crowl, the nearest of the warriors hiding with him; but as the king spoke, Platt reappeared at the door of the lodge and began to walk back with an exaggerated care not to leave footprints.

"Are you really going to let Platt live?" Crowl asked. Instead of the external speaker, he used the radio built into his battlesuit's circuitry. Platt, wearing only the ragged jacket and fur trousers in which he had reappeared at court, could not overhear them.

"As long as he's useful," Hermann said.

The party consisted of six warriors including the king; a dozen freemen with bows or spears; and almost a hundred slaves. The slaves had been necessary to carry the battlesuits the last three kilometers to the lodge so that the sound of baggage animals would not alert the smith.

The warriors knelt in their armor, flanked by the freemen. The slaves huddled a kilometer away, keeping as silent as possible. If the overseer told Hermann that the slaves had made any commotion while they waited, they would all be killed.

Platt the outlaw entered the lodge alone to determine whether or not the householder was present. A part of Hermann's mind whispered to him that the best result would be for Platt's body to be flung back out the door in pieces. . . .

But the smith was absent.

"It's empty, majesty," said Platt, wringing his hands nervously. He dipped as though he intended to kneel on the mold of leaves and needles. "We can wait now, and when he returns, we'll have him."

"Well, when *does* he come back?" Crowl demanded. "I don't want to sit in this damned suit for the next fortnight."

"There's no way to tell, milord Crowl," the outlaw mewled. His voice had the same choppy, high-pitched timbre as that of the head-down squirrel complaining from a nearby treetrunk. "He may come back in minutes, or he may have just—"

"I want to see the interior," Hermann said abruptly.

Platt's face froze in a rictus. The king started forward.

"Milord!" the outlaw wailed, throwing himself flat on the ground as King Hermann's boot rose to crush forward with several hundredweight of armor behind it. "Milord, you'll leave marks and he's a hunter and he'll see and he'll, oh my lord, we'll miss him!"

Platt was terrified. He knew that if the ambush failed for whatever cause, he would pay the price.

And he was right. A battlesuit's weight and the sputtering discharge wherever its forcefield touched a solid object left browned, deeply-impressed footprints on any surface but solid rock. If their quarry returned by daylight, he would have to be blind to miss the tracks.

The king sighed and stepped backward. Platt was scum, but he was cunning scum.

"All right," said Hermann, reaching for the catch of his armor. "I'll take this off."

"I'll go too," said Crowl.

The outlaw got up from the ground, dribbling flecks of forest debris. From the look in his eyes, he was doubtful about the safety of this course also.

But Platt knew there was no doubt at all as to what would happen to him if he tried to block his monarch's whim again.

The lodge had a breathy, lived-in-but-empty quality which worried Platt but only made Crowl's lip curl. Crowl hadn't seen the smith, moving with the power and arrogance of a bear.

King Hermann halted three steps into the long room. He was impressed despite himself by the unique objects scattered in careless profusion.

Crowl paused at the moving lights. He poked, then flailed his arms impatiently beneath them, trying to find the invisible pillar. "What in hell holds these up, Platt?" he demanded. Before the outlaw could answer, the warrior leaped into the air with his hands cupped.

"Don't!" Platt shrieked. "You'll—"

The air snapped like the popper of a drover's whip.

"YEOW!" Crowl bellowed. He came down in a crash, one hand gripping the other.

The air smelled of burned meat. The hole seared through the warrior's hand was as neat as could have been pierced with a white-hot wire.

The beads of light continued their slow, undimmed circles.

"—break something . . . ," Platt concluded.

The outlaw's voice trailed off. He maneuvered to put a tall silver spiral that sang like a waterfall between him and Crowl's angry reflex.

"Stop fooling around, Crowl," Hermann grunted, very possibly saving Platt's life for the moment.

The king stopped in front of the battlesuit. He fingered its lining of padded leather. It was a big suit, but Hermann was a big man himself. The jointed arms lifted and fell to his touch with a feeling of jeweled smoothness, as though inertia alone restrained the motion without any friction between segments.

"Did he *make* this suit?" Hermann wondered aloud.

"He must have done, majesty," Platt said, wringing his hands again. "And all this, must have made them because how else would they be here, one man and no baggage train?"

Crowl drifted across the hall to stare at a construction of gears and pivoting levers. Its purpose was beyond the warrior's imagination. He kept his hands thrust firmly through his back, though at intervals he withdrew the injured member and pressed it against his belly. The cauterized hole did not bleed.

Platt bent over the pile of scrap and ore beside a bench.
He prodded with the point of his long knife. At the core of
the heap was a section of tubing decorated with lightly-etched
flowers.

"You see his work?" the outlaw said. "Have you ever seen
a smith who could make *this*?"

"Toys," King Hermann grunted. "But this . . . ,"

His hand ran over the battlesuit's surface, a finish as smooth
as that of a pool of black ice.

The king stepped back to see the armor complete. His eye
caught a wink from the floor between the boots; he bent
to retrieve the mirror. "What's this, do you suppose?" he
asked.

Platt was covering the object in process more or less the
way it had been when they arrived. "Oh, that's another wonderful thing, majesty," he said, lifting a last pebble of ore
onto the pile. "It shows you the owner, wherever he is."

"No it doesn't!" Hermann snarled; but as the king spoke,
the reflective metal suddenly cleared into a vision as sharp
as that in a diamond lens.

Platt looked over his shoulder and frowned. "That's not
the smith . . . ," he muttered.

The mirror showed a scene in the royal hall. Princess
Miriam sat at leisure in a chair inlaid with ivory and gold.
A slavegirl teased out her long hair, and ladies-in-waiting
played a soothing trio for lute, recorder, and solo voice.

"I just wondered what Miriam was doing, and there she
is," the king murmured in an awestruck tone.

"Truly a marvel, majesty," Platt said in nervous approval.
"Like all the objects here, treasures beyond imagining, just
as I said."

Hermann stared into the mirror, which now showed his
sons. They were in the palace kitchen. Bran tipped a ladleful
of hot broth down the back of a scullery maid sleeping in a
corner.

"But perhaps we should, ah . . . ," the outlaw murmured,
"ah, go back into concealment so we don't lose our prey?"

The miniature image trembled again. Each scene had its
own internal light, so even in the gloom of the lodge's interior

the intruders could see every detail of the smith, who strode through the forest, seemingly unaffected by his load.

"He's a mean-looking one," the king muttered.

"Stella said to chop him," Crowl said as he joined the other men at last.

"That's a whole stag," Platt said, unable to keep bitterness at the smith's strength and ease out of his tone. "That's a hundred kilos dressed out—besides what else he's carrying."

"And if he's carrying it like that," King Hermann said in sudden decision, "then he's probably coming home. We'd best get into position."

The mirror blanked suddenly into a circle of polished bronze again. The king hung its carrying loop around his neck.

Platt paused halfway to the back door of the lodge. "Ah . . . majesty?" he said.

"Well?" Hermann snapped.

Crowl was in the doorway. The tone of the king's voice turned the warrior around, his face tense with the chance he would be called on to finish Platt.

"Are you . . . majesty, ah, going to take that mirror with you now?" Platt blurted in an agony of indecision.

"Yes," said King Hermann. His lips pursed. "It's—" he went on with a hint of doubt "—just one little thing, after all. He won't notice it, and . . . Anyway, we'll be waiting."

"Yes, majesty," the outlaw said, bowing and mopping in terror. "Yes, of course, majesty."

But instead of leaving immediately, Platt hopped back to the work in progress. His fingers poised for a moment. He removed a piece of flint no larger than a pea and carried it across the room to the battlesuit.

"What are you . . . ?" King Hermann said in wonder.

Platt set the chip of flint carefully in the joint of the lower hinge of the frontal plate.

He gave a great sigh as he straightened. "Now . . . ," he said.

The polished surface of the battlesuit reflected his relief.

≡ 18 ≡

THE HOUSE OF Assembly was an echoing confusion of voices and battlesuits.

Warriors got into and out of their armor, clashing the frontal plates. Helmet speakers amplified their shouts in metallic dissonance.

The coffered ceiling was still decorated with a Pageant of Trade from the days when Frekka was an independent trading port ruled by a syndicate of merchants. Frescoed Syndics frowned down on the warlike babble.

Occasionally one of the levies would light his cutting arc. That created a snarling dazzle and thunderous orders to, "*Shut it off or eat it, dickhead!*" from the armored professionals overseeing Marshal Maharg's examination.

Other warriors argued face to face with the staff officers who trailed along behind Maharg. The officers were hard-faced men who jotted down notes and explained what the marshal's cryptic remarks meant to the levy he had just examined.

Almost every warrior had a complaint. Some spoke in disbelief, some in anger; and not a few in a desperate hope that surely they could be raised a little in the roster, their suit was surely better than a *sixth* ranking (. . . fourth ranking . . . seventh ranking . . .), wasn't it?

The officers never raised their voices, except to be heard over some exceptional commotion; and they never took any notice of the complaints except to deny with the cool firmness of marble slabs that there would be any change in Marshal Maharg's dispositions.

Some men would have argued further, but the professionals following the staff officers wore battlesuits. These escorts gave every indication of being willing to end a problem within seconds of when it started.

The marshal finished with the warrior to the left of Arnor and, beside him, Hansen. He looked at Arnor and asked, "Name?"

"I'm the Champion of Peace Rock," said Arnor with an obviously manufactured assurance. "Obviously I have the right to demand the front rank in the name of Lord Waldron, but in view of the circumstances, I'm willing to accept a s-sec—"

Arnor's flood of confidence waned under the pressure of the marshal's gaze. "Ah," Arnor concluded in a softer voice, "a third-rank posting."

Maharg's eyes were brown and as hard as polished chert.

"Buddy," he said with the air of a man repeating what he'd said to *every* damn warrior he'd examined this morning, "if you'll let me do my job, then you can get around to yours when the time comes at Colimore. Now, get in your suit but *don't* switch on the bloody arc."

"You ought to list the levies separately from the household," Hansen said.

He pitched his voice to carry, but he kept the tone as cool as that of Maharg's staffers. "People are going to get their backs up about ranking anyway. There's no reason to make it worse by maybe three steps each time."

The marshal turned with no more haste than the first boulder of an avalanche. "And just who the hell are you, buddy?" he asked.

One of the armored professionals stepped around the staff officers—in case of need.

"I'm the guy who just gave you good advice for the next time," Hansen said. His right arm was at his side. He leaned on his left hand against the thorax of his battlesuit.

Maharg was a tall man with broad shoulders. He wasn't paunchy, but his waist was thicker than that of his father.

Of course, I knew his father as a much younger man.

The marshal's complexion was just dark enough to suggest that his father Malcolm was an octoroon; his eyes hinted that his father's quirky intelligence had passed to the son as well.

"There won't be another time," Maharg said. "Not after what we're going to do at Colimore."

Hansen shook his head gently. "There's always another Colimore," he said. "Peace doesn't happen. It's something you make and keep."

Maharg turned away. "Close up your suit," he said to Arnor, peering from his open battlesuit. "Take a couple steps forward."

An expert—Maharg was certainly an expert—could determine a battlesuit's quality from visual examination. If there were any doubts, the artificial intelligence of any battlesuit could provide either a relative or an absolute ranking of any other suit within an observation range of several kilometers.

Maharg wasn't examining the armor alone. He was checking the way each suit behaved when its owner was wearing it. Hesitation, awkwardness; overcompensation for the inertia which servo motors did not quite eliminate—all would be evident to the marshal's practiced eye in a matter of a few seconds and a few steps.

Hansen watched the current demonstration as critically as Maharg and his staff officers did.

Arnor had good armor. Had he wanted it to, his battlesuit would have earned him high rank in a household that was less of a backwater than Peace Rock.

But that was the point: Arnor *didn't* want to duel his way to a position, even if that meant bruising, half-power contests instead of arc weapons at their full lethal intensity.

The Peace Rock champion was skillful enough. He stepped forward, then pirouetted on one foot; a tricky maneuver even on a surface as solid as this floor. Despite that, each of Arnor's movements started with a jerkiness which indicated mental uncertainty rather than a power-train lag in his armor.

"All right," said the marshal wearily. "You're done for now."

He turned to an officer who carried a notebook made of boards planed thin and bound with leather thongs. "Call him a five and put him in White Section," Maharg said. "And get his damned name, will you?"

The officer flipped a board over and dipped his writing brush into the pot of oak-gall ink attached to his belt.

"And what," the marshal continued, sliding his eyes over Hansen and onto Hansen's armor, "do we have here, smart guy?"

"Put on your own suit, Marshal," Hansen said, still leaning on his armor, "and I'll show you exactly what we've got."

Maharg ran his fingers over the battlesuit's forearm, then worked the elbow joint from the outside. The bearing surfaces slid like fitted diamonds.

The marshal snapped his fingers and gestured, still concentrating on the suit's finish. Hansen moved his hand and stepped aside obediently so that Maharg could examine the frontal plate.

Maharg looked at Hansen. "I wonder, smart guy," the marshal said in a tone that would have brought the armored bodyguards to attention again if the words had not been spoken so softly, "just where you got this suit?"

"I took it from a rover who didn't need it any more," Hansen said evenly.

"That's right, Marshal," Arnor put in as he climbed from his battlesuit. "I saw him."

Everyone ignored the Peace Rock champion.

"He thought I was a smartass," Hansen continued, his eyes on Maharg's eyes and neither man blinked. "I thought he'd lived long enough already."

Maharg ran his fingers over the faceplate and thorax, the parts of a battlesuit that normally received damage in combat. He glanced down at the legs to be sure that neither of them had been burned off and patched with the inevitable scarring and degradation of performance.

He looked at Hansen again. "Were you wearing suits when you killed him?" the marshal asked.

"He was," said Hansen.

Maharg began to grin. "You *are* a smart sonuvabitch, aren't you?" he said, but this time there was a certain respect in the words.

He rang his knuckles off the thorax plate. It gave no more than the stone wall behind it would have done. "Pretty good piece of hardware," he said. "Pretty *damn* good, I'd say."

Hansen also relaxed. "Thing is . . . ," he said.

He ran his fingers across the epaulet plate, found the point he wanted. "Here," he went on. "Feel the join line? And the same just above the hip joints."

Maharg placed the tips of two long, well-formed fingers at the point Hansen indicated. Arnor and the staff officers watched; Arnor in curiosity, the others in amazement.

Maharg's lips pursed. "That's not bad," he said.

"It's not bad," Hansen said, "but it's not in a class with the rest of the workmanship, believe me."

He gave the marshal a hard, professional smile. "But yeah, it's a good suit. It's a real good suit."

Maharg patted the battlesuit again while he continued to look at Hansen, curious now rather than challenging. "You wouldn't happen to know something about team tactics, would you, smart guy?" he asked at last.

"As much as anybody in this room does, I guess," Hansen said. He smiled, but he could feel all his muscles start to quiver with the prospect of imminent action.

"As much as any of the levies do, you mean," corrected the officer with the notebook.

Hansen raised an eyebrow. "*Is* that what I mean?" he said.

"Right," said the marshal in sudden decision. He nodded to the officer who had spoken. "Patchett," he said, "take over here. I may or may not be back before you're done."

"What?" said the staff officer. "Ah, yessir, but—"

Maharg had already switched his attention back to Hansen. "Do you have a name, smart guy?" he demanded.

"Hansen."

"Is that what it is?" Maharg said without particular emphasis. "Bring your suit, then, Hansen. You can wear it or I'll get a crew to carry it for you to the practice ground, it's all one with me. You and I will each lead a three-man team, and we'll see just what you do know."

"But sir!" Patchett interjected. "Where should we place this Hansen?"

Maharg scowled over his shoulder at his subordinate. "I'll know when I've seen him on the field, won't I, Patchett?"

He grimaced and added without enthusiasm, "After all, *somebody's* got to lead this lot of stumbling levies."

≡ 19 ≡

"WELL, COME ON, Hansen," the engineer demanded, showing his nervousness in an excess of enthusiasm. "It's time to go!"

Ritter knew only that the next few minutes would involve a situation different from every situation of his past life—and that there would be some danger. Anybody sane would be nervous under those circumstances.

Hansen looked around one more time. The image of the dragonflies sat placidly in the image of their thicket.

Hansen scowled and changed the window back to normal viewing with a quick brush of his hand. The falsely innocent landscape irritated him.

"Don't worry," he said in a voice closer to a growl than he'd intended. "We'll get there."

Hansen was nervous also. He *did* know what to expect on a visit to the Lomeri.

The aircar squatted on the other side of the observation room's clear windows. Penny sat in the vehicle, her head raised and her back turned ostentatiously to the men.

If you looked carefully—and Hansen always looked carefully, even when his eyes swept and his expression stayed as flat as the finish on his pistol barrel—you could note that a plane of air formed a reflecting surface in front of the woman.

Penny might have been viewing her own appearance. That was probably the act she performed most often. But it rather seemed that her eyes followed the activities of the men she appeared to ignore. . . .

"Yeah, right," Hansen muttered to himself. "Look, stick close, do what I tell you to. This oughta go slicker 'n snot."

He put his left arm around Ritter's shoulders; checked the fit of his pistol in its breakaway holster; and—

The engineer reached down toward his own weapon in imitation.

—they inserted.

The air was warm and humid. Some of the flies buzzing among the pink magnolia blooms lighted on Hansen's cheeks. They flicked away and returned moments later as sweat popped out of his pores. The soil underfoot was pebbles and grit, well enough drained to keep the magnolias comfortable despite the horsetail marsh within twenty meters.

Hansen couldn't see the horsetails. He couldn't see jack shit because of the mass of blossoms and shiny green leaves in all directions including up. Some of the damned magnolia bushes were three meters high.

Especially, Hansen couldn't see any sign of the Searchers' vehicles which he knew had to be parked here.

Ritter fluffed his loose garment away from his chest without any sign of discomfort. The engineer kept the humidity of the controlled climate in which he lived at 50%. Static had been more of a problem to his tests than contaminating water vapor was.

"Which direction?" he asked Hansen. As he spoke, he took a small magnetometer from his sidepocket to answer his own question.

Ritter didn't realize anything was wrong.

Hansen was very calm. He didn't know what the *fuck* was going on, and you never let yourself get into a flap when it's that bad. That could get you killed.

Something bellowed a kilometer or so away. The sound seemed to come from the west, but in this tangle of branches, ramifying to interweave like a puzzle, there were no certain directions.

"That's funny . . . ," the engineer said as he peered at his magnetometer. The loops holding his pistol holster to his belt were long and flexible. He raised and lowered the holstered weapon, checking the motion against the read-out.

Hansen thought about the image he had seen from his house. He didn't know much about vegetation, but the shape of the surrounding magnolias seemed correct for the brush he'd glimpsed from the window's higher vantage. He put out his hand, his left hand, because Krita's vehicle *should* be—

It wasn't.

"Do you have the place and time correct?" the engineer asked as he frowned at his instrument. "Because I'm not getting—"

"Hell, that's it!" Hansen shouted.

Sparrow's instinctive understanding of the Matrix had led him to twist his concealment of the dragonflies one step further than Hansen had realized. When the smith lifted the dimensional vehicles from his plane to this one, he'd also set the time horizon a millisecond out of phase with the spatial controls.

Hansen's window conflated the partial spacetime realities, but that was an image and this—

A two-tonne megalosaur, long-jawed and carnivorous, crashed through the magnolias at a dead run.

Ritter bawled in surprise. He juggled his magnetometer from his right hand to his left so that he could draw his pistol.

Hansen's instincts were different—*nothing* is as important as clearing a weapon when a weapon is needed—and his gun was pointing within a quarter second at the eyes and yellow-white palate tearing into sight.

Hansen didn't fire. The megalosaur was fleeing, not charging, and it ripped past several meters away.

The beast's tail and spinal column were almost parallel to the ground as it ran. The hips, covered with flattened scutes in a leathery, bronze-on-brown hide, were higher than either man's head.

Fleeing. Which meant—

"What was that?" the engineer shouted.

Part of Hansen's mind was viewing a present concealed

from Ritter. His left hand blurred out of sight. His fingers touched a dragonfly's controls.

—*something was chasing it.*

Hansen had reholstered his weapon. The practiced reflex of drawing and firing was actually quicker for Hansen than it would be for him to aim a weapon in his hand. Ritter waved his own pistol toward the flutter of quivering branches the megalosaur had left as it disappeared through the tangle.

A gun isn't a magic wand that you wave and hope something desirable happens.

The dimensional vehicle popped into sight. Magnolia branches wove through its angled legs.

In a gap through the upper foliage—

Hansen drew and fired. The thicket exploded in actinic radiation that crisped the nearest flies and stung the exposed skin of the men twenty meters away.

The Lomeri scout was mounted on a saddled iguanodont. The five-meter height advantage permitted the lizardman to look over the tops of the magnolia bushes. The Lomeri's instruments had warned it that the intruders were nearby—

But instinct and the fleeing carnivore had done the same for Hansen. He fired at sunlight winking through the foliage from the visored helmet that covered the Lomeri's flat skull.

"Get on the dragonfly!" Hansen screamed over the hissing echoes of his shot.

Hansen was carrying a directed-energy weapon. Though his bolt loaded the Lomeri's forcefield to a dazzling coruscance, it did not penetrate. The energy, rebroadcast all across the electro-optical spectrum, seared the iguanodont like a bath of live steam.

The bipedal beast honked and curvetted as it tried to paw its injured forequarters. The lizardman, thin as a wire armature, tried simultaneously to control his mount and point his short-barreled shoulder weapon in the direction of the shot.

Hansen fired again, down the track of foliage withered by his first bolt. The Lomeri forcefields were normally directional, convex bowls of protection which faced the front and danger.

The scout, broadside to Hansen as the iguanodont spun,

took the shot in the middle of his rib cage. The creature's head and shoulders toppled backward. His long feet retained the stirrups.

Reflex discharged the lizardman's weapon in a thunderclap of shredded vegetation.

"Get aboard!" Hansen shouted. *The engineer swung his leg over the dragonfly's saddle, but there were more Lomeri coming. He aimed at them instead of—*

Hansen shot again.

The scouts had seen what happened to their leading fellow. They dismounted with predatory grace, slapping their mounts aside to avoid being set up by the beasts' gyrations. Hansen's bolt re-radiated like a minuscule nova, but it did nothing to disrupt the attackers' movements.

One of the lizardmen managed to fire in the air, aiming along the ionized track of Hansen's bolts. He hit the injured iguanodont. This time the explosion was accompanied by a mist of blood, scales, and bone fragments. The beast whooped a gout of lung tissue.

"Get—" Hansen said.

Ritter fired as his buttocks settled on the dragonfly's seat. There was a high-pressure *crack!* at his pistol's muzzle, doubled instantly by a *crack!* that cut through the shouts and echoes.

Hansen expected a ricochet from the forcefield of the arching lizardman. The duplex projectile struck the Lomeri shield with a blue spark at the point of impact and a tiny jet of radiance *through* the forcefield where kinetic energy had already loaded the unit to maximum output. There was nothing unsophisticated about Ritter's equipment.

And nothing wrong with his aim, though the way his miniature plasma beam pierced the target's slit-pupiled eye might have been luck.

Hansen's left hand slapped the dragonfly's engagement control, hoping that he'd set the coordinates correctly despite the confusion—

And certain as he followed Ritter through the Matrix that there was no worse place to be than the thicket detonating in orange fury as the humans fled.

• • •

The dragonfly's legs flexed as the vehicle settled in the center of Hansen's observation room. Penny stared from outside. Her moist palms were pressed against the crystal barrier.

Hansen's exposed skin prickled. It would peel in a few days unless he chose to cure the harm by manipulating reality—

Which he would not do, because he'd been so sure he could dodge the Lomeri that he'd gone underequipped. *When you screw up, a minor injury like a UV burn from your own weapon was maybe worth your life the next time. That made it a lesson to be treasured.*

Ritter was gasping. A twig or a fragment from an explosive projectile had gashed the engineer's sleeve into rags, but the skin beneath appeared unharmed.

"Were those—" he said and hacked to a stop.

Hansen tried to adjust the dragonfly's controls left-handed. Now that he and Ritter were safe, he was all thumbs.

"Those were the Lomeri," he said. The inside of his throat had been savaged by ions released when he fired. "Pray you never get a better look at the bastards."

The barrel of Hansen's pistol glowed. He laid the weapon on the floor and set the controls with his right hand.

Penny strode into the room radiating fury and sexual excitement. The men and the borrowed dimensional vehicle were already phasing back to Ritter's home.

≡ 20 ≡

IT WAS NEARLY midnight when Sparrow entered his home. He started to unsling his pack, then paused.

The betrothal gift he had given Krita was missing. His bride must have returned while he was hunting.

"Krita?" he called softly.

"K—" and his voice caught. "Krita?"

His pack slipped the rest of the way and thumped. Sparrow didn't notice it as he ran to where the mirror had been, like a bear making its short, unstoppable rush onto prey.

The crossbow was still in Sparrow's left hand. He flipped the uncocked weapon away with a motion that skidded it across the puncheons.

The crossbow could as easily have smashed to fragments on a wall. Sparrow didn't care.

The smith knelt on the bare floor and ran his fingers over the wood as if he could touch past events. For minutes he remained in that attitude of subjection.

Sparrow's body blocked light from the illuminating spiral which rotated in the center of the hall. There was nothing to see in light or shadow, only in the big man's memory.

A breeze made the door of the lodge creak on its leather hinges. The night air felt cold on the skin of a man who had hiked twenty kilometers with a heavy load.

Sparrow stood up. "Krita!" he called. "I've waited for you!"

A crow, wakened by the shouting, squawked from a pine tree.

"I'll still wait!"

Sparrow made a fireset of punk and kindling in the corner of the hearth beneath the smoker cage. He lighted the set with an object which looked like a silver salamander and spat a blue spark from its jaws when Sparrow moved its tail.

Sparrow went outside again. He looked tired but steadfast, an ox near the end of the day's plowing. When he returned, he carried the stag's carcass and a large square of mammoth hide, stiff and reeking with old blood.

The smith tossed the hide on the floor with a clop like a wooden pallet falling; fed up the fire; and finished butchering the deer beneath the slowly turning lights. He used his belt knife for the job, a sturdy tool with deep fullers to keep the suction of raw flesh from gripping the blade on long cuts.

Occasionally a sound made Sparrow look up, but it was never more than wind or an animal scrabbling.

As he separated each strip of venison, the smith hung the piece on a hook in the smoker. The slatted cage was indoors to protect it from scavengers—which could include a bear. The low heat began to drive out meat juices in a tangy perfume that replaced the scent of death.

Sparrow wrapped the stripped bones in the deerhide and carried them outside with the butchering mat. He kept his offal in a safe of fieldstone and lime cement until he could dispose of it in a gorge two kilometers away.

A scavenger is almost any predator who's between meals. Sparrow was confident in his strength and agility; but he was a methodical man, and there was no reason to increase the risks he took. Logic, not immediate ease, governed his choices.

When he had finished the clean-up and washed his hands with a gourd of water from his cistern, Sparrow closed the lodge door. He called a harsh command. The beads of light darkened, though they continued to move in blackness relieved only by the coals beneath the smoker.

Though the night was cool rather than cold, the smith took a huge white bearskin from a chest and wrapped himself in it. For a time, he sat beside the fire, staring toward the shadowed emptiness between the feet of his battlesuit.

Then, eventually, Sparrow fell asleep.

The doorlatch clicked as it opened. Sparrow jumped like a bear awakened by hounds.

They were in battlesuits, fumbling through the front door. At the back, wood splintered as gauntleted hands failed to work the latch mechanism in their haste. The image-amplifying screens of the powered armor would turn scraps of moonlight to day, but Sparrow knew his home.

"*He's*—" bawled a warrior's amplified voice.

The intruder would have continued 'awake' or 'moving' or simply 'there,' but Sparrow *was* moving, toward his own battlesuit, and light glinted from steel as he flung his knife like a bolt from a catapult.

The darkness ignited in harsh, ripping light. The knifeblade struck the leading warrior and burned because it could not penetrate the battlesuit's forcefield.

Breaking through the back door were two warriors and a third. There were three more at the front, much closer to Sparrow, but the leader of that trio staggered backward from the white dazzle of the knife and blocked his fellows.

A man with a face like a jackal and no armor shouted as he ducked away from the afterimage and fading red sparks.

Sparrow was at his battlesuit and in it, launching himself and turning in the air with the grace of a dancer or a lunging wolverine.

Static discharges popped around the intruders' feet as they clomped forward in their armor. The gauntlets of several warriors glared with dense arcs to cut and kill.

"*Don't hurt him!*" squealed the little man without armor as Sparrow slammed the thorax of his battlesuit closed and—

The vision screens did not brighten into life. The suit's forcefield did not glow with a lambent aura that could block the weapon of any of the warriors, maybe of all six together.

And the arc which should have sprouted from Sparrow's right hand to shear forcefields, metal-ceramic substrate, and the blazing flesh of the intruders—

The arc did not light, because Sparrow's armor had not latched closed.

The leading intruder gripped the edge of the thorax plate and pulled. The smith resisted with all his strength; but Sparrow's strength was human, while his opponent's steel gauntlet was driven by the energy of the Matrix itself.

The smith let the frontal plate go. He tried to leap clear of his battlesuit. Armored hands gripped him before he could get his legs free. He was dragged into the center of the hall.

Freemen carrying torches and supple withies entered through both doors. While warriors held the smith firmly, the freemen wove the captive's limbs with bindings that could have hobbled a mammoth.

Only when that task was completed did the leading warrior open his armor and get out. He was a big man, almost as big as Sparrow, though his face held a hint of softness despite the cruelty of the lips.

Krita's mirror hung from its loop around his neck.

"Well," the intruder said. "I'm King Hermann, lord of this domain. Who are you who've been robbing me all these years?"

"My name's Sparrow," the smith said. "There's no king over this valley. Or over me."

His gaze touched but did not linger on the mirror. His face looked like a fragment of nature, a boulder or a wrack of clouds rising into a thunderhead.

The jackal-faced man spit on him. "Treat your master with respect, scum!" he shouted in a shrill voice.

"Move back, Platt," King Hermann warned without emotion. The little man scuttled away.

Hermann knelt beside his captive. "Of course I'm king here," he said. "And you're a thief, because it's only from me your king that you could have gotten treasures like these."

He gestured calmly, palm upward, at the wonders winking in the torchlight.

"I made everything here!" Sparrow shouted. "I've stolen nothing!"

A warrior who'd taken off his armor stepped forward. He raised his foot.

The captive twisted to glare at him. The man blinked and eased back without kicking.

Sparrow turned his face to the king again. "Why would I need to rob a poor princeling like you?" he demanded. His voice sounded like rocks sliding. "I'm a king's son myself!"

King Hermann straightened. "No," he said in a tone of finality, "you're a slave. And if it turns out that you really are a smith . . . then you'll use your craftsmanship for *me*, Sparrow."

≡ 21 ≡

RITTER, SLUICING THE last of his cider around his mouth, turned from contemplating the craftsmanship of the dimensional vehicle on the central examination stand.

A woman had entered the workroom. She was watching him.

"Look, do I have to lock the damned door?" the engineer snarled. "When I want you, I'll call—"

He broke off. Though the woman's features were unfamiliar—pretty but rail-thin, scarcely sixty kilos on a height of a meter sixty-five—he recognized the jewel glowing on her transparent choker.

"I thought I'd pay you a visit at home, you know," Penny said.

She was dressed as though she were a concubine: her black hair teased high on a framework so that she seemed to be wearing a shako; groin and oxters depilated; gold sandals and belt; and a baggy blouse and trousers which were transparent except for the hundred-millimeter net of metallized fabric woven in to flash as she moved.

"Look, not here, Penny," Ritter said in irritation. "I'm busy, and—"

A chime over the suite's outer door rang, a cheerful sound only if you didn't know what it meant. The screen showed a procession of courtiers who wore brocade and weapons decorated to catch the light. They were coming down the hallway in respectful attendance on Lord Greville.

"It never rains but it fucking pours," the engineer snarled. "Look, Penny, just disappear again or you'll cause all damn sorts of—"

But he wasn't speaking to Penny any more; not speaking to a concubine, that is. The woman before him was stooped and old, a housemaid. Her gray smock hid the jewel around her neck. The electrostatic broom she held in her gnarled fingers was reasonable enough, but—

"Get that damned thing out of here!" Ritter said. "Don't you know what it could do to some of these instruments?"

The outer door opened. "All rise for noble Lord Greville!" caroled the four courtiers in front.

The engineer had added a secret interlock which could prevent even Lord Greville from keying the mechanism against Ritter's will. Ritter was saving that modification for a great need which he hoped would never come. When Lord Greville *did* manage to batter through, lock or no lock, it would be with the fixed intention of flaying his insubordinate servant alive.

Ritter waited a moment until the Lord of Keep Greville had entered and seen him, then bowed. Otherwise the engineer would have disappeared within his dense clutter of equipment, creating an absurd situation.

That was never a good idea when dealing with an arrogant master who held the power of life and death.

The slavey bowed also. She held a long-handled duster of feathers from cranes like those which fished the marsh beyond the keep.

"Ah, there you are, Ritter," Lord Greville said amiably as he wove a path through the banks of instruments and test pieces. "I've just come to congratulate you on those triplex charges of yours. They penetrated the forcefields of Lord Worrel's tanks almost every time we hit."

Greville was a young man, clean-limbed and extremely handsome except for the white scar trailing up his cheek and deforming his left ear. He'd gotten that ten years ago, in the same skirmish which put paid to his uncle and made a fifteen-year-old Lord of Keep Greville.

The new lord's first act had been to execute his uncle's

chief engineer and put Ritter in the victim's place. Since then, Keep Greville had been uniformly successful in its squabbles with its neighbors.

"Very glad to hear that, milord," Ritter said, nodding where a commoner of lower status would have bowed.

"Yes, I took two of them myself," Greville continued. "And damaged Worrel's marshal. Thought I had him too, but—"

Lord Greville's handsome face darkened; frustration bit as deeply from memory as it had during the event. "But he managed to restart and back away. It was a *perfect* shot. I saw his hatches lift, but he drove away."

"Well, milord," Ritter said, "it's a trade-off. Penetration or punch. I'll see what—"

"I'll tell you, I don't much like this new shit," interjected Colonel Maynor, one of the courtiers. He was a grizzled man who'd reached his rank because he was a favored drinking companion of the previous lord. "The old ammo opened 'em a treat every time we got home."

Ritter looked at the man who'd spoken. In theory, any soldier was the superior of any commoner. In practice *here*—

"Yes," Ritter said coolly, "the duplex rounds did pack more of a punch inside the forcefields. When they got there, that is. Which would be about one time in twelve with the beefed-up armor of Worrel's current production."

The soldier glared at Ritter, then glanced aside in willingness to end the exchange.

"Of course," Ritter continued, because he *wasn't* willing to let challenges to his professional judgment end as draws, "having gone over your accuracy records, Colonel Maynor, I don't think your personal experience with hits is enough of a sample for any meaningful generalization."

Lord Greville smiled. Several courtiers guffawed openly. Maynor turned and kicked an instrument console.

The engineer chuckled. He built his equipment to last. From the sound the boot made on the console, Maynor had broken a toe.

Lord Greville's eyes wandered toward the dragonfly in the center of the lab. "What on earth is this, Ritter?" he asked.

One of the courtiers put his hand on the dragonfly's saddle. He pumped the vehicle up and down against the shock absorbers in the legs.

"Oh, that's just a notion, milord," the engineer said calmly. "It may or may not pan out."

Lord Greville pursed his lips. "Doesn't look very sturdy," he said. "But—"

His face brightened into a patronizing smile. "—I suppose we can let you have your little surprise. You don't let us down very often, Master Ritter."

The engineer bowed.

"Come along, you lot," Greville said to his entourage. "Maxwell's creating a moving diorama of yesterday's battle, and I want to see what he's chosen for his color scheme."

Ritter's visitors swept out of the laboratory. The engineer wiped his hands on his trousers, leaving sweaty streaks across the electric blue fabric.

"You're really good at your job, aren't you?" Penny said sadly. "I suppose I should have known that, or Hansen wouldn't have . . ."

Ritter turned. She was beautiful again. Perfectly formed, at least. The puzzle-solving part of his mind traced the network of gold accents in Penny's clothing back to sunbursts centered at her nipples and vulva.

"Good?" the engineer snapped. "Do you want to know how good? I could design weapons that would *vaporize* Lord Worrel's tanks. I could vaporize Keep Worrel from right here, give me a year and the budget. And he tells me that I'm doing pretty well, I can keep it up!"

Penny took Ritter's left hand. She slid the loose sleeve above his elbow, checking critically to be sure that the firefight with the Lomeri had not left a permanent injury.

"Why don't you, then?" she asked. "Build the weapons?"

Ritter snorted and turned to look at the dragonfly again. The motion pulled him away from the woman's hands.

"Because if they even dreamed I could do that," he said, "they'd shoot me before I had time to blink. They don't want to upset the balance, you see."

Penny snuggled close to Ritter's side. The pistol holster interfered with her attempt to press their hips together.

"They just want to blow up a few of their neighbors' tanks and have a few of their own blown up too," the engineer continued, oblivious to his companion except as a wall from which he could echo his frustration. "And then all the survivors go home to drink and brag and get ready for the next pointless skirmish!"

"Do you think I'm pretty this way?" Penny asked abruptly.

Ritter blinked and looked at her. She stepped back obligingly and did a pirouette.

"Yeah, you're fine," Ritter said. Actually, she was too thin for the squat ideal of beauty here on Earth—

On Northworld, as Hansen and the ancient colonists called it.

—but Ritter's interest was in function, not form, in sex as in all his other pursuits. No one was likely to object to Penny's ability to function in that category of activity.

"I mean," the woman pressed, "because you said you wanted me the way I was, the—way before we came to Northworld and I got this."

She clutched the jewel at her throat, hiding for a moment the brilliance that flashed like a sun's core.

"I told you I didn't care," Ritter said, frowning at her misquote. Penny took his hands. "I said I'd as soon see you the way you really were. This is fine."

"Come on," she said, tugging him toward the door to his living quarters.

He might as well. The first thing he had to do about the dragonfly was think, just think, and he wasn't going to be able to concentrate anyway after Lord Greville's interrup—

Whoops.

"No," Ritter said, pulling back, but Penny was already within reach of the latchplate. "Don't—"

Penny opened the door. The concubine on the bedside chair was a sultry brunette. She had thrown back her robe while she did her toenails.

"Are there going to be two of us tonight, then?" she asked.

Then, with a catty smile, she added, "Or one and a half, I should say, unless you've got another skinny one to come later."

"Look, you can leave—" Ritter began. *It was always this way when he wanted to get stuck into a project, one balls-up after another—*

Penny leaned forward, swept up the footstool, and went for the concubine.

Ritter didn't realize what was happening for an instant because the other woman—the woman who *belonged* in his bedroom—was twice Penny's size. The concubine raised her hand to keep Penny from clawing at her eyes and bleated, "What—"

Penny clouted the larger woman above the temple with the stool.

The concubine sprawled to the floor. Penny jerked the robe's sash of multicolored silk out of its loops and began to choke her rival with it.

Ritter grabbed Penny's wrists from behind. He squeezed and twisted until the garotte slipped out of her hands. He backed up, ignoring the way Penny kicked his shins with her slippered heels.

The concubine got slowly to her feet, rubbing her throat with her palms. She was wheezing.

"Go on, get out," Ritter snapped. "Next time, hold your smart remarks until somebody calls for them."

The concubine looked as though she might speak. Either her throat or the look in Penny's eyes convinced her to keep her mouth shut. She banged closed the door in the opposite wall.

Ritter let Penny go. He was breathing hard. She turned and struck at his face. He blocked the blow.

"Do you let her suck your cock?" Penny screamed. The puffed sleeve had torn loose from her left shoulder seam. It dangled around her wrist. "You do, don't you?"

"Look," said Ritter, "you better leave too. I should've listened to Hansen."

"Hansen?" the woman repeated, turning the name into a curse. "Oh, you think he'll save you, do you?"

She pointed her index finger at the engineer's chest.

"He never said he'd save me, Penny," Ritter said softly.

He wondered whether he would feel death. His mind clicked over and over like a tumbler lock. "But I guess he'll do what he did say."

Penny stood like a statue of Nemesis. "Do you think I'm afraid?" she shrilled.

"*I'm* afraid, Penny," Ritter said in a burst of dry-lipped honesty.

She lowered her hand.

Ritter took a deep breath.

"Look, lady," he said. "This doesn't make any sense. Pussy's cheap, so's dick, I suppose. You go find your Myron or whoever and we don't ever have to look at each other again. All right?"

Penny laced her fingers together like a knot of vipers. The dangling sleeve got in the way. She tugged at it. "What did Hansen say about me?" she demanded in a husky voice.

"Noth—" the engineer began, but he paused when he saw the spark ignite in her eyes.

"That you liked men," he continued flatly. "That you had a temper."

The woman lifted her chin in a brief nod of acceptance. Another time, she might have argued with the obvious.

"Look," Ritter went on, "I don't want trouble for you or him either. He didn't give me orders, he just . . ."

He smiled wryly. "Hansen treated me like a man," he said. "I don't get a lot of that from Lord Greville, you see."

"Or from me, you mean," Penny said bitterly.

Abruptly, she sobbed and threw herself against the engineer's chest. "Oh, darling," she said, "I'm sorry, I just—"

She leaned back so that she could meet Ritter's eyes. "Look," she went on, "I don't care who you fuck, just so you fuck me, all right? And, you know, you don't tell me about it . . . and I won't go looking."

As Penny spoke, she slid down Ritter's body and opened his trouser fly. She paused for a moment with his penis in her right hand, then began to lick it as she tore away the remnants of her blouse with the other hand.

"Does she take you up her ass, darling?" Penny murmured. "Does—"

"For god's sake, woman!"

"Oh, darling, I'm sorry, I won't . . . "

Tears sparkled like jewels on her cheeks. "It doesn't matter."

Penny wiped her eyes quickly with her left wrist. "Look," she said, bright and controlled again. "I'll get you really good and slippery—"

She paused to engulf the shaft of his penis, then slide it back out and tongue it firmly.

"—and then I'll kneel on the bed and show you how much fun somebody who's *really* had practice can be!"

≡ 22 ≡

WARRIORS ALREADY ON the practice ground lit the air with the blue *c-c-crack!* of their arcs as Maharg led his group onto it.

The field outside the old walls of Frekka was roughly square and nearly five hundred meters on a side. More than sufficient room remained for six more men to hold a mock duel.

"All right," said the marshal. "Get kitted up and we'll start."

The boundary was marked by posts—and by the stumps which remained when a warrior tested his arc against a post. Eight slaves carried each battlesuit. The coffle set down its burdens gratefully at the margin of the field.

"It'll take a moment," Hansen said. "I need to talk with my troops, here."

He gave a terse, friendly smile to Culbreth and Lee, the warriors Maharg had picked for Hansen as they strode past the levies whom the marshal had already examined. The levies glared back at Hansen with flat-eyed insolence.

Culbreth turned deliberately to Maharg. "I came here," he said, "in response to the *royal* levy, to serve the king. I didn't come to take orders from some underling from Peace Rock, of all places."

Hansen's face smiled. His muscles quivered, and his vision blurred in a moment of red haze while he waited for Maharg to deal with the problem.

It was Maharg's problem. Until it became Nils Hansen's.

The marshal had chosen two professionals for his own team. They got into their armor without wasting motion, then ran preliminary checks of the sensors and displays.

"Yes, indeed, champion," Maharg said in a tone that might not have been mocking at all. "You came here on your lord's oath to serve the king and the king's officers . . . and I'm sure King Prandia is as grateful as I am that your lord is no oathbreaker."

He put his hand gently on Culbreth's shoulder. The levy was no taller than Hansen and of a slimmer build, but he did not flinch at the marshal's touch. Culbreth's muscles were firm; his wrists bore the calluses of a man who had spent long hours inside a battlesuit.

" 'Serve' doesn't mean you rush off to die in single combat against Colimore," Maharg said, lowering his hand.

His voice had changed, hardened. Hansen's mind nodded approval because the other tone had been mocking. You might break a man by sarcasm, but that wouldn't make him a soldier; and Culbreth had too much potential to waste unless—

Hansen wiped his palms against his thighs.

—he *had* to be wasted.

"Look—" said Culbreth. The other levy, Lee, pretended to examine the exterior of his battlesuit.

The sky was gray-white. The clouds were too thin to mean rain, but they turned the sun into a milky blur which could not warm the wind gusting across the field.

"Your oath—and your lord's oath," Maharg said, his voice crackling like the arc which the professional beside him tested at that moment, "means that you obey orders. King Prandia's orders, my orders—anybody he or I put over you."

"Look—"

"Otherwise you're an oathbreaker!" the marshal said. "Otherwise you'll get better men killed. And I—"

"I—" said Culbreth, white-faced.

"—will have you executed *now* as an oathbreaker and leave your body for the dogs!"

"Marshal," said Nils Hansen.

Everyone stared at him. He heard his own voice from a distance.

"He's a man I want at my side," Hansen said. "We'll do fine. You don't need an army of people who don't have any balls."

Maharg stared at him. Hansen could almost hear the marshal wondering whether this was a clever variation on an interrogation technique: bonding the subject to a gentle questioner after the harsh member of the team had threatened—

Or whether Hansen really *was* trying to prevent Culbreth from making the wrong response and being executed as an example to the whole army.

Hansen grinned. He wasn't sure himself.

Maharg relaxed. "Yeah," he said. "Get into your armor. I've got work to do."

"Wait a sec," Hansen said, holding out his hands, palm down, to Lee and Culbreth to get their attention. "You both know the basics of team tactics? Everybody strikes at the target the leader designates. And *only* that target."

The levies nodded warily.

That was about as much as you could hope for. The warriors from scattered holdings might be as experienced as those of the Royal Household in individual combat, *but*—

There was no honor in group evolutions, and group training didn't help a man survive the lethal personal duels that occurred in the absence of war. Warriors would practice as teams only if a hard-fisted leader insisted that they do so. The few days before the army set off for Colimore weren't going to make the levies expert in the tactics that would multiply their effectiveness in war.

Though Duke Colimore's warriors weren't likely to be a damned bit better.

"Right," said Hansen. He grimaced unintentionally.

This was going to be a ratfuck, and the campaign that followed was going to be a bigger ratfuck . . . but that's what wars were, individual ratfucks multiplied by the number of combatants.

"I'm going to lead," he continued briskly. Maharg had already slammed his battlesuit closed. "They'll try to split us up, then concentrate to take us one at a time. Block cuts aimed at you, but don't strike till I mark the target."

Culbreth gave Hansen a tight grin and nodded. Lee looked blank, but he might do all right, as well as could be expected.

"If you don't get moving, Hansen," said the marshal coldly, "I'm going to see how long you last without armor."

Hansen made a chopping gesture with both hands. "Remember," he said to his men, "it's practice. And don't lose your cool, because that's the main thing these bastards want."

An arc snapped high from Maharg's right palm.

Hansen slid quickly into his battlesuit. It was quite possible the marshal *would* prod one of the levies if they delayed further. Even at practice power, the arc weapon would sear through flesh as easily as its blue lambency danced in the air.

When Hansen closed the frontal plate over him, his battlesuit switched on. The screens gave him a visual display both brighter and more clear than that of his unaided eyes.

The practice battle had attracted spectators besides the band of slaves who carried the battlesuits. Most of the warriors on the field interrupted their training sessions to watch. A surprising number of others—civilians and off-duty warriors alike—had come out of the city as well.

All right, they'd get something to look at.

"Suit, secure commo for Team White," Hansen ordered. His suit's artificial intelligence set up a lock-out channel for Hansen, Culbreth, and Lee—perhaps the first time the other levies had even heard of such a thing, though the capacity was built into every battlesuit. The AI also tagged the three of them with a white carat on the team's vision screens so that the friendly elements could identify one another instantly.

"Ready?" demanded Maharg. He used his external speaker rather than spread-frequency radio to communicate. Arcs quivered from both his gauntlets, crossing without quite intersecting in front of his thorax.

Hansen stood in the center of his team with Culbreth to his right. No time now to talk.

"Practice," Hansen ordered his AI. "Cut." A low-power arc spluttered from Hansen's right gauntlet, extending and then condensing to a higher flux density as he scissored his thumb and forefinger.

Maharg and his two professionals stepped forward in unison.

The teams were well matched in terms of equipment. The marshal himself wore a suit of royal quality, the creation of a master smith on a long series of good days. Its overall finish was flawless, though Hansen was confident that the armor he'd taken from the Solfygg rover could equal it in terms of offense and protection.

The other four battlesuits were clustered on the boundary between third class and fourth—better than 90% of the suits in the royal army, and inferior only by contrast to the nearly unique armor worn by the team leaders. Hansen doubted that there would be any advantage to his team if Culbreth and Lee swapped equipment with Maharg's two subordinates.

But equipment doesn't fight wars: men do. And these professionals were very fucking good.

"Mark!" Hansen shouted to his AI with his command field centered on the professional fronting Culbreth.

The warrior's image pulsed red in Hansen's display and those of the other levies, but Maharg wasn't waiting for Hansen to drill his subordinates in the fine points of teamwork. Each of the professionals moved against his opposite number.

Maharg slashed at Hansen with his arc extended two meters from his glove. The weapon was too attenuated at that distance to endanger a royal suit even if Hansen hadn't parried the stroke with his own dense flux.

The arcs crossed with a dazzle. Sparks flew and the air itself fluoresced for the instant before Maharg's overloaded weapon died with a sputter. The marshal stepped backward to relight it with a command.

Hansen's screen was set to a 120° wedge to his front. At the left margin of his vision, he saw Lee parry a stroke skillfully and step forward to chop at his opponent in turn. The professional locked arcs with him.

Maharg cut sideways. His weapon took Lee waist high while all the power of the levy's battlesuit was concentrated on beating down the arc of the warrior in front of him.

Circuit breakers tripped. Lee toppled, his battlesuit as cold and dead as a steel coffin. Had the combat been real instead of an exercise, the marshal's arc would have cut Lee and his armor into a pair of smoldering pieces.

"Strike, Culbreth!" Hansen shouted as he cut at the warrior he'd marked on the displays.

There wasn't any good thinking about the ones who didn't make it through, not while the fighting was going on. Not afterward either, but Hansen did, he always did.

The professional backpedaled and parried, but Hansen's arc licked out three meters to soak up the power available to the lesser suit in a blaze of protective sparks. The man started to fall because his servo motors couldn't react at the expected speed, and Culbreth slashed across his ankles to trip the suit off-line.

One down from either side, but there wasn't any time to think about it because Maharg, an instant too late to save his subordinate, cut at the peak of Hansen's helmet. Hansen barely blocked the stroke with an arc from his left gauntlet.

The roaring *thrum* of the hostile weapon vibrated through Hansen's battlesuit. His displays broke into snow. He kicked, overcoming the inertia of drained servo motors with the strength of his thigh muscles.

Hansen felt but could not hear the clang of his boot striking something. Maharg's suit had been as near overload as his opponent's. The marshal staggered backward and broke the contact.

Hansen's vision display cleared in time to show Culbreth stepping in to stab Maharg—

Not now! Maharg was free!

—with a straight thrust to the belly which Maharg parried. The other professional cut Culbreth down while the levy focused, mind and battlesuit, like a gadfly eager to die so long as it can drink blood first.

Culbreth didn't get his drink of blood this time, but his depowered suit was still falling toward bruising contact with the ground when Hansen dropped the professional who had gotten between Hansen and the marshal.

Hansen stepped onto rather than over the professional and cut at his remaining opponent. This time it was Hansen's arc within a hundred millimeters before the marshal was able to block it.

Their suits crashed together. The physical shock was lost in the electrical roar that bathed both men. All the power the battlesuits sucked from the Matrix snarled out again through the locked right gauntlets as arc cut arc.

"Poplin and Branch!" the marshal shouted through the deafening static. "Reset and join me! You others, you stay where you are."

"Bastard!" Hansen wheezed and lurched sideways to break the contact.

One of Maharg's subordinates was already on his feet with his weapon lighted. The other warrior was getting up also.

Hansen's right arm was in an oven. As good as his battlesuit was, the amount of power being channeled through the gauntlet heated the current pathways and soaked into the flesh of the man inside.

The bastard Maharg was determined to win. He was going to shut down Hansen's suit even if that meant changing the rules mid-way.

It wasn't dangerous to lose a practice round. You bounced around like the pea in a whistle when your suit hit the ground—bruises, pressure cuts; maybe a bloody nose.

Not really dangerous.

Hansen flashed the arc from his left gauntlet in a long stroke toward the marshal's face, then waved the other arc toward the subordinate on his right as if ready to parry an attack from that side.

Maharg laughed. The sound from his external speaker had a metallic cruelty. He strode in. His two fellows were a step behind to either side.

Hansen flicked the left-hand arc high, clamped it off, and lunged with all his suit's power toward the marshal's left knee.

Three arcs hit him simultaneously, overloading even Hansen's armor in a fingersnap.

And it didn't matter a damn, because of what Hansen's

display showed him in the last instant before it went black:
his thrust had gotten home. Maharg was dropping also, as
sure as a barrel-rider in a waterfall.

Hansen hit face-down. His nose and forehead rapped the
vision display. His eyes watered, but he didn't think he was
bleeding anywhere from the impact.

He would have liked to rest where he lay, dragging air
into his blazing lungs, but the heat cooking his arm was too
much to bear.

"Reset," Hansen said to switch the battlesuit live.

The display flooded Hansen's world with light. He wasn't
interested in that or even in getting to his feet. He used the
suit's servos to roll him over on his back; then he unlatched
the frontal plate and shut the power off again.

The outside air was cold and comforting, though it made
him shiver uncontrollably. Hansen dragged both his arms
from the battlesuit. He tried to lever his body clear and felt
his muscles quiver uselessly under the strain.

"You there!" he shouted toward the slaves goggling at the
edge of the field.

*Hell, his voice was cracking also. He felt like death, like
meat through a grinder.*

"Come fucking help me out of this coffin!"

Lee and Culbreth had already taken off their battlesuits.
They reached Hansen's side before the slaves did and supported him while he pulled his legs from the armor.

Maharg lay on his side. He opened his suit without having
to power it up again. His subordinates stepped close, then
backed away from the marshal when they saw his face.

"Smart guy," Maharg muttered. He'd cut his lip on a tooth
when his suit hit the ground.

Hansen offered him a hand, though god only knew whether
Hansen wouldn't just fall back down if the marshal put any
weight on him. He hadn't hurt like this since . . .

Since the last time he'd been in action, and nothing had
mattered except whether he nailed the ones he was after.

"Naw, that's all right," Maharg rasped. He set his palms
on the ground to support his upper body. His biceps were
trembling.

"Are you okay, sir?" asked one of his subordinates. Both of them were still suited up.

"Oh, I'm bloody wonderful," the marshal grunted. "Will you get out of that damned armor before you step on somebody?"

He looked at Hansen. "That's a pretty good battlesuit, buddy," he said; paused; and added, "And you're not so bad yourself."

Hansen managed to smile. "When I don't hurt all over," he said, "I'll thank you for the compliment."

Maharg swore and got to his feet in a series of determined movements that didn't quite overbalance and make him fall again.

"Think you can lead the left wing with all the levies when we meet Colimore, Hansen?" he asked.

Hansen nodded. "Yeah," he said. "I think so."

"Then I guess you got the job," the marshal said, as nonchalantly as if they had discussed the time till sunset. His eyes swept the crowd, then focused on Hansen again. "Where did you say you served before you came to Peace Rock, buddy?" he asked.

"I didn't say," said Hansen.

Maharg nodded. "Yeah," he agreed. "That's what I remembered too."

He laughed. "Come on," he said. "We've got three days to train these levies well enough to keep them alive."

≡ 23 ≡

"Why is he still alive?" Stella demanded as she saw hate as cold as black ice glistening in the eyes of the prisoner bound in the palace courtyard. "Hermann, you're a fool!"

"Don't use that tone on me, woman," the king replied. His tone was too querulous to be an order. "Anyway, you don't understand. His work is—"

Sparrow smiled at the queen.

King Hermann saw the mirrored expressions on their faces, his wife's and the smith's, and looked away quickly. "Get the loot brought in at once!" he shouted to the servants already unloading the baggage mammoths.

The evening sky was pale and streaked by high clouds that threatened an early snow.

"You're the one who doesn't understand, Stella," Hermann resumed, drawing strength from the protectively-wrapped bundles which slaves lifted from the baggage nets. "He's too valuable to lose."

"What did you bring for *me*, Father?" asked Miriam. The princess wore an ermine cape, clasped at the throat with gold and garnets. She flared it open with her elbows to display the gown beneath, scarlet silk brocaded with gold.

"Oh, there'll be wonders for you, darling," Hermann said. "Wait till we get things in—Bran! Don't do—"

The king shouted too late, though the twins rarely paid attention to commands anyway. The twins had stretched a boot thong at ankle height between them, in the path of the burden bearers. A wizened slave in rags tripped, grunted as he tried to catch his balance—

—and crashed forward on his bundle. Metal tinkled into junk despite the layers of deerhide.

"Hell take you!" Crowl shouted as he kicked the fallen slave. The slave tried to rise. Crowl kicked him again.

"I want my things now!" cried the princess.

The remainder of the slaves had frozen. They resumed moving, but they stepped well off the usual path in order to skirt the incident.

The twins had run away. Their laughter chirped from an alcove of the stone-built palace.

"You're a fool, Hermann," Queen Stella repeated with her eyes still locked with the smith's, "if you think a few baubles are worth the risk of leaving this one alive."

"Bring that battlesuit over here at once!" the king shouted. "At once!"

"Daddy!"

"Darling," Hermann said to his daughter desperately, "you'll see it all, every bit of it very soon. And you can have—ah!"

Eight slaves approached, carrying the considerable deadweight load of Sparrow's battlesuit. Platt led them.

"Here is the suit I won for you, Your Excellency," said the outlaw with an unctuous bow.

"Well, open it up, then!" cried the king. He turned to his wife and continued, "You'll see, my dear; you'll see what I mean."

"I've seen armor before, Hermann," said his wife as she watched tight-lipped. The slaves carefully set the battlesuit down on its own legs and held it while Platt opened the frontal plate. "I'm sure it's very nice. It's this *man* that—"

"Mother," snapped Princess Miriam, "can't you make—"

"Hush, dear," said the queen.

While mother and daughter faced one another beneath the slowly darkening sky, King Hermann clambered into the undecorated battlesuit and closed it over him. The edges of the thorax and faceplate mated with the remainder of the suit like layers of rock in a cliff face.

The battlesuit's sensors gave a visual display sharper than the same scene by daylight. The suede lining was initially at air temperature, but the suit's environmental control began quickly to warm the pads.

Hermann swung his arms. Normally there was inertia, a lag before the suit's servos converted the operator's motion into movements by the powered armor itself.

Not with this wonder. The whole mass of steel and circuitry slid through the air as if it were Hermann's own skin.

The slaves who had been holding the armor ducked away. One of them slipped. The king pirouetted like a dancer and kicked out. The armored boot lifted the man a meter in the air, then dropped him like a burst grainsack.

Hermann laughed like a god.

"Look at me, Stella!" his amplified voice thundered. "Look at me!"

He raised his gauntlet and said, "Cut!" to the artificial intelligence controlling the battlesuit. A flaring arc ripped into the air, ten meters, twenty meters—

Hermann continued to narrow the angle between his thumb and index finger, controlling the flux that leaped from them and seared still higher without the arc breaking. "Is this a bauble, Stella?" he shouted. "Is this a—"

He swept the arc down across one of the palace's projecting roof drains, ten meters above him. The stone cracked. Rock fragments and a bright blazing spray of quicklime flew in all directions.

Onlookers flattened and cried out; even the queen flinched. A scullery maid watching from across the courtyard knelt with her eyes closed and her hands over her ears. She screamed like one of the damned until the cook clubbed her silent for fear that the maid would bring royal displeasure on his department.

"—a bauble?"

Stella looked upward. The fractured stone still glowed. Streaks of molten lead from the drainpipe had twisted a meter down the face of the wall before cooling.

"Hermann," said the queen in a distant voice, "get out of that armor before you hurt somebody."

The king unlatched his battlesuit. His face was flushed with the power he had worn. "You do see," he said with assurance.

Platt and a slave—both of them hesitant—jumped to Hermann's side to help him out of the armor. "I know you do."

The mirror flashed against Hermann's chest as he was lifted from the battlesuit. Princess Miriam pointed toward it.

"Daddy, what's that?" she demanded. Her voice was thinner than usual because of the way her father's demonstration had frightened her.

"This?" said the king, lifting the loop over his head and showing it to her. "This is a wonder too. Just hold it in your hands and think of anything."

Miriam took the mirror. Her expression was a mix of her normal petulance with anger at the recent fear. Her face cleared. "Oh!" she said. For a moment she was truly beautiful.

"Oh, darling!" her father gasped. Even Queen Stella's face softened.

"It's my room!" Miriam squealed. "Oh! And it changes! It's my garden and it's springtime again! Oh!"

Suddenly a more normal emotion drew the princess' lips back in a feral grimace. She pressed the mirror against her brocaded bosom. "This is mine, isn't it?" she insisted. "You *have* to give it to me!"

"Of course, darling," said the king, stroking his daughter's ermine shoulder.

"King Hermann," said a voice like a tree splitting with the cold, "don't do that."

They all glanced around. It took a moment to identify the speaker—the prisoner lying on the ground where the slaves had dropped him.

"Not that piece," Sparrow said. His eyes were the same color as the lead had been while it dripped over cold stone.

Miriam continued to clutch the mirror tightly. She backed a step, looking down with horror and disgust.

Hermann turned to his wife and said with the false brightness of unease, "You see, my dear, what a smith like this can mean to the kingdom?"

"He's too dangerous," Stella muttered. Her glance now

vibrated between the mirror in Miriam's hand and the face of the man who had made it.

"There won't be any danger," the king wheedled. "We'll put him in the old tower, the citadel my grandfather built, and he'll work for *us*."

"If he has to live," said the queen slowly, "then at least be sure that he stays locked up forever. And—"

Her smile was as cold as winter dawn. "—why don't you just cut his hamstrings, too?"

"Of course, of course," said King Hermann, beaming. He glanced at Platt and snapped, "Well, what are you waiting for, you?"

The outlaw drew his knife and knelt beside the prisoner. Sparrow tried to kick him. Withies bound the smith's thighs as well as his ankles.

Platt dodged back from the clumsy blow and gripped the prisoner's feet. "Hold him!" Platt shouted.

Half a dozen slaves piled onto the bound smith like dogs on a bear. Sparrow twisted in speechless fury, but Platt waited his time. The knife slid forward as smoothly as a viper's fang. It cut the backs of the supple deerhide boots and withdrew.

Blood followed the knife, but not much blood.

Platt sprang away. "All right," he said. "You can let him go."

Sparrow's muscles bunched like steel hawsers, but his feet lolled loose now that the tendons to them were cut.

Hermann looked at his prisoner in satisfaction—and looked away, because Sparrow's face was the face of a beast.

≡ 24 ≡

THE BEAST SABURO rode to Hansen's home was a dinohyid that looked like a huge pig. The slim god with oriental features sat doll-sized in his saddle on the creature's bristling, two-meter back.

Hansen waved from his crystal enclosure. When Saburo dropped the dinohyid's reins and sprang lightly from its back, the beast snorted and began to browse morosely. The grass that covered much of the rolling plain was of little interest to it.

"Just thought I'd visit and see how you were getting on," Saburo said as he entered the observation room.

The giant hog the young man rode was at variance with the fussy niceness Saburo projected in all other respects. His clothing was in muted taste, layers of translucent robes which were mostly shades of gray. The black-and-orange tiger stripes of the innermost garment were smothered into a suggestion, not a highlight.

The ensemble had been high fashion in Saburo's section of the Consensus of Worlds—before Saburo came to Northworld as part of an exploration unit and found godhead.

"Moving along," said Hansen. "Can't complain."

Hansen gestured to the image on part of the observation room's windows. There was no point in trying to hide the scene from his visitor. If Saburo was interested enough to come here, he had doubtless been following the events already.

To the east of the building, the dinohyid nuzzled soft-bodied flowers from among the grassblades. On the lower side, the view plunged toward the distant arroyo which was dry except when Hansen's whim brought the rains down in thunderclaps and sheets of sky-splitting lightning.

Between the landscapes, instead of a sideslope, an image of Ritter caressed instruments that probed Krita's dragonfly.

"What's he doing now?" Saburo asked.

Hansen shrugged. "I'm not sure," he said. "Just looking it over so far, I suppose."

He grinned at his visitor. Neither man was big, the way the bulky Ritter or North, almost two meters tall, were; but Saburo looked like a sparrow—

While Hansen was a sparrowhawk, blunt-featured and strong and assuredly a predator.

"After all," said Hansen, "if I knew what he was doing, I wouldn't need him to do it, would I?"

Saburo checked the hang of his robes critically, then smoothed the pleat of the fourth layer between his thumb and forefinger. His hands were slender but corded with sinew.

"That's rather the problem, isn't it?" he remarked as he returned his attention to the engineer. "Having the power to accomplish anything we want doesn't mean that we know what we should want."

Hansen had arranged the image to look down on Ritter from a slight angle, with a panorama of the entire engineering complex beyond as though the walls did not exist. A dozen under-engineers worked in separate alcoves or lounged, chatting or staring at the ceiling—which was very possibly work also. From the number of empty cubicles, as many more of Ritter's personnel were out on the shop floor, supervising construction.

Ritter touched his controls. A beam of cyan light vanished into the ultraviolet, then reappeared as pure magenta as it rotated about the surface of one of the dragonfly's legs. A greatly magnified hologram of the leg's internal structure appeared in the air behind the engineer and in a small screen inset into his console.

"You think that one's good, do you?" Saburo asked without looking at Hansen.

Hansen smiled at the indirection. "He *is* good, Saburo," he said mildly.

"I don't suppose you'll need him after your game with North is finished," his slender visitor said. "Will you?" Saburo pretended to watch intently as Ritter's console hummed and the holographic information dissolved into its central file for analysis.

Hansen's expression did not change, but his face was suddenly harder as all the muscles beneath the skin grew minusculely more taut. "It's not a game, Saburo," he said evenly.

Saburo fluttered a hand and met Hansen's direct gaze. "Not to you, I'm sure," he said.

"Not to North either," Hansen snapped. "And most particularly not to the people in the West Kingdom."

Saburo could not have been either a coward or a fool and still qualify for a place in an exploration unit. He straightened but he did not back away from his host's sudden cold anger. "Yes," he said, "of course, in the Open Lands. . . . But let's not argue, Commissioner. I wish you well, though—" neither his face nor his voice changed "—with our leader on the other side, I don't know how optimistic you can be about success."

Hansen relaxed with a chuckle. "Yeah, well," he said. "There aren't any guarantees in life, are there?"

Hansen continued to smile, but there was a slight edge in his voice as he went on, "Care to tell me what brought you here?"

"You're so very direct, Commissioner," Saburo said with a brittle laugh. "It's a wonder to me that you don't get along better with poor Penny."

He waved a dismissive hand, a flutter of gray robes, as he saw Hansen's face go cold again. "Please forgive me, we all have our ways. I came because I could use a servant who understood how to make things. I was rather hoping—"

Saburo turned aside, having forced himself as far as his

personality could go into flat statement and direct eye contact.

Ritter's probe was now chrome yellow. It wriggled in a narrow line across the dragonfly's saddle. The mass of gray patterns in the engineer's hologram could have been a complex parking lot, but it was more probably a map of the vehicle's microcircuitry.

"I was rather hoping," Saburo continued to the image, "that you might give this servant of yours to me. When you're finished with him, of course."

"He's a human being, Saburo," Hansen said. There was just enough steel in his tone to make sure his visitor would listen and understand what he was being told. "I won't *give* him to anybody."

Robes fluttered.

"But if you want to cut your own deal with Ritter when he and I are through," Hansen continued more mildly, "then I won't have any objections, no."

He grinned and added, "Penny might have ideas of her own, of course. But that's between you two."

"Oh, I'm not worried about our Penny," Saburo said. He gave a high-pitched giggle. "At the rate she goes through men—even if duration mattered to us, I wouldn't be concerned about the wait."

He looked at the engineer and pursed his lips. "One can't really say that Penny has a *type,* of course. But it still seems a little odd that she'd have any real interest in a dwarf from the Fifth Plane, doesn't it?"

"Maybe she's more interested in what he is than in what body he comes wrapped in," Hansen suggested with no apparent emotional gloss over his words.

"Penny?" said Saburo in amazement.

He stared at Hansen, then giggled again. "Oh, you caught me that time, Commissioner. You see, I can never tell when you're making one of your little jokes."

Saburo looked back at the engineer. Ritter stood and stretched with his fingers locked behind his short, massive neck. His elbow blurred a portion of the hologram which continued to scroll upward in a dense array, meaningless to either Hansen or his visitor.

"The tricky part," said Saburo with a slight narrowing of the eyes, "will be to prevent Penny from disposing of Master Ritter in some final fashion when she gets tired of him. That would be such a waste! He makes things so well."

≡ 25 ≡

"WELL, SPARROW," BOOMED the king from the polished magnificence of his battlesuit, "what have you made this time?"

"What you asked for, Hermann . . . ," the smith said quietly. "What you expected. No more and no less."

"I wanted him to make something for me," said Princess Miriam. "Has he made something for me?"

Platt tripped near the outer door. The citadel's attendant— the smith's jailer—had been backing to prevent either of the twin boys from getting behind him. He had forgotten the slops bucket which he had yet to empty.

"Pee-ew!" Bran shouted as he scampered back to his parents in false innocence. "See what he did, Mommie?"

"Have him beaten, Mommie!" his brother cried. "Have him beaten!"

"Boys, be quiet," Stella said sharply, seizing each of the brothers by the hair. She held them for only a moment, but long enough for them to try to pull free and start to shriek.

"Platt, you whorespawn," she continued in a voice whose syllables crackled, "clean that up!"

"At once, lady," Platt murmured, bowing and looking around desperately for something to mop with.

"Now!" the queen shouted. "If you have to use your tongue!"

Platt pulled off his shirt and began to scrub. He scooped up the bigger chunks and wrung the rest out into the bucket.

"You see, darling," boasted the king from his armor. "The prison is perfectly safe."

Stella looked around in a mixture of distaste and disapproval. Though it was much as her husband said. . .

The citadel seemed from the outside to be a large building, but its stone walls were three meters thick. The circular internal cavity was only half the outside diameter; it was bisected now by a barrier of close-set iron bars each of which was as thick as a man's wrist. The ceiling—the floor of the upper level—was five meters high.

Sparrow crouched on a pile of furs on the other side of the bars. A dog whose hind legs were withered lay beside him. Sorted heaps of ore and scrap metals, the raw materials for the smith's work, filled almost all the remaining floorspace.

"Well, open the gate, man!" Hermann snarled at the citadel's attendant.

Platt leaped up from his cleaning. There was a look of controlled desperation in his eyes. The key to Sparrow's cell was chained to his waist. Platt fumbled for it, then thrust it into the lock and twisted.

King Hermann used the powered strength of his armor to open the gate against the friction of its massive hinges. The metal shrieked, making everyone in the citadel wince—

Except for Sparrow.

The smith looked from the king, who wore the battlesuit Sparrow had fashioned for himself, to Princess Miriam, who wore the mirror Sparrow had given Krita as a betrothal gift. His face was as still as a broken cliff.

"Get on with it," Hermann ordered.

The six slaves accompanying the king entered the cell one by one, bent under wicker baskets of stone and metal. They knelt to deposit their burdens, then snatched up part of the finished work. This time Sparrow had formed the thorax plates of battlesuits.

The slaves watched the smith warily. They moved with a clumsy quickness, as though they were mucking out a sabertooth's cage. The dog whined softly.

"Not bad," King Hermann murmured as the slabs of armor

passed under his protection, though he knew that the pieces were excellent rather than merely good.

Sparrow's work was always excellent.

King Hermann checked his prisoner every week. Any other smith would have required a month to accomplish the amount of work that the slaves were now removing. More important, the consistent quality of Sparrow's work was higher than virtually any rival could have managed no matter *how* long he took.

Princess Miriam watched the procession of slaves with increasing irritation. At last she shrilled, "Father! Why did you bring me here if there's nothing for me?"

"I just wanted you all to see how well I've—" Hermann said.

"Do you want gifts, lady princess?" the smith interrupted. His voice carried over the king's amplified words. "I'll make you a wonder, Princess Miriam. Give me back the mirror, and I'll make you any number of wonders."

Sparrow had calluses on both knees. A short pair of sticks helped him to stump around his cell, but he could not have walked even with full-length crutches. He could balance for a moment, perhaps, on the crutch tips and the flopping baggage that had been his feet; but not walk.

Never again.

The princess crossed her hands reflexively over the mirror hanging from her neck. "What?" she said. "No! Make me things anyway. After all, this isn't any good to you. It would just show you where you can't go."

"This is what you have him making?" the queen asked Hermann in puzzlement.

"I have him making battlesuits," the king explained. "But not all the parts at one time. You—"

"Make him give me more jewelry, Father!" Miriam interrupted.

"—see how careful I'm being."

"Will you let me go if I make a bauble for your daughter, King Hermann?" the smith asked. His voice was calm and his face still; but there was a gleam of frozen Hell in Sparrow's eyes.

The last of the slaves left the cell carrying the prisoner's slops bucket.

The king clashed the gate closed. "Don't be stupid," he muttered, quietly so that Princess Miriam would not hear him over the clang.

While the adults looked at Sparrow, Brech again overturned the bucket into which Platt had been mopping. The attendant grabbed the full bucket to prevent it from suffering the same fate. In theory, Platt was still a noble. In practice . . .

But he was alive; and he had his legs.

"I don't see why you worry, majesty," Platt said with a chuckle. "Even if Sparrow here did build an entire battlesuit, it still wouldn't help him walk!"

He laughed, and they all laughed at the despair on Sparrow's face.

≡ 26 ≡

THE ONLY THING that kept Hansen from open despair was his knowledge that the Colimore army a kilometer away was no better prepared for battle than were the levies Hansen led.

Intellectual awareness wasn't the same as emotional belief. Hansen believed, whatever his mind told him, that warriors on royal left wing—his wing—were going to charge without any discipline at all and be sliced six ways from Sunday by a Colimore phalanx.

Freemen mounted on ponies galloped back from a sortie toward the Colimore lines. It had been more bravado than reconnaissance. One of the riders lifted his curved bronze horn from its neck sling and blew a trill of meaningless excitement.

"God help us all," Hansen muttered as he stood in his battlesuit with the frontal plate still open.

Culbreth was at Hansen's side, already suited up. "Sir?" he boomed. "The marshal says, ah, would you get into your armor so he could talk to you."

Maharg had said to tell his left wing commander to get his thumb out of his ass, there was a job to do—if the marshal had been so polite.

Maharg was right. Hansen swung his battlesuit closed.

"Suit," he ordered to switch on his artificial intelligence. "Schematic overlay, opposing forces." He paused, then added, "Thirty percent mask."

"Hansen," snapped the command frequency in Maharg's

voice, "what do you make their numbers as being?"

The same thing your suit's AI does, Marshal.

"A hundred and forty-six, Maharg," Hansen said, keeping his voice cool. "We've got a clear margin of forty warriors. That's not the problem."

The normally diamond-sharp visual display of Hansen's battlesuit was now covered by a thin overlay which showed the two armies disposed across the terrain. At the edge of the screen, the artificial intelligence tabulated the relative strength of the forces, both total and by class of battlesuit.

"There's no possible way Colimore could hire more than fifty warriors!" Maharg said sharply. "Not if he sold the whole bloody duchy."

Maharg had chosen to let off steam with Hansen, a levy from nobody-knew-where, on a closed push where no one else could hear them. It was one of the greatest compliments anyone had ever paid Hansen.

It also spoke pretty well for the marshal's ability to judge men.

"We knew Solfygg was behind all this, Maharg," Hansen said. "We've still got them by numbers, and I think we're generally better man-for-man, even my crew."

Hansen kept his tone that of the calm advisor; a man whose guts *weren't* a gray turmoil at the thought of leading warriors whose idea of group action was persuading a scullery wench to pull a train before everybody was too drunk to stand up.

"Generally better, I'll grant," the marshal said. "But my read-out says there's twelve Class 1 suits on their left flank. *Twelve* royal suits."

"Yeah," said Hansen. "That's the thing that bothers me, too."

It was going to rain before the day was out. Earlier storms had beaten down the prairie's autumnal grasses, though tussocks of brown and gray and remembered green still remained. The field, a traditional battle area for the generations before the Peace of Golsingh, was nearly flat, but visibility would still be tricky.

The Solfygg armor was one *of the things that bothered Hansen.*

"It had better bother you," Maharg grumbled. His voice had lost the particular harshness of concern Hansen had noticed at the beginning of the discussion. "I was expecting to be able to give your wing some support. I don't know how quick I'll be able to take care of those royal suits."

"Look, my boys'll hold up their end, never fear," Hansen said, his voice sharp with pride despite himself. "You can call us levies if you want to, but if we weren't the damned best warriors in our households, our lords would've sent somebody else!"

And that was flat truth.

Hansen suddenly realized how much he cared about the men he led . . . and how much he hoped they wouldn't let him down.

Horns and bugles blew across the field. Thirty or forty mounted freemen armed with lances and crossbows advanced through the Colimore line. The warriors in battlesuits remained motionless for the moment.

Hansen's overlay showed that the Colimore warriors were spaced irregularly, like beads strung by an infant. Duke Ontell was using his freemen to entice the royal forces to advance first.

The royal army wasn't in parade-ground order either, but its four-to-three advantage in numbers gave Hansen a feeling of comfort as he glanced through the overlay—

So long as he ignored the twelve Solfygg warriors who stood out from the Colimore left wing like the teeth of a saw. Those champions wore suits as good as Hansen's own . . . or just about anybody else's.

A hundred or more royal freemen charged to meet the Colimore riders. The latter immediately turned tail and galloped back toward their own lines.

"All right," said Maharg in a tone of calm determination. "This is as good a time as any, I suppose."

Hansen visualized the marshal as he stood in his armor at the center of the right wing. Maharg's face would be set, his eyes knowing. The marshal was betting numbers against quality, and he was perfectly aware of the casualties that always resulted from that trade-off.

"Hey, buddy," Hansen said softly.

"What, then?"

"That's a lot of royal suits," Hansen said. "More than you've seen in one place before, probably more than anybody has. Don't push. If they come to us, they'll get separated and you can handle them just like you did me on the practice ground."

Maharg snorted. "Who's the marshal?" he demanded. "You or me?"

And then he said, "Thanks. We're going to take care of these bastards."

Or die trying—

But that thought was lost in Maharg's command over the general frequency, "Warriors, remember to keep your line and hold your intervals. All forces, advance!"

Bellowing with amplified enthusiasm, the royal army strode forward. The warriors' battlesuits sizzled blue halos in the humid air as they went forth to kill and die.

≡ 27 ≡

RITTER WAS PACING back and forth behind his console when
Hansen appeared in the workroom. The engineer took the
staccato, frustrated strides of a caged carnivore.

"Thought I'd drop in and say hi," Hansen said.

His ultramarine trousers and cream-colored shirt made him
look like one of Ritter's underlings. The pistol he carried was
part of the uniform also. The weapon was in a heavy flap
holster very different from the breakaway unit Hansen had
worn against the Lomeri.

"Drop in and check up on me, you mean," the engineer
snarled.

If I wanted to check on you—

Hansen waved his left hand. An image of Ritter in his
laboratory hung in front of the man whom it pictured. The
color was full and rich, the resolution crystalline. The image's
face went blank, then grimaced in embarrassment as though
it were a non-reversing mirror.

Hansen waved the image away. "Hi, Master Ritter," he
said with a slight smile.

"Hell, I'm sorry," the engineer said.

He slapped the chair built into the console. It spun on its
gimbals, but the blow wasn't a serious one, just a flick of
irritation. "I'm not usually that dumb. Hell, maybe I'm just
too dumb to do your job, Colonel Hansen."

Hansen shrugged. "I doubt that," he said.

He sat down on the bed of a milling machine, shifting a tray of jigs carefully so that they didn't fall onto the floor. "Anyway," he continued, "I'm no colonel. Just Hansen. Or—"

He smiled. "—Nils, if you want to, but that formation's not much in favor on Northworld, I've found."

Ritter gave a deep sigh, not so much relaxing as expressing a willingness to relax. He seated himself with his back to the console's screens and controls. "Penny calls you 'Commissioner' sometimes," he said. "It seemed to mean 'colonel,' in the ranks here."

" 'Commissioner' was . . . ," Hansen said.

He quirked a corner of his mouth, trying to hook the correct words. "That was before I came to Northworld. I was a . . . type of policeman. For oh, well; violence, I suppose you could say."

"You were Civic Patrol?" the engineer translated, cautiously trying to avoid contempt.

Hansen grinned. "Close enough," he said. "It wasn't a high-status job where I came from either, Master Ritter. But maybe not quite as low as it is here, where military elites run the keeps and the police only have authority over the laboring class."

Ritter shrugged. "Well," he said, "none of that stuff matters anyway, does it?"

"Status doesn't matter?" Hansen said. "Balls."

He laughed, stood up, and stretched. The knuckles of his left hand bumped the suction hood that would close over the workpiece during operations. "You wouldn't say that after you told Lord Greville to go piss up a slope."

Hansen's smile was as hard as the diamond cutters of the milling machine. "Or," he added, "if one of your party girls said the equivalent to you."

Ritter grimaced at the backs of his hands. "You know what I mean," he said. "*You* know that getting the job done is the only important thing. And I've hit a stone wall on your job."

"What's the problem?" Hansen asked equably. "I don't know jack shit about the hardware, but you do; and talking helps a lot of times."

The engineer shrugged. "Okay," he said. "I can't find the

bloody power supply. And I know there is one, because I've seen the unit work."

"You made a liar out of me," Hansen said. "I *can* help there."

He got up again, smiling at an unexpected win. "The dragonflies draw their power direct from imbalances in the Matrix. Same with the battlesuits. You remember them?"

Hansen waved his hand. Men in armored suits weighing a hundred kilos and more moved uphill at a swift, staggering pace toward another similarly-equipped force. Blue radiance sprang from the warriors' gauntlets. The lines crashed together in a blaze of arcs on protective forcefields like the lightning-lit core of a tornado.

"The problem those men have running," Hansen continued, "isn't the weight, it's the control circuits. There's lag time between moving your leg and the servos obeying, especially in the cheap suits."

Ritter swore and pounded the console behind him. He used the side of his hand, but there was nothing petty about the blow. He stood up again and walked around the console to put his back to his visitor.

"Problem with that?" Hansen asked mildly. His lips were the only portion of his face that moved.

"Look," said the engineer, "I know the Matrix exists, I've, I've been in it. But—"

He turned. "It *doesn't* exist for me, do you see? It's bloody magic!"

"Oh, yeah," said Hansen. He stepped forward, almost gliding, and put his arm around the engineer's shoulders. "Yeah, I do know what you mean. But look, friend—"

He waited until Ritter met his eyes, then continued, "It's what we've got. Pretending reality doesn't exist can get you killed in my line of work. Or yours."

Ritter began to laugh. "Civic Patrol!" he said.

Hansen laughed also. "Hey, man, try me one-on-one with your Lord Greville and we'll see who has a better idea which end of a gun goes bang. Is it my fault that your cops only carry nets and clubs?"

"Okay," Ritter said, "I'll build your magic horse, now that

I'm sure I've got all the pieces." The laughter had broken his mood into good humor. "Reverse engineering isn't as easy as it looks. People don't realize that."

"If it was easy," Hansen replied, "I wouldn't have had to come to you, right?"

"So you figure I'm the best, do you?" the engineer said, half mocking but half in justifiable certainty of his own worth.

"You're the best I could find," Hansen agreed. "Of what you do, I mean."

He waved an image to life in the air before them. "In the Open Lands," he went on, "there are smiths who use the Matrix to create things. Some of them might be as good in their way as you are in yours."

In the image, a big man in a filthy garment lay on a bed of furs. His legs were scabbed, and his feet sprawled like a seal's flippers.

The viewpoint slid downward to cut a slice through the pile of gravel and metal arranged beside the man. Solid matter shifted, then re-formed from chaos into intricate patterns of circuitry and sheathing.

Hansen rotated the image viewpoint to a close focus on the man's face. His mouth lolled open, and the pupils of his slitted eyes were rolled up out of sight.

"His name is Sparrow," Hansen said. "And he's probably as good as you are."

≡ 28 ≡

PLATT CLUTCHED THE flaccid wineskin in both hands and said, "You know, Sparrow, I don't see what good you get outa making all this for King Hermann."

The smith shuddered on his pallet of furs.

"Hey, you!" Platt shouted. He pounded his hand on a bar. The metal rang. The attendant cursed the pain in his hand. He picked up his stool.

Sparrow's dog lay with its head across its master's belly. The beast growled and bared its teeth without lifting its head. Sparrow was still in the outer fringes of his trance, but his hand stroked the dog back to silence.

The crippled animal tracked Platt with hate-filled eyes.

Platt rang his stool across the bars in a clatter like a bridge falling. "Hey!" he bellowed. "Hey, you legless bastard!"

Sparrow's eyes snapped fully open. For an instant, the smith's expression was the same as that of his dog. His face calmed in quick stages, as though control overlaid hatred in a series of nictitating membranes.

Platt stepped back from the bars and belched. He tried to squeeze another dribble from the stolen wineskin. Scarcely enough remained to wet the tip of his tongue. He threw the container down in anger.

Sparrow stroked the head and neck of his dog. "What are you doing with wine, Platt?" the smith asked. His tone held no more emotion than the sound of a distant landslide.

"None of your business, is it?" Platt shrilled. The question had surfaced fear in his drunken mind like a shark slicing up from murky seas.

He turned and picked up the wineskin, then paused for a moment to regain his balance. At last he plunged the container deep within his slops bucket. It would stay there unnoticed until he had a chance to empty the bucket unobserved in the community cesspool.

Platt stared again at the prisoner he attended. "What I wanna know . . . ," he said.

He blinked and glanced down at his hands. After a moment, he wiped them on his breeches.

"What I wanna know," he resumed as he traced the thread of his intention, "is why you do it? Make the stuff. Seeings they treat you like shit."

Platt belched again. He caught the bars to keep from falling down.

The dog growled. Platt stared owlishly at his hand, then removed it with care from the metal.

You didn't cling to the bars of a bear's cage. Not even if the bear had been hamstrung.

"Seein' as they treat you worsen 'n they treat me," the attendant muttered. "And they treat *me* like shit."

Sparrow sat up; his dog perked sharply onto its haunches and front legs. It was not immediately obvious that either of them was crippled.

The smith smoothed the dross away from the piece on which he had been working in his trance. Some of the rocks crumbled to grit and dust as he touched them.

Bits of the crystals forming the rocks' structure had been rearranged into the core of a metal/ceramic/metal sandwich: the left calf of a battlesuit. Scrap metal—a broken scythe, a worn plow coulter, a grill from the palace kitchen which long use had warped and thinned—had been added to the pile. Most of the metal had vanished into the sheathing of the workpiece which Sparrow withdrew from the dross and eyed critically.

"You think I should refuse to work for King Hermann, do you?" the smith asked in a voice too flat to be calm.

"I didn't say that!" Platt cried.

He hadn't said it, the wine had been talking; and anyway, he'd deny the words with the experience born of a life of lying denials.

Sparrow set the workpiece down and laughed. It was not a pleasant sound. "Are you worried I'll tell the king?" he said. "Who would believe *me*?"

Of course, who would believe that crippled husk?

"And besides," the smith continued with a smile as brutal as his laughter, "you're too useful to be chopped for what you spew when you're drunk. A slave would run away if they kept him like they do you—"

The smile again. "—but the king knows that if you ever leave the protection of his palace, there's a hundred men waiting to kill you in the slowest way they can think of. See how useful you are?"

Sparrow's fingers caressed the upper ball of the armor's knee joint. He would form the thigh piece in a few hours. The join would be so perfect that only the creator himself would know where one section stopped and the other began.

But even Sparrow needed rest and food.

He looked in his bowl for the remainder of his noon feeding. The crust and porridge were only a memory.

A hog thighbone had arrived the night before with some fat and skin. The bone remained, lying between the dog's forepaws. The animal's jaws had worried but could not crack the dense bone. He whined hopefully as his master lifted the thighbone.

"Tell them I need more food," Sparrow said. "The Matrix is cold. . . ."

Sparrow's mouth trembled with the memory. He controlled it. "If they want the work out of me, they'll have to feed me better."

"You'll get whatever the king chooses to send you, crippled scum!" Platt cried in an attempt to assert the authority both men knew he lacked.

"They will send me more food," Sparrow said.

His right thumb pressed against the ball of the hog thigh which snapped like an arc breaking. The shaft of the bone splintered between his palm and fingers.

"Not because they love me," the smith continued with his eyes focused on his attendant's. "But because they want what I make."

Sparrow smiled. He opened his right palm and gave one of the bone fragments to his dog. He put another in his own mouth and began to suck the marrow.

"So they must feed me," he concluded.

"I . . . ," Platt said. He was suddenly very queasy. He could steal wine only rarely, and there was no place to hide a part-finished container. He'd drunk his spoils too quickly.

"You tell them yourself when they come next," Platt said in the bitterness of sudden self-realization. "They won't listen to me, whatever I say."

Sparrow picked out another splinter for the dog. It growled in anticipation.

"You want to know why I work for King Hermann?" the smith said with his usual lack of affect. "Because in the Matrix—"

Platt knelt and began to vomit, onto the floor and onto the tumble of his own bedding. The spasms wracked him as though they were trying to bring his bowels up through his throat.

"—I'm not a slave any more, Platt," Sparrow continued.

The smith smiled, but his dog drew away from him with a sudden yelp of concern.

"In the Matrix, I'm free," said Sparrow in a harsh, terrible voice. "And there are no walls around me!"

≡ 29 ≡

"HANSEN?" RITTER ASKED suddenly. "Can you take me out-side the walls?"

The laboratory held numerous duplicated pieces from the dragonfly, though the only set obvious to an outsider was the four legs. They were mounted upside down on a testbed which flexed them rapidly in three planes. The hydraulic pump driving the test rig whined, but the articulated legs performed without complaint.

"Sure," Hansen said, shrugging in his loose blouse. The local fashion was so comfortable that he'd begun wearing similar garb back home. "The only thing is . . . "

Hansen's voice trembled. His mind reviewed the muzzle of the lizardman's weapon and the fireball enveloping the veg-etation as he and Ritter shifted from the dimension. "We're going to be carrying more gear this time," he continued, "if you want to go back to visit the Lomeri. Forcefield projectors, for a start."

The engineer looked at him in honest surprise. "Why on earth would I want to do that?" he asked.

To prove you weren't really frightened by what scared the hell out of you and me both.

"Why does anybody do anything?" Hansen replied aloud.

Ritter shook his head in amazement. "Well," he said, "all I want to do is see what's out there—"

He reached behind him and touched a switch on the con-sole. The control replaced laboratory walls with a panorama of lake and vegetation. A number of large animals sported in the shallow water.

Laboratory equipment and some feed lines had been run along rather than within the walls. They stood out in eerie contrast to the natural scene.

"—under an open sky."

"Sure, no problem," Hansen said, checking his holstered pistol by reflex to be sure that the flap was unsnapped. Hansen had been practicing with the clumsy rig, not that he expected ever to need the weapon. "Ah—it's raining out there just now."

"I won't shrink," Ritter said. He flipped up his armrest to access an array of hidden controls. "Just a minute while I seal the doors so that nobody stumbles in while we're gone."

"Don't bother," said Hansen. He put an arm around the engineer's shoulders. "I'll bring you back the same time we leave. Only you'll be—"

Reality became two-dimensional, then flip-flopped into infinite pathways—

And shifted back along a different plane of reality, into soft ground and the smell of living things.

"—a little damp," Hansen concluded. It wasn't so much rain as a mugginess so thick that droplets condensed out of the air.

"Oh . . . ," said Ritter. He looked around slowly.

Keep Greville rose behind them, a great blue hemisphere of force that hissed in the damp atmosphere. At its peak, the dome's vague glow merged with that of the mid-morning sun.

The red, gritty soil supported a knee-high cover of grasses and broad-leafed vegetation. There were many palm trees in clusters of two or three. Ritter walked over to the nearest. Something with long, fawn-colored fur scampered up the tree as the engineer approached; it chittered its irritation from among the fronds.

Ritter patted the treetrunk. The surface was as coarse as concrete, but where concrete would have been cool to the touch, the bark was warm.

"I used to spend a lot of time out here when I was a boy,"

he said. "I sneaked out with the creche leader's pistol in case I ran into any of the carnivores that hang around the keep's waste outlets. Shot a few of them too, though just when I had to."

The sky was clearing. When one of the hornless rhinos suddenly galloped from the lake, the spray its short legs stirred up made a sudden rainbow. The beast must have been playing, because it immediately plunged back in with its fellows.

"I was afraid the creche leader would notice the missing shells, you see," Ritter continued softly. He explored the bark with his fingertips while his eyes followed the rhino's antics. "But he never checked the magazine. Not once."

"Not many people go outside the keep, then?" Hansen asked.

He was keeping a careful watch around them. The carnivores of Plane Five weren't any great shakes compared to those on Plane Two with the Lomeri—or in the Open Lands, for that matter. But something that weighed upwards of fifty kilos, with long jaws and a nasty disposition, was worth blasting before it got within fang range.

"Not except for the soldiers," Ritter agreed.

He stepped around the palm, looking up toward the chittering. The animal making the sound retreated around the trunk. Hansen, standing still, got a good view of a little rodent with black rings on its slender tail.

"The soldiers are always in armored vehicles," the engineer added. He walked slowly in the direction of the lake. "So that isn't really getting outside either."

The rhinoceroses noticed Ritter's approach. One barked a challenge, then ducked under the surface. In a moment, all of the half-tonne animals had vanished. Regular wheezing from the beds of water hyacinth indicated that the rhinos had not gone far.

"There's no *need* to go out, after all, though it's not prohibited for most people," Ritter said. "There just isn't much reason to bother. The colonizing vessels had efficient hydroponic systems, and we've improved the technique since then."

Mud squished onto the uppers of the engineer's short boots.

He changed direction slightly to parallel the shore. Hansen stayed a few steps inshore of Ritter, though even so there were occasional wet spots to hop over.

"But I liked the outside," Ritter continued.

He bent and plucked a spray of something fernlike, though Hansen wasn't sure it was really a fern. "And you know, Hansen, the Lords Greville—this one and his uncle—haven't allowed me out of the keep in twenty years. They were afraid—"

Ritter savagely stripped the leaves from the frond he held, leaving only the bare stem. "—that something might happen to me. Even a kidnapping attempt by another keep."

"You're good enough they need to worry about losing you," Hansen said evenly. "I guess you were good even twenty years ago."

Hansen felt uneasy. He slipped the pistol up and down in its holster, but it wasn't the approach of anything tangible that his subconscious feared.

"Oh, you bet I was," the engineer said. He squatted and poked at the soft soil, twisting until his finger had almost disappeared. "Do you know . . . "

Ritter's voice trailed off without completing the question. He rose and wiped the muck from his finger against the bole of a deciduous tree.

"I'm treated well," he continued harshly. "There's almost nothing in Keep Greville that I couldn't have if I demanded it. But do you know, Hansen . . . do you know what it's like to be unfree?"

The back of Hansen's neck prickled. He heard his voice saying, "I don't suppose I've ever been free, Ritter. Surely not before I came to Northworld . . . and even now. . . ."

Hansen gripped a sapling slender enough for him to close his hands about its trunk. He wasn't trying to experience its nature, the way the engineer had been doing ever since he left the constructed reality of the keep.

Hansen just needed something safe against which anger could work his muscles.

"Look, I'm . . . ," he said. His hands went white and mottled with the sudden strain.

"I always did my job, the job right in front of me," he said. His voice sounded like gravel sliding through a sieve. "Now I can do anything, *anything*. And it scares me."

Hansen's whole body shuddered. He released the tree and hugged his arms to his body. His eyes focused on Ritter, but all that entered his conscious mind from the sight was a vague impression of the bigger man's concern.

"I look at the others," Hansen said, "the other *gods,* and they're caricatures, Ritter, they're warping themselves into one little slice of whatever they musta been when they came here. Look at Penny! She's got all the power there is, and look what she does with it."

"Ah, Hansen . . . ," the engineer said.

"So what I do is pretend that nothing's changed for me, do you see?" Hansen went on. "Pretending that I'm no more than what I used to be when I, when, when they sent me here."

It had come on him unexpectedly, a combination of what the engineer meant as a rhetorical question and the process of watching the other man peel off the layers hiding his past life. Hansen knew he was speaking loudly, because dozens of birds exploded from the undergrowth in panic, their wingfeathers clattering. He couldn't stop.

He didn't want to be talking about this, he didn't want to think about this; but he couldn't stop.

"I pretend I'm just a cop," he said. "Just a troubleshooter. The one they call in when the job's going to mean serious violence, do you see? Because there's nobody in the human universe who's better at *that* than Commissioner Nils Hansen!"

His hands were shaking. His whole body was shaking.

Ritter wrapped Hansen in his muscular arms. He held him, gently but as firmly as a crash harness, until the multiple spasms passed.

Hansen drew a deep breath. He began to laugh. He felt the engineer's arms tighten again.

"No," he said, "no, it's all right, Master Ritter. I'm okay now."

Ritter released him cautiously, as though he were afraid that the slighter man would jump for his throat as soon the engineer's grip slackened.

Hansen squeezed Ritter's shoulder affectionately. "Hey, look," he said, "it's really all right. I'm as crazy as the rest of them, I guess . . . but I'm under control. That's all that really matters, isn't it?"

The sun blazed down, making the atmosphere even more humid as heat lifted water from the foliage and the surface of the lake. The rodent in the palm tree had at last grown silent.

"Let's get me back to my lab," said Ritter. "I've got a dragonfly to make."

≡ 30 ≡

WHEN HE SAW Bran and Brech at the citadel doorway, Sparrow took from beneath his bedding the piece he had made in anticipation.

"Hey!" cried Platt in alarm. "Nobody's supposed to come here unless the king brings them himself."

"Here, boys," Sparrow called from his cell. "You wanted me to make something for you. Isn't that right?"

King Hermann might or might not be trailing a few meters behind his sons. Even if the king was present and Sparrow's plan could go no further forward for the moment, a hint of wonderful toys would bring the twins back like dogs scenting a bitch in heat.

"Shut up, you!" snarled Platt.

The attendant snatched up his half full slops bucket. He went on in a voice compounded of fear, hatred, and a horrible oily subservience, "Now, boys, you know your father wouldn't want you to be up here with this nasty man, would he?"

Light danced on Sparrow's right palm, within the cage of his fingers.

"Oh!" said Bran and kicked Platt on the ankle.

The attendant yelped. The bucket swung on its handle, splashing out a little of its contents.

The twins ran up to the bars. "He threw *shit* on us!" Brech caroled. "We'll tell Daddy he threw shit on us!"

The crippled dog edged back against the stone wall. It bared its teeth and growled at so deep a level that only a hand on the beast's chest would have disclosed the vibration.

"Yes . . . ," Sparrow said. He rose to his knees and stumped a little closer to the bars. The barrier was still a hand's breadth beyond his reach. "Look what I made for you boys."

The smith opened his fingers. Two beads of yellow light began to rotate in separate figure-eight patterns around a common center.

Sparrow cupped his hand behind them as if to give the insubstantial display a push. The speed of rotation increased, and the beads drifted toward the twins.

"Ooh, no, please . . . ," the attendant moaned. He clutched the bucket to his chest as if it were treasure being snatched from a holocaust.

"Ooh . . . ," said the twins together.

The spinning beads reached the barrier. Part of the diameter of the circle they described passed through a gap between bars, but the rest of their motion took them into the iron itself. The light vanished while the beads were within solid matter, but they reappeared unchanged on the other side of the bars. They continued to slide forward.

"Please," whimpered Platt. "Please, please. . . ."

Bran and Brech snatched simultaneously at Sparrow's creation. Neither of the twins quite touched it, though their hands collided where the thing of light had been a moment before. The object bounced a meter into the air and continued in roughly its previous direction, sinking slowly.

"There . . . ," murmured Sparrow in satisfaction. "Isn't that a wonder, boys? Isn't that a marvel for you?"

The twins ignored him as they squealed in pursuit of the gleaming construct. Brech leaped high to grab the object. He only succeeded in swatting it toward Platt.

The attendant stutter-stepped to the right, then the left, and finally threw up one of his hands with a shriek. At the moment the spinning lights should have touched Platt's splayed fingers, the object's rotation increased to a blur and it shot straight up.

The lights vanished into the high wooden ceiling.

"He broke it!" Bran cried in genuine fury. "He *broke* it!"

Wailing in anger, both the young princes began to kick and pummel Platt. The terrified attendant yelped and broke for the outside door.

"I'll get it!" he called, instinctively reaching for an explanatory lie even in a moment of panic.

The slops bucket hit the doorframe and spilled half its contents. Platt dropped the container onto his bedding and continued to run. The children started to follow him.

"Here, boys!" Sparrow called.

Brech turned. His face was screwed into an expression of inhuman rage. Bran took another step and looked back also.

"I have things much lovelier than that, my royal darlings," the smith said. His husky whisper was as terrible as the arc ripping from a battlesuit.

"Show me!" Brech cried. He ran to the barrier and hammered at the gate with his bare hands. Iron rang on iron, nearly drowning out the boy's repeated, "Show me now!"

Sparrow's dog began to howl. The beast's eyes were slits; it thrashed its tail against the stone.

"Hush, lad," the smith said. He stepped forward on his knees, over a pile of brass and pewter scrap, and stroked Brech's head.

"Don't touch us, you slave!" Bran shrieked. He jumped to the barrier and clawed at Sparrow's hand where it lay on Brech's fine, fair hair.

"Ah, my error, darling boys," Sparrow said, snatching his hand away and raising it, palm outward in token of submission.

"Show us, then!" Bran demanded. "The toy!"

"Shh . . . ," Sparrow warned, gesturing toward the outer door with an index finger as solid as a pick handle. "Don't let him hear or he'll break the new toys too, don't you see?"

"My daddy will *fix* that dirty slavebastard," Brech said with grim certainty.

"No, we'll do better than that," the smith warned. The light in his eyes would have chilled any adult who saw it; but there were no adults to watch, only a dog and two young boys . . . and the crippled dog lolled its tongue out like that of a wolf closing on fawns.

"If you come back tonight, boys," Sparrow continued, "Platt will be asleep, and I'll show you things that not even your father and mother can yet imagine. But you'll have to do something for me, all right?"

Though he spoke without haste, Sparrow glanced frequently toward the door, afraid that his attendant would return at any moment.

"We don't have to do anything!" Bran announced shrilly.

"He wants us to let him out," his brother said. "He wants us to take the key from that old slavebastard."

"No, no-no, my lads," the smith said. "Where would I go—" he gestured toward his feet, as loose as the tongue of his dog "—a cripple like me?"

"We could make Platt give us the key," Bran said to his brother. "We could have Daddy beat him if he didn't."

"Not the key, lads," Sparrow said with a face like vengeance become a god. "Only wine, only a little skin of wine, that you can hide in the kitchen midden at dusk, is that not so? You can steal a skin of wine and hide it?"

Brech sniffed with simulated maturity. "Sure," he said. "We can get through the ventilator into the buttery. We do it *lots* of times."

"Oh, I thought you might, lad," the smith whispered. "It was a thing I thought you might do. And then—"

There was shadow on the doorjamb. Platt was returning.

"—come to me at midnight," Sparrow concluded quickly. "Not before, but at midnight, and you'll see wonders."

Platt peeked around the jamb. "What are you doing?" he demanded. "You get away from those boys, you cripple!"

"Run along, lads," Sparrow said in a voice as bright as the sun on a glacier. "And remember what I told you."

"What?" the attendant demanded in renewed panic. "What did you tell them?"

The twins darted past him, gurgling their delight at a plot and the promise. Bran kicked at Platt as he went by, but the little boot only brushed the attendant's jerkin.

"What . . . ?" Platt repeated, looking out the door after the twins' disappearing forms.

"Oh, they're lovely lads, Platt," Sparrow said. "And so generous. Would you believe that they offered to steal me a skin of wine?"

Platt's head snapped around. "What?"

"Yes, a skin of wine," the smith continued. He spoke in nearly a falsetto, so high and thin was his voice. "They'll hide it at dusk in the kitchen midden, so that when you go to fetch my supper tonight you can bring that as well."

He gave the attendant a great, twisted smile. "Is that not generous, Platt?" he said. "To offer wine to a crippled slave like me?"

Platt laughed; first a sharp bark of sound, then cackling, echoing peals of mirth.

"Did the gods make you such a fool, Sparrow?" the attendant said after he regained control of his merriment. "Don't you know that stolen goods have no owner but the one who holds them?"

"Ah, but the lads mean the wine for me to drink, Platt," the smith said softly as his eyes gleamed with his own hellish laughter.

"Maybe they do," Platt announced. "But *I* mean it for my own throat!"

He began to bellow his amusement again.

"If that's what you really want, my deserving friend," Sparrow whispered as his hand stroked the ears of his crippled dog, "then I'll see that you get it."

≡ 31 ≡

A COLIMORE WARRIOR, chasing honor or pursued by it, got five meters ahead of his fellows and died as three arcs slashed his battlesuit to sparks and molten metal.

"An omen!" Hansen bellowed over the general push. "Peace and Prandia! An omen!"

Not because he believed in omens, but it was a good thing to shout to his troops. Anyway, it was one fewer opposing warrior and a champion besides—though his suit hadn't been good enough to absorb the simultaneous strokes of levies who had, after all, learned something about teamwork in the past few days.

And besides, anybody who needed luck to live knew that omens *did* count, at least when they were in your favor.

The battlefield stuttered into electrical brilliance. Clumps of sodden grass began to burn, sending drifts of smoke across the fighters like veils of dirty cobweb.

No one else on Hansen's wing of the army fell. Warriors probed one another at a few meters' distance, steeling themselves to lunge close to a range at which their arcs could be effective—

And where their opponents' weapons could gut them like trout, giving them just enough time to scream in sizzling agony as they died.

The lines eased together, as nearly parallel as the rolling prairie and variables of human nature allowed. Every third man or fourth stood a little in advance of his fellows, twitch-

ing his arc toward an enemy who was doing the same, just
out of effective reach.

Hansen, with Culbreth to his right and Arnor on the left,
followed three paces behind the center of his line. He was
trying to keep the whole wing in view on his overlay while
he continued to step forward. He paused when the warriors
ahead of him stopped advancing.

There were commanders, and there were leaders. Nils Hansen had never been very good at ordering other men to go
die.

"Suit, straight visuals!" Hansen ordered his AI, clearing the
display. "Team, follow me!" he added as he drove forward
between two levies.

He wasn't really confident that Culbreth and Arnor would
follow him. He was pretty sure that he could handle alone
what was about to happen, pretty sure, but he'd seen too many
men die in too many places to believe that he was invulnerable
either.

A pair of Colimore champions met motion with motion,
striding forward behind points of dense blue flame.

What happened didn't matter as much to Hansen as the
fact he was moving now and not just watching.

The arc from Hansen's right gauntlet parried one stroke
and started to burn back toward the helmet of the warrior
who made it. Hansen's weapon paled to a fraction of its initial
density as the other warrior slashed at his ribs and Hansen's
suit redirected power to the defensive screen.

Culbreth thrust at the warrior whose arc Hansen was holding. The man's defenses fluoresced a microsecond before the
angel painted over his thorax went black and the steel beneath
burned.

Instead of doubling Culbreth's stroke, Arnor cut at the warrior whose arc lit a coruscant blaze from Hansen's screen.
That wasn't the way Hansen had trained them, but it was all
right, the Colimore man stepped back—

*Hansen's left side burned like the wall of a furnace, but the
servo motors had power again and the flux from his gauntlet
was blue fury.*

—and Hansen pivoted to follow him, slashing at the neck

joint, shearing *it* and down through the *thorax* plate and *out*.

The body toppled. The head, still attached to the warrior's right arm, fell separately.

Real close. Real close to Hansen's final mistake.

Hansen's battlesuit was an oven, though the environmental control whined to cool it. There was a bubbled patch on the sheathing above his left ribs, and his vision display took a moment to regain its normal crystalline precision.

The less enthusiastic warriors formed a second half-line behind the Colimore champions. Six of them had surged forward when their leaders did. Now they were trying to retreat from the sudden carnage. Smudgy grass fires lapped at their feet like a flood of thick liquid.

This was the chance to turn local success into a sweeping rout.

"C'mon!" Hansen croaked. He lurched forward, hoping his team would follow.

Culbreth was already a stride ahead, cutting at a Colimore warrior who turned to run.

Culbreth's weapon sprayed the smoldering grass with bits from the victim's shoulder armor, violating the battlesuit's integrity and probably killing the man inside. Arnor followed with a quick downward cut which ended the latter doubt by burning a chin-deep wedge in the Colimore helmet.

Hansen had his footing and his suit at full power again, but the warriors he'd passed to break the hostile line were moving now also. Hansen almost slashed a royal warrior who stepped between him and a Colimore champion.

Both the suits were good and well-matched. The point-blank grapple created a spray of sparks and radiance, ending an instant later when Arnor stabbed the Colimore warrior under the arm and blew the victim's screens with a double load.

Warriors were down all across Hansen's end of the field. Some of them royal levies—half a dozen of them royal levies. *The people who talk about light casualties are the ones who've never had to mop a man's body from the interior of his equipment.*

But the Colimore line was unraveling like a knit garment.

Twenty or more of the duke's warriors sizzled on the ground as power continued to short through their ruined armor. The remainder were backing in nervous desperation or had taken the risk of turning to run.

"Suit, overlay!" Hansen said, letting his men flare past him to right and left now that the wing needed an officer more than it did another shock troop.

What the 30% mask told Hansen was chilling. The battle *was* by god a rout on the left wing. It was damned close to a rout on the right also—but there it was the dozen Solfygg warriors in first-class armor who had hammered the Royal Household to the verge of cracking.

One of the Solfygg champions was down, but smoldering fragments of five of Maharg's professionals lay around him. White carats on Hansen's display marked other friendly casualties, all along the original line of contact.

The surviving eleven champions strode forward. The remainder of the Colimore right wing followed rather than supported their splendidly armored leaders, stepping over the blackened armor of royal troops who failed to retreat in time from the Solfygg advance.

Hansen opened his mouth to shout an order. He remembered that his radio was still on White Band, the general frequency for the levies on the left wing.

"Blue push," he directed his AI. He jogged up the rolling slope to his right, behind and paralleling the triumphant line of his own troops. The last thing Hansen wanted to do was to drag those men along with him.

The levies would hunt their fleeing opponents until disaster slammed into them from behind. There was nothing they could do against the Solfygg champions except die . . . and they would do that soon enough if the right wing collapsed and left them unsupported.

"Aim at the hip and shoulder joints!" Hansen ordered as he saw—direct vision and the overlay as well, it was still blurring the sight he needed now—three of the royal professionals make a desperate sally against the champion on the right of the Solfygg line. "The suits have weak spots at the joins!"

Duke Ontell had deployed his shock troops against the Royal Household, discounting King Prandia's levies as no more than a match for his regular warriors. That had been a misjudgment—

But maybe not a fatal one.

The eleven champions were arrayed together on one wing of the army. Because they were concentrated, they supported one another even though they appeared to have no more notion of team tactics than so many snarling tigers.

Maharg's three men made a well-coordinated attack. It stalled when the Solfygg champion lashed the leader with an arc so powerful that it froze his suit at three meters' distance. The other two royal troops stepped in from either side. Their enemy's battlesuit held for the moment their weapons licked it; then another Solfygg warrior struck the man on the right.

"The joints!" Hansen screamed again.

Running in a battlesuit was like running in liquid: though the motors did the work, the massive inertia of over a hundred kilos of armor required soul-deadening effort to make it move quickly. Hansen's thigh muscles pumped, anesthetized by the adrenaline that would leave them pools of fire as soon as the crisis cooled.

Unless he died in the next few minutes.

Either the professional on the Solfygg champion's right heard Hansen call or else he got lucky. He shifted his arc from the champion's helmet to the line between arm and thorax where a lesser smith had mated the pieces.

The leader of the royal team died as the supporting Solfygg champion struck from the side. Everything between the victim's neck and diaphragm flared into saffron plasma in the powerful arc.

But in the instant the other Solfygg warrior's weapon was locked by the leader's, the surviving royal professional struck home. The Solfygg armor failed at the join line.

The arm of the Solfygg suit spun away in a devouring flash. The black stump of a humerus poked from the open end, but the muscles had shriveled in a current so hot that even the battlesuit's ceramic core burned.

The Solfygg champion who had killed the other two team

members rushed the third at a lumbering run. The royal professional backed as quickly as he could, knowing that his suit could survive his opponent's weapon for only fractions of a second.

Hansen stepped between the hunter and his prey.

The royal army was falling back; Duke Ontell's forces pressed on faster. Two more of the champions from Solfygg moved up in support of the warrior on the right of their wing.

This was going to have to be fast.

Hansen was at close quarters before the Solfygg champion realized he had another opponent. The champion's arc was already extended several meters to lick the lesser suit of the man he was chasing.

Hansen held the Solfygg weapon with the merest flicker from his right gauntlet. His main blow was with his left, a thrust that ended only when the steel of his glove clanged on the sheathing of his opponent's hip. A white-hot collop exploded from the Solfygg battlesuit.

Another Solfygg warrior in top-quality armor slid to a startled halt a few meters away when he saw his fellow's blazing corpse topple into the smoldering grass.

"At the joints!" Hansen screamed.

Instead of pressing in against Hansen, the Solfygg champion shouted for another of his peers to join him. Hansen went for him, coldly careful to step between the armored legs of the man he had just killed.

The Solfygg warrior tilted his foot to retreat, then lunged forward in what was either desperation or fury. His arc was so dense it was nearly palpable. He thrust at the center of Hansen's chest.

Hansen blocked the stroke with his right hand. His gauntlet began to heat immediately. Blue-white discharges heated the air into sudden vortices, lifting ash from the ground. Colimore supports moved up behind a curtain of smoke and diffracted light.

Hansen's vision displays degraded as the AI diverted still more of his suit's power into the flux that protected his life. He twisted slowly against the mass of his armor and cold servos, shifting his torso and directing the arc from his gauntlet down rather than up as it continued to lock the Solfygg weapon.

Hammering vibration from the two full-power arcs overwhelmed any chance of Hansen's screaming fury being heard except by his artificial intelligence.

The tip of Hansen's arc touched the soil. Both discharges shorted to ground in a cataclysmic uproar.

Hansen switched most of his suit's power to his left gauntlet, leaving only a trickle to keep the current path open and his opponent's weapon safely grounded. He struck at the hip joint. The gout of flame in which the Solfygg champion died was less dazzling than the spouting effulgence a moment before as both battlesuits discharged at their full capacity.

There was another Solf—

There wasn't.

The third champion was down, a gaping wound in the shoulder of his armor. Two of Maharg's professionals were down also, one's helmet a molten ruin, but they'd got the bastard, they'd *got* him.

Eighty meters from where Hansen stood, brilliant light danced skyward as Maharg in his own royal suit faced two Solfygg champions. The marshal had been covering the retreat of the Royal Household. It was a miracle that he'd lasted so long, but now several of his warriors scrambled back to his aid.

"Peace and Prandia!" shouted somebody who ran past as Hansen gasped to breathe before he staggered on toward Maharg. *Arnor, and that was fucking Culbreth, they were going to get themselves—*

The nearest Colimore troops hadn't yet made up their minds what to do when their Solfygg leaders fell. Arnor and Culbreth, Hansen's *team*, hacked at an opponent together. He fell.

The next Colimore warrior wore a silver battlesuit, itself of nearly royal quality. He blocked Arnor's thrust, parried a stroke by Culbreth—

And died when the professional that Hansen saved as he

rushed to the right wing struck between the two arcs and finished the job.

"Aim at the joints!" Hansen called as he stumbled forward. He couldn't feel his legs, just lances of fire into his groin every time he took a step, but that didn't matter as long as he moved.

A lightning storm snarled across the surface of the battlefield. Men died, and most of them were members of the Royal Household attempting to engage the Solfygg champions.

Six of the latter still stood. The Colimore line had wavered, but now the Solfygg warriors resumed their advance.

Hansen was under no illusions about the situation. He had dropped two of the Solfygg champions, but the only thing wrong with their armor was that it hadn't been worn by a killer as experienced as Nils Hansen. Hansen couldn't deal with six more of the bastards alone, and—

Death rippled in blue fire. Three professionals had run to Maharg's side. All were dead now. The legs of one man were intermixed with those of another; the torsos lay at a meter's distance.

—there weren't going to be many surviving friendlies to help him.

A Colimore warrior got in Hansen's way, not trying to stop him but caught in the flow of battle. Hansen swiped the enemy aside in two pieces, slowing his rush only for the moment his battlesuit reduced current to the servos.

It was suicide to go up against royal-quality armor while wearing a lesser suit.

"Maharg, I'm—" Hansen shouted.

The marshal, ten meters away, held a Solfygg champion at bay with either gauntlet. He stepped back, a grudging retreat that changed into a thrust as one Solfygg warrior slipped on a corpse's armored hand and Maharg shifted full power to his other weapon.

"—coming!"

The Solfygg battlesuit failed in a blaze of light. Maharg's remaining opponent turned his stumble into a lunge toward the small of the marshal's back. Maharg's suit exploded.

Hansen hacked from behind, severing the Solfygg champion's right leg. The warrior sprawled forward onto Maharg.

The ruined battlesuits of the marshal and the man who had killed him spluttered on soil which their struggle had burned to glass.

"C'mon," Hansen wheezed. "Come—"

He took a step and stumbled because his foot did not, *would not,* lift high enough to clear the body of a man Hansen didn't recognize.

"Oh god," he whispered on his knees. "We've gotta go on. We gotta finish. . . . "

The Colimore forces were in full retreat. Many of the levies Hansen led had scattered in pursuit of the Colimore right wing, and the Royal Household had been butchered in its attempt to stop the Solfygg champions.

The warriors who fled toward Colimore outnumbered the forces Hansen could bring against them. Three Solfygg champions survived to shepherd them home.

"We gotta finish them!" Hansen cried as he lurched upright and ran toward the enemy: two strides, ten strides.

Two or three royal warriors followed him. None of the rest were able to.

Hansen toppled forward. He lay among the dead until Culbreth and a pair of freemen managed to turn his suit over so that they could open it.

It had begun to drizzle. The rain settled ash from the air and washed the tears from Hansen's upturned face.

≡ 32 ≡

BRAN'S FACE PEEKED around the edge of the outer door as they pushed it open. The massive hinges groaned so softly that the sound might have come from Platt, snoring as he sprawled on the floor.

Bran slipped through the opening. Brech grabbed his arm and tried to pull past. The twins struggled for a moment in whispered anger.

The attendant, dead to the world, continued to snore. Instead of ordinary wine, the boys had stolen a small cask of liquor made by freezing a portion of the water out of raw wine.

Platt had gulped down the whole contents, chortling to Sparrow in successful greed until drink stupefied him. He vomited in the night and now lay in his own spew, but his system had absorbed enough of the alcohol to keep him comatose till morning.

"Here, boys," called Sparrow softly as he spread his huge right hand.

This time the object that lifted from Sparrow's palm was material, a skein of silvery threads which wavered in slow undulations around a common center. The skein rose slowly as it moved toward the boys. When it neared the barrier, it hesitated as if it were repelled by the iron bars.

"Oh!" cried the twins together, forgetting the need for secrecy in their delight.

Their short capes, scarlet satin with fur linings, flared out

like wings as they ran to the barrier. Brech trod on Platt's
outflung hand, but the attendant was too drunk to twitch.

Sparrow's dog trembled like a motor straining against the
brake. The dog's teeth were bared, but no sound came out
of the jaws glistening with nervous drool.

"Here, lads, I'll help you," said the smith as he hitched
himself closer to the bars and raised his hand toward the
skein. The threads seemed to have a light of their own in
addition to that of the tallow lamp guttering in the niche by
the outside door.

Individual strands bowed farther out from the center. The
skein lifted another twenty centimeters, but it would not
approach the iron.

"Give me!" Bran cried as he pressed himself against the
barrier. He flailed his right hand toward the object.

"Me!" shrieked his brother, waving also, his face red with
effort and frustration.

Platt snored.

Sparrow reached out with both hands. The motion was as
swift and perfectly gauged as that of a bear swiping trout
from a stream. His fingers closed on the throats of both twins
simultaneously.

The boys did not scream. Nothing, not even a burble of
surprise, could pass the grip of fingers that could break lime-
stone into powder.

Sparrow leaned forward so that the twins' thrashing feet
did not ring against the bars. Death had been assured from
the first instant in which he crushed the cartilage of the boys'
windpipes, but he continued to squeeze with his full force.

If he let them go, they would wheeze and kick in a commotion that might arouse even Platt—

But the real reason Sparrow did not release his victims was
that this act was the first he had done by his own choice since
Hermann trapped him.

The boys' faces turned purple, then black. Their tongues
protruded. The smith continued to squeeze. Increased pressure made drops of blood seep from the victims' ears.

When Brech's right eye started from its socket and hung
by the optic nerve, Sparrow opened his hands. The bodies

slumped to the angle of the floor and the barrier. The bars rang softly.

Sparrow took a deep, shuddering breath. He did not realize he was crying until a hot droplet splashed on the back of his wrist. He didn't know why his body—not his mind; certainly not his mind—was acting that way.

It didn't matter. . . .

The dog crept over to Sparrow and thrust its head onto his lap, whining softly. After a time, the smith began to stroke the animal's ear between his thumb and forefinger. His breathing returned to normal.

The silvery toy continued to spin in the air, just as it had when it decoyed the twins into reach. Sparrow pointed his forefinger at his creation.

The filaments drew in. The skein drifted purposefully, between the bars and across the outer room until it hovered low over the sleeping attendant.

The smith snapped his thumb and middle finger. The sound was like that of a treelimb cracking. Platt stirred but did not rise.

Threads extended from the skein. One of them hooked the guard of Platt's knife and tightened as a snake does when it seizes prey. The remainder of the toy spun at an increased rate until it drew back toward the barrier, dragging the knife along.

The blade dangled from the filament holding it, skittering just above the floor. Occasionally the point touched stone with a faint *tsk!*

Sparrow spread the twins' clothing on the floor and set the bodies on the garments. Their skin was smooth and white, except for the lividly swollen faces. Both the boys had fouled themselves as they died, but the smell was indistinguishable for the thick reek of Sparrow's cell and Platt.

The smith took the knife from the waiting toy and began to butcher the small bodies so that they would fit between the bars enclosing him. The job required very few cuts. The blood had not had time to extravasate, but the wadded clothing absorbed most of it.

Sparrow had already arranged hollow ovals of scrap and

ores like a pair of shallow graves. As he cut away each portion of a body, he set it within a hollow.

The heads were a problem: they would neither pass entire nor could Sparrow section the skulls with a knife. But the skulls would crush between the palms of his two huge hands. . . .

When he completed the task, Sparrow sat back. He was crying again.

He wiped the knife and set it down, then used the least saturated of the boys' clothing to wipe down the bars. He laid the wet cloth on top of the bodies, then covered the fabric in turn with more chunks of metal and rock. The skein, its tasks complete, slid between the interstices of one of the mounds and disappeared.

The smith's last act of concealment was to upset his slops bucket over the scene of the murder and butchery. Platt would probably require the prisoner to clean up the mess with his bedding, but Sparrow's furs were already filthy anyway.

Sparrow lay on the floor between the two oval mounds. The corpses took up surprisingly little space when sectioned and piled part upon part.

The attendant continued to snore. Sparrow used the rhythm of Platt's rasping breaths to jog himself into a trance in which the Matrix opened its infinite series of pathways and patterns.

The dog was asleep also. Its belly was full, for perhaps the first time in the animal's life.

The mounds shifted and clicked as the structure of what was within them changed. Fluid soaked its way across the floor—demineralized water, a waste product beneath the notice of the most suspicious of observers.

The master smith was creating something again; but not a battlesuit this time. . . .

≡ 33 ≡

"THIS TIME . . . ," RITTER said to himself in confidence and wonder. He stood up slowly from his chair as he stared at the two dragonflies rotating like mirror images in an all-angles view. "*This* time I think I've got you where you'll work, you cunning little devil."

"So she's ready for a test—" said a voice from behind him where nobody was. The engineer turned and groped for the pistol slung over his chair back.

The fingertips of Hansen's left hand rested on Ritter's holster flap. "—ride, is she, Master Ritter?" the slim, cold-eyed man concluded.

"I don't like that," Ritter said flatly. "I wish you wouldn't do that."

"I'm sorry," Hansen said. "I—"

He didn't look away from Ritter, but his eyes were no longer staring into the same universe. He was wearing a suit of velvet dyed a muddy blue, breeches and a jerkin cinched with a broad leather belt. The garments were obviously handmade, and they seemed to have been cut for a bigger man.

"There's been some things going on," Hansen went on with no more emotion than a voice synthesizer could supply. "Nothing to do with you, friend. Not even going that bad—"

Hansen shuddered. His face changed and he attempted a smile. "For the survivors, at least, and that's about all you can ever say, isn't it?"

"Your work is going all right, then?" Ritter said. Given his own focus, that was the most positive thing he could suggest to the other man without seeming to pry.

"That *is* my work, Ritter," Hansen said. His smile was wistful for a moment. "And yeah, like I said, it's going pretty well."

That wasn't what Ritter's visitor had said before.

"But the main thing," Hansen continued, "is how your project's going. Think you've got a handle on it?"

"Why don't you ride what I've built?" the engineer suggested proudly. "Then you can tell me."

He touched a control on his console. The pair of dimensional vehicles stopped turning on their invisible pedestals.

Ritter continued to manipulate his joystick. An invisible overhead beam slid one of the dragonflies out of the examination area. When the engineer thumbed the control downward, the crane deposited the dragonfly on the floor of the laboratory between the two men.

Hansen ran his hand slowly over the dimensional vehicle. The saddle was smooth, but it had a slight tackiness to the touch. He rubbed his fingertips together and found no residue on them.

Ritter smiled with quiet pride. "There's a suction system that works through tiny pores to help the rider keep his seat," he explained. "I'll bet you couldn't tell mine from the original."

"*Her* seat mostly, friend," Hansen said as he checked the control panel. "But I take your meaning."

He looked at Ritter. "I'm really impressed. You built it all here?"

He gestured around the huge workroom.

"Some of the smaller, one-off pieces," the engineer said with a shrug. "Most of it, though, I just piped the specs down to fabrication—"

He touched a switch. A wall became a full-scale window onto Keep Greville's manufacturing level.

Thousands of technicians and laborers worked in the interconnected bays. Occasional splotches of bright clothing marked Ritter's under-engineers, performing set-up or overseeing particularly complex operations.

"—as normal," Ritter concluded. "Does it matter?"

Hansen laughed. "I was worried somebody might find out what you were doing," he said. "For your sake, I mean. But I've always been told the best place to hide a needle is with a million other needles, not a haystack. Forgive me for trying to tell you your business."

Ritter shut off the wall image. "You didn't," he said. "And anyway, I'd have done what I pleased anyhow."

His smile was half humor, half challenge.

Hansen raised an eyebrow. "Like I say," he said. "It's your business, Master Ritter."

The slim man swung aboard the dragonfly.

At rest, he didn't look dangerous. It was only when Hansen moved that Ritter remembered the way the pistol was in the other man's hand and firing before the engineer knew an enemy had arrived.

"Are you going like that?" Ritter asked. His voice caught on the first syllable. He cleared his dry throat to finish the question.

Hansen plucked his jerkin between thumb and forefinger and peered at the material critically.

"Oh, this would fit in where I'm going," he said. He patted the saddlehorn. "The dragonfly would raise some eyebrows, but I'll hover just out of synchronous the way the Searchers themselves do over a battlefield. Anyway, it's just a quick test run."

"It . . . ," Ritter said.

He licked his lips. "Look," the engineer went on, "I'm good, but this is a complex sonuvabitch. I don't want you stuck in the middle of those lizardmen with no way to defend yourself."

He gave Hansen the holstered pistol which hung from his chair. "Take this at least. I'll find you a forcefield projector to go with it."

Hansen's mouth opened to protest.

Look, if I thought I needed hardware, I've got my own that'd make this look like a pop-gun.

Then he remembered Maharg standing within arm's length,

and Hansen unable to save his life. Hansen *failing* to do what was necessary to save Maharg's life.

"Thanks," Hansen said. "Not the forcefield, though. An untuned unit might interfere with the dragonfly's own projector."

The belt was sized for Ritter's waist. Hansen hung it over his left shoulder like a bandolier. He adjusted the containers of spare magazines so that they did not chafe bone.

He gave Ritter a thumbs-up. "See you soon," he said.

"Good luck," said the engineer. He smiled tautly.

"I don't need luck, Master Ritter," Hansen said. "I've got you."

He stroked the dragonfly out of the present continuum, using the manual controls rather than voice operation.

To a Searcher, the Matrix was merely a blur of light. The dimensional vehicle shielded its user from the medium instead of merging her with it the way Hansen or even a smith on the Open Lands could do.

Dragonflies did not convey information about the Matrix, any more than a hovercar permitted its rider to levitate unaided—but that was beside the point. All a Searcher needed to know was that her vehicle would take her where North or her own whim decided she should be.

And that was all Hansen needed now as well.

The dragonfly shifted out of the veils of light. That was expected, a momentary pause on the next plane of the Matrix—

But this was Plane Four, which was Hell in truth as well as in appearance; and the dragonfly did not pause on the cold, milky ice sheath—

It stopped dead.

Hansen moved the thumb switch to its neutral setting, then rolled it forward again in case Ritter had simply failed to copy the original vehicle's repetitive-input setting. Nothing happened.

Nothing happened inside the dimensional vehicle's bubble of force. The ice was warted with milky stalagmites the height of men. They stretched to the blank horizon in all directions.

The stalagmites were turning toward Hansen with glacial slowness.

"Control," said Hansen calmly, activating voice operation. "Shift to Plane Three."

The dragonfly was alive with the normal complement of electronic quivers; it had not depowered. The force bubble was at full strength. The nearest stalagmites began to press against the invisible barrier, deforming as exterior sections of a perfect sphere.

"Control," Hansen said, "Plane Two!"

The holstered pistol was in his way as he groped for the saddle-edge controls again. He swore and slung it behind him, then toggled the switch forward against its stop.

Nothing was bloody happening with the dragonfly. The sunless horizon humped up slowly and began to sag with cavities which hinted at the eyesockets of a skull.

Hansen swore by the god of his childhood. He gripped the vehicle's unified in-plane control, a wheel that moved in three dimensions as well as rotating on its axis.

He lifted the unified control on its column. He'd hover ten meters in the air—or a thousand meters up if the tumor growing on the horizon was what Hansen thought it was. Some safe altitude, so that he'd have time to figure out what the hell was going on with the bloody—

The dragonfly didn't lift.

Hansen spun the control column forward and gave it a vicious twist. The vehicle had plenty of power to smash through the wall of stalagmites—

But it didn't move, wouldn't move, and the milky peaks of the stalagmites were forming human features.

"Control!" Hansen shouted. "Plane One!"

He bumped the pistol butt again as he groped for the manual control because the dragonfly had done *nothing* this time either. The weapon was in his hand before he thought—

Nils Hansen never had to think about a weapon.

—but he didn't shoot because he knew the faces growing on ice colder than Death were the visages of dead men.

Men he had killed. Women—but only a few women, not

many at all compared to the male faces, stretching to the horizon in every direction.

The skull at the edge of vision turned and cloaked itself in a milky semblance of flesh. Hansen stared at his own face.

He screamed then and—

His hand reholstered the pistol without conscious command.

—rocked the toggle switch back, to return the dragonfly to Plane Five.

If that control worked, while all the others had failed. It was Hansen's last resort.

The Matrix was magenta light as warm as love. Hansen caught the saddle with both hands as the dimensional vehicle purred and slipped from nowhere to rest on the floor of Ritter's workroom.

The dragonfly bobbed as its legs telescoped, accepting the pull of gravity that it had escaped in the Matrix.

"Oh my god," Hansen said. He was gasping.

He closed his eyes. "Oh my god."

"What is it?" the engineer demanded. "Come on, man! Are you all right? Tell me!"

"I'm all right," Hansen said in a voice that shuddered into normalcy. "Just keep the fuck away for a minute."

He opened his eyes and swung off the dragonfly. The vehicle's force bubble collapsed automatically as its rider's weight left the saddle. Condensate formed on all exposed surfaces.

The engineer's face was plastic; his need for information shimmered under a crust of rigid control. "Okay," Hansen said, "we've got a problem. Two problems. The unit switches to the next plane down, but it won't go farther."

He shuddered despite himself. "It does come back. That's a big one. It came back just fine."

"The other problem?" said Ritter.

"The in-plane controls, the physical movement ones," Hansen said. "They don't work either. Zip. Nada."

He could have abandoned the dimensional vehicle in Hell and entered the Matrix himself.

He thought he could have.

He had been safe all the time. He thought.

Hansen shuddered again. He unslung the gunbelt and handed it to Ritter.

"Right," said the engineer emotionlessly. "Well, there's full telemetry on the unit. I'll get to work on it right away."

"There's always glitches," Hansen said to his trembling hands.

"Sure," said Ritter. "We'll take care of it."

Then he turned and slammed his fist into the console, hard enough to crack the dense plastic top.

≡ 34 ≡

PRINCESS MIRIAM LOOKED bored and angry; Queen Stella looked cold and angry; King Hermann's expression was hidden by the battlesuit he wore—but Hermann was so nearly blind with fear that a stumble slammed him into the doorjamb as he entered the citadel.

"Majesty, milady," Platt said, bowing to rise and bow again, as quick and graceless as a bird drinking. "Milady princess—"

Stella trod on his foot without noticing the contact. The attendant jumped out of the way with a stifled yelp. King Hermann, equally oblivious, swept through the vacated space like Juggernaut's carriage.

"Sparrow!" boomed the king's amplified voice.

"Where is he?" demanded the queen, though she was looking at the cell rather than Sparrow's attendant. "Where's the prisoner?"

"Why are you dragging me to *this* filthy place?" the princess said in a tone as hot and clear as live steam.

"Your Majesties!" Sparrow cried in apparent amazement. It was just after noon. Light through the door the king had flung open was dazzling to eyes adapted for the citadel's normal gloom. "What's the matter?"

An under-cellarer, one of the freemen now accompanying the royal family, pointed toward the smith.

"When I came here searching for the boys this morning,"

the servant said/accused, "he told me he had to see all three of you right away!"

"Where are Bran and Brech?" Stella asked in a glassy, echoing tone. She would have stepped to the barrier, but her husband's armored body blocked her away from the danger.

"Where are my sons?" Hermann shouted.

"*I* don't see why *I* have to be here!" Miriam said shrilly.

"Your Majesties?" the prisoner said. He clung to the bars to hold his torso upright, blinking and apparently bewildered. "Has something happened to the boys? I only asked you to come because I've made wonderful presents for all of you."

"But I thought—" the queen said. The quivering distress of a moment before gave way to her more usual look of cruel anger as she stared at the under-cellarer.

"But he said—" the servant blurted before terror dried his voice in his throat. Other freemen in the entourage, most of them carrying bows or edged weapons, backed away from their fellow.

"I know nothing of this!" Platt cried from as far out of the way as he could cringe. "I didn't speak! I didn't see the boys!"

Platt had awakened this noon to sunlight, a pounding head, and the toe of the cellarer's boot kicking him. The freeman was demanding something about the boys—*might they freeze in Hell, wherever they were*—which Platt was too nauseously hung over to understand. Sparrow had called something to the questioner, but Platt hadn't caught that either.

"I didn't really notice what your servant said when he came here," apologized Sparrow, no longer the focus of his visitors' eyes. "I've spent the entire night in the Matrix, creating your presents. But of *course* I know nothing of your sons, King Hermann. Perhaps it's a prank of theirs."

"I said, 'Are the princes here?' and *he* said I must bring you at once!" the under-cellarer bleated.

He looked from the king to his wife. There was no more mercy in Stella's expression than there was on the steel face-plate of Hermann's battlesuit.

The queen drew a gold-toothed comb from her hair and raked it toward the freeman's face. He lurched sideways. The king's armored fist crushed his skull.

In the sudden silence, Princess Miriam said, "What's this present you made for me, prisoner?"

Before Sparrow could reply, the princess clutched the mirror against her heart and added, "But I'm not giving this up! It's mine!"

Platt's head rang with each beat of his pulse, but the death had set his mind to working again. He had seen Bran and Brech . . . *when?* A day ago, the previous noon; but they'd been their normal selves, vicious and cruel, when they left.

And they had hidden the liquor as Sparrow said they would, so above all things Platt must know *nothing* of what the boys did or thought or went. . . .

"Of course you won't, princess," Sparrow said.

He turned, rotating awkwardly on his buttocks. His legs swept aside the remains of the materials he had worked into his latest creations, merely powder and grit.

"This is for you," the smith continued, holding a glittering something to a gap between bars, "because so fine a lady as you deserves to have it."

Miriam stepped forward.

"No!" her mother said with a voice like a whiplash.

Hermann raised his hand. An arc licked from the gauntlet, out and back and out again in snarling threat.

Platt threw his forearms across his face so that he would not see Death come if it were coming for him.

"I ask your pardon, Majesties," said the smith calmly.

Sparrow raised his hands—one empty and the other holding a pattern of lights and motion between thumb and forefinger. He set the object on the floor between the bars and slid himself backward, away from the barrier.

The dog, brighter-eyed than usual, dragged itself to Sparrow and licked his great, calloused hand.

King Hermann switched off his arc weapon. He bent forward and picked up the thing the smith had made.

The object was a doubled loop of golden light. The circles tilted at a slight angle to one another along a hidden axis.

They pulsed with increased brightness in a pattern like that
of the surf, never quiet but never the same.

The loops encircled Hermann's armored forearm without
touching the metal at any point.

"It's a necklace for the princess," Sparrow explained softly.

"It's mine!" Miriam cried and snatched at the object before
either of her parents could stop her.

The necklace came away in her hand as if it were a material
thing, but the golden light had slipped *through* the battlesuit.

Hermann flexed his gauntlet. He had felt nothing. He tested
his arc. It snarled out with full lethal intensity.

Miriam raised the necklace over her head. Stella caught
the girl's arm, but the necklace dropped past and through
the queen's flesh as easily as it had King Hermann's armored
forearm.

The joined lights pulsed their perfect circles around Miriam's neck. They woke rich color from her complexion and
the sable trim of the dress she wore.

"Oh!" the princess cried, delighted even before she saw the
result. She lifted the mirror on its chain and used the polished
bronze surface to view herself with still greater enthusiasm.

"And for you also, King Hermann," the smith said with
a courtier's diffidence, "and your lady wife. Just call for it,
Your Majesty. Call, 'Come, chair.' "

"What?" said the king.

" 'Come, chair' " Sparrow repeated. "No more than that."

"Wha . . . ?" King Hermann began. After a pause, his
voice grunted from the battlesuit, "All right: come, chair."

Dust stirred within Sparrow's cell. Stella screamed.

A network of silvery filaments rose through the filth and
litter beyond the barrier. The wires were so fine that they
looked for a moment like the sheen of oil on water. They
spread into an interlocking pattern of lines describing a three-
dimensional object, a chair with back and legs and curving
arms. The creation slid toward the bars.

Hermann's arc blazed out in readiness.

Sparrow seized the object with one powerful hand. "Only
a chair for your comfort, Your Majesty," he said. The chair

tried to move away from him, but the smith's arm was too strong.

"Only a chair, Your Majesty," Sparrow repeated.

He levered his body onto the seat. The sketchy cushions sank and shifted, molding themselves to the heavy body they now supported. The chair resumed its motion toward the barrier and stopped only when it touched the bars.

The smith raised himself again and swung onto the floor. "A gift I think you will treasure," he said.

As he spoke, the chair's wire fabric tightened. The shimmering construct squeezed between the bars and halted expectantly behind King Hermann.

The king turned to look at the chair. It scuttled on hollow, castored feet to stay in back of him.

"Don't . . . ," the queen said. Her eyes were on the chair also, and her voice trailed off without completing the warning.

"Hell take you, woman!" Hermann grunted. "I'm in my armor."

Hermann lowered himself cautiously. The chair remained motionless until the battlesuit touched it. Then it deformed into a perfect match for the armored curves, accepting the weight and holding it as easily as light lies on the surface of a pond.

King Hermann leaned back.

"It would carry you if you wanted it to," the smith said in an obsequious tone. "It was a pleasure to create it for you, Your Majesty. One of the greatest pleasures of my life."

The king jumped up in a sudden fit of terror. The chair helped him rise, lifting his torso and buttocks until he was planted firmly on his feet again.

"And another for you, my lady queen," Sparrow continued. "As fine as the first."

Stella licked her lips. "Come, chair," she said in what was little more than a whisper.

The ores and waste material shifted as a second chair surfaced and slid toward the barrier. The filaments were so fine that when the chairs were at rest, they quivered like pools of liquid rather than solid objects.

"You'll never sit in anything else so comfortable," the smith said. His voice was soft, and it trembled with unholy joy.

"I only ask, Your Majesties," he continued as those outside the iron barrier stared at the wonders that had taken their minds off the missing children, "that you think of the service I have done you every time you use these marvels."

A terrible blue light moved in Sparrow's eyes as he spoke.

≡ 35 ≡

THE TRUNKS OF mammoths moved ceaselessly to squeeze rain from the fur where their bodies were not covered by cargo nets. The slight sounds the huge animals made as they padded through the main gate of Frekka were lost in the human cries within the walls.

Hansen's pony whickered in irritation as it waited, unable to find even a twig to crop so close to the gate. Hansen stroked its neck absently. Life wasn't perfect, even for a horse.

But maybe it was better for a horse.

"Ah," said Culbreth, who had halted a cautious three meters away from his leader. "Ah, I think that's the lot of them, sir."

Rain had turned the sky black, though it was still an hour short of sundown. A lantern hung from a pole above the pack saddle of each mammoth, above and behind the driver. The red glow which marked the last animal in line swung into view.

"I'm not keeping you, Culbreth," Hansen snapped.

Culbreth did not reply.

Arnor began to hum a song that Hansen had taught him around the campfire two nights before the battle, when it was safe to be drunk and not so safe to think soberly about the future. Taught Arnor and Culbreth; and Maharg was there too, joining in the choruses. . . .

"Sorry, Culbreth," Hansen said. "I'm on edge. I thought maybe I'd let the crowd thin."

Maybe some of the tearful, accusing faces would have gone back to their empty rooms by the time Hansen rode through the city gate.

"Yet I've always sort of missed her," Hansen murmured under his breath as Arnor hummed, *"Since that last wild night I kissed her. . . ."*

On the way to battle, the mammoths carried the army's provisions and the battlesuits to be worn by the royal army. Now, on the road back, the cargo nets slung from the pack saddles were swollen with loads of booty besides: armor stripped from the enemy dead, often in separate pieces.

Virtually any damaged suit could be repaired more easily than complete new armor could be constructed. The result would be a battlesuit whose quality was lower than the virgin unit before high-amplitude currents surged through its circuitry; but it would do for somebody to wear.

There had been battles where the margin of victory was one warrior more or less in the line.

"Left her heart and lost my own," Hansen whispered as cold trickles of rain ran down his spine. *"'Adiós, mi corazón. . . .'"*

The red lantern swung under the archway at the mammoth's smooth, ground-devouring stride.

Much of the armor that had gone out of Frekka whole was returning gouged with molten fury, and freemen led strings of ponies whose riders had gone to North or Hell in a great pyre after the battle. The dead men's families waited inside the gate, hoping against hope. . . .

"You weren't responsible, sir. You weren't in charge."

"I was there, Arnor," Hansen said. "Don't tell me I wasn't responsible."

Fathers with stiff faces and dry eyes. Sons trying to copy the old men, succeeding well enough but not understanding why it had had to happen to *their* father.

Hansen knew why it had happened. It had happened because Nils Hansen hadn't been good enough to stop it from happening.

Culbreth laid his fingers on the back of Hansen's hand.

Hansen jumped. He hadn't heard Culbreth cluck his pony

closer. He hadn't realized how hard he was gripping the saddlehorn until the other warrior touched him, either.

"Yeah," said Hansen. "Let's go."

He nudged the pony with his heels. "Somebody's got to explain to King Prandia why the Searchers took so many of his men," he muttered, "and it may as well be me."

≡ 36 ≡

THE WALLS OF Ritter's workroom displayed a dozen views of the original dragonfly in action, ridden by the Searcher in her black battlesuit. It swooped, hovered—then faded through planes. Each scene was a computer simulation created from data in the vehicle's flight recorder.

On the examination stand in the center of the room rested Ritter's copy, which had done none of those things when Hansen rode it into danger.

Penny appeared on the other side of the examination stand. She was a leggy blond whose breasts, secured by a transparent bandeau, looked too large for her rib cage.

Ritter touched a key. Vertical sections through the original dragonfly and the copy appeared beside one another in front of the engineer, then merged. Colors highlighted the incongruities between the pairs; a sidebar tabulated those differences.

None of the colored masks was farther up the spectrum than bright red. At the sensitivity setting which Ritter had chosen, chips from the same production batch might vary into the green level, and a ten-thousandth's variation in wall diameter would make the image of tubing glow yellow.

Penny's jewel flashed. She became a brunette with broad hips and a small bosom, then a black-haired woman as squat as Ritter himself.

The paired sections slid through the dimensional vehicles from the front backward. The mask stayed within the red level. The engineer balled his fist silently.

Penny walked around the viewing stand. "What are you doing, then?" she asked.

"There's a control problem," Ritter said, still watching the holograms. "The software was copied directly, so that leaves the equipment itself, probably somewhere in the control circuits. But I'm *damned* if I know where."

"What, ah . . . ," Penny said. She leaned against the engineer. Her nipple became erect when it brushed his triceps. "What sort of shape do you particularly like me in, darling?"

"Huh?" said Ritter. He glanced over at her. He put the display on pause reflexively for the moment he looked away from it. "Tall and thin's unusual, I suppose, but I've told you—I don't really care."

The images began to scroll forward again. "And look, Penny," he added. "Time may not mean anything to you, but it does to me. I really don't have time for recreation just now."

The woman's head jerked back as though Ritter had slapped her.

The engineer continued with his painstaking search. He had performed the operation several times already, slicing the vehicles at a different viewing plane for each attempt.

"It'll descend only one level of the Matrix from wherever you start it," the engineer said. "We've tried it from several planes, and it's the same each one. It'll go from here to Four, or Eight to Seven if Hansen lifts it up to his house to begin with. But not down to Six from Eight."

Penny brightened when Ritter first began to speak, but she soon realized that he was using her as a living wall from which to echo his own thoughts. One of the engineer's concubines would have done as well; or a skivvy.

"Now that wouldn't thrill me," Ritter continued. "It means there's something wrong in my set-up . . . but by this time I could live with that, because we can work around it. Hansen can take the vehicle to Plane Two and drop into the Open Lands from there. But the other thing is, the bird won't move *within* the dimension, and that means it's no good at all."

Penny shivered at mention of Plane Two. She was now a tall red-head, almost skeletally thin. She crossed her arms

over small breasts with jewels depending from the nipples.
"The Lomeri are too dangerous to interfere with," she said.
"Hansen could have killed you when he took you there
before."

Multiple images of the Searcher on her dragonfly raced
over a battlefield on the walls of the laboratory, framed by
conduits and fittings within the room. Below the Searcher,
battlesuits shorted incandescently. Delicate antennae on the
underside of the vehicle's saddle received and copied men's
minds at the moment of their dissolution.

Ritter scowled at Penny in irritation. He resumed running
the paired sections.

"We were there longer than we'd expected, that was all,"
he said. "The fellow who stashed the dragonflies there had
set them a millisecond out of phase with the surroun—"

His body grew rigid. His mouth was suddenly dry.

"Ritter?" Penny asked. "Ritter? Are you—"

"Oh my *god*!" the engineer said.

He turned, seized Penny beneath the elbows, and lifted her
tall form another half meter in the air without showing any
strain. "That's it! Hansen fetched the unit back by using the
override switch, but the software still thinks it's out of synchronous. It won't *let* any of the in-plane controls operate!"

Penny twisted her legs around the big man's waist and
drew her groin tightly against his diaphragm. "You've fixed
it, then?" she asked, reflecting his delight like the full
moon.

"Well, next best," explained the engineer with a slight
frown.

He set the woman down and returned to his keyboard. She
barely got her feet beneath her in time to avoid dropping onto
the smooth floor.

"There's no way to reprogram the software," Ritter continued, muttering in the direction of his console. "Not from
what I have. But the override switch will work, I'm *sure*, so
long as it's detached from the chassis and operated back on
Plane Four!"

"Now that you've done that . . . ," Penny said. She knelt
to fumble with the engineer's fly.

"Not now, for god's sake!" Ritter snapped. "I need to check this while it's still clear in my mind."

He shifted his groin. When the woman's hands tried to follow, he slapped them away.

Penny sat on the floor beside the console. She drew her knees up to her chin. Her body flickered through a series of forms before settling on a statuesque blond with an hourglass waist and high, firm breasts.

Holographic images, both schematics and solids, shifted in quick succession on Ritter's holographic display. Possible redesigns vanished into limbo or were lifted higher in the air for comparison with other ideas.

The engineer whistled between his teeth as he worked.

Silent tears ran down the cheeks of the woman at his feet.

≡ 37 ≡

"I WOULD HAVE come out to greet you at the gate, Lord Hansen," the king said in concern at the silent anger on Hansen's visage. "But I'd summoned another advisor when I received the first reports of the battle, and he just arrived. No disrespect was meant."

Hansen blinked. "Excuse me?" he said.

Why was the king apologizing?

Formal functions were held in the House of Audience. The houses of two of the Syndics who ruled Frekka in past times had been knocked together to form a royal residence across the square from it.

The entrance hall into which Prandia strode with a bustle of nervous menials was decorated for comfort rather than show. Clerks with parchment scrolls and tablets of wood peered from side corridors, whispering among themselves.

"Ah, I'm sorry about the delay, sir," Hansen resumed. "I . . . wanted to be sure all the baggage train got in. It—"

He shrugged to loosen the words which tension held back. "We'll need the armor, even the suits that really got chopped up. We'll—that is, you'll want to get all the smiths in the kingdom working on repairs immediately. You'll need to gather warriors—and raise new ones or, or . . . "

Hansen's face twisted. "Or else the next defeat will be a lot worse than this one."

Two professionals in battlesuits guarded the door to the

residence. Half the Royal Household had remained in Frekka when Maharg marched, a necessary reserve.

Between the surviving portion of the Royal Household and the much larger number of warriors available in an emergency from the kingdom's individual landholders, King Prandia had the makings of a very impressive army.

"You weren't defeated," said Prandia. "You won. The army won because of you, Lord Hansen."

Hansen's mind went white. "Balls," he said.

"Sir!" Culbreth hissed desperately as he gripped his leader's shoulder.

"Duke Ontell holds Colimore," Hansen continued harshly. "Our campaign objective was to remove him. We failed."

"But Lord Hansen—" the king said with a look of pained uncertainty.

"Look," Hansen said. "I don't mind giving things their right names! It makes it easier to change them."

"Lord Hansen?" said Arnor. "We killed Ontell. Me and Culbreth."

"And Tapper from the Household," Culbreth put in. "Ontell had silver armor."

"Why—" Hansen shouted in amazement. "—*didn't you tell me?*" died in his throat.

Because you didn't bloody ask, his mind sneered. *Because you were too deep in doom and guilt to behave like a commander and learn the facts.*

Hansen started to laugh. Prandia's jaw dropped. Culbreth thought his leader was going into hysterics and grabbed Hansen in a bear hug.

"No, no, it's all right," Hansen said. "I'm fine, Culbreth, I'm not going to go berserk."

Culbreth stepped back uncertainly.

"Your Excellency?" Hansen said to the king. "Could I trouble you for the loan of something dry to wear? My clothes're somewhere back at my billet. I'd like to discuss your future operations now—but without catching pneumonia."

Prandia snapped his fingers.

"See to it," he ordered. He didn't bother to look around at his train of servants, several of whom were already scrambling to obey. "For all three of the lords. Do forgive me, Lord Hansen. I'm not myself with, with the press of events."

Arnor reached behind Hansen to nudge Culbreth. "We don't need to stick around," he murmured.

"And I did indeed hope that you would join me and my new marshal immediately," King Prandia continued. "It was an emergency appointment, of course . . . but I think the right one. He just arrived."

Hansen reached out and hugged Arnor and Culbreth. "Thanks, troops," he said quietly. "There's worse things than a battlefield, sometimes."

He released his team and met the king's eyes. "Yes sir," he said. "I think that's just what we need to do. There isn't a lot of time."

Servants sprang away like startled quail as the king turned with Hansen beside him. Prandia strode into a large chamber behind the hall. He held a whispered conversation with a gorgeously-dressed usher.

A servant carrying a set of clothes pranced up to Hansen, who tossed his sodden cloak toward the floor to get rid of it. Another servant snatched it out of the air and disappeared down a side corridor.

Hansen began to change. He took clothing from the servant's pile every time he stripped off one of his present garments.

"We'll go to him, if that's acceptable with you, Lord Hansen," the king said. "He's very tired from his journey to Frekka."

"What?" Hansen said. "Hell, of course."

The servant held out soft slippers with pointed toes, velvet rather than fur. Hansen accepted them with a smile and patted her hand. She was only about eighteen, pretty in a frightened sort of way.

Hansen padded behind the king barefoot rather than spend the time to pull the slippers on.

The usher threw open the door to a luxuriously appointed chamber. There was a separate hearth; a curtained bed in place of the bed closet normal in communities less sophisticated than Frekka; and a high-backed armchair in which huddled a shrunken, aged figure swathed in quilts.

"Foster father," the king said, "Lord Hansen has arrived. Lord Hansen, this is Malcolm, Duke of Thrasey and marshal of my armies in place of his son."

Hansen froze.

"Ex-duke," said the man in the chair. "Glad of that, too."

His voice was cracked, but his brown eyes were as bright as they had been two generations before, when Hansen first met the man.

"And as for marshal, we'll talk about—"

"You agreed, foster father!"

Malcolm looked straight at the king. "Another outburst, Your Royal Majesty," the old man said, "and I'll tell you to leave the room while the grown men speak."

Prandia opened his mouth, then turned his head with an expression of frustration and chagrin. After a moment, the king began to smile.

Malcolm grinned also. "Hansen . . . ," he said, rolling the name across his tongue. "I knew a man of your name once, Hansen. He was older than you."

The room was illuminated by the hearth and a flaring rushlight, a lighted reed whose pith was soaked in tallow. It made Hansen nervous to watch the rushlight's tongue of pale, tremulous flame; but these walls were stone rather than wattle, and the plastered ceiling was high enough to be out of danger.

Hansen and the king stood in front of the door. Servants huddled in the hall, unable to enter the room with their superiors in the way.

Two of the servants carried extra chairs. Hansen glanced over his shoulder at them, then stepped close to Malcolm and sat cross-legged at the old man's feet.

Malcolm looked down at him. "*I* can't marshal the kingdom's troops," he said. "You know that, don't you, Hansen? I can't even walk."

"You can be carried, foster father," Prandia said.

The king waved away the servants with their chairs, but he squatted instead of sitting on the rush-strewn floor. "It's your counsel I need, not your legs."

"You, Hansen," Malcolm said as if he had not heard his king speak. "My son put you in charge of the left wing. Why did you leave your post?"

"Our side of the fight was under control," Hansen said. He met the bright brown eyes squarely. He avoided blinking, because blinking looked shifty, and you never wanted to look shifty when you reported to a superior.

God, how old was Malcolm now?

"The right wing was having problems," Hansen went on, "because of the, of the champions from Solfygg."

"Alone though?" Malcolm demanded. "You left your men and went haring off by yourself?"

"My men were levies," Hansen replied deliberately. "I knew what the weak points of the opposition's suits were. All my men could have done was die, a little faster even than the Household troops were doing already."

"Ah, foster father?" Prandia said. "Lord Hansen restored the—"

Hansen gestured at him with a spread left hand. He did not look away from Malcolm.

"—right wing," Prandia continued, ignoring an attempt to silence him in his own residence, "and won the battle for us. All reports agree on that."

"And at the end, then, Hansen?" the old man said in his cracked, piercing voice. "When you decided to charge the Colimore rear guard alone?"

Hansen licked his dry lips. "Yeah," he said. "I screwed up."

The king jumped to his feet. "Marshal Malcolm!" he said hotly. "All the men talk about that charge. Lord Hansen is a hero!"

"Do they talk about it—*son*?" Malcolm said. "The man *I* knew, *Lord* Hansen—he would have said that was a fool's act. The sort of trick a warrior pulls, not a trained soldier who wins battles for his liege."

"If—" the king said.

Hansen turned to the king. "If I'd managed to get myself killed," he said harshly, his voice full of the power that Malcolm's had lost with age, "we might have lost the field and all the armor there to salvage. And that would have been our ass."

He chuckled without humor. "Your asses, milords."

Malcolm cackled in delight. "Not mine either, Lord Hansen. I have nothing to lose."

He reached out with the care old bones require. Hansen opened his hand and clasped Malcolm's gently.

"I'm supposed to know things, Malcolm," Hansen whispered. "I should have seen it coming and warned him."

"My son wouldn't have lived forever," Malcolm said. "If the gods were good to him, he wouldn't have lived—" Hansen felt the wizened fingers tighten in senile fury "—as long as I have."

The rushlight beat like a slow pulse, stroke and stroke and stroke, while the two men gripped one another's hand.

"Maharg has a son, you know," Malcolm added. "Named after me, he was. Only ten years old now, but a fine lad . . . and the only immortality that *men* find, my friend."

"Have you two met before?" Prandia said uncertainly.

"In a matter of speaking, Your Excellency," Malcolm said.

He lifted his hand free and made a peremptory gesture at Hansen. "Get up, get up," he said. "I'm not a god that you should be sitting at my feet."

Malcolm turned to the king. "Make Lord Hansen your marshal, lad," he said. "Your grandfather had a warchief of that name. Perhaps it's an omen."

He cackled until a fit of coughing interrupted his laughter.

"Ah, foster father?" King Prandia said. He was careful not to let his eyes fall on Hansen as his lips formed the words of disapproval.

Malcolm shook his head sharply. "No," he said. "Your Excellency. Son. You said you wanted my counsel. Look at me."

Prandia met the old man's eyes. He nodded.

"Sometimes the gods give men one chance," Malcolm said softly. "The survivors are the ones who are smart enough to take it when it's offered."

The king sighed, then straightened his shoulders and turned to Hansen.

"Lord Hansen," he said formally. "I ask that you accept your duty to your liege and your kingdom by becoming Marshal of the Royal Army."

"If you've got any women around that you feel personally about, lad," Malcolm said to the king, "then you'd better keep them locked away tight." He laughed.

Hansen looked at the old man flat-eyed. "We still may not win," he said. "If they had twelve royal suits to send to Colimore, then they've got a lot more besides."

"Oh, I've got faith in you, Marshal," Malcolm said.

The flame of the rushlight was so pale that the texture of the stone was visible through it. It gave Malcolm's *café au lait* complexion a patina like that of old ivory.

"And it may be, Marshal," he went on, "that you're not really younger than the Hansen I knew in times past after all."

≡ 38 ≡

THE YOUNG WOMAN opened the door suddenly and spilled light past the barrier in the middle of the citadel. Glare turned the black iron into a grid of silvery reflection. The smith's dog whined.

Platt sneezed and jumped to his feet in surprise. "P-princess!" he blurted and sneezed again. "I—that is, is your father here?"

"Phew!" Miriam said, wrinkling her nose.

She waved dismissively to the attendant. "I don't want to talk to you. Go stand outside."

The princess carried a sable muff and wore a short sable cape over a coat of creamy silk brocade which covered her to the ankles. The ornament of light which Sparrow had made for her oscillated around her neck in golden radiance.

The mirror that Sparrow had given Krita was a bulge beneath Miriam's cape instead of being worn in plain view as was her wont.

"Lady princess," Platt said as he knelt with his head bowed. He peered up at Miriam from the corner of one bright, cunning eye. "Your father the king was most speci—"

"Shut up!" Miriam said. "I told you to go outside. I don't like the way you smell."

"But I mustn't—" the attendant whined.

He raised his head as the princess strode toward the barrier. A quick glance through the open door proved that she had come by herself. To her back Platt continued, "Anyway, you can't talk to the prisoner now, lady. He's in a trance. His mind's lost in the Matrix."

Miriam turned like the nut of a crossbow rotating to loose the string.

"Then we'll have to wake him up, won't we?" she snapped. One of her perfect hands slid out of the muff and snatched the empty bowl from Platt's three-legged table.

Miriam's ring twined like a snake on her middle finger. Its gold scales and garnet eyes quivered on the pewter as she rang the bowl along the barrier. The racket was as loud as the gates of Hell crashing open.

Sparrow woke up. His body rose upright before the mind returned to light his pale eyes. The event was more similar to a glacier calving icebergs than it was to the movement of a living thing.

Princess Miriam stepped backward. Her shoulder bumped Platt, who had approached behind her.

Miriam screamed and struck the attendant with the bowl. "Get out!" she shrieked at him. "I told you to get—"

Platt scuttled to the outside door with the graceless haste of a frightened spider. Miriam hurled the bowl at his head.

"—out of here, Hell take you!"

The pewter dented on the transom instead.

She turned back, recovering her aplomb with a shiver like the motion of a fore-edge book being thumbed to release its hidden scene. Sparrow smiled at her.

The princess blinked. Whatever expression she thought she had seen on the prisoner's face was gone as suddenly as it appeared. It could have been a trick of the light. . . .

"You," she said haughtily. "Prisoner! I need you to do something."

The smith rubbed the spot between the dog's eyes. The animal licked his huge calloused hand.

"What can I do for you, lady princess?" Sparrow asked. His voice was a rasping caress.

"I—" Miriam said.

She paused to look back at the door. Platt's shadow was visible, though the attendant himself was concealed behind the stone doorpost.

The princess stepped up to the bars again. She unpinned her cape and held it with one hand as she lifted the mirror from around her neck. The ornament of light quivered as Miriam's hand and the gold cord slid through it, but the helix continued its dual track unimpeded.

"It's my mirror," Miriam whispered. She waggled its face toward Sparrow. Since the light was behind her, the reflection was never more than a pale blur. "It doesn't work any more."

The smith locked his hands behind his neck and stretched.

"I see myself in it, lady princess," Sparrow said. Cords of sinew stood out on his neck. "What could be wrong with that?"

"You fool!" the girl snapped. "I mean it's *only* a mirror! It doesn't show me the places I want to see, the way it should."

"Ah," said Sparrow wisely. "Show it to me, then, lady."

He pointed to the filthy floor between the bars. "Set it there and step back while I take it," he said. "We can't have my jailor telling King Hermann that I put you at risk, now can we?"

Miriam spun on her heel. "You!" she cried to the eye that slid aside an instant too late to go unseen. "Get out into the courtyard, you little foulness! Or I'll have Daddy flay you!"

The attendant's shadow bobbed away from the doorjamb. Platt was mumbling something exculpatory.

The princess set the object down. She did not move back. Sparrow leaned only as close as necessary to pinch the cord between his thumb and forefinger, then rocked to his former position as he inspected the mirror.

"Ah," he said. "Ah, I see what the problem is."

The mirror had stopped working because the ornaments Sparrow had made for Princess Miriam interfered with its ability to take power from the Matrix.

Just as the smith had intended.

"You can fix it, then?" Miriam said, unable to keep a tone of concern from her voice. The mirror was unique and uniquely wonderful. Even the princess in her arrogance had realized that.

"Very difficult, lady princess," the smith lied solemnly. He closed the mirror again and set it where Miriam had placed it. "But I think . . . yes. But in two weeks, at the new moon. Not during daylight. And not now."

"I don't understand!" Miriam said, making the words an accusation rather than a confession of ignorance.

"The Matrix, lady princess," the smith said. He waved his hand dismissively. The dog smelled the hormones Sparrow was exuding and growled in anticipation.

"Well—" said the princess. She drew herself up in a regal pretense that her will had not been thwarted.

"One thing, lady princess . . . ?" Sparrow added.

"What?" she snapped.

"For this particular task," the smith said, his voice rasping softly like a dog's tongue, "I'll need a skin of strong wine. Can you bring that when you return with the piece that I will repair?"

"I don't see why I should bring you anything!" the princess said. "You're only a slave."

"Ah, not for me, lady," Sparrow said. "For the task. Only for the task."

"We'll see," she said coldly; turned, and swept out of the citadel. She paused on the threshold for a moment and called back over her shoulder, "You'd *better* fix it!"

When the princess was gone, Platt slunk back inside.

"What was that all about?" the attendant asked spitefully. He did not expect an answer.

Sparrow smiled at him. "Oh, she's a fine girl," he said. "She came to thank me for the ornaments I made her."

"*She* did?" said Platt in puzzlement.

"Oh, yes, a fine girl and worthy of her family," Sparrow said. "And to prove how grateful she is, she'll come back when the moon is dark and bring a skin of wine for us. Is that not a fine girl?"

Platt shook his head. He found his bowl. He morosely attempted to press out the dents, using the butt of his knife as a mallet.

The smith lowered himself onto his furs and slipped back

into his trance. Platt glanced through the bars, then returned to his own task.

He supposed that Sparrow was making some piece of a battlesuit.

≡ 39 ≡

SOMEWHERE IN THE ruck of hundreds of men exercising on the plain below Hansen, Culbreth wore Hansen's own battlesuit.

The warriors of the royal army were going through tactical evolutions in small groups. The troops particularly needed experience in how to deal with armor of exceptional quality. When Hansen was too exhausted to go on, another trusted warrior took his place in the suit.

The skin was raw over Hansen's joints, the places where his body first touched the interior of the battlesuit as he moved. He was wrung out physically and mentally. Though he trained his eyes in the direction of the troops as he chewed a grassblade on the bluff above the exercise field, he wasn't really seeing the men.

He had been this tired before. He was sure he must have been, sometime or other.

Black wings beat through the Matrix. He could feel Searchers coming closer. . . .

On the field sunlit below, warriors fell battered—their armor stunned, their bodies bruised by hitting the ground.

But they weren't dying—and as with ravens, little but death would summon the Searchers.

Hansen turned without rising as the dragonflies, two of them, changed from shadows to matter more solid than that of the scrub grass on which they landed—

And vanished again a millisecond out of temporal phase,

leaving their riders behind. The Searchers wore linen rather than their powered armor.

"Race," Hansen said. He crossed his legs beneath him, then straightened them like the arms of a scissors bridge to lift him upright. "Julia."

He gave the women a smile that was not so much careful as ready for whatever came next. The Searchers were North's minions, but Hansen had the powers of a god. . . .

"Does North have a message for me," Hansen said, "that he doesn't choose to bring himself?"

"Who knows what North does?" Race said.

"We came for ourselves, Lord Hansen," Julia added in a gentler tone. "Nobody sent us."

The women were like enough to be sisters, though not twins. Race's nose was a little higher than that of her companion. Her eyes were blue rather than gray, and her body looked vaguely more taut than Julia's—though Julia moved like a cat, while Race had more of a birdlike jerkiness.

Both of the Searchers were beautiful; and both were hard, by the standards of the warriors battering one another in training below.

"Look, we . . . ," Race said.

Thanks did not come easily to her tongue. She paused to watch the movements on the practice field, her hair flying in the breeze that came up the bluff and broke in turbulence.

"Look, we may as well sit," said Hansen, indicating the ground.

Herds being driven to slaughter in Frekka pastured often enough in the area to keep the grass on the overlook cropped. Neither beasts nor herdsmen were in sight at the moment.

"You gave us our dragonflies back," Julia said. "We came to thank you."

"I liked Sledd well enough," Race said. "But I'd been *free* before. You don't know what it's like to be . . . held. When you've been free."

"You may like having the wind blow in your face . . . ," Hansen said. He sat, recrossing his legs and lowering himself in the same fashion as he had gotten up. "But I don't. And—"

His tone became softer, partly because he was below the level of the constant breeze and no longer had to speak over its keening. "—I really didn't do anything that requires thanks."

The Searchers settled also. Race squatted; Julia sat on one hip, curling her feet behind her and supporting part of her weight on her left arm.

"Krita said she wouldn't come unless you ordered her to," Race said, scowling at her interlaced fingers. She wore rabbit-leather slippers and a chemise that fell to mid-thigh when she stood but hiked up to the hip joint in her present position.

"I did nothing important," Hansen said in a sharper voice. "I showed Krita that her mirror was a doorway as well as a window—that she could touch anything she could see through it. That's nothing."

Julia said, "You are a god, Lord Hansen. We're only servants. For you to think of us at all was an honor."

Unlike her companion, Julia wore a loose shirtwaist belted over a pair of trousers. The belt was of gold worked into a broad strap and clasped by a sapphire-eyed dragon swallowing its tail.

Hansen laughed. He was amazed at how bitter he felt at the images called up by the Searcher's words. "Be thankful you at least know who you serve, Julia. And don't—"

He stared critically at the rubbed spot over his left wrist-bone, then patted it with his fingertips. "Don't ever think that I'm not still human."

"Your warriors are pretty good," Race said neutrally as she watched the practice field. "Are they the whole army?"

"About a third of it," Hansen said, turning sideways to look over the bluff. "Every warrior in the kingdom has been mustered. It costs Prandia a fortune just to feed and maintain them, but it's the only way that they're going to get the training they need."

Julia eased forward so that she also could see the field. Viewed from the bluff, the arcs and glowing forcefields were a work of art; but all three of the watchers could add the reality of their own experience to the distance-blurred portrait.

Dust, sweat; the bitterness of lactic acid cramping muscles. Ozone scouring mouths and nasal passages, making eyes water even before the tears of fatigue started. Blood from pressure cuts and lips bitten in the shock of falling. Bruises and raw skin.

And above all, pain. The same constant, enervating pain which was as certain a concomitant of battle as death, and which practice trained warriors to accept until death or victory released them.

Hansen shivered.

"It's going to be a slaughter," Race said. Her voice held no loading but that of professional experience. "If all your men are as good as these—"

"More or less," Hansen said.

He turned to squat beside the Searcher, facing the practice field. "This is Wolf Battalion, but Bear and Eagle started with personnel as nearly equal as my staff and I could pick."

"Then you may win," Race continued. "But the Solfygg champions in royal suits will cut your lines to ribbons, no matter how good your training is."

"North will be pleased," said Julia. They now perched on the bluff like the three wise monkeys. "There will be a slaughter like the world has never known."

Hansen turned to her. "Do you think I don't know that, Julia?" he said very softly. He was shivering again.

Race cleared her throat. She continued to face over the edge of the bluff. "Krita learned that the mirror was open to what it showed," she said. "Because she kissed your image through it, Lord Hansen."

Hansen's head rotated. "She can do as she pleases!" he snapped. "That's none of my business!"

"Lord Hansen?" Julia said. She put her right hand softly on his shoulder. "This is what *we* please, Race and I."

"I'm jumpy," Hansen said in embarrassment. He backed into a sitting position a little farther from the edge of the bluff. "I'm sorry. I—"

Julia was smiling. Her free hand released her dragon-clasped belt. She stood up for a moment to let her trousers slip down about her ankles, then stepped out of them.

Race tossed her crumpled singlet on top of the trousers while Julia was still lifting her shirtwaist over her head.

"We could try spreading clothes to cover the ground," she said. Her pubic wedge was light red, almost orange. "If the grass bothers you."

"It never has yet," said Hansen as he and Julia reached together for the waist tie of his shirt.

Hansen started to laugh with real humor for the first time in too long. He laughed several times more in the next hour and a quarter.

≡ 40 ≡

RITTER HAD BECOME used to seeing visitors appear from the air before him, but the laughter in Hansen's eyes was a surprise to the engineer. Hansen was always grimly purposeful. For that matter, Penny had more often than not been sullenly gloomy the past several times she visited.

If he made her so miserable, why the hell didn't she stay away?

"How are we doing, Master Ritter?" Hansen asked, hitching his felt trousers around to a more comfortable position.

Hansen was not dressed to fit in with the personnel of Keep Greville, though Ritter knew he could vanish again into the Matrix as quickly as he appeared. Besides the obviously hand-sewn trousers, the slim man wore a shirt of coarse gray wool with bits of dry grass clinging to it—and a belt of flexible gold with a dragon-head buckle which combined function and artistry in a fashion that Ritter approved.

Still, the combination of coarse garments and intricate belt was as unexpected as Hansen's cheerfulness.

"I've completed the modifications," Ritter said.

Normally it didn't make him nervous to turn hardware over to users—the soldiers of Keep Greville—for testing. Ritter knew, and Lord Greville knew, that there would always be flaws in new equipment. Field testing was the only way that designs could be refined to meet actual needs—or be scrapped as certainly useless because the flaws uncovered were insuperable.

But Lord Greville didn't personally test new equipment against the weapons of his neighbors . . . and that was just what this thin, cold-eyed *god* intended to do.

"That was your job," Hansen said, raising a quizzical eyebrow. "That makes it a win, friend. What's the problem?"

"I wish . . . ," said the engineer.

He touched his console, idly rotating an image of the dragonfly directly above the unit itself. "I wish that someone else could test its operation. Especially after the last time. Don't you have servants?"

Hansen's face was briefly immobile. A tiny smile played at the corners of his mouth and his nostrils were flared.

Ritter had seen the look before on his visitor's face. That time it had been directed at the Lomeri, not at him.

"Send somebody where it's too dangerous for me to go, Master Ritter?" Hansen said in a whisper like whetted steel. "It was always me that they sent."

He licked his dry lips. "I'd rather die than be one of *them*, Master Ritter."

The engineer lowered himself to one knee and bowed his head. "Forgive me, my lord," he said.

"Hey," said Hansen, stepping around a rack of testing equipment. He gave Ritter's arm a friendly tug upward. "You're doing your job to warn of the risks. But, you know, I'll carry out my end my own way."

Ritter stood and nodded appreciatively. He gestured toward the dimensional vehicle. "Well . . . ," he said.

Hansen was lost within his memories again. "I've lived a lot longer than I ever thought I would, Ritter," the slim man said as he stared into the past. "Maybe longer than I should have, too."

His hand still lay on Ritter's left shoulder. The engineer clasped it with his right hand and said jovially, "Well, just watch yourself on your end, and I'll keep my thumb on the override button here."

Hansen's eyes focused again. "You bet," he said. "But not *here*, exactly. We're going to do this safely this time. I'll run you and the hardware up to Plane Seven and drop the dragonfly back to Six where there won't be any, ah, problems besides what may happen with the equipment."

"Glad to hear it," said Ritter, relieved at more than the plan of operation. He followed his visitor, through the narrow aisle and onto the examination stand where the dimensional vehicle waited.

"Climb into the saddle," said Hansen, "but don't fool with the controls. I'll take it and you both with me."

The engineer obeyed his instructions. Hansen's mouth quirked into a lopsided smile and he added, "You know, I made a pretty good choice in you."

Ritter guffawed. "I've pulled in my horns since the screw-up the last time," he said. "But—" serious again "—I don't think you were going to find a better engineer within a thousand kilometers of Keep Greville."

Hansen spread his fingers to touch the saddle and Ritter simultaneously. "Yeah," he said. "That too."

The Matrix hardened around them, turning the workroom into a memory as slight as chaff drifting through a steel cage.

Only illumination surrounded Ritter. Bars of light branched in infinite directions, each a pure color and different from every other.

His guide had vanished. The dragonfly had vanished. The light had form and power and—

The dragonfly rocked under Ritter's weight. Its feet ground into the sandy loam of a ridge above the tide line. Large-headed grass waved to the height of Hansen's chest, and a line of palms leaned their coconuts out toward the surf.

"Oh!" said the engineer, reacting to the Matrix rather than the world he now overlooked.

The atmosphere was alive in a fashion that the air of Ritter's own countryside lacked. Near the horizon, the sea changed color; gray-green replaced the inshore gray-blue.

For as far as Ritter could see from twenty meters above sea level, a great circular storm arced around the horizon. Lightning crackled silently, back-lighting the clouds, and slanted bars of rain joined clouds and sea at intervals. The sparkling tang to the air was more likely ozone from the storm than salt alone.

"Where are we?" Ritter asked.

"This was the plane that the original exploration team under Captain Rolls found," Hansen explained. "Thousands of islands but no large continents. When Rolls vanished, the Consensus of Worlds sent North and his troubleshooters to find out what had gone wrong."

The engineer shook his head. "I heard all that when I was little," he said. "And a colony was sent—"

"To the Open Lands," his guide agreed. "To Plane One, where all the other planes impinge without going through the Matrix."

It appeared that a great wave was swelling at the juncture of blue water and green. The mass grew still further, streaming seawater in all directions to assume its own dense black color.

The thing was alive. It spouted a double plume of spray which hung in the air after the beast itself had resubmerged.

"And the colony vanished too," Ritter said. He was beginning to shiver. "And we were sent, my ancestors, ten thousand years ago, in a fleet to find them."

"After you, a fleet of androids," Hansen agreed softly. "And after the androids, a fleet crewed by machine intelligences. They're all here, each on its own plane; and the Lomeri, who came before there were humans in the greater universe."

He laid his hand on the engineer's hand. After a moment, Ritter stopped trembling.

Last of all, the Lords of the Consensus sent Commissioner Nils Hansen alone, to go where fleets had disappeared to no avail. But the engineer didn't have to know about that. . . .

"But that's mythology!" Ritter shouted. "That isn't real!"

Hansen bent down and pinched up a portion of soil. He turned Ritter's hand palm-up with his own free hand and dribbled the sand and dirt into it.

Ritter rubbed the grit between his palms.

"Yeah," he said. " 'What?' is more important than 'Why?' isn't it? Sorry."

Hansen chuckled. "For people like you and me it is, friend," he said. "Now, trade me places and let's see how our noble steed—" he patted the dimensional vehicle "—handles in a nice, safe pasture like Plane Six."

Ritter swung himself off the dragonfly. His mass dwarfed that of the vehicle, but its spindly legs barely twitched when his weight came off them.

The engineer detached the control panel from the saddle. "I'm ready, my lord," he said.

Hansen waved from the saddle—left-handed by instinct, though he wasn't wearing a pistol that his right hand had to be free to grasp. "Let's do it," he said.

Ritter pressed the override switch. The vehicle and its jewel-hard rider shrank out of sight.

The veils of color that surrounded Hansen were identical to those when he slid down into Hell. They were not a description of the Matrix, merely an artifact of the dragonfly's passage.

Even so, Hansen flicked his eyes around him like a beast which suspects that it may be in the slaughter chute. . . .

The vehicle touched down on a gravel beach, rocking gently. The landing was soundless because there was no air here, only rock; and, motionless in the sky, a huge red sun.

So far, so good.

"Control," Hansen ordered. "Drop to Plane Five."

The dragonfly's mechanisms whirred softly within themselves, but the vehicle remained where it had been.

As expected. Ritter hadn't thought he'd be able to cure that part of the unit's problem.

Light winked on a distant corniche. There was life of a sort on Plane Six: the great crystalline descendants of machine intelligences which the Consensus had sent to Northworld within Hansen's lifetime—

Or in the unimaginably distant past, depending on the vantage from which one viewed temporal duration.

The creature on the cliff edge was too far away for Hansen to see it directly, but light striking the myriad facets of its body amplified the slightest motion.

Hansen drew a deep breath. The force bubble surrounding the dragonfly was firm. Even if that protection failed, Hansen could walk unaffected across this airless waste chilled to within a degree of absolute zero. He had the powers of a god. . . .

Hansen lifted the in-plane controls. The dragonfly lifted also, as smoothly as water spouting from a fountain.

Hansen cocked the column forward and sailed over the gravel, speeding or slowing as he chose. The bloody light transmuted all colors into shades of red and gray, but bands of texture paralleled the ancient shoreline to mark the stages by which the sea had vanished.

The skeleton of something terrifyingly huge lay on a bed of ooze which had frozen to the hardness of basalt. Most of the bones were scattered on the ground, but toothless jawplates gaped upward like some work of man. Hansen thought of the spouting creature he had watched from the beach where Ritter now waited.

The in-plane controls worked. He had learned what he came for.

Hansen sighed and swung the dragonfly back the way he had come.

"Control," he said as the frozen waste blurred past beneath him. "Plane Seven."

Hansen swam through color into sunlight that seemed brighter because there was an atmosphere to scatter it. He drew back on the control column when the surf foamed to fleck his legs.

With a dragonfly, apparent duration was the same at either end of the dimensional contact. While Hansen maneuvered over the waterless sea, the storm had swept closer to the beach on Plane Seven. The first big drops pocked the sand like miniature asteroid impacts.

The engineer released the override switch. "How did it go?" he asked anxiously.

Hansen grounded squarely on the marks from which the vehicle had lifted. "Like a charm!" he said. He hopped out of the saddle. "Now, let's get you home before we get soaked."

Ritter climbed aboard the dragonfly. His movements were graceless but adequate to his need. "So there won't be any problem with the actual operation?" he pressed.

"No hardware problem at all," Hansen said cheerfully.

But because of the limited dimensional control, the insertion would have to be made from Plane Two . . . and whoever operated the override switch from the Lomeri's home risked more than the chance of being soaked by a storm.

≡ 41 ≡

THE STORM HAD banged the shutters of the royal residence throughout the night, but a part of Hansen's subconscious must have heard the pattern of outer door, inner door, and nervous voices. He was up and dressed when someone rapped on his bedroom door.

"Lord marshal?" a servant called. "L—oh!"

Hansen pulled the door open from the inside swiftly enough that the servant's lantern guttered. The man's knuckles, raised to knock again, almost struck Hansen instead of the doorpanel.

"Oh, I'm sorry, m-m-m," the servant stuttered. "M-milord!"

There was a crisis. Prandia would want Malcolm in crisis discussions, and Hansen's old friend didn't move very quickly any more. Therefore—

"In Malcolm's suite?" Hansen demanded.

The servant nodded.

Hansen was already trotting down the corridor toward the other wing of the residence.

"Alert my battalion commanders!" he threw over his shoulder, though he couldn't take time to be sure that the servant knew where those warriors were billeted. If the fellow did, it might save a little time.

The message that spurred this crisis almost certainly meant war. That was good. During the past several days, Hansen had been waiting for an excuse for war.

For the last twenty meters to Malcolm's door, Hansen could have followed the trail of wet footprints on the flagstones. Prandia's major domo stood outside the suite with a handful of flunkies carrying lanterns.

"Yes, milord marshal," he called. "His Majesty is waiting for you!"

The major domo had managed to pull on a velvet robe and cinch it with his sash of office, proving that it wasn't only military men who could move quickly in a crisis.

Malcolm had gotten up from his bed. He sat in one of the chimney seats. Servants had built up the hearth fire before they scurried out of the way.

With Malcolm when Hansen entered were the king and another man, both standing. The stranger was of middle height and had a facial scar which showed as a white worm across his dark beard. He wore rain-soaked leather garments. There was a crude bandage on his left hand. It was leaking blood.

"This is Kraft," said King Prandia. "He's, ah, a scout from the Solfygg border."

Hansen looked at the spy. "Your hand?" he asked.

"It'll wait," Kraft grunted. "I took a forest shortcut I shouldn't have. Wolves got my pony."

"The Duke of Gennt is about to switch his allegiance from my foster son to the King of Solfygg," Malcolm said. He looked like a bedroll in the corner of the hearth—unless you noticed the glitter of his eyes. "If our friend here is correct."

Kraft grinned at the old man. The expression suggested that not all of the wolves had survived to eat Kraft's pony.

Hansen said, "Yeah, let's operate on that assumption."

The spy had risked his life to deliver the information. That didn't *prove* he was right about Gennt's intentions, but it sure-hell predisposed Hansen to believe him.

"Well, then," said the king crisply. "I don't think this is any time for half measures. Lord Hansen, all the forces available to the kingdom have been mustered for the past month. Have they not?"

"Yessir," Hansen said, nodding.

His eye caught on Kraft. The spy was losing the nervous energy which had sustained him thus far; he looked all in. Hansen gestured to him, then pointed at the other chimney seat, opposite Malcolm.

Kraft hesitated. He glanced at the king. Prandia was still standing.

"Sit," ordered Hansen. "We've been asleep while you rode."

And fought the wolves. And god knew what all else.

"What's the state of training, Marshal Hansen?" Malcolm asked. He ended with a sound somewhere between a cough and a giggle.

Hansen shrugged. "You've seen them, Malcolm," he said. "They're a hell of a lot better overall than they were a month ago when we pushed the training."

Malcolm wore a stocking cap of wool dyed red. The pompon on the end of it bobbed as he nodded. "They're at a plateau, though?" he said in his cracked voice.

"Yeah, that's right," Hansen agreed. "I don't think we can expect any significant further improvement in less than another six months. And we don't have six months."

"Because Solfygg will invade us before that?" Prandia asked with a frown. The king's head shifted from his former marshal to the current one and back.

"It's their royal suits that're the problem," Hansen explained, drawing Prandia's attention again. "At the rate Solfygg is getting them, they'll have hundreds in six months' time."

"I don't understand that," the king said, shaking his head. "A royal suit is a year's work for a master smith!"

"It doesn't matter whe—" Malcolm said. He subsided in a fit of coughing.

Hansen stepped over to the fireplace and ducked under the mantel. He put an arm around the old man and held him gently.

Malcolm thrust a crabbed hand out of the quilts and clasped Hansen with it. "We don't have to understand, lad," he said to the king. "The world does what it pleases, whether we understand or not."

"Kraft," said Hansen. "Will the King of Solfygg be sending warriors to Gennt?"

The spy nodded. "That's how I learned what was going to happen," he said from his seat. "There's a party of fifty warriors on the way now. Ten of them have the new armor."

Kraft was shivering from reaction. The fire on the hearth cooked moisture out of his leather garments in a miasma of sweat and the chemicals used in tanning.

"Solfygg can't have that many good warriors!" Prandia snapped. "They may have armor, yes. But warriors of the first rank are just as rare as royal suits, and I haven't heard that Solfygg has gotten around *that*."

"They don't have to be good, Your Majesty," Hansen explained wearily. "You're thinking of a battle like you're used to, where the top warriors fight one another and the rest of the armies hack around. When there's this many first-class suits . . . it's slaughter. I've seen it, and it's bloody slaughter."

He rubbed his eyes, trying to erase the memory.

"A god couldn't have done better with your warriors than Marshal Hansen has," Malcolm mumbled from Hansen's arms. "But that won't keep them from dying, lad. Ten for every one they kill, that'll be the way the battle goes."

"All right!" Prandia said harshly. "All right. We'll take the full army to Gennt except for a guard detachment here. At least Thurmond of Gennt will regret his treachery."

"No," said Hansen, "Your Majesty."

"How *dare* you!" the king shouted.

Kraft shifted in his corner. The knife handle projecting from the top of his right boot was suddenly close to the spy's uninjured hand.

"Listen to him, lad," Malcolm cackled. "*This* one doesn't threaten any better than a dying old man does."

"King Prandia," Hansen said. He cleared his throat. He'd *always* made a horse's ass of himself in situations that required tact.

"Ah, Your Majesty," he resumed, "I think it's time to win. We don't go to Gennt—we go to Solfygg. And we finish this instead of letting those bastards nibble you down till there's only a nub to swallow."

Prandia made a moue of apology for his outburst. "Ah, can we win against the main Solfygg army, Marshal Hansen?" he asked. "I understood from what you said . . . "

"Easier now than later, lad," Malcolm whispered.

"And the contingent split off and sent to Gennt is a bonus," Hansen added. "But—what Malcolm said is the truth. There'll never be a better time to try."

"Very well," said the king. "Give the orders, Marshal Hansen. I will accompany the army, but it will be under your command."

Prandia shivered. "And may North be with us!" he added.

"No, lad," Malcolm said. "Pray that Hansen be with us." He giggled. "The god, I mean. Of course."

Hansen held his old friend while the laughter turned into spasms of coughing; but in every pause, Malcolm's laughter resumed.

≡ 42 ≡

ONE PANEL OF the observation room showed a vehicle speeding toward Hansen. The panels to either side gave close-ups of an aircar driven by a lone woman.

The driver's features were unfamiliar, but the jewel between the full breasts left no doubt of Penny's identity.

The three-quarter frontal angles in the magnified images showed Penny's face was set with grim determination. That would have been normal enough for North—or Rolls, or almost any other member of their teams, the men and women who had become gods when they came to Northworld. But not Penny.

Perhaps the expression, like the visage itself, was merely a shape formed by her necklace.

The sky behind the aircar turned black. A squall swept across the plain.

Rain-cooled air slammed down in a column, then spread over the ground as a fierce wind which flattened grass. In the far distance, black-backed grazing animals the size of the aircar faced the storm. Their Y-shaped nasal horns lifted as they bellowed challenges to the lightning.

Hansen smiled as he stepped out into the wind. The titanotheres were as stupid as the aircar, and the vehicle had no brain at all.

But then, Hansen's own recent behavior had a lot in common with what the beasts were doing now.

Penny pulled up hard and let the vehicle fall twenty centimeters with the fans cut off. Its shock absorbers protested. The driver herself hung inertialess in the air for the time it took for the results of her lack of skill to settle down; then she got out of the car.

Penny had grace and—which was harder to recognize—intelligence. She drove badly because nothing, either animate or machine, mattered to her except for her own appearance and her own lust.

At least until now.

"I have a favor to ask you, Hansen," she said.

The squall hit.

The huge drops of the leading edge were massive enough to batter through layers of warm air and chill it so that the rest of the storm could follow. They smashed and splattered silently on the bubble of protection covering the aircar and the two gods beside it.

There was no thunder, but lightning rippled every few seconds. Penny's face looked terrible in its blue-white glare.

Hansen said, "Let's go inside, then," and led the way into his home.

Penny looked with distaste at the extruded furniture and blank walls of the lower chamber, not because the decor would have been cheap on any of the 1,200 planets of the Consensus of Worlds, but rather because it was austere to the point of asceticism.

Hansen smiled. The walls became a mass of pink, gold, and mirrors, while the furniture sprouted carvings so florid that they almost hid the underlying purpose of the items.

"Oh, I don't care about any of that!" said Penny with a wave of her jeweled hand. She sounded as if she meant it . . . but if she did, it was for the first time since Hansen had met her. "I came about—something else."

"All right," said Hansen.

He'd wait for her to get to the point . . . but this was his home. He wasn't going to hop around in it like a nervous client in a fancy cathouse.

"I know that duration doesn't mean anything to us," Hansen said. "But . . . ?"

He sat on the floor, not a chair, and stretched out on his left hip and elbow.The surface looked hard, but it gave slightly under his weight.

"Yes, well," said Penny, making washing movements with her hands. She turned almost instinctively to one of the mirrors now adorning the walls and checked her appearance. "I, ah . . . "

Penny's right hand touched the beehive of red hair she currently wore. She was full-bodied with a dusting of freckles on her shoulders and cheekbones. Her skirt and scoop-necked blouse were made of tiny gemstones, strung rather than attached like sequins to a fabric backing. They rustled minutely as she moved.

The woman realized what she was doing. Her face contorted into an expression Hansen would have described as self-loathing on anyone but Penny.

She turned and snapped to Hansen, "I don't want you to take Ritter with you against the Lomeri. That's what I came for."

"Oh . . . ," said Hansen as he got to his feet again.

Lying down was about as awkward a position as you could find for drawing a pistol. Intellectually that made no difference here, where the two parties controlled the Matrix and powers which dwarfed the destructive capabilities of any artifacts.

But Hansen's subconscious knew it was going to be the kind of conversation that had made Hansen very thankful for guns in the days when he was no more than human.

"We aren't attacking the Lomeri, Penny," he said. He looked at a Cupid-decorated pilaster instead of his visitor, who stood near it. "It's just that we need to launch from Plane Two to get where, ah, I need to be in the Open Lands."

"The lizardmen think you're attacking," Penny said coldly. "And anyway, they wouldn't care. They *like* to kill, just the way you and North do!"

I don't like to—

Hansen grimaced. "I guess if I didn't like killing . . . ," he muttered, aloud but to himself, "I'd do something else. Other people manage, most of them."

"All I'm asking is that you not take Ritter with you," Penny said with careful precision. "I can give you any number of servants, thousands of them if you like."

Hansen snorted. "That *would* convince the Lomeri that the Final Day had come, wouldn't it?" he said. "Look, Penny, I didn't tell Ritter he had to come along and mind the override. He *wants* to come."

"Because he thinks it's his fault that the damned machine doesn't work!" the woman blazed. "Anybody could do that! Anybody!"

"Not anybody," Hansen said, clipping the syllables. "And—"

There were a few of the West Kingdom warriors Hansen could train into the job; Culbreth certainly, and maybe Arnor. They had the courage, but the technology of war outside the Open Lands was alien to them.

That technology was crucial. On Plane Two, the Matrix was only a gateway—not a weapon to turn against the lizardmen, who would swarm toward any intrusion they detected.

"—if it comes to that, it *is* Ritter's fault that the dragonfly won't work unless somebody minds the shop on Plane Two for a couple minutes."

"So for that you make him—"

"No!" Hansen snapped. "He did everything a human can who doesn't work in the Matrix. But for that I *let* him volunteer to help me. Because I sure-hell need the help."

Penny looked at him. Her gaze was as smooth and opaque as polished granite.

Instead of speaking, she lifted the jewel on her breast by its transparent neck band and held it out to Hansen.

"Go ahead," she said at last. "Take it."

"I don't understand, Penny," Hansen said. His voice was thinned by the truth of the statement. He kept his hands at his sides.

Without the necklace to transform her appearance, the woman before him was what genetics and about nineteen standard years had made her: soft though not fat; blondish hair, but not blond by several shades. Her areolae were small and very pale. Despite her youth, her breasts sagged, and there was a mole near the left nipple.

"I'm giving it to you!" she shouted. Her eyes were clamped shut, but tears streamed out beneath the lids anyway. "Only give me Ritter! That's all I ask, just give me Ritter."

"Penny," Hansen said. He didn't know what to do with his hands. "Penny, listen, it's not like that."

He put one arm around her plump shoulder. She collapsed against his chest, sobbing.

"Please," she whispered. "Please, Commissioner. . . . "

Hansen eased the woman's head back and guided her hand so that the necklace dropped around her neck, where it belonged.

"Penny," he said, "listen to me. Ritter thinks he's responsible for the problem. I don't think he's responsible; there's just so much you can do working back from a piece of hardware."

The woman stepped away from him. Her form shifted reflexively through a number of choices before settling into someone with black hair and austere, aristocratic features.

Someone as different from the real Penny as Hansen could imagine meeting.

"Ritter says it's his duty to back me up," Hansen went on, knowing that she didn't—*couldn't*—understand what he was saying. "I can't tell him he's wrong, because I'd feel the same way myself if I stood where he does. And I'm going to let him do what he wants to do, because I like him well enough to let him make his own decisions."

He swallowed, then added the rest of the truth: "And because I need him."

"You're a bastard, Hansen," Penny said distinctly but without raising her voice. "You're doing this because you hate me. I don't know why, but you hate me."

She turned and walked with stately grace to the lift shaft which would return her to the upper level where her vehicle waited.

"I don't hate you, Penny," Hansen called to her back. "I don't hate anybody."

Except myself. And that's never stopped me doing whatever was necessary.

≡ 43 ≡

THE SKY WAS clear and windless, and the bright sunlight was all that was necessary to raise the spirits of the Eagle Battalion. It would be bitterly cold tonight in the lean-tos of leather and brushwood—and colder still for the slaves stoking the fires around which the warriors' lean-tos would cluster; but this was now.

The three battalions of the West Kingdom army were spaced across a ten-kilometer front. Hansen didn't like to divide his forces, but the need for haste made a multi-pronged advance necessary.

A dozen warriors and a larger contingent of freemen trotted by on ponies. They were going off to hunt, both for pleasure and to supplement the expedition's rations. The hunters would have no difficulty rejoining, since the main column was limited to the stolid pacing of the draft mammoths.

"Hey, Marshal Hansen!" called Tapper from the hunting party. "Why don't you tell Wolf and Bear to go home and whittle by the fire? We'll take care of Solfygg ourself!"

Hansen waved to them cheerfully from the back of his pony.

"Damn it, Malcolm," he muttered. "I'm leading lambs to the slaughter."

A mammoth carried the one-time Duke of Thrasey in a modified baggage basket rather than a howdah on the beast's back. The trails beneath the huge conifers were broad, free from undergrowth that might scrape off the cargo.

And the low-hanging basket permitted Hansen to ride alongside Malcolm, the only person alive in the Open Lands with whom Hansen shared enough background to think of as a friend.

"Not children, Hansen," Malcolm replied. "They're all old enough to know what they're doing. We were, when we were their age."

Hansen clucked his pony on a wide circuit around a tree. When he closed with the mammoth again, he said, "They're well trained, but the West Kingdom's had peace for—"

His tongue stumbled. He'd almost said, 'too long'; but that was the whole point of what he was trying to do.

Wasn't it?

"For a long time, Malcolm," he said. "They don't know what a real war's like, the way w-w-you do."

Malcolm gave a cracked, crippled laugh. It sounded much like the squirrels who occasionally chattered from out of sight in the branches; but the squirrels were louder and vibrant with health.

"Colimore wasn't war, then, laddie?" Malcolm said.

"Colimore was war," Hansen replied grimly. "But most of these men—" he waved his hand in the direction of the hunting party and the head of the column "—weren't there."

"You're always looking for a stick to beat yourself with, laddie," the old man said. "I didn't understand it before, and I don't understand it now."

"I—" Hansen said.

Another giant tree separated them. As he rode around it, Hansen realized he didn't know what he had been going to say next.

"How many of the men who served at Colimore," Malcolm asked in a voice as jagged and cutting as broken glass, "deserted after you got back, Marshal?"

"We lost a couple," Hansen admitted.

"And we didn't lose a hundred and some others," the old man said, "who knew sure as *hell* what a real war was like. We didn't lose Tapper, for one."

"Yeah," Hansen said. "That's true."

Ravens flew silently down the column.

Hansen started. The birds' broad wings made them seem shockingly huge, more like aircraft than their lesser relatives the crows.

"You made Tapper the sub-commander of Eagle Battalion," Malcolm continued. "Good choice, that. He's twice the man his father ever was. . . . But what are his chances of surviving Solfygg, Marshal Hansen?"

"Right," said Hansen.

Malcolm's formal phrasing brought up the coldly analytical part of Hansen's mind, much the way a code word switched on a battlesuit's artificial intelligence. Hansen weighed variables—the terrain, the Solfygg array; and then factored in the certainties, the way Tapper had fought at Colimore and the way he would behave now that Marshal Hansen had honored him by promotion for his skill and courage.

"I've upgraded his armor," Hansen said. "He's got the least damaged of the suits we took off Solfygg bodies at Colimore."

He wet his lips. "But the odds aren't good. Tapper has as much chance of surviving a full-scale battle at Solfygg as you do of living another century."

The wicker container rattled softly. Malcolm shifted within it to look squarely at the man riding beside him. "And you think he doesn't know it, laddie?" he asked.

Hansen said nothing.

"Go on," the cracked voice demanded. "You know the answer. I've told you the answer."

"I lead them to *die*, Malcolm!" Hansen cried bitterly.

"No friend," Malcolm said. "You lead the lucky ones to die."

The basket creaked again. The old man was working a hand out of his fur wrappings with the stolid determination of a butterfly emerging from its cocoon.

"Some of us grow old and useless," Malcolm continued in the whisper that was all the voice which age had left him. "But none of us get so old that we forget we were led by Lord Hansen—back when we were men."

Hansen did not reply. He reached out and held Malcolm's hand until another tree parted them.

≡ 44 ≡

WHEN HE SAW Hansen, Ritter clapped his hands in amazement. "Don't tell me you're wearing *that* when we go see your lizardmen!" he said.

A thought crossed the big engineer's mind. He added, "Unless you want me to kit you up? I can, you know—weapons and a force screen as good as anything you're going to find anywhere."

Hansen grinned slightly, absently. "Almost as good," he said.

Hansen wore hand-loomed wool trousers, a knitted wool pullover, and a short cape. A resident of the Open Lands would have exclaimed at the costly scarlet and indigo dyes, then noted that the cape was sewn from prime sables. To Ritter, the cloth was coarse, the colors muddy, and furs of any sort unhygienic and unsuited for the climate with which he was familiar.

More important, the short dagger slung from Hansen's belt wasn't a weapon in the engineer's technologically sophisticated terms.

"But, ah . . . ," Hansen mumbled. "I thought you and I ought to talk before, ah, I insert."

He looked around the workroom. There were tools and materials in such profusion that the huge expanse looked crowded. It looked like a junkyard.

There'd been a firefight in a junkyard once while Hansen was still in the Civic Patrol. Him carrying a needle stunner, and three villains with energy weapons.

This room was probably home to the engineer, but it depressed the hell out of Hansen.

"Look," he said, "why don't we go for a walk? Would you like to see somebody else's swamp?"

Ritter raised an eyebrow. "Sure," he said. "You mean over to Keep Worrel?"

"A little farther than that," Hansen said with a smile. "I'm thinking of visiting Plane Three, where the androids that followed your ancestors' fleet wound up."

He grinned more broadly. "And though I don't intend to meet any of their descendants, I *will* borrow a pistol and personal forcefield."

They landed on what looked like solid ground. It was so soft that Hansen sank in to his ankles. Muck rolled almost to the top of Ritter's half-boots under his greater weight.

They were on a spit of land between shallow watercourses. Reedlike horsetails sprouted around them, growing only waist-high or less. There was no grass, but the mud itself showed the green tinge of algae between the bases of larger vegetation.

Ritter wrapped the stems of several spike-branched horsetails together in one broad hand and tried to use the plants as an anchor as he walked up the gentle slope. Their shallow roots pulled out with a squelching sound as soon as he put tension on them. Muttering under his breath, the engineer stepped upward unaided.

"You can clean off at my place before we go back," Hansen said. "Never fear."

He stared at the similar mud shoreline across the water. The bank was less than fifty meters away, but mist drawn from the swamp by the red sun overhead was almost thick enough to turn all its features into a blur.

"See?" Hansen said, pointing.

Ritter followed the gesture. The flicker of eyelids made a lump of mud coalesce into something alive: stumpy legs, a barrel-shaped body, and a head that seemed huge even for the size of the body.

The creature was several meters long. It was hard to be certain about the length, because the tail merged with mud, mist, and vegetation.

"A crocodile?" Ritter asked.

"Nothing so advanced," said Hansen. "An amphibian. A big salamander."

He cleared his throat. "You know," he resumed, "I've been thinking. There really isn't any need for you to come along on this project. You've done your—"

"Like hell I've done my job!" said Ritter, anticipating the next word. "If I'd *done* my job, you wouldn't need somebody manning the control panel while the vehicle shifts planes!"

"One of the Searchers can handle that," said Hansen. "They're used to hardware, it won't be a problem."

"No," said Ritter. "We had a deal, you and I. I'm going to do my end of it, and I damn well expect you to do yours."

The giant amphibian emitted a great burp of noise. It sounded as though a truck had skidded to a hard stop. The beast slid into the water with unexpected grace, leaving behind only a roiled patch on the surface.

Hansen sheepishly reholstered his borrowed pistol. "Look," he said, "there's no question about you getting the freedom you want. I can set you up with a keep on your own plane, if that's what you like—"

The engineer grimaced. "I don't like taking orders from fools," he said. "That doesn't mean I want to act like a fool myself."

"—or," Hansen continued with a nod of approval, "you can take service with any of a number of . . . "

He cleared his throat. "Of gods," he said. "Me—I would be honored. Saburo has asked after you. I think you would find him undemanding and . . . not a fool, in most fashions."

Hansen bent as if to examine the large millipede crawling over the algal mat. "And of course there's Penny."

The engineer touched Hansen's elbow. Hansen met his eyes again.

"I told you I'd make your dragonfly work," Ritter said. "I figured that I could manage that in the lab, but I was wrong. I *will* do what I said."

Hansen slapped the engineer's hand away. "Do you *want* to die?" he snarled.

Ritter's left fingertips massaged the red mark Hansen had raised on the back of the other hand. "No, I don't," he said mildly. "Do *you* want to die, Master Hansen?"

"Sorry," Hansen whispered. "Yeah, that's a fair question." He managed a wry smile. "It's just, you know . . . There's nothing in this that requires somebody of your talent. There's no point in you risking yourself for nothing."

Ritter squatted and tweezered up the millipede between the thumb and forefinger of his hand. The animal twisted its shiny black body furiously while its legs quivered in the air.

"Not for nothing," he muttered to the arthropod. "Sure, I'm scared, but I . . . "

Ritter put the millipede back on the ground carefully and stood up again. "I wasn't as good an engineer as I thought I was," he said. "Don't make me think I've failed as a man too, my friend."

Hansen squeezed the web of the engineer's hand where the red patch was still fading. "If you're not a man," he said, "then I'm sure-hell not fit to meet somebody who is."

He cleared his throat. "Like I said, there's no need for you to come. But if you want to—I'd be honored to have you covering my back. Friend."

≡ 45 ≡

TWO WARRIORS WITH short blond hair accompanied King Prandia and a guard of honor to where Hansen sat on a camp stool in his open tent.

"This is my marshal," the king said. "He'll formally enroll you in our forces."

Hansen held in one hand a dispatch from Wolf Battalion which he was reading while he sipped broth from the wooden bowl in the other. Arnor and Culbreth were nearby on a felled log. They rose, and the coterie of lounging servants and freemen jumped to attention.

Hansen put down the tablet of planed wood. He continued to drink his soup, watching his visitors over the edge of the bowl.

"Marshal Hansen!" Prandia called. "Excellent luck! Even in this near wasteland there's a pair of warriors who want to join us against Solfygg. And better yet—"

"They both have royal suits," Hansen supplied.

His sidemen, Arnor and Culbreth, looked at him.

King Prandia blinked in amazement. "How did you know that?" he asked. "Did you see them come in?"

"I'd been expecting them," Hansen said dryly. "Though I thought they might have tried to join one of the other battalions."

"Then you know them?" the king said, increasingly puzzled at finding his marshal knowledgeable—and cold when Prandia expected enthusiasm.

Hansen finished his broth and stood up. "I'll deal with

them, Your Majesty," he said. His voice was quiet, but the anger underlying it made all those in earshot blink.

The two warriors were stocky. They wore heavy fur cloaks, wolfskin and wolverine. Though their features were regular enough to be conventionally handsome, their eyes were hard.

Nearly as hard as Hansen's own.

"Lord Marshal," said the warrior in wolverine fur, "my name is Race."

"And your companion is Julius, I suppose," Hansen said grimly.

Julia nodded meek assent.

Hansen glanced up at the sky. It still lacked an hour of sundown, though the ground among the great trees was in shadow.

"Let's the three of us go walk in the woods," he said in a neutral voice. He looked at his sidemen and said, "I'll be back in good time."

"Milord marshal?" called a courier, probably the man bearing Bear Battalion's situation report.

"Later!" Hansen snapped.

Hansen walked for more than a minute in silence. The Searchers followed him, one to either side and a step behind.

A squirrel called nervously. Hansen stopped. A moment later the animal's chattering stopped also.

Confident that the rodent would warn them if anyone crept close enough to overhear, Hansen turned and said, "I appreciate what you two are trying to do, but you've got no business here. I hope you'll leave quietly. You *will* leave."

Race opened her mouth to object loudly. Julia touched her arm to silence her.

"We've been watching the Solfygg army," Julia said. "The state of training isn't nearly as good as yours, Lord Hansen—"

"Not as much difference in numbers as I would've thought, though," interjected Race, calm and professional again. "Solfygg has been planning for this war."

She grinned a hawk's grin. "But they didn't expect you to strike first, that I'll bet. They don't have all their levies in yet."

Julia nodded the interruption away. "They have seventy-three battlesuits as good or better than the ones you faced at Colimore."

Hansen winced despite himself. He felt as though he'd been punched in the pit of the stomach.

"We thought," Julia continued, "that you could use a pair of warriors with first-class armor."

"I really appreciate it," Hansen said. "But I can't accept your help. My arrangement with North—"

"This is no action of yours, Lord Hansen," Race said. "This is *our* choice, with nothing of you or any god to do with it."

The squirrel began to click and yammer in response to the Searcher's harsh tone.

"Well, let me put it another way," Hansen said coldly. "When North learns that you're fighting against his interests, he will punish you—rightly, to my way of thinking, because you've taken his service."

"That's our—" Race began.

"I won't have that happen on my account," Hansen continued, trampling her voice beneath the steel in his own.

"Lord Hansen," Julia said. She bit her lower lip, then reached out and took Hansen's right hand in hers. After a moment, he returned the pressure, then patted her and broke away.

"Milord," Julia continued, "at the end of the battle—and I expect you to win it, I would never bet against your ability, milord . . . but there won't be enough survivors to burn the dead. It will be like nothing until the Final Day."

"Lord Hansen," Race said softly. "Let us stand beside you. Please."

"No," said Hansen.

He stepped forward and put an arm around the hard shoulders of each woman to embrace them.

"But I won't forget," he whispered. "Some day you'll learn how much your offer meant to me."

• • •

Hansen walked back to the encampment alone. No one asked him about the two warriors.

No one who saw the controlled look on Hansen's face asked him anything at all until well after sunset.

≡ 46 ≡

HANSEN USED THE manual controls rather than the aircar's artificial intelligence to settle them in front of the palace's gold-barred gate. String instruments inside played lushly.

"I feel," said Ritter acidly, "like a load of protein being delivered to the commissary."

Penny's palace was a gingerbread creation of marble and gold. It sprouted upward from a dozen turrets and a great, onion-domed tower in the center. Now, close on to midnight, lights concealed in the machicolations illuminated swathes of the pink stone. The creation seemed even more of a fairytale castle than it did by daylight.

"I need to talk with her," Hansen said mildly. "When I've done that, I'm going to leave. You can come straight back with me if that's really what you want to do."

The gates opened. A dozen male servants in pink and white livery marched out carrying trumpets festooned with pennons. The servants did not step in close unison, and a few of them did not seem to realize that they were even supposed to.

"I don't owe her anything, you know," the engineer said truculently. "I never asked anything from her, and I never promised anything either."

Hansen got out of the car. "I'm not arguing with you," he said. "I just need to talk to the lady."

Penny's servants raised their instruments to their lips. Instead of crashing peals of brass, sophisticated electronics within the seeming trumpets sang like harps and violins.

Trumpets *looked* right, but Penny was not to be balked of her saccharine string music.

Hansen strode between the two lines of musicians. The engineer was still in the aircar. Hansen didn't look back.

Penny's reception hall had a thirty-meter ceiling. The walls were of mirrors; gold panels—antiqued bronze would have been far more attractive—with love scenes in low relief; and internally-lighted sconces of frosted glass.

More liveried servants lined the walls. They serenaded the visitor with music that might have been Wagnerian before being transmuted through the tastes of the palace's mistress.

Six red-plush steps rose to another portal at the far end of the hall. The doors were closed, and no one stood on the upper landing where Penny normally greeted male visitors.

Hansen paused, just within the outer set of doors. Penny's major domo scurried to his side. The man was plump, balding, and ridiculous in his costume: pink tights and body stocking, with white pompons on his toes, shorts, and sleeves.

For all that, the major domo looked less harried than most of the other male servants, probably because his duties to his mistress were unlikely to include the most basic one. Penny was quite particular about the performance of her lovers, and a fit of godlike pique could have horrifying results for the victim.

The major domo bowed to Hansen. "The mistress has asked me to conduct you to her in the garden, sir," he said over the murmur of the music. "If you'll follow me . . . ?"

They went out through a side door concealed in the paneling. Behind them, servants continued to play, but the walls thankfully muted the sound.

The walls of the service corridor were pink stucco, decorated with swags and Cupids and highlighted in gold. Neither the walls nor the floor were particularly clean. The building could have been constructed to maintain itself—as Hansen's utilitarian home did—but Penny cared too little about such details to bother.

A couple was making love in an alcove. When the woman suddenly realized that Hansen wasn't just another servant, she shrieked and knocked over a potted fern in trying to rise.

By the time her partner looked around, Hansen and the major domo were out of sight around a corner.

Hansen heard the chuckle of water even before his guide unlocked the wrought-gold wicket gate and ushered him through. "Milady," the major domo called. "Your visitor is here."

Warm twilight hung over the garden, though there was deep night beyond the palace walls. Bowered roses and wisteria perfumed the air; lotuses bloomed in the spring-fed pond.

There was a gazebo in the center of the pond. A bridge of gold bars led to it. Penny stood hipshot in the gazebo's doorway, wearing her own form and draped in a single off-the-shoulder length of translucent silk.

For the first time since he met her, Hansen felt a touch of desire for Penny.

Her half-closed eyes opened. "Hansen!" she cried. "What are *you* doing here?"

The major domo staggered as though shot. "B-but milady!" he whimpered. "You said to show your visitor—"

"Not *him*!" the woman shouted. She pointed her finger.

Hansen stepped between Penny and the servant.

"Wait, for god's sake, Penny!" he snapped, thinking as he did so that his choice of words was as unfortunate as everything else about this situation. "He just did what you told him."

The woman remained poised to send her major domo to death or a worse fate . . . and there assuredly were fates worse than simple death at Penny's godlike command.

"Ritter came along, Penny," Hansen said in a calmer voice. "He's out in the car for the moment, but I think he'll come in later, after I talk to you."

Penny lowered her arm and turned away. After a moment, her figure changed to that of a tall, slim woman with a skull-cap of blond hair. She was dressed in a high-necked black chemise.

Hansen stepped onto the bridge. It creaked softly, making him wonder how it would perform under the engineer's great weight. Behind him, he heard the wicket click as the major domo fled, safe at least for the moment.

"You won't give him up, will you?" the woman said sadly. Her back was straight, but she dabbed at her eyes with one hand.

Carp with streaming fins and scales of mottled gold and silver stared open-mouthed from either side of the walkway, hoping for scraps of food.

Hansen reached the gazebo. "*Ritter* won't give up," he said. "And I won't order him not to go."

Penny walked across the octagonal building and sat on one of the ermine-fur couches. She crossed her legs at the knee and said brightly, "Ritter doesn't love me, you know. Isn't that amusing? I love a man, and he doesn't love me."

"People are different, Penny," Hansen said. He licked his lips, hoping to find words that would help him—

Explain? Apologize? He didn't know. Maybe just show sympathy.

"Look," he said aloud, "I asked him to come along so you could, you know, see him off. All I want is that you bring him back in good shape, because he's got a tough job to do."

Penny flared her aquiline nostrils. "Very magnanimous, aren't you, Commissioner?"

"Look, Penny," Hansen snapped. "If you treated him like a man instead of the latest goody in the candy store, it might be that he liked you better than he does!"

He paused and grimaced. In a softer tone he continued, "You might find that you liked him better, too."

The wicket squeaked open. Ritter stood in the gateway, filling it with his massive body.

"Guess I'll leave now," Hansen murmured as he turned.

He heard Penny get to her feet. "Like him better, Hansen?" she said. "That's the biggest joke of all. I *couldn't* like him better than I already do. The bastard."

The engineer waited at the gate until Hansen reached it.

Hansen nodded. "Thanks," he said to Ritter. "She's not a bad kid."

Ritter snorted. "The hell she's not," he said. "But she's a human being. And it's not as though it costs me anything I can't afford."

Hansen closed the gate behind him. He took one last look over his shoulder at Ritter crossing to the gazebo.

The engineer was doing his duty, because he was a responsible man.

≡ 47 ≡

HANSEN SETTLED HIS commo helmet and grinned like a death's head at the engineer. "Still time to change your mind," he offered with a lilt.

"Screw you," Ritter muttered.

Ritter's heavy form was as lumpy as the deck of a warship. Hansen had offered to equip him for the insertion, but Ritter preferred to carry hardware of his own design and construction. Hansen's forcefield and weapons might have been superior in some absolute sense—

"Ah, you're not my type, Master Ritter," Hansen said. He wore close-fitting coveralls with a flat forcefield generator that looked like a breastplate. His pistol rode in a cutaway holster high on his right hip, and a stocked, short-barreled energy weapon was slung muzzle-down over his left shoulder.

Hansen's voice trembled as if with laughter or madness, but that was only the adrenaline coursing through his blood.

—but in a firefight, the shooter was more important than his equipment. Hansen was too experienced to choose to send somebody into combat with hardware that the user didn't know by instinct.

Ritter's laboratory clicked and sizzled with the sound of ongoing processes, tests and experiments and computer-directed refining steps; mechanical life which continued whether its creator was present or not.

"Well," Hansen said softly. He lifted himself onto the dragonfly's saddle. "Let's do it."

The engineer stepped close to his mounted guide and touched his hands, skin to bare skin; but in the moment before Hansen took them into the infinite perfection of the Matrix, Ritter's mouth opened.

"Yeah?" said Hansen.

His voice was calm, his face calm. His hands shivered with hot fury.

"You're going to carry us to Plane Two," Ritter said. "This isn't going to—be a problem with North?"

Hansen's face glared ice through the mask of his smile. "I *have* powers," he said with brutal calm. "I've agreed not to use them for a time in the Open Lands. Period."

For a moment, Hansen's smile was touched with humor. "If North has a problem with what we're doing with the Lomeri," he said, "then he can come visit us on Plane Two. This is one time I wouldn't mind his company."

Ritter managed a grin which the taut muscles of his face turned to blocks and angles. His body's response to tension differed from Hansen's. "We don't need North," he said. "You and I can handle any trouble the lizards start."

Both of them knew that if the Lomeri managed to react in time to the brief intrusion, Ritter would have to face them alone.

"Hang on," said Hansen.

The walls became sharper, clearer. The network of reinforcing rods expanded in all directions until—

Ritter hung in a void at the base of an enormous tree. The roots spread to borderless infinity, forking again and again into hair-fine tendrils that split still further as Ritter surged along their pathways, dragged by a touch he could not feel toward—

They landed in a magnolia thicket. The ground was black with charcoal from the fire which had cleared the hill a few years before. Limbless stumps up to five meters high remained as grave markers for the forest that had once existed here.

Ritter stepped away from the dragonfly and took the separate control panel from one of his cargo pockets. The color-coded read-out was in the middle of the green zone, as expected.

"Ready!" he said to Hansen. He thought his voice sounded thin.

Horns sounded, clear and terrible in the humans' ears. The Lomeri were already on the trail.

Hansen nodded curtly. He and the dimensional vehicle started to fade.

"Good hunting!" the engineer shouted.

The read-out started to edge toward the upper yellow zone. Ritter thumbed the roller switch to center it again, then concentrated on his own defense.

There was low ground to the north and west of the hill. At the moment it was a band of lush meadow. There must have been standing water in it when fire swept past where Ritter now stood, since the forest on the other side was undamaged.

The trees were conifers. On the side facing the meadow and full sunlight, the trunks were lapped in lesser vegetation, brush and vines and white-blossomed dogwoods. Only a few meters deeper into the forest's heart, the gloom of great trees would open paths as broad as cathedral aisles among the pillared boles.

That was the direction from which the horns had called.

Ritter pushed his way downhill. Where possible he squeezed through or ducked under the tangled, odorous branches. When necessary, his powerful arms tore a passage. He was used to moving swiftly in the complex passages of his own workroom.

On standby status as at present, none of the engineer's equipment had an electromagnetic signature on which the lizardmen could home, but their instruments had obviously registered the intrusion itself. He needed to put some distance between himself and the insertion site.

A cloud of insects, flies or dull-colored bees, rose from the magnolia stems and swarmed around Ritter's face. Some of them settled on his skin, drinking his sweat or sticking to it. He squinted, hoping the insects would stay out of his eyes.

The dragonfly read-out was sliding toward the low end of functional. Ritter corrected it.

If he'd done his job, there wouldn't have been any need for the override switch.

Ritter had coupled his passive sensors to a mechanical plotting table because he didn't want to risk the electronic signature of even a liquid crystal display. Three styluses jolted suddenly onto a positive bearing.

Ritter unslung his shoulder weapon and pumped the fore-end to chamber the first round. The *click-clack,* scarcely louder than the insects' buzzing, made him wince.

A horn sounded its brassy challenge from the forest margin. Three Lomeri scouts riding ceratosaurs strode into view. Vines and bits of undergrowth fluttered behind their powerful bipedal mounts.

Ritter held his breath. The leading scout clucked. The trio charged across the meadow in line abreast, aiming their short carbines one-handed as if they were lances.

The lizardmen were headed for the hilltop. They would not pass within twenty meters of where the engineer huddled near the lower edge of the magnolia thicket.

Ritter moved only his head, trying to keep the Lomeri in sight through gaps in the branches and dark green leaves. He hadn't had time to deploy the miniature optical periscope he'd brought along. Anyway, it might have gotten in his way if he needed to snap off a shot. . . .

For a moment the engineer wondered what would happen if the dragonfly reappeared just as the lizardmen reached the hilltop.

He'd seen Hansen move when it was time to kill. Ritter would bet on him again.

Muddy dirt splashed up beneath the ceratosaurs' great clawed feet. The ten-meter-long carnivores moved with bird-like jerkiness. Each beast had a short, blunt nose horn and a mouthful of daggerlike teeth.

They were passing him by. . . .

The nearest of the ceratosaurs paused. Its Lomeri rider snarled and kicked it with spike-roweled spurs. The carnivore ignored the punishment and twisted its head toward Ritter's hiding place. Its rider tugged on the reins.

The beast flared its nostrils. It had scented warm-blooded prey.

The Lomeri leader turned to chirrup a complaint to the lagging scout. Nictitating membranes clouded and cleared as the slit-pupiled lizard eyes followed the line of the ceratosaur's interest.

Ritter fired at the nearest scout.

A magnolia branch caught the muzzle of his rifle as he swung it on target; the powerful duplex round struck low, in the carnosaur's haunch behind the protective hemisphere of the Lomeri force screen. The initial explosion blew a hole the size of a washtub in the beast's hide, and the follower projectile smashed the pelvis like a dropped glass before exiting on the other side.

The Lomeri leader swung his weapon past the crests of his mount and fired. A bolt of saffron energy crisped ten square meters of bushes, halfway between Ritter and the lizardman.

Ritter aimed and squeezed the trigger. There was a blue flash on the Lomeri forcefield, a second flash in the center of the lizardman's chest, and a spray of bright blood in the air as the creature went over the crupper of its saddle while its mount curvetted.

Though Ritter had missed the nearest scout, the lizardman's crippled, dying mount thrashed on the ground where it had thrown its rider under the bullet's goad. The beast's slashing legs flung leaves, magnolia branches, and bloody dirt in the air.

The third scout was aiming his—

The air in a spherical section around Ritter went bright yellow.

The engineer could see nothing but the enveloping afterimage. The back and breast pods of his forcefield generator glowed white with the overload, searing Ritter despite their thick asbestos padding. Deflected radiance blasted a tenmeter semicircle from the thicket, reducing the thick stems to carbon skeletons and completely vaporizing the foliage.

But the forcefield which Ritter designed and wore held against the direct hit.

He couldn't see the Lomeri scout because his retinas still pulsed from the lizardman's bolt. The engineer fired twice, aiming roughly along the radius of the blackened arc.

His bullets snapped blue sparks against the blur of light. As vision returned, he saw the third ceratosaur running riderless across the meadow.

The dragonfly's control read-out had risen into the red zone. Ritter screamed a curse and thrust it back into the green with the rotary switch.

He stumbled deeper into the magnolias. The thicket which had sheltered him was a charred waste that would draw the attention of every lizardman on this side of the planet. Of course, now that his forcefield generator was live, Lomeri instruments could home on it.

Three steps into the undisturbed magnolias, Ritter ran head on into another Lomeri on a ceratosaur.

The lizardman shrilled a curse and tried to aim his energy weapon over the head of his mount. The ceratosaur's gullet was mottled black and yellow; its breath stank like an abattoir.

Ritter pointed his short rifle as if it were a pistol and fired reflexively. The heavy recoil would have torn the weapon from the hand of a weaker man. The engineer noticed only the flash of heat as his initial projectile struck the Lomeri force screen and vaporized.

Metal plasma recondensed on the nearest solid objects, plating Ritter's gun muzzle and freezing in black microcrystals over his leading hand and wrist. The back of the ceratosaur's high-domed head blew away.

The dinosaur leaped high in an autonomic spasm. One of its legs flung Ritter backward, though the engineer's own forcefield prevented the black claws from rending him.

The lizardman spun out of his saddle, his weapon flying in an opposing parabola. Magnolias crackled when the Lomeri hit, then continued to rustle as the disarmed scout fled in panic.

Ritter got to his feet and ran toward the hilltop. The dragonfly's read-out was still in the green zone.

Bellowing and the calls of brass trumpets sounded from the

forest. The Lomeri main force was coming up swiftly. From the sound the draft animals made, they were much larger than those the scouts had ridden.

Ritter wondered how far he could run before they caught him.

And he wondered when the dragonfly would return.

≡ 48 ≡

HANSEN FELT HIS dragonfly struggle as though the Matrix had material substance instead of being a skein of possibility.

The wash of surrounding light should have been monochrome. Instead, the enveloping blur shaded from yellow straight ahead of him into green at the corners of his eyes.

Hansen's face was calm, but his brow was cold with sweat. *Like being stuffed in a garbage can and rolled into a firefight.*

The dimensional vehicle broke into a realtime universe with the suddenness of an equatorial sunset.

It was night. He floated twenty meters above the roofs of a walled city. Torches flared yellow and a dull, smoky red. Men walked the streets between dwellings and taverns. No one seemed to be looking up, but—

Hansen touched the temporal trim control, adjusting for the microsecond advance which would permit him to see without being seen. The vernier rolled easily beneath his thumb.

The dragonfly's electronics did not obey. If Hansen looked carefully, he could see his shadow thrown across the slate roofs by the quarter moon. A dog began to howl.

Hansen swore softly. While the meaningless syllables tripped off his tongue, his vehicle lurched as if it were being hauled through a wire-puller's template. Time drew a faint mask over the scene below.

Hansen drew a deep breath. He couldn't really be said to have relaxed, because his eyes kept flicking in one direction, then another, as though a gunman was waiting, might be waiting . . . but he knew that the first trial was over.

"Control, locator," he ordered the vehicle's AI. The holographic display that sprang to life above the in-plane controls was as crisp as that of the unit Ritter had copied. It gave a vector and a distance, 837 meters, wobbling between .44 and .50 as Sparrow moved within the confines of his cell.

Hansen pivoted the column forward. He could already see the dark mass of the citadel ahead of him.

The controls moved as easily as if they were disconnected. For a moment, Hansen thought that might be the case, but the dragonfly *was* moving, very slightly, slower than the smoke drifting from chimney pots.

Instinct made Hansen want to push the column harder. His conscious mind told him that the problem was in the override panel, not any of the controls over which the rider had mastery here in the Open Lands. He waited, moving only to scan the terrain—and to switch his left hand onto the control column, though he had no intention of clearing his weapons.

The dragonfly began to slide through the air at the speed of a man running. The force bubble protected its rider from the wash of winter air.

He kept a light grip on the control column, avoiding any input so long as his vehicle proceeded more or less as he wanted it to do. He was overflying the waste of rubble and rubbish between the modern part of the city and his destination.

The wall of the ancient citadel loomed. Hansen drew the column back—no change in velocity; pulled the column straight up on its axis and felt the dragonfly respond instantly by swooping higher than the brutal, lichen-splotched stone an instant before the vehicle's forward motion trembled to a halt.

The time lag was irritating.

The time lag was damned dangerous; but then, so were most of the things Nils Hansen had found himself doing with his life.

He pushed the control column slowly into the pommel. The dragonfly dropped in obedience to the controls. The distance read-out was still operating—6.59/6.60/6.61—so Hansen decided to trust it.

He edged the vernier clockwise another three clicks of the detent. The city faded. The Matrix's foggy illumination returned.

The dragonfly was no longer *quite* a part of Plane One. Hansen tilted the control column forward again, only a hair, and watched the metered distance to Sparrow reel down the holographic digits.

He was sweating again. There were judgments, uncertainties; none of them serious if his vehicle performed as it should, but—

Ritter's copy worked flawlessly. Hansen centered the in-plane controls at three meters and brought the vernier back three clicks, a fourth. The only light was moonglow through a high slit window, but Hansen could see well enough by it.

He could smell the interior of the cell also. The dragonfly hovered just across the iron barrier from Sparrow. The attendant, Platt, snored in filth as complete as that in which he compelled the prisoner to live.

Hansen's fingers tightened on the grip of his pistol; but he remembered his plan. He was not here for vengeance, only from necessity.

He smiled like a shark killing.

Hansen rotated the vernier one last point to bring the dimensional vehicle into perfect synchrony with the Open Lands.

"Master Sparrow," he called in a low voice. "I have an offer for you."

A dog growled low. The smith touched the beast's throat with huge, gentle hands and stilled the threat. "Krita?" he whispered into the dark. "Have you come for me at last?"

"Not Krita," Hansen said. He would kill the attendant if necessary, but even the flies walking over Platt's face seemed unable to rouse him. "There are gods who would employ you, Master Sparrow. All you have to do is leave your prison."

"I *can't* leave, you fool!" the smith snarled. "I'm—"

His voice changed. "But you could take me on your vehicle. It will pass through the bars. Take me and I'll—"

"I won't take you, Sparrow," Hansen interrupted. "But if you're the master smith you claim, you could find the template in the Matrix yourself, couldn't you?"

Hansen felt a buzz in the dragonfly's saddle, sure sign that the override control had slipped out of the safe zone. The vehicle began to sink, almost imperceptibly.

There was a tiny metallic sound. The crippled prisoner had gripped the bars with both hands and was squeezing them in an access of emotion. The particular cause was uncertain in the darkness.

"Why did you tell me that?" he asked.

"Because you didn't think of it for yourself," Hansen replied.

"I didn't think of it . . . ," Sparrow said in a tone of mingled wonder and fury.

"Control, Plane Two," Hansen ordered his dragonfly.

Nothing happened for seconds, tens of seconds.

It gave Hansen far too long to wonder whether he would come back to Ritter in time.

≡ 49 ≡

"I WONDER IF she's coming," Platt muttered as he stared out the citadel door.

He rubbed his hands together nervously. The backs of his fingers were ulcerated from poor diet and poor hygiene. "The moon's dark tonight," he added.

He turned around. "That's what you said, isn't it?" he demanded. The only light in the citadel came from the small lamp near the doorway. "At the new moon?"

Gravel ticked as a pile collapsed on itself. Its internal structure had been modified by the template into which Sparrow's mind forced it.

"Sparrow, damn you!" the attendant shouted. He strode toward the barrier. "Answer me, you half-man!"

The smith's dog backed against the stone wall, growling. Sparrow rose onto the support of his hands. "Wha . . . ?" he muttered. "Wh . . . "

"Where is she?" Platt said.

Sparrow chuckled like a falling tree.

The crackling, crunching sound went on too long for the attendant's temper. Platt tried to shout over the laughter, but the smith's deep lungs were too powerful.

"I want to know what you're making these past nights," Platt demanded in the final silence. "It's not armor. I know it's not armor."

"It's a gift," Sparrow said. "Aren't the king and queen happy with the gifts I made them?"

The smith's hand hovered over the pile of material on which he had been working in his trance. For the moment he did not disturb the covering of excess material to check his progress.

"How the hell would I know?" the attendant muttered sullenly. "D'ye think they talk to me except to curse?"

Platt's weasel eyes focused on the prisoner again. "Anyway, it doesn't matter. I'm to make sure you don't do anything but what the king tells you. You'll stop it now, or—"

Sparrow smiled. "Our guest is here, Lord Platt," he said.

Platt turned. "The hell she is," he snarled.

As he spoke, Princess Miriam flung back the half-closed door and cried, "Platt, you filthy fool! Why didn't you put a lamp outside the door? Did you think I was going to come here with a train of linkmen?"

"M-m-m princess!" the attendant blurted. "I didn't—"

"Close and bolt the door, Platt," Sparrow said/ordered. "The city's full of warriors tonight. We don't want them disturbing us while I provide for the lady princess."

"Yes, that's right," the young woman agreed haughtily.

Instead of dealing with the door herself, Miriam stepped aside so that Platt could get by to accomplish the menial task. She wore white suede boots. They were muddy to the ankles. "And you—Sparrow. Be quick about it. I don't want to spend any longer in this disgusting place than I have to."

Miriam was wrapped in an ankle-length cloak of mottled sealskin; a matching shako covered her head. Although she wanted to avoid attention in the dark streets of the city, she still wore the glowing ornaments Sparrow had made for her. Every time the princess tried to remove the loops of light, they slipped back through her fingers to continue their slow, lovely spirals around her neck.

"Put more fuel on the hearth, Platt," the smith ordered. "The lady princess wants to be comfortable while she waits."

"I want—" Miriam snapped.

"The wait," Sparrow continued with an easy power that overwhelmed the girl's sharper accents, "will be only as long as necessary."

He smiled again. "You brought the mirror, lady?" he asked.

"Of course I brought the mirror!" Miriam said. "Why else would I be here? And I brought—"

She swept back the sealskin. She wore a jumper of scarlet linen over a blue silk tunic which showed its sleeves, high neckline, and hem. The mirror was on its neck chain.

A skin of wine hung from a broad shoulder strap, waist-high where the princess' cloak had concealed it.

"—this," Miriam continued. "As if I were some sort of servant!"

She slung the wineskin toward Sparrow. It struck the bars with a squishy sound and flopped to the floor. The stopper remained seated in the wooden mouthpiece.

The attendant knelt by the hearth on one wall of the building. It had no hood or chimney. Fagots of pine popped and sizzled, multiplying the amount of light within the citadel but throwing shadows in ghastly patterns as well.

Platt stared at the wine with eyes turned orange by the reflection.

Sparrow grinned. "It's necessary, lady princess," he said. "Now, give me the mirror."

The attendant jumped to his feet. "I'll take it to him!" he said sharply. His eyes were still on the wineskin.

Miriam made a moue of distaste. She lifted the mirror over her head and headgear, then held it out to her side without looking to see Platt's scabrous hands take it from her.

Platt minced toward the barrier and knelt so that his body was between the princess and sight of the wineskin. As the attendant slid the mirror through the barrier, his free hand slipped toward the wineskin.

Sparrow took the mirror. "Why don't you open the wine and try it, Master Platt?" he said in a playful voice.

"What?" Miriam cried. "I didn't bring—"

She broke off. The attendant was already guzzling at the mouthpiece. A drop of the strong red wine spurted across his cheek. He squeezed the fluid out of his whiskers and licked the edge of his hand to lose as little as possible.

"It's all right, lady princess," the smith said. His voice was gentle, but there was a current underlying it that made his dog's hackles rise. "You will see."

Sparrow removed rods and small wedges of less definable shape from their concealment among his piles of raw materials. He began to arrange them into a linked pattern on the floor of his cell.

"What are you doing?" Princess Miriam demanded. She looked at the attendant, then glanced in the direction of the door. Platt had barred it securely.

"I have everything under control now, lady princess," Sparrow said. "You will see."

The smith shuffled purposefully around the confines of his cell. He had made himself thick leather kneepads for walking. Gravel between the pads and the stone floor must still have been painful, but he showed no sign of discomfort.

Platt noticed that the princess was no longer watching him. He lifted the wineskin surreptitiously to his mouth.

Sparrow put the mirror in the center of the partial objects he had already arranged. He covered the array with carefully-chosen bits of ore and scrap metal.

"What are you *doing*?" the princess demanded. She stepped closer to the bars and tried to peer past her own shadow.

"What is necessary, lady princess," the smith said flatly. "When I have completed it, then you can tell me how much to your taste the result is."

"You'd better make my mirror work again!" Miriam said in a venomous whisper.

Sparrow smiled at her. He lay back on his bed of furs. His eyes remained open, but after a moment they glazed as the master smith's mind slipped into the Matrix.

The man and woman on the other side of the bars watched Sparrow. Platt glanced sidelong as he squirted more wine down his throat.

Though the rekindled hearth was warming the room quickly, Princess Miriam shivered and pulled her sealskin cloak more tightly around her.

≡ 50 ≡

THE COLORED AMBIANCE surrounding Hansen shivered like glass struck by a brick. Sunlight and the glare of energy weapons made the hillside quiver.

The dragonfly emerged at the edge of the unburned forest, half a klick north of where Hansen had inserted. The undergrowth was torn. Facing away from Hansen were six lizardmen.

The Lomeri were mounted in pairs on blocky, broad-frilled triceratops. The beasts were in line abreast with about fifty meters separating each from the next. Containers with black, gray, and bright shimmering copper finishes were slung to their flanks.

The modules carried defensive electronics—and fed the wrist-thick barrel of the energy weapon which protruded above each triceratops' own triple horns.

The nearest Lomeri had reached the low ground between the forest and the magnolia-covered hill. They were the reserve line. Five more pairs of their fellows, also on heavily-burdened ceratopsians, had blasted their way through the brush to the hilltop.

The dragonfly's force bubble was made for general protection, not combat. Its controls would not spin an opening automatically when Hansen fired out. Hansen shut the bubble down, trusting to the lighter personal screen projected from his breastplate. His left hand swept the dragonfly toward the middle triceratops.

Hansen's right hand held the pistol he'd drawn as naturally as he breathed. He opened fire.

The ceratopsians carried forcefield projectors powerful enough to provide all-round protection against bolts from Hansen's pistol. Because the Lomeri thought they had only one intruder to deal with, they had shifted their defensive arrays so that the frontal arc facing Ritter was nearly opaque even to the optical spectrum.

Hansen shot the nearest pair from behind. The second lizardman died before his brain registered the actinic dazzle which had killed his fellow mounted at the console on the rear saddle.

The triceratops trundled on. It was not disturbed by the fact one of its riders had fallen to the ground and the other was slumped over his control console with a hole in his flat skull.

The instrument crewmen of the flanking teams both noticed the spike on their screens as a second intruder entered their plane almost on top of them.

Hansen shot at both ceratopsians, flicking his pistol barrel from one side to the other like a conductor's baton. He aimed at the large copper modules containing the power supplies.

One unit collapsed silently when the white bolt punched through its center. The shell of light distorted by the forcefield vanished from in front of the triceratops. Hansen fired twice more to finish the screaming riders before they could clear their personal weapons.

He didn't have to worry about the crew of the other beast. The power supply exploded in a sun-bright flash which devoured the lizardmen as well as the rear half of their mount.

The dragonfly skimmed past the tail of the beast whose electronics were intact. "Control," Hansen shouted. "Stop!"

The dragonfly was inertialess; its rider was not. Hansen slammed forward against the locked control column, bruising his palm.

He jumped off and ran to the triceratops. The mounting ladder which hung from its saddle was designed for longer, narrower feet than Hansen's. He snatched at it with his free hand, then holstered his pistol to get a better grip with his right. The beast continued to walk forward.

The pistol's ceramic barrel was white hot. The holster was extruded from refractory material which withstood the heat, but the fabric of Hansen's coveralls began to melt.

A volley of explosive projectiles raked across the dragonfly, sending up spouts of dirt. The little vehicle disintegrated.

Hansen pulled himself into the forward lobe of the saddle and swung the pintle-mounted energy weapon.

The magnolia thicket burned sluggishly wherever the Lomeri had not blasted it away as their mounts advanced deliberately on Ritter. The underlying soil had a great deal of silica in it. In some places the lizardmen had melted the ground to cups of glass around which even the triceratops' horny feet had to detour.

The air stank. The basic odors were of smoke and ash, but those were underlain by the complex, sickening molecular by-products of explosives through which stabbed ozone and other ions.

One of the lizardmen stood on his saddle and fired at Hansen with a shoulder weapon while his fellow tried desperately to turn their beast so that the forward-mounted main gun would bear.

The force screen of Hansen's ceratopsian muted to gray the flash of bullets hitting it. Even the *crack*s of the bursting charges were pillowed into thumps.

Hansen centered the sights of his hijacked energy weapon on the flank of the shooter's mount. *The trigger guard is meant for slender, scaly fingers, but that isn't a serious problem.*

Hansen's weapon jetted a line of blue radiance for as long as he held the trigger back. The target's forcefield held for a millisecond, then overloaded. Both power supply modules vanished in a huge green fireball, leaving a crater where eight tonnes of flesh and equipment had been a moment before.

Hansen didn't know how to control his mount, but the rate at which the beast plodded forward was faster than a man would walk. He didn't bother asking his helmet AI for a vector on his companion. He could be quite sure that the lizardmen had already pointed the triceratops in the right direction.

Two of the leading Lomeri teams had disappeared over the hill before they realized they were under attack from the rear, but the other pair were an immediate danger. One lizardman fired his main gun before it could bear on Hansen.

The Lomeri's blast raked the swale twenty meters away into a hell of smoke and steam, making himself the human's next target. Hansen aimed and fired at the sphere of protection.

Because the Lomeri was shooting out, there was already a hole in the forcefield. Hansen's bolt licked across the weapon and both riders, crisping them.

The triceratops squealed and lurched up on its hind legs alone. The top ten centimeters of its frill burned off in a razor-sharp line, but the beast was essentially uninjured. When its forefeet hit the ground again, it galloped away at racehorse speed.

The remaining driver had spun his mount to three-quarters frontal by the time Hansen rotated his weapon on target. The rear-seat crewman remained at the controls of his defensive electronics instead of jumping up to fire useless shots with his personal weapon at Hansen's full-density forcefield.

Hansen triggered a long burst anyway, lighting up the opposing armor just in case a portal opened as the lizardmen tried to shoot out. The forcefield remained solid. It pulsed across the spectrum, easily reradiating the energy Hansen's weapon poured into it.

The hostile ceratopsian now faced Hansen squarely. It strode forward. At any moment, one or both of the other Lomeri teams would trot back over the hill. Hansen would have to stop shooting or be caught in a crossfire while there was an aperture in his own forcefield.

Hansen lowered the muzzle of his weapon and blew a trench in the soil beneath the forefeet of his opponent's mount.

The triceratops plunged knee-deep in a pit of bubbling glass.

The beast screamed like the earth splitting. It threw itself backward and lifted its front legs into the air. Hansen ripped the triceratops' uncovered belly, killing the animal instantly before cutting upward into the module which controlled the forcefield.

When the protective hemisphere vanished, the Lomeri riders leaped from the saddle in opposite directions. Hansen's stream of blue fire turned them both to ash in midair.

The world around Hansen had slowed, but his body could not keep up with the kaleidoscopic impressions filling his mind. His triceratops continued to stride uphill, unconcerned by nearby bolts and burning flesh.

Hansen drew a slim-bladed knife from his boot and rammed it through the trigger guard of the pintle-mounted weapon, jamming the weapon to fire continuously. Then he jumped from the saddle and ran for the hilltop at an angle diverging from that of the triceratops. As he moved, he unslung his shoulder weapon.

The hillside was a smoldering, ash-strewn waste. It was hard to remember that this had been an expanse of magnolia flowers and the exuberant life which buzzed around them. Sparks stung Hansen's bare skin and melted speckles into his coveralls.

The corpse of a saddled dinosaur lay on its side with one stiffening leg in the air. It was a carnosaur of some sort, not a ceratopsian like those the present Lomeri rode. Ritter had been busy.

A laden triceratops strode over the hilltop ten meters from Hansen. The lizardmen riding the beast were concentrating on the animal Hansen had hijacked, then abandoned. The Lomeri force screen was a narrow wedge, dark as a moon in eclipse, facing what they thought to be the threat.

Hansen shot from the flank and killed both crewmen with a single bolt. He continued to run.

Horns sounded from the forest. Another troop of lizardmen was arriving.

The hill's farther slope had not been stripped by energy weapons, though the crew Hansen just killed had blackened a tunnel through the gorgeous foliage. A knob of higher ground to the left protected Hansen from the surviving Lomeri fire team.

That was also the direction toward Ritter, according to Hansen's AI.

A projectile weapon fired nearby. It was either semiautomatic or set to cycle very slowly. Despite the muffling vegetation, the muzzle blasts seemed sharper than those of Lomeri carbines, and Hansen was sure the impacts had the characteristic *cr-crack!* of the engineer's duplex rounds.

A triceratops blundered through the brush just in front of Hansen. He had to jump aside to avoid its hooves. The force screen was a hemisphere of smoky crystal shadowed by the animal's beak and black-tipped horns.

Hansen poised with his weapon aimed up at a 45° angle, waiting for the discontinuity behind which he could hope to penetrate the lizardmen's front-focused protection.

If the lizardmen didn't fire first, through an aperture they could form by pointing a gun.

One of the Lomeri lay slumped over his console. Most of his skull was missing. His fellow had fallen out of the saddle. They had turned away from Ritter to meet the sudden threat of Hansen's arrival, but the engineer was not a toothless victim. . . .

"Ritter!" Hansen bellowed. "It's me! Don't shoot!"

He wondered if the engineer could hear after firing his high-powered rifle repeatedly. If Ritter shot at any movement, Hansen's personal forcefield might block the impact, but the damage Ritter had done was convincing proof of the effectiveness of his duplex ammunition.

"Ritter, I'm—" Hansen shouted and almost fired by reflex into the figure that loomed in front of him. A squat troll of a man, singed and blackened except where perspiration had runneled paths through the soot—

But a man. Ritter was alive.

Hansen threw down his weapon and stretched out his hand to touch the engineer. A lizardman mounted on a ceratosaurus crashed through the thicket five meters to Hansen's left. The creature's carbine was already aimed.

Ritter turned and brought up his own weapon.

"*No!*" Hansen screamed.

He was too late. The *crack!* of the engineer's shot merged

with the devouring radiance of the Lomeri bolt which streamed through the hole in Ritter's force screen.

Hansen threw his arms around his friend and hurtled out of the plane with him. In the cold radiance of the Matrix, he could not hear the engineer screaming.

But black wings hovered nearby, a Searcher whom North had sent to carry away the soul of a dying hero.

≡ 51 ≡

DAWN WAS A pale warning, and the waning moon was a sliver on the black western horizon.

"Milord!" the voice demanded again. "Marshal Hansen! They're coming!"

Several trumpets sounded together from near Hansen's tent and the field headquarters.

Hansen shrugged out of his cocoon of furs and pulled on an additional linen sweater. He'd slept in shirt, breeches, and felt boots, suitable for either light use around the camp or for wearing within powered armor.

"*Who's* coming?" Hansen demanded as he slipped into his battlesuit. It would begin to warm up as soon as he closed it over him, but for the moment the suit's interior was at the ambient temperature of a night in late fall.

"A Solfygg army!" said Culbreth. He was already in his armor. "Ah, Baron Vandemann of Ice Ford and some of the other local lords!"

Hansen slammed his battlesuit closed. He was already shivering, but that was partly in reaction to the news. He'd counted on avoiding battle until he encamped beneath the walls of Solfygg, but the enemy wasn't obeying the West Kingdom's war plan. . . .

"Suit," Hansen ordered. "Hostile forces in red, map location."

Hansen's servants had thrown open the tent flap to admit Culbreth. The marshal stepped outside as a dozen high-

ranking warriors including King Prandia arrived in their
armor. Brightly-painted battlesuits gave the bustling throng
the look of giant insects.

The suit's AI overlaid Hansen's immediate surroundings
with a terrain map and three groups of tiny red dots converging
on the blue pip at center. The nearest of the Solfygg forces
were within a kilometer of the Eagle Battalion camp.

The artificial intelligence provided a numerical read-out
in the upper left corner of the screen without being asked.
According to that sidebar, the attackers totaled ninety-seven
warriors. Roughly half of them were in the central group, with
the remainder evenly divided among the flanking forces.

"The chief baron in these parts is attacking," the king said.
"I can't imagine what he's thinking. We have twice his numbers in this battalion alone."

The three West Kingdom battalions were almost within
mutual supporting range now that the invasion had penetrated so close to the enemy capital. That shouldn't be
necessary, but Hansen was more concerned than King Prandia
appeared to be.

Hansen had fought more battles than King Prandia had.

"They were trying to surprise us," grumbled Wood, a warrior from Prandia's combat team. "That's ungentlemanly!"

"Suit," Hansen muttered. Part of his mind listened to the
words his officers spoke, but he had more important things
to do at the moment than join pointless conversations. "Rank
hostile suits on the map by color code."

Parties of mounted freemen were bivouacked along the
approaches a kilometer or so from each battalion's camp.
Inside the camps, at least six warriors were on duty throughout
the night, watching through their battlesuit sensors for the
enemy.

The entire battalion was in armor by now. Ponies and draft
mammoths added their separate brands of noise to the confusion. Hansen hadn't *expected* an attack any more than Wood
had; but Hansen had made sure his forces were prepared for
the unlikely.

"Section leaders," Hansen ordered, "this is the marshal.
Deploy your troops to meet attack from the west. Odd sec-

tions by the north gate, even numbers by the south. Sections Nine and Ten are the reserve. Out."

"Baron Vandemann must be mad," Prandia muttered. "What can he hope to achieve with so few men?"

The sections were units of eighteen or twenty-one men. Hansen's AI reduced the responses of their leaders to a bar of green light across the top of the marshal's screen. There was certainly a great deal of chatter as the troops advanced to meet the unexpected threat, but again the marshal's artificial intelligence protected him from the distraction.

Hansen concentrated on the new overlay the AI provided at his request. He swore softly.

Ten of the forty-four pips in Baron Vandemann's central formation shone pure white: suits of royal quality. The flanking formations were probably conglomerations of lesser nobles from the neighborhood. None of them were marked higher in the spectrum than a dull blue, the AI's shorthand for third-class armor.

"What Vandemann's counting on, Your Majesty . . . ," Hansen said.

All the section leaders and the high-ranking warriors in Hansen's immediate vicinity could hear him. That was fine.

" . . . is that his ten champions wearing royal suits will slice straight through our line, kill you and me, and panic the rest of the battalion."

Which they just might have been able to do if we hadn't been keeping a good watch.

"Also," Hansen added aloud, "it's because he's a jackass. Our foragers drove off most of Ice Ford's herds yesterday. Instead of abandoning his own lands and joining his king like he ought to do, Vandemann's going to teach us a lesson personally."

"Instead of which we're going to teach him one, hey?" suggested Arnor.

"No," said Hansen. "We're just going to kill him."

He took one last look at the map, then said, "Suit, straight visuals. Your Majesty, gentlemen—let's go do it."

As Hansen led the command group out of the camp, he

noticed an ancient, wizened face peering from a fur cloak by the south gate. He waved his armored hand.

Malcolm waved back. The despair in the old man's eyes was pitiful to see.

≡ 52 ≡

HANSEN'S EYES WERE slitted when he burst into Plane Five on the examination stand of Ritter's laboratory, as though what he couldn't see clearly had not really happened. He was too numb to realize that he carried a hundred-and-fifty-kilo body, almost double his own weight.

The laboratory should have been empty. Instead, a woman waited. "Is he—" she called.

The smell was as sickening as it was familiar to Hansen. "For god's sake, Penny!" he shouted. *"Don't look!"*

He placed Ritter on the stand. The engineer's left forearm was burned to a stump. His ribs were showing, except where lung tissue had bubbled out through the gaps, and he no longer had a face.

Penny screamed as she stumbled toward the men. That was good, because otherwise Hansen would have had to scream for himself.

Ritter went into convulsions. The blast had seared open his esophagus. His dying breath wheezed through the gap, blowing out charred flecks of cartilage as the engineer's muscles contracted in their final spasms.

"Get away from him," Penny said.

Hansen looked up. "Penny, we can't—" he said.

Can't bring the dead to life. Can't modify events embedded in the Matrix.

Can't change the will of a woman named Unn or a man named Ritter, though a god's powers could have forced their bodies into any slavery the god desired. . . .

"Get away from him, Hansen," the woman said as she knelt beside the body. "Or I'll kill you. If I have to collapse the Matrix to do it."

Hansen nodded and backed away. He knew the feeling too well himself to doubt the truth of her words.

He hadn't noticed Penny's appearance when he entered the plane; now she wore her own form. Her body was naked except for the jewel hanging between her breasts.

She lifted Ritter's head onto her thighs, ignoring the blood and ash which smeared her skin.

Penny turned her head. "Will you leave us, please, Hansen?" she said in a cold, regal tone.

Hansen looked at her. Penny had the face and body of a teenage girl, but her eyes were as old as death.

"I'm sorry," he muttered.

There's nothing you can say, but you've got to say something.

Hansen let himself slide into the Matrix. The icy terror of the transition was almost pleasurable, a bath to wash away the stench of death and failure.

For a time, Hansen watched the scene from the observation room of his dwelling. He'd thought Penny would immediately carry the body of her lover back to her palace. Instead, she remained in the darkened workroom until Ritter's assistants entered at dawn to receive instructions for the day's work.

Penny set her jewel on the corpse's ruined chest, but the engineer had no mind to direct its activities. The body remained as life had left it, cooling slowly and congealing.

Penny kissed it repeatedly, though her lips touched only blood and charred bone.

≡ 53 ≡

SUNRISE TURNED THE Solfygg battlesuits blood red, whatever the underlying markings might be, when the Vandemann contingent strode out of the morning haze half a kilometer away.

The attackers were not preceded by the usual screen of freemen mounted on ponies. Baron Vandemann was an innovator, a rare thing on Northworld. It was his fatally bad luck that he had chosen to experiment against a force led by Nils Hansen.

A few of the Solfygg warriors hesitated when they saw Eagle Battalion was not only aroused but that most of Prandia's greatly superior numbers were already deployed outside the palisaded camp. Vandemann, a scarlet-suited warrior in the center of the line, turned and shouted a command. He used the battlesuit's speaker instead of its radio. The sound echoed to the camp, though distance robbed the words of meaning.

The central body resumed its advance.

"The courage of them!" Arnor said.

Because Arnor stood beside Hansen, the marshal heard his fatuous words even though the artificial intelligence cut them out of the radio net.

They're idiots!

The Solfygg flanking forces straggled into sight. Each of the smaller bodies was separated from Vandemann's force by nearly a half kilometer of flattened yellow pasture. When *they* saw the West Kingdom array, they stopped in their tracks and began to edge backward.

Arnor's job was to cover Hansen's back, not to deploy troops. Hansen didn't need to correct his sideman's words, and he had no time now for anything unnecessary.

"Suit," Hansen said, "display schematic. Undermarshal Tapper, advance at double-time with Sections Three, Five, and Seven toward the northernmost hostile force."

As Hansen spoke, his AI drew a pale blue arrow from Tapper's right flank units toward the clot of red beads. The Solfygg warriors were already retreating to put a rolling hill between them and the battalion they were supposed to attack.

"Undermarshal Patchett," Hansen continued, "advance at double-time—" another blue arrow "—with Sections Four, Six, and Eight toward the southernmost hostile force. Both undermarshals, screen the hostile flanking forces with one section—"

The blue arrows flattened into lines which were slightly concave in the direction of the hesitant Solfygg flanking units.

"—and hit the hostile main body in the rear as soon as it's fully engaged with our center."

The forces under Vandemann's personal control became a red arrow that flattened against the blue line of Hansen's remaining sections. Blue arrows curved back in from the flanks and squeezed the red patch into electronic limbo.

Reality wasn't going to be nearly that clean.

"Suit, send schematic," Hansen ordered. He'd learned not to trust words alone when trying to get across a complex, utterly vital concept. "Undermarshals, move out!"

Vandemann's main body was within three hundred meters. A warrior directly in front of Hansen turned. "What about *us*?" the man demanded in a voice that would have growled even without amplification.

The undermarshals' sections streamed forward at a jog. The lines lost cohesion almost immediately, but for the current purpose that wasn't crucial.

"Suit," Hansen said. "Straight visuals. Sections Nine and Ten, remain in reserve under the King Prandia."

Because Vandemann's troops were concentrated on a narrow front, Hansen could use no more than two sections effectively in the front line himself.

"Sections One and Two, advance under my command. *Peace and Prandia!* "

Hansen stepped forward. He slapped the warrior who'd spoken on the shoulder to move him sideways so that his marshal could stride by. The fellow yelped, but he must have sensed that it would be a very bad time to get in Hansen's way.

Arnor and Culbreth were to either side and a pace behind. Sections One and Two were in motion. Hansen had intended to advance at a walk, but sight of the undermarshals' forces jogging drew the center into the same gait.

And hell, he was leading the line himself.

"Marshal Hansen!" yelped the king's voice over the command frequency. "You can't leave me——"

Behind with the reserves, Prandia no doubt continued, but Hansen's artificial intelligence cut him off. The AI knew the marshal didn't care squat what the king or anybody else felt about his deployments; and Prandia himself had put Hansen in command.

"Cut," Hansen ordered, forming his right gauntlet into a scissors which quivered with blue fire.

His hand tingled pleasurably. All along the lines, Hansen's and that of the Solfygg force, arc weapons sawed through dawn's slow brightening. The opposing numbers were roughly equal, but the quality of the armor was——

The lines crashed together. Vandemann's ten champions strode onward with none of the hesitation which warriors normally showed just before the moment of impact.

Hansen parried Baron Vandemann's high cut. The blaze of light paralyzed both men in their overloaded battlesuits. Culbreth thrust at Vandemann's left shoulder. Arnor stepped close and hacked at his right ankle.

Vandemann's suit failed with a loud bang. Arnor's arc blackened all the paint from toes to knee. The baron's right foot flew away from a ball of plasma.

The baron toppled. "I got him!" shouted Arnor.

The Solfygg champion beside Vandemann cut Arnor's head off.

Hansen's battlesuit was hot and reeked of ozone. He switched his arc to his left gauntlet and stabbed at the killer's helmet. He had to pull the blow when a second champion pressed from his right. He didn't know where Culbreth was.

Hansen backpedaled, waggling a three-meter arc in the face of each opponent. Several of the Solfygg champions had fallen. The survivors of Hansen's front line stumbled in retreat.

One of Hansen's immediate opponents slashed through his arc. Hansen relighted his weapon and tried to step backward. It was like trying to push a dreadnought.

Hansen's suit was using all its power to defend against the hostile arcs. The joints of his armor were stiff, and if he stumbled—

His heel clanged against a battlesuit. He guessed he'd found Culbreth.

—Hansen was dead.

King Prandia's battlesuit was bright gold. He and his sideman Wood struck together, chopping the opponent on Hansen's right into three pieces.

Hansen transferred full power to the arc from his left gauntlet. When he tried to lunge into the blow, his legs trembled instead of obeying smoothly. The king and another warrior, the left-side member of his team, stepped around the marshal and finished that Solfygg champion also.

The battle area shrank into a dazzle like that of a megawatt transformer shorting out. It was over almost immediately. The undermarshals' forces had swept in behind Vandemann's troops and hammered them to scrap metal.

Just like it was supposed to happen. . . .

Hansen unlatched his battlesuit and opened it wide to the morning breeze. The wind was already dispersing ionization products in the air, but the smell of charred flesh would remain for months.

Hansen tried to get out of his armor. His muscles wouldn't obey. He wasn't sure he could have stood upright had not the legs of his battlesuit been firmly planted on the soil. He began to sob.

Two of Hansen's freemen ran over to lift the marshal out of his suit. On their second attempt, they succeeded.

King Prandia had stripped off his battlesuit. He walked toward Hansen, taking short, precise steps.

There was a windrow of armored bodies where the lines met. The remainder of the dead all lay in the direction of the West Kingdom encampment.

Even as they died, Baron Vandemann's warriors continued driving their opponents back.

"How . . . ?" the king mumbled. "Marshal Hansen, how many men did we lose?"

"We won the battle, Your Majesty," Hansen said. His eyes were closed. "That's all history's going to care."

He opened his eyes again. The smell and the memories behind his closed lids were worse than viewing the carnage.

Prandia put his arm around Hansen's shoulders. "I don't mean to seem ungrateful for your—your wisdom and your courage, Lord Hansen," he said. "But their battlesuits were, were . . . "

The king swallowed. "Were what you warned me they would be. What if the rest of the troops had supported Vandemann the way they were supposed to?"

"They didn't," Hansen said harshly. "They won't. You have a kingdom, Your Majesty. Solfygg has only a con-glomeration of barons. They mostly hate each other worse than they hate you."

"Yes, but—" Prandia said.

A man stumbled toward them, through the wandering free-men and blank-eyed warriors who muttered about what had just happened.

Culbreth! Hansen's sideman wore a numb expression and his forelock was shriveled by the arc that slashed into his helmet, but he was still alive.

"What could've happened doesn't matter, Your Majesty!" Hansen said. "All that matters is that we've won!"

The ranks of silent dead threw the lie back in his face.

≡ 54 ≡

SPARROW MOANED, BREAKING the silence. His dog licked his face while it stared watchfully at Platt and the princess beyond the bars.

The smith had stacked ore and pieces of metal over his partial construct. The arrangement shivered. Bits fell to either side, and a puff of dust spurted from the interior.

Miriam turned from the barrier. "What's he *doing*?" she hissed, an apostrophe to her own frustration rather than a question for the attendant.

Platt lowered the wineskin. He stared goggle-eyed at the princess. The skin had been empty for more than an hour, but at intervals the feral attendant lifted it again to his lips.

Miriam grimaced in disgust. She spun on her heel and cried, "You! Prisoner! What are you doing?"

Sparrow had been dipping in and out of his working trance. Now he awoke slowly but completely. He rose into a sitting position and stretched his mighty arms—straight out from his sides; back as far as they would go; and then forward, crossing in front of him.

The smith's blue eyes snapped with the lively humor which had been lacking since his capture.

"What are you doing?" Princess Miriam repeated in a less assured tone.

"I'll show you, lady princess," Sparrow said. He reached into the slag and lifted out his workpiece.

"What the bloody hell is it?" Platt mumbled.

The attendant rose from his stool and stepped heavily toward the barrier. Drink had not impaired his coordination, but his face was a mask of truculent evil.

Sparrow lifted the broad saddle with his left hand until it was more than a meter in the air. The four legs dangled loosely.

"Don't you recognize it?" the smith asked with patronizing amusement. "But then, I don't suppose you've ever been on precisely the same timeline as one before."

His right index finger made an adjustment at the base of each leg. Mechanisms clicked into place. The leg joints locked into self-supporting springiness.

Sparrow lowered the dragonfly. He brushed bits of rock dust from the saddle.

There was no sign of the mirror in the pile of slag. Its material had provided elements necessary to create the dimensional vehicle.

Sparrow's dog whined in curiosity and concern.

"I'm leaving!" shrilled the princess. She turned and collided with Platt.

The attendant cursed and grabbed at the girl reflexively. When he realized what he had done, he snatched his hands away as though they had touched hot metal.

Sparrow chuckled. "She's the nicest piece *you'll* ever have in your life, Platt," he said. "Why are you letting her go?"

Miriam broke for the door.

Platt snatched at her. He caught a handful of the sealskin cloak. Miriam clutched convulsively at her throat and bent open the pin of her gold clasp. The cloak fell away and tangled the attendant's legs.

Miriam took two steps and tripped over the slops bucket. Her head and right shoulder crashed into the heavy doorpanel. The shako fell off.

As the princess crouched on her knees half-stunned, Platt gripped her shoulder and flung her onto her back on the floor. The necklace of light winked on steel as Platt slit Miriam's clothing from hem to neckline.

The princess began to scream. Platt's clenched fist knocked her head against the stone floor. Her eyes unfocused.

Sparrow used the strength of his arms to pull himself onto the dragonfly's saddle. His dog whimpered and tried to climb up with him. The animal's scarred hind legs would not support it; it could only nuzzle its master's feet.

Platt had lowered his leather breeches. The half-rotten tie-string parted under his desperate enthusiasm. He knelt between the woman's legs.

Princess Miriam turned her face away from the attendant. Her eyes followed without understanding the smith's activities beyond the bars.

Sparrow leaned over and scooped up his dog with one hand under its rib cage. The animal whined and thrashed its limbs, but it settled again when Sparrow rested it on the saddle ahead of him.

"Prisoner!" Princess Miriam whined. "Help me! You've got to—"

Platt hit the princess again, bloodying her mouth. He attempted to enter her. In his excitement, he instead ejaculated across her white belly. He screamed a curse and slapped her, front and backhand.

"I would rather leave on my own legs, princess," Sparrow said in a tone of inexorable calm. "But your parents denied that to me."

Miriam sobbed at a pain so intense that it penetrated her state of borderline consciousness.

Sparrow touched a control. The dimensional vehicle faded from sight, then reappeared on the other side of the barrier, hovering in the air as Hansen had done when he visited the smith.

Platt did not look up. He removed the knife hilt with which he had forced the virgin and bent to his work again.

The dog looked around brightly. It gave no sign that it was concerned at what was happening to it.

Sparrow slid into the curtains of the Matrix again. The light was sharp and pure, perfect. He had duplicated the dimensional vehicle with a skill that no other smith in the Open Lands could have imagined.

The dragonfly returned to synchrony with the world around it. The waste ground between the citadel and the modern city was dark and silent. The eastern sky lacked an hour of dawn, and the stars were feeble tremblings above the haze of smoke that trickled from chimney pots.

Sparrow slid the in-plane controls forward, heading for the stone mass of the palace. The dragonfly rose as he proceeded. It climbed until the vehicle was almost two hundred meters in the air and the great gargoyles carven on the palace roof were insect-sized blotches.

"King Hermann!" the smith shouted. "Queen Stella!"

Sparrow's words were little more than a suggestion in the cold night. From within, the walls echoed, "*King Hermann! Queen Stella!*" in childish voices, terrible and terribly loud.

"King Hermann!" Sparrow cried. "Run to the citadel to find your children!"

The voices from the palace repeated Sparrow's words. Lights winked through the cracks in shutters as servants ignited rushlights on the hearths.

King Hermann and a dozen of his barons in battlesuits poured out of the front door of the palace. The king wore the armor he had stolen when he captured Sparrow. Stella, throwing a cloak over her night dress, ran after the men.

"Quickly!" the smith urged. "To the citadel!"

His dog howled. Sparrow began to laugh.

The two mobile chairs the smith had built for the royal couple slid through the palace gates behind them.

The chairs had voices. They echoed Sparrow's laughter, but they did so in the cruel, childish tones of Bran and Brech.

≡ 55 ≡

IN THE HOUR before dawn, a cruel wind blew from the West Kingdom army toward the walls of Solfygg. Warriors in battlesuits kept watch from the walls, but Hansen had no intention of committing his forces to unfamiliar streets in the face of a hostile army.

"They'll be marching out soon," said King Prandia. He let his voice trail off as his mind considered what would happen next.

"We've got to assume that," Hansen said. He thought he could hear shouting from within the city, but it might have been the wind which skirled around the rooftops.

"We're ready for them," said Wood, the king's sideman. He used his helmet speaker rather than the radio, so only the two teams—the king's and the marshal's—could hear his words.

"Marshal, this is Tapper," said Hansen's earphones. "Eagle Battalion is fully arrayed. Over."

"Report accepted," said Hansen, knowing his AI would do the rest.

Just like a good secretary.

"Ready to die, you mean?" said Culbreth in what seemed to be no more than a tone of idle question. Culbreth hadn't been *right* since the morning Arnor killed Baron Vandemann, but there was nothing physically wrong with him.

Hansen had offered to remove Culbreth from the line on the grounds that the army had no time to repair his damaged battlesuit. Culbreth refused. He now wore an equally good suit, one abandoned by a Solfygg warrior in one of the units which had failed to support the baron.

"Marshal Hansen," the king said formally over the channel to which only the pair of them had access, "this time I will not be left with the reserve. You'll need my armor in the front rank."

"Marshal, this is Sears," said the right wing commandant over the general command channel. "Wolf Battalion is fully arrayed. Over."

"Of course I'm ready to die," responded Wood in a tone of wonderment. "I'm a warrior. We're *all* warriors."

"Report accepted," Hansen said. Then, "Your Majesty, I'll need first-class warriors in the reserve also. Without you at Ice Ford—"

"We lost twenty-five men from the front rank at Ice Ford!" Prandia interrupted angrily.

"We won!" Hansen said. "Your Majesty, your job today is to do what I tell you to do. Dig *latrines* if I tell you to do it!"

The net passed a spurt of sound, a brief snippet before the AI realized that it was a shocked intake of breath rather than a syllable.

"They'll be coming out anytime now," said Culbreth softly. "I can feel the Searchers gathering. Can't you?"

"Marshal, this is Epson. Bear Battalion is fully arrayed."

There was definitely an uproar within the walls of Solfygg. It might have been warriors jockeying for the order in which they would march from the city and fall upon the West Kingdom attackers.

"Report accepted," Hansen said.

The eastern sky hinted dawn. Arc weapons quivered in Solfygg, lighting the battlements into momentary silhouette like summer clouds in a distant storm.

And the black wings of Searchers trembled just out of sight, waiting for the slaughter to begin.

≡ 56 ≡

WARRIORS ARMED FOR slaughter stamped from the houses of Solfygg in which they had been billeted. Shouts from the palace area had aroused the Solfygg forces before dawn, the hour of assembly which King Hermann had set.

Arcs flashed in the confusion. Warriors were testing their equipment nervously. The streets of the city were too narrow for arc weapons, even when used cautiously.

Sparrow watched in cold amusement as a warrior brushed the lower edge of a house with his arc. The stone footings shattered, causing the building front to sag.

Roof tiles slid into the street. Some of them broke on the battlesuit of another warrior who wheeled about, cursing and flailing his arms.

The warrior's armored right hand smashed plaster from the half-timbered facade of a house. He lit his arc in shock at the impact. The dense flux blew a hole completely through the wall, igniting both the wattlework core and tapestries inside the structure.

Sparrow surveyed the city. Dense blue sparks marked a dozen repetitions of the same scene. He didn't care about the Solfygg warriors, not even those champions who wore armor the smith had been enslaved to create. They could live their lives without his let or hindrance.

The royal family, though. . . .

Hermann and his entourage stumbled across the rubbish tip toward the citadel, lighted by several torchbearing servants.

Besides the queen and the armored barons, there was a score of freemen with lights or weapons.

The chairs followed.

The chairs glided behind the humans as if drawn by cords. Their wire bodies gleamed softly in the torchlight and the occasional snap of a distant arc weapon. Servants and even warriors glanced sidelong at Sparrow's eerie gifts, but the royal couple were oblivious of everything save their goal.

A freeman tried the door. The inner bar was shot through its staples. King Hermann raised his right gauntlet. The servant barely had time to leap aside before Hermann's arc shattered both panel and bar.

Iron—the bars and studs within the doorpanel—burned white when the flux touched it, but the glow faded as soon as the weapon sliced away. Splintered wood flew out in a blazing five-meter circle, causing servants to yelp and swat at the sparks on their garments.

Queen Stella's cloak smoldered. She ignored it and pushed past her armored husband in the narrow doorway.

Sparrow twisted his in-plane controls. The dragonfly slid through black air toward the citadel.

"Are you pleased to have robbed me, King Hermann?" the smith shouted. Cradled in his left arm, the dog shivered and whined.

The interior of the citadel blazed and echoed with the arc Hermann swept across it. Platt had started to rise. Blue fire from the battlesuit Sparrow had crafted for himself ripped the attendant's torso into vapor and glowing carbon.

Platt's severed head bounced on the stones. His mouth was open, but the intended curse had burned away with his lungs. His legs and dangling genitalia toppled in the opposite direction.

The king continued to slash the citadel's interior, severing the iron barrier in fire and deafening noise. His weapon melted the piles of slag and ignited the bedding on which the master smith had lain.

Queen Stella stumbled out the door. She carried her daughter. Miriam's head dangled, mindless or lifeless. After a moment, the king followed them.

"Do you remember telling them to cripple me, Queen Stella?" Sparrow called. "*I* remember, lady."

King Hermann looked at Sparrow, three meters above his head. He slashed his arc upward.

The vehicle's protective systems resisted easily. An opalescent globe surrounded the dragonfly and defied Hermann's efforts for over a minute.

The king shut off his weapon. His right gauntlet shimmered, glowing from the current it had carried in its failed attempt.

"Would I had killed you in your lodge," King Hermann whispered.

"Would you had killed me in my lodge," the crippled smith whispered back.

Queen Stella looked up from her silent daughter.

"Sparrow," she said on a rising inflection. "Sparrow? Where are my sons?"

"With you now, lady queen," Sparrow said.

He pointed with the first and second fingers of his right hand. The chairs shifted into wire simulacra of small boys.

"Hello, Mother," squeaked one in Bran's voice, stretching out its arms to the queen.

"I'm here, Father," said the other as its wire legs walked toward Hermann. "It's me, Brech."

Stella began screaming. She buried her face in the mud, but even that was unable to stifle her shrieks.

King Hermann cut the approaching wire figure in half at the waist. Until the arc weapon had completely devoured the creature, the legs continued to walk and the mouth to chirp, "It's me, Father!"

The eastern sky was lemon-colored. Fires were breaking out all over the city. Some conflagrations had grown to the point of showing open flames rather than just a rosy glow.

Metal clanged as Baron Tealer gripped the king's forearm. "Your Majesty," Tealer said, "it's almost dawn. The West King—"

Hermann shrugged away. He spread his right gauntlet and wiped the remaining wire figure away in a hissing electrical fan.

"I'm getting out of here," Baron Salem said. He spoke softly despite the suit's amplification. Three more of the armored warriors slipped away from the group when he did.

"Your Majest—" Tealer attempted.

King Hermann stabbed his vassal in the thorax. The unexpected, point-blank attack burned a hole the size of a fist through Tealer's own excellent armor.

Tealer toppled backward from the force of the blow. Other barons lurched away, then jogged at their suits' best speed toward the safety of their own retainers.

The king turned. He began methodically to erase his daughter's body as he had the armatures which spoke in his sons' voices.

Queen Stella babbled hysterically. Her face was turned toward the sky. Neither her eyes nor her mind held any image.

The dragonfly rose higher in the air. If there was an expression on Sparrow's face, it was pity; but there may have been no expression at all. His great, capable hands petted the crippled dog.

Below them, battle and chaos raged within the walls of Solfygg.

≡ 57 ≡

THE SOUNDS OF battle from within the city were unmistakable. Arc weapons were a constant nervous flickering. The guards on Solfygg's battlements turned to watch what was happening behind them. Some deserted their posts.

"Marshal?" said Blancy, the warrior who had replaced Arnor on Hansen's left side. "What the hell is going on in Solfygg?"

"Marshal," said Hansen's earphones, "this is Tapper. Do you know what's going on in the city?"

"Hold one," Hansen said. His artificial intelligence correctly keyed the response both over the command channel and through his battlesuit's speaker, answering both men's question.

"Suit," Hansen said, "patch the vision inputs from King Hermann's battlesuit into the left half of my screen."

This wouldn't work if Hermann had secured his inputs. . . but the AIs did *that* only if their operators told them to do so. Very few warriors in the Open Lands understood that their battlesuit's artificial intelligence was as valuable—if properly used—as the forcefield or arc weapon.

"But—" said Blaney.

King Prandia touched a finger to Blaney's vision pick-ups. "Silence," he said.

The left half of Hansen's viewpoint was the interior of Solfygg:

The ancient citadel blazed like a chimney. Wind ripped

*through the doorway and slit windows. The draft fed flames
fueled by everything inside the stone walls, including the floor
joists.*

*A body lay sprawled in what had been a first-class battlesuit
before an arc destroyed the breastplate and the heart of the
man wearing it.*

*An empty-eyed woman screamed hysterically beside a
trench burned into the broken ground. Her body was uninjured, but her mind had shattered like a lightning-struck
cliff.*

"Montage view," Hansen directed his AI. "Four top Solfygg leaders, your pick."

The center of the vision screen remained a view of Hansen's
immediate surroundings. King Prandia and the other West
Kingdom warriors, faceless in their battlesuits, stared at their
marshal.

The four corners of Hansen's screen each flashed with a
different scene of panic and strife. *The Solfygg barons hate
each other more than they hate you,* Hansen had told King
Prandia. Now that central control had disintegrated, those
hatreds flowered.

A major battle with at least twenty warriors on either side
was taking place in the square in front of Solfygg's royal
palace. Two of the viewpoints Hansen's AI had chosen were
reverse images—barons hacking at one another, while beside
them their retainers did the same.

In another quadrant, the viewpoint was a sea of flames. A
Solfygg baron turned and turned again, looking for safe passage between buildings which had blazed until they collapsed
across the street. The screens degraded as the battlesuit heated. Even if the images had been perfectly clear, they would
have been images of death.

The fourth corner was a scene of flight. Servants quickly
loaded their lord's movable possessions—and a quantity of
obvious loot—onto baggage mammoths near the east gate of
Solfygg, the side opposite King Prandia's drawn-up army.
The baron and his warriors watched and guarded them.

"Suit," Hansen said. "Set all the friendly suits to receive
these images unless overridden."

He took a deep breath. The warriors around him began gasping in wonderment.

"All units," Hansen said. "This is the marshal. Hold your lines until your section leaders re-form you. We've won, gentlemen. There will be no battle. We've won."

His teeth were chattering violently. It was with difficulty that he managed to add, "Out."

He'd won. Now there was nothing to save Hansen from the memory of what victory had cost.

The sky was growing brighter. As if in reaction, smoke from the burning city rose into the clear air. West Kingdom warriors cheered to watch chaos through the eyes of their enemies.

Hansen unlatched his battlesuit. He lifted himself out of it. A freeman jumped to Hansen's side and offered his shoulder for support.

"Shall I have the armor carried to your tent, milord?" the man asked.

Hansen blinked. The freeman was Kraft, the spy who had brought Prandia warning of Gennt's treachery. Kraft's left hand was no longer bandaged, but there were angry pink scars where a dire wolf had chewed until Kraft severed the beast's throat to the backbone.

"What are you doing here?" Hansen asked.

Kraft shrugged. "I like to go where it's interesting," he said. "When I met you, I thought I'd stick close till my arm healed."

He smiled tightly. "As I said—are you finished with your armor for today?"

"I'm finished with it forever," Hansen said. "It's yours. I give it to you."

"Marshal Hansen?" said the king. Like all the other warriors, Prandia still wore his battlesuit. "Shouldn't we attack now? While the enemy is confused, I mean."

"*No!*" said Hansen more sharply than he intended. "No, Your Majesty. March back home as quick as you can, so that you don't get caught up in the fighting."

"But they're ripe for finishing, milord!" the king protested. "Even I can see that."

"No, Your Majesty," Hansen said. "Anything that needs to be done, they'll do themselves—Hermann's barons and their own vassals."

"But—"

"Go home and enjoy your peace, King Prandia!" Hansen said. He had to shout to interrupt Prandia's amplified voice.

"God knows we've paid enough for it," he added bitterly.

Hansen strode back toward the West Kingdom camp. The crackle of Solfygg burning had mounted into a dull roar.

"Marshal Hansen!" the king called.

He turned only his head. "Just 'Hansen,' Your Majesty. You don't need a marshal any more."

"But where are you going?" Prandia called to Hansen's back.

"To see Malcolm," Hansen replied. "To say goodbye."

Wind drove a curl of smoke westward. It wrapped Prandia's army in smoke and the stench of death.

Nils Hansen had done his job.

Again.

≡ 58 ≡

SPARROW SAT IN the saddle of the dragonfly he had built, looking down on the rest of what he had done. The smoke was so general that only strong gusts swept it from the roofs of Solfygg, and those same winds whipped flames across the tiles.

The army arrayed to the west of the city was disengaging cautiously. Servants had struck the tents. Warriors, a score at a time, handed over their battlesuits to be loaded on draft mammoths.

The sky around Sparrow darkened. His dog wormed into the fold of the smith's tunic. The beast opened its mouth as if to howl, but its jaws closed again each time with a dry smack.

Sparrow thought for a moment that a column of smoke had enveloped him, but the dragonfly did not respond when he lifted the control wheel on its axis.

He—they; he stroked the dog, to reassure it and to assure himself of its presence—were in a globe of deep amber light. Sparrow could see hints of motion through the surface in one direction.

It was a tunnel, not a globe. A figure appeared, walking toward the dragonfly and its riders. A woman—

Not a woman. A man with fine oriental features, wearing flowing robes.

The hem of each sheer garment showed beneath the hem of the next above. There were at least a dozen robes. All of them were basically green, but the shades were graduated by what seemed to be no more than a few hundred angstroms.

The dog shivered.

"Who are you?" the smith demanded.

"My name is Saburo," the slender man said. "I'll guide you. You're to be my servant now."

"Am I, milord . . . ?" Sparrow said. He had no feeling of motion, but striations in the wall of the tunnel suggested that something was happening. The color slipped down through the spectrum into orange.

"I was recently in the service of the King of Solfygg . . . ," Sparrow's tongue added.

Saburo looked into the smith's eyes and jerked back from what he saw there.

"Of course, of course," Saburo muttered. "I should have known, given where the recommendation came from."

He smiled formally at Sparrow.

"Nothing like that, master smith," Saburo explained. "You do, after all, have to go somewhere now. I am offering you a home with me, with better conditions and services than you could possibly find anywhere in the Open Lands. In return, you would be expected to act for me in those instances when I need a skillful craftsman."

He cleared his throat. "And you could leave my service at any time," he added with his face slightly averted.

"You said 'recommendation,' " Sparrow said. "Whose?"

Saburo smiled again, minutely looser than the first time. "From Commissioner Hansen," he explained. "He says that you are as skillful as the servant he recently lost himself. I trust his judgment implicitly on anything of this sort."

"Actually," Saburo added with a frown at the memory, "Hansen said the *friend* he recently lost. But he meant servant, I'm sure."

Sparrow still said nothing. His face was opaque. His fingers moved, gently massaging the fur of the dog huddled to his warmth.

"Ah . . . ," said Saburo. "Ah, Master Sparrow, you would honor me if you accepted my offer of employment."

"All right," Sparrow said at last. "We'll come with you willingly. My lord."

The walls of the tunnel now were a streaky red, as bright as the flames which devoured Solfygg.

≡ 59 ≡

As Nils Hansen lay on the dead grass of Unn's grave mound, watching the red sun set beyond the silhouetted pines, he felt the subliminal tremor of black wings behind him.

The dragonfly halted with a soft *pouf* of displaced air. Hansen waited for the second vehicle to land, but this time there was only one. He rose to a sitting position and turned.

Krita walked toward him. The sunset deepened and enriched the color of her lips and long, lustrous hair.

Hansen nodded, then looked back toward the west again.

The woman sat down beside him. She raised her knees and locked them with her forearms, holding her torso upright.

Krita wore a suede singlet. It was a light garment for the season, but Hansen himself was dressed in only the linen shirt and breeches he had worn at Solfygg that morning in his battlesuit.

The flattened ball of the sun disappeared. The ragged pines stood out sharply against the red and purple light it bled across the sky.

"Do you come here often?" Krita asked.

An owl banked close to the humans, hunting for voles. The bird's soft-feathered wings were soundless, but it made a *krk-krk-krk* sound deep in its throat as it passed.

"Yeah," Hansen said. "I . . . "

After a moment, he added, "I should've come more often before. While she was still alive."

"I miss her too," Krita said. "But I couldn't stay in the

palace, knowing she had you."

Hansen looked at the woman. "Nobody *has* anybody," he said harshly. "Nobody *owns* anybody."

Krita reached out and touched his cheek, brushing her fingertips down the whiskers Hansen had allowed to grow while he lived as a warrior in the Open Lands.

"I miss her too," the woman repeated.

Hansen put a hand on Krita's shoulder, then leaned forward to kiss her as the first stars came out in the sky behind them.

≡ Afterword ≡

The *Volundarkvida* is one of the oldest, finest, and most grim of the poems of The Poetic Edda, but the tale of Volund the Smith can be traced back well before the Eddas. Probably the earliest extant account of the legend is non-literary: a seventh-century Frankish casket shows the crippled smith hiding the corpses of twin boys beneath his hearth.

The themes of *Northworld: Vengeance,* like those of its predecessor in this series, are largely drawn from the compilations of Norse myth in The Poetic Edda and The Snorri (or Prose) Edda. *The Lay of Volund* provides the core episode for the novel.

The remaining strands of *Vengeance* have come from quite a number of sources within the Eddas. The structure of Northworld is that of the *Alvissmal*. This short lay is of no interest as literature, but it provides tabular data (which the stunning, magnificent *Voluspa* lacks). Perhaps because of my eight years as a practicing attorney, I feel a manic need for structure in the fictions that I create.

Alvis himself is one of the Black Dwarfs, the cunning craftsmen who do work for the gods of Asgarth—and generally have time to regret the fact before they die.

The *Hyndluljoth,* a source that surprised me, provided the circumstances to which Penny's behavior leads.

The Peace of Frothi is an incident of the *Grottasongr,* a very powerful lay which I expect to figure largely in the next novel I set on Northworld.

One major incident was imported from outside the Eddas. The scene within Waldron's hall was borrowed/re-searched/stolen (you pick your own verb) from *Killer Glum's Saga*, an anonymous work written in Iceland at about the time The Poetic Edda was taking its final form.

Let me emphasize that the sensibilities of the Eddas are in large measure those of Dark Age warriors in some of the bleakest terrain that humans have chosen to inhabit. Volund was not a civilized figure even at the time his legend was created: he was a force as stark and implacable as the rivers of ice which crush their way downward until they calve icebergs into the sea.

But it is well for those of us living in the soft lands of our own day to remember that there are still cultures to whom vengeance is a way of life, and to whom an enemy's women and children are targets as acceptable as they were to a red-handed Viking.

—Dave Drake
Chapel Hill, NC